PLEASING MINDY

BEYOND GRANITE FALLS - BOOK 3

ANA E ROSS

CEDAR TREES PUBLISHERS

PLEASING MINDY

Copyright © 2017 by Ana E Ross
ISBN: 9780986339967
Cedar Trees Publishers

Edited by Crazy Diamond Editing
Cover Design by Najla Qamber Designs
Cedar Trees Publishers

ISBN: 9780986339967
ISBN-13: 978-0-9863399-6-7

www.anaeross.com

BOOKS BY ANA E ROSS

Billionaire Brides of Granite Falls Series

The Doctor's Secret Bride – Book One

The Mogul's Reluctant Bride – Book Two

The Playboy's Fugitive Bride – Book Three

The Tycoon's Temporary Bride – Book Four

With These Four Rings: Wedding Bonus – Book Five

Hot & Sensual Billionaires-Billionaire Brides: Volumes 1-4

Beyond Granite Falls Series

Loving Yasmine - Book 1

Desire's Chase - Book 2

Pleasing Mindy - Book 3

Hot & Sensual Billionaires Take II - Beyond Granite Falls: Volumes 1-3

Billionaire Island Brides: Akilina Connection

Seduced by Passion - Book 1 (2021)

Untitled - Book 2 (2021-2022)

Untitled - Book 3 (2022-2023)

❧

To my dearest, one and only sister, Delores, who passed away this year. Thank you for sending me those True Story, Ebony, Black Romance, and Jive magazines when I was a teenager. I can say without a doubt that those stories inspired me to become a romance writer.

May your soul Rest in Peace, my lovely sister. You've been my delight in life. I miss you terribly. You will forever live on in my heart and soul.

"*For what is it to die but to stand naked in the wind, and to melt into the sun? And what is it to cease breathing, but to free the breath from its restless tides, that it may rise and expand and seek God, unencumbered?*"

- Kahlil Gibran - The Prophet

CHAPTER ONE

Evergreen, New Hampshire, USA...

"I don't like it here, Mommy. Can we go home now?"

"In a few minutes, hon." Mindy smiled down at her five-year-old daughter huddled against her legs as they stood in subfreezing temperatures in Evergreen Cemetery.

She took a deep, unsteady breath as her eyes fixated on the limestone headstone. *Kyle Grainger. Loving Son and Father. Gone Too Soon. 1993 - 2013.* She wished she'd had the luxury of adding *Loving Husband* to his headstone. *Loving Fiancé* would have been her next best choice, but his mother had objected, blaming Mindy for her only child's death.

Virginia Grainger had claimed that if Kyle hadn't gotten mixed up with Mindy—*the little trailer park trash*—he would still be alive. If it was strictly up to Mrs. Grainger, Mindy would have been banned from attending Kyle's funeral altogether. Dudley Grainger, Kyle's father, had come to Mindy's aid and forced Virginia to back down. He'd told his wife that their son must be so ashamed at the way she was treating the mother of her grandchildren.

1

Mr. Grainger had been very kind to Mindy, and he'd loved and spoiled his grandchildren every chance he got. After Kyle died, he'd begun paying Mindy's portion of the rent on the apartment she and Kyle used to share with two of his friends. He'd become the father Mindy never had, and she'd ravenously soaked up the attention. Then tragedy struck again when Mr. Grainger suffered a heart attack and died three years after his son's death.

Mindy's gaze hesitantly traveled to the gravestone on the left of Kyle's. Mrs. Grainger had blamed her for that death too, claiming that her husband had had to work overtime at Grainger & Son Painting to make up for Kyle's absence.

For the past five years, Mindy had carried the guilt for Kyle's death in her heart, and then for his father's for the past three. Taking another deep breath, she pushed the regrets and the guilt aside, knowing that if she dwelt on that period of the past, if she gave it one moment's attention, she would not be able to get up the next day and take care of the two beautiful children she and Kyle had created from their young crazy love for each other. She had to stay positive, cheerful—the devil-may-care kind of girl that Kyle had fallen in love with during their high school years.

She wiped at a half-frozen tear on her cheek. She missed him so much still, and even more on two specific dates every year.

"Why do we have to come here every week?" Her son's contentious voice pulled her out of her cave of bittersweet memories.

"We come here twice a year, Kyle," she said, understanding that a six-year-old's concept of time was somewhat warped, especially when he was forced to do something he didn't want to do. "We visit your father on his birthday and on the anniversary of his death. It's a sign of respect," she continued in a gentle voice. "We want your father to know that we haven't forgotten him. Now, say 'Happy Birthday' to him."

"But he's dead. He won't know if we come here or not. And I don't know him."

"I knew him. I loved him," Mindy said emphatically. She wanted her children to have a sense of belonging, something that she'd never had since her own mother hadn't told her who her father was until she was fifteen, and by then he'd been diagnosed with lung cancer brought on by chain-smoking since he was a teenager. She'd only had a few months with him before he died, but he hadn't seemed to care one way or another that she existed. Mindy still couldn't decide if it was worse to have had one parent who just completely ignored her existence, or the other who'd constantly told her that she was an inconvenient mistake.

One thing she knew, though—she never wanted her children to feel that they were mistakes or inconveniences in her life. They would always know that they were wanted and loved by both their parents, even if one of them lived in the afterlife.

She'd loved Kyle and he'd loved her, and if he hadn't died, they would be married today. Theirs was a love that would have stood the test of time. They'd been saving up to get married and rent their own apartment when he died suddenly and tragically. It was his love for her, and his protection toward her that had caused his death. So in that regard, his mother was right. Kyle was dead because of her. She so wished that she'd lied about how she'd gotten her bruises when she'd walked into the apartment that day.

"You don't have to know your father, Kyle," Mindy said, passing her hand over her son's mop of curly dark hair and gazing into his gray eyes. He was the image of his father, making it impossible for her to ever forget the wonderful but so few years she'd loved and was loved by his father. "All you need to know is that your daddy knew you. He held you in his arms, he hugged you, he kissed you. He loved you very, very much, and I loved

3

him just as fiercely. Our love for each other made you and your sister."

"How, Mommy?" Britt asked, staring up at Mindy through warm brown eyes. "How did you and my daddy make us?"

"With sex." Kyle glared at her as if daring her to refute him. "That's where babies come from."

"What's sex, Mommy?"

"Something you don't need to worry about just yet," Mindy told her five-year-old daughter. *What do you know about sex?* was what she wanted to ask her six-year-old son, but she tucked the question away for later when they were alone. "Say 'Happy Birthday' to your daddy," she reiterated, smiling down at her children. And say 'Hi' to your grandfather," she added, glancing at the headstone next to Kyle's.

"Happy Birthday, Daddy. I love you," Brittany said in her sweet angel voice. "I hope you like the flowers we brought." She glanced at her grandfather's grave. "I love you, Grandpa. I hope you like the flowers, too."

Kyle silently stared at the headstones of his father and his grandfather, his lips drawn into a tight line, just like his father's when he was upset, Mindy thought.

"I'm cold, Mommy." Britt pressed her slender body against Mindy's thigh in an effort to stay warm. "Can we go back to the car now?"

"It doesn't matter," Kyle stated in a vehement voice. "The car is just as cold. I hate my life!"

Mindy shuddered as she watched him stomp down the narrow path toward the car that was parked in a clearing a few yards away. He was hotheaded like his father had been, and that one particular trait scared her. She hoped to God that he would grow out of it.

"Wait up, Kyle," Britt called, as she chased after her brother.

Alone for a few moments, Mindy pressed her lips together to

stifle the cry that threatened to erupt from her throat. "I miss you," she said, tears blurring her vision as she bent down to rearrange the fresh flowers in the mason jar on Kyle's grave. "I'm sorry. I should have known that you would have gone after him, but I couldn't lie to you. We'd promised never to lie to each other or to our children no matter how much the truth might hurt. I just didn't know that *that* truth would hurt so much, that it would take you away from us." She blinked as fresh tears pooled in her eyes. "You were my first love, Kyle, and I will always love you." Her heart ached at the thought that she hadn't even had the chance to say goodbye to him. "I'll take good care of our beautiful kids."

She choked on a sob as she recalled the day of Kyle's funeral when she'd stood in this very spot for the first time with a fussy two-month-old Brittany in her arms, and a crying twenty-two-month-old Kyle Jr. hanging onto her legs. "Britt has your smile, you know—the kind that lights up a room like yours used to. She's so sweet, Kyle, like the little angel you used to call her."

She paused, leaned forward and ran a finger along the groove of Kyle's name in the limestone. "I'm worried about our son, though. He's so angry, and I don't know what to do. I wish you were here. I try to make up for it, but I'm not enough. He needs a man in his life, a father figure…"

A father figure. Mindy shot to her feet and took a step back from the grave as if the very idea of a father figure for her son was an affront to Kyle's memory, or perhaps she was conflicted because she'd messed up. Two and a half years ago, Mindy thought she'd finally found a man she could open up her heart to and love again, one who would love her children like his own. But Galen Carmichael, bastard half-brother of Massimo Andretti, CEO of Andretti Industries—a multibillion-dollar textile company—had turned out to be the worst mistake of her life.

Her second-worst mistake was supporting Galen when he tried to sue Massimo for half of the Andretti fortune. Mindy was aware that her decision could have cost her her job since her boss, Adam Andreas, was Massimo's cousin. Miraculously, it hadn't, but it had definitely dampened Mindy's relationship with Tashi, Adam's wife, who Mindy suspected was the only reason she still had a job.

However, her coworkers at Arabella, the boutique at Hotel Andreas—Granite Falls, where Mindy worked weren't so forgiving. They saw her as a traitor and they shunned her for it, even to this day. Adam Andreas was the CEO of Andreas International that was comprised of Hotel Andreas and Ristorante Andreas, a chain of exclusive hotels and restaurants that spanned the globe. Adam's employees were loyal to him, and with good cause. He cared about the people who worked for him and he treated them fairly and respectfully. He'd even remained courteous to Mindy after she'd betrayed her loyalty to his family.

In hindsight, Mindy would have chosen differently, but sometimes people in love make the worse choices. It was love at first sight for Mindy, and for Galen too, she thought, recalling one of their first conversations.

"What do you want from me?" she'd asked after Galen's fifth trip in three days to the boutique. "Are you some kind of stalker?"

"Not a stalker, an addict."

"What?"

"I'm addicted to you. You're unlike any woman I've met, Mindy Marshall." He flashed her a disarming smile as his sexy hazel eyes gazed deep inside her, unlocking doors she hadn't even realized had been shut for years.

"Then you must not have met many women." His laugh resonated deep inside Mindy's belly, sending an army of butterflies fluttering wildly about.

"I just want to please you, Mindy Marshall."

"Please me how?" She indulged him, loving the way he said her name in his smooth English accent. Not to mention the titillating attention he was giving her—attention of the kind she hadn't received since Kyle.

"I'll please you in any and every way you want to be pleased."

A hot ache had throbbed in the dormant place between Mindy's thighs at his words and, despite her attempts to move slowly, she'd quickly succumbed to the charms of the handsome Brit, and had accepted an invitation to dinner at his lakeside villa in Granite Falls. They'd dined on takeout from Ristorante Andreas the best restaurant in town. The food was scrumptious, as expected, but halfway through dinner, Mindy had found herself lying naked in Galen's bed, and he was holding true to his promises—pleasing her every which way, and then some, all night long. It had been sweet, and wild, and delicious.

Mere months after they'd begun seeing each other, Galen mentioned his decision to sue Massimo for half of Andretti Industries. Mindy hadn't hesitated to throw her support behind him, despite her mother's disapproval and warnings that Galen wasn't worth putting her job security in jeopardy. Their difference of opinion had widened the already existing rift between mother and daughter, but Mindy had followed her heart. Wasn't that what a woman was supposed to do? Stand by her man? Take risks in the name of love? But love, as Mindy had later come to realize, was completely blind and stupid.

She'd stood by Galen even though she and the rest of the locals, except for those who'd been called as witnesses, had no idea what was going on inside the courtroom since both Massimo and Galen had agreed to a closed arbitration with a private judge. All parties involved, including Mindy's mother, who'd been called as a witness because she was an employee at Andretti

Industries when Galen's mother worked there, had been prohibited from discussing the case with anyone.

Mindy had tried, unsuccessfully, to get Galen to talk to her. His irritable mood, sullenness, and aloofness each time he returned from court suggested that he might have been losing to Massimo. The case was put on hold when Galen immediately left for London after receiving a call that his grandfather had suffered a stroke and had been hospitalized.

Mindy expelled a harsh sigh. Her stupidity and irresponsibility had crippled her son's sense of security. She knew that Galen's prolonged absence was one of the reasons Kyle had become so angry. He'd been a very happy little boy before Galen swept into his life, bonded with him immediately, treated him like a son, and then disappeared. He'd broken Kyle's heart, and after eight months, Mindy still couldn't figure out how to heal the hurt her son was going through. He'd shut her out, probably blaming her for his pain, and rightfully so since she was the one who'd introduced him to Galen, made him vulnerable and subject to hurt.

It wasn't the fact that Galen had left so abruptly that bothered Mindy. After all, he was close to his grandfather, the only living relative he had from his mother's side. In actuality, the only living relative he had in the world since he and Mass were at odds with each other. What bothered her was that in the eight months since she'd dropped him off at the airport, he'd only called her once to let her know that he'd arrived in London and was on his way to the hospital to see his grandfather.

After that, nothing—no calls, e-mails, texts, video chats—nothing but absolute silence. She'd tried to reach him, but each call had gone straight to voicemail. She'd left messages asking him to call her. Eventually, an "out of service" message had put an end to her efforts to contact him. It had crossed Mindy's mind that Galen might have gotten back with his ex, Trix, the woman for whom he'd been buying a present the first time Mindy had met him at Arabella, but she'd squelched that idea at the memory of the love she and Galen had shared for almost three years.

Out of her concern for him, she'd swallowed her pride and asked Tashi if she knew whether Galen had been in contact with Massimo. As far as Tashi knew, he hadn't. Mindy had taken her concern one step further and asked Tashi if she thought he'd died, to which Tashi had responded, "We would all know if he had."

As the silence grew louder and the weeks turned into months, Mindy's concerns had slowly turned into anger, anger into pain, and now pain into hate and self-loathing for allowing herself to be conned by that lowdown, lying Brit.

He'd shown his true nature as an Andretti. He might not carry the Andretti name, but he carried their blood. The whole world knew that the male members of the Andretti family were faithful only to two things—money and power. Galen's very existence proved his father's unfaithfulness to his wife— Massimo's mother. Maybe their creed was that when money and power—neither of which Galen had—weren't at their disposal, they just weren't faithful to anyone or anything.

If Mindy Marshall never saw Galen Carmichael again, it would be too soon.

A dusting of snow from an overhead tree branch landed on Mindy's forehead, bringing her awareness back to her surroundings. She brushed the snow away and stared apologetically at Kyle's grave. "I'll choose better next time. I promise. I have to go now," she said as Kyle and Britt's laughter penetrated the dead silence of the cemetery. She touched her fingers to her lips and pressed them on the headstone. "I'll see you in November." She pushed her hands into her coat pockets and made her way toward the car and her children, who were chasing each other around it.

Before he died, she and Kyle had dreamed about leaving Evergreen, even New Hampshire, for a better life somewhere. They'd considered Boston, New York—cities that were filled with life and excitement. Those dreams had died with Kyle. And it wasn't until four years ago that Mindy did leave Evergreen behind, not for New York or Boston, but for the next town over to live with her brother, Billy. Even though she'd lived in a rundown section of Granite Falls, it was better than being in the then lazy town of Evergreen where nothing was happening, and where as a single mother she'd had no hope or opportunities to improve her life and provide a better future for her children.

If she hadn't left Evergreen, she would not have met Tashi Holland, the aloof girl who'd lived next door in the dilapidated, rodent-infested apartment building where Mindy and her brother lived. Tashi's accidental collision with Adam in a cafe almost three years ago had changed the course of both their lives forever. It was because of Tashi that Adam had offered Mindy a job at Arabella.

Mindy made a good wage for a one-person household, but not good enough for a one-income family of three. Nevertheless, she'd been able to move into a nicer section of town, but she'd had to be wise and frugal with her spending. Her employment also came with excellent medical and dental benefits and a full college scholarship, so she really couldn't complain. She was in her third year of school, and Adam had promised her a promotion once she earned her degree in Office Management, so she did have that to look forward to.

"You want to play tag with us, Mommy?" Britt yelled as Mindy got close to the car.

"I wish, baby, but we have to leave now." The Graingers also visited Kyle's grave on his birthday and on the anniversary of his death. When Mr. Grainger was alive, they'd all come together, and Mrs. Grainger had kept her resentment for Mindy in check. But in the past three years she'd made no attempt to disguise her hostility. She'd even upset the children. So that they could both honor Kyle in peace, Mindy had suggested that they split the days in two sessions, and alternate visiting with the children each year. Mindy had the morning sessions with her children this year, but it was almost one o'clock and Mrs. Grainger would be arriving soon. Mindy had no desire to see that dragon's face today, or any other day for that matter.

"Can we go get pizza, Mommy?" Kyle asked.

"I'm sorry, honey, but I have a test tomorrow night, so I have to study for the rest of the day." *Besides, we have food at home. I don't have money to splurge on a pizza.* With a heavy heart and a tired soul, she opened the back door to let her children in.

"You can study while we're in school tomorrow," Kyle said as he scooted to the far seat and buckled his seatbelt. "You do that sometimes."

"Yeah, when I don't have to work the morning shift. Tomorrow isn't one of those days." She tucked two blankets tightly around them.

"You're always working, or studying, or going to school. You're no fun," Kyle said.

"Yes, she is, Kyle. Mommy is fun," Brittany said, coming to her aid. "She plays dolls with me."

"That's because you're a girl. She never does any boy stuff like Galen used to do with me. Grandma said you chased him away, 'cause that's what you do with men. She said you're a loser. That's why you had to move back to Evergreen. I want Galen to be my daddy, not some dead guy." Kyle pulled the blanket over his head.

Mindy closed the door and leaned against the car as she tried to catch her breath. She didn't need to ask which grandma her son was referring to since they called Mindy's mother Nana.

Mrs. Grainger had ridiculed Mindy for losing yet another man who was obviously too good for her. She'd even called Mindy some terrible names, right to her face, for getting pregnant at sixteen, and again at seventeen. Mindy knew the woman was poisoning her son against her, and if she didn't need her to watch her kids when her own mother couldn't, Mindy would have cut her access to them—grandma or no grandma. But beggars couldn't be choosers.

One more year, just one more, she thought as she walked around the car and got behind the wheel. She turned the engine over three times and, when it sputtered to life, she breathed a sigh of relief. She backed out of the cemetery then immediately slammed on her brakes when a black SUV turned abruptly into the parking area.

"Damn!" Mindy's entire body went numb. One second earlier and she would have been in a serious accident.

"That's a bad word, Mommy," Brittany said. "Not nice."

Mindy set the car in park and turned around. "I was just scared that you could have been hurt if we had an accident. I'll try not to say it again." *In your presence.*

"It's Grandma." Kyle tossed off his blanket. "I'm going home with her. She's got heat in her car." He opened his door and jumped out.

"Kyle, get your little butt back in this car," Mindy grated between clenched teeth. "Now!" she barked when he glared at her as if he would disobey her order.

He grumbled something under his breath, climbed back in, slammed the door, and burrowed down under his blanket.

Deciding to deal with him when she got home, Mindy turned and rolled down her window as the medium-built, dark-haired woman walked toward them.

Mrs. Grainger stopped beside Mindy's car and peered in through the window. "Hi, babies, you okay?"

"We're fine, Grandma. Can I go—"

"Kyle!" Mindy warned.

"Mommy said a bad word because we almost got in an accident," Brittany said.

"What are you trying to do, Mindy? Kill my grandchildren? Isn't it enough that you've—"

"Okay, that's enough!" Mindy rolled up her window and turned to her children. "Mommy will be right back. Stay in the car. Understand?"

They both nodded, their eyes wide with uncertainty and fear.

Mindy yanked her door open, forcing her nemesis to jump back. She grabbed her by the elbow and hauled her toward the shiny black SUV. She was done being afraid of this woman. She would not let her put the blame for Kyle's death on her anymore. Come to think of it, Kyle had had a choice. He didn't have to go after Danny, but he did. "I am so tired of you belittling me in front of my children, blaming me for Kyle's death. I won't tolerate it anymore."

"Well, if you hadn't been at Danny's apartment, he wouldn't have attacked you. If you ask me, I'd say that you were begging for it. The way you used to dress like the little tramp that you are. You were a walking invitation."

"You're blaming me for my boyfriend's friend offering me a ride from the supermarket. But instead of driving me home, he takes me to his apartment where he lives with his girlfriend—one of my best friends—and asks me to come in to approve a gift he'd bought for her, just so he could make his move on me, then beat me up when I refused his advances."

Mindy swallowed the humiliation as she recalled that rainy afternoon, and how she'd had to fight off a six-foot-plus, hundred-and-eighty-pound boy with her five-foot-five-inch, one-hundred-and-five-pound body. Oftentimes, Mindy had wished that she'd just let Danny have his way. If she'd just lain down and taken it, Kyle would be alive today. She could just have kept the shame and pain bottled up inside, carried the internal bruises forever, but she couldn't have hidden the physical bruises that Danny had left on her body. She'd promised never to lie to Kyle, and so she'd told him the truth.

"It still doesn't change anything, Mindy. My son is dead because of you. If you hadn't gotten yourself pregnant, he wouldn't have stayed with you. He would have gone on to college and made something of himself like his father and I had been planning since the day he was born. I don't wish this kind of pain on any mother, not even you."

Mindy sniffled and wiped at the tears that rolled down her cheek. "Virginia, I begged Kyle not to go after Danny. I knew the danger of him riding his bike on the slippery roads. I begged him to wait until the next day when the rain had stopped, but he didn't listen to me. I loved your son. I miss him every single day, especially when I hold my son and my daughter in my arms. I struggle to raise his children, to make a decent life for them. I deny myself so they can have what they need. You call me a tramp when you know that Kyle was my first and only boyfriend until Galen came along. I denied myself love and romance because I didn't want to expose my kids to someone who might mistreat them."

Virginia scoffed. "See how that turned out. What did you do to make him leave you? Face it, you're bad news when it comes to men."

Mindy decided to ignored her insults. This wasn't about her. This was about Virginia's grandchildren. "You hate me so much that you think helping your grandchildren, buying them a pair of shoes or a backpack for school once in a while would be helping me. You buy them toys and clothes that they are only allowed to keep at your house. You punish them to punish me. You are a selfish, vindictive woman, Virginia Grainger. I have often wondered how you could have given birth to a child as kindhearted, honorable, and loyal as Kyle. I guess he took after his father."

Virginia grabbed her by the elbow. "You listen here, you little—"

Mindy shook her arm free and glared at Virginia. "Don't you ever touch me again, woman!" She wagged her finger in her face. "Now, *you* listen! You will stop poisoning my children against me. You will stop telling them that I'm a loser. I'm their mother. I'm a good mother. Think or say whatever you want about me behind their backs, but you will respect me when in their presence, whether or not I'm with you. Or I swear to God, you will not see them anymore."

"You can't keep me from seeing my grandchildren."

"You want to bet, Virginia? I have friends in very high places." *Yes*, she thought, as the words spewed from her mouth, *I am playing the Tashi card*. "Tashi Andreas, my boss' wife, for one. I'm sure you've heard of her. Why do you think I still have my job after I sided with Massimo's half brother?" she added, refusing to mention Galen's name. "You have until Thursday to apologize for trying to turn my children against me, or your weekend visit with them will be postponed until further notice. Now, go wish your son a happy birthday, and while you're at it, apologize to him for being a jerk to the mother of his children."

While Virginia's mouth hung open, Mindy marched back to her cold old jalopy, and her children. She inhaled deep breaths of the crisp air. God, she felt good. Light as a feather as if a two-ton load had been lifted from her shoulder. Why the heck hadn't she done that years ago?

You weren't ready, a tiny voice said to her. *You're not caged anymore. You got your wings back.*

Mindy got into her car and sat for a moment watching Virginia as she slowly made her way down the path to her son's and husband's graves, her head bowed in defeat or shame, Mindy had no idea. But she did feel sorry for the woman. No mother should ever have to visit her son's grave.

"Did you and Grandma have a fight?" Britt asked.

"Yes," Mindy said without even contemplating her response. "Grown-ups sometimes fights, but we'll be fine," she added, as her car backfired when she eased it out onto the street.

"People laugh at your car, you know," Kyle stated, almost comically.

Mindy smiled. "I know. And some of them who're laughing don't even have cars. So there."

Her car was twenty years old—almost as old as Mindy—rusted and dented with slightly over three hundred thousand miles under its belt. She'd say that it had been ready to retire when she'd bought it at an auction for five hundred dollars with her first paycheck from AI. She realized now that she should have gotten a cheaper apartment and a better car back then. Nevertheless, it had served her well for those two and a half years. It had warned her that it wouldn't last much longer when it stopped producing heat two months ago and then last month when the exhaust system began to fail. She was grateful it was still running, though.

Perhaps she should have taken Galen up on his offer to buy her a car. At least she would have gotten something good out of their relationship. *She was so stupid.*

"It's embarrassing," Kyle said, when the car backfired again, leaving a trail of smoke behind them.

Brittany giggled. "I think it's funny. *Putup, putup, bang!*"

"Laugh all you want," Mindy said with a chuckle. "This old thing takes me to work and school, and you, to wherever you need to go. We must always be grateful for the things in our lives and treat them with respect and kindness," she added on a serious note. "Sometimes, it's only when they're gone that we realize how much we needed them, loved them."

"Like Daddy, Mommy?" sweet Brittany asked. "He's gone to heaven, but you still love him, right?"

Mindy nodded. Her little girl was so smart to understand symbolic language. "Yes, Britt, like your daddy," she said in a choked voice.

And the sad thing is, I might never find another man to love us as unconditionally as he did.

CHAPTER TWO

Ashford, Surrey, England...

"Sign here, here, and here, and then we'll be all set."

Galen held his breath as Trix signed the places on the forms where the solicitor pointed out. When the ink began to dry on her last signature, he let out a slow breath.

The solicitor took back the pen he'd loaned Trix, stacked the piles of paper that had been scattered around the table, and placed them into his briefcase. He stood hurriedly to his feet as if he couldn't wait to leave.

"Thank you for traveling all this way, Mr. Peabody," Galen said, standing, and offering his hand to the middle-aged man on whom he'd recently come to depend for legal counsel.

Mr. Peabody gave Galen's hand a hearty shake. "I will have everything ready for you to pick up tomorrow afternoon, Mr. Carmichael. I must leave now if I want to avoid rush hour back to London." He turned to Trix. "Good day, Miss Noyes," he said, tipping his head before moving toward the exit.

"How much is he costing you?" Trix asked Galen as he reclaimed his seat.

"A bloody lot."

"You could have gotten a cheaper one."

"I could have, but the stakes were too high for anything less," he stated in response to the reproof in her voice and silver eyes. *How dare she?*

"How are you going to pay his fees? Especially now that you—"

"Perhaps you should have thought of that before you destroyed my life," he snapped.

"I've said I'm sorry, Galen, several times, but I know it will not erase what I did, the trouble I've caused you."

"You're right about that." Galen crossed his arms and stared at her, thankful for the umpteenth time in the past eight months that he'd never revealed the identity of his biological father to her. Call it instinct or foresight, but he'd always been wary about sharing private information with her. What a freaking bigger mess this would have been if he had.

All Trix knew was that he'd grown up believing his father was dead when in fact he'd been alive for the first seventeen years of Galen's life. But she didn't know that his father was the late Luciano Andretti who owned one of the most successful textile companies on the planet. She didn't know that the half brother he'd spoken of was the infamous reformed playboy, Massimo Andretti, the current CEO of the Andretti multibillion-dollar corporation.

Growing up a penniless bastard had been bad, but the embarrassment of discovering that he was the penniless bastard of one of the richest men in the world—a man who didn't give a fig about him—had kept Galen from broadcasting the news of his lineage to the world. And neither had Massimo, the only legitimate heir to the Andretti fortune.

Only family, close friends, and a selected few in the States knew he was an Andretti. His deceased mother and aunt, and his recently deceased grandfather, were the only Brits who'd known the truth. Telling the world that he was an Andretti might have helped with the trouble he'd found himself in when he returned to England eight months ago. But it would have been humiliating if Massimo, with whom he'd been locked in a court battle for the Andretti fortune and who'd called Galen a conniving little usurper a few days before Galen left Granite Falls, had refused to come to his aid.

Galen wished he'd kept even less important private information from Trix. He wished he'd never told her about his grandfather, or told her where he was living.

He wished he could say that he wished he'd never met her.

He glanced at his watch. "Listen, I need to get on the road. It's been a long day."

"I know. But before you go, tell me you won't let him forget me. I know you're a man of your word. I need to hear you say it."

Galen looked around the visitor's room at HMP Bronzefield Women's Prison located on the outskirts of Ashford in Surrey. The murmur of adult voices and the enlivened chatter of children swirled around him. He couldn't wait to end this debilitating chapter of his life once and for all. He turned back to her. "No, I won't let him forget you."

It was a promise he wished he didn't have to make.

She gave him a bland smile and combed her fingers through her short crop of dark hair. "Thank you. I'm glad I named him after you."

"Not really. You gave him my middle name."

"Would you've been happier if I'd given him your first name too?"

"It's not as if you gave me a choice," he said in a mildly contentious tone.

"I don't want to argue about his name, Galen. I'm just saying that I'm at peace because I know you'll take good care of him. I've always known you had a good heart. You're kind and responsible and one of the most honorable men I've ever known."

The jury is still out on that one. Especially one juror in particular. A different kind of wretchedness settled into his heart. He cleared his throat and shifted his weight on the chair. "It will be difficult for me to explain why his mummy isn't around in a way that he can understand. He's still a baby."

"Just tell him that I went to heaven, that I'm with the angels."

Heaven? Angels? There's a gross misstatement of the facts if ever there was one.

With an opposing mixture of indifference and gratitude, Galen stared at the woman who'd given him an unexpected and beautiful gift—a one-and-a-half-year-old son—who was now the center of Galen's world. Geoffrey was the one and only reason that Galen could not say that he wished he'd never met Beatrix Noyes.

Their first encounter had happened about four years ago at a London pub where Trix worked as a cocktail waitress. Five years his senior, Trix wasn't what most men would call physically attractive, but she was sociable and highly intelligent. Immediately after he sat down at her bar, she'd engaged him and a few other patrons in conversation about domestic politics, world affairs, history, and a host of other engaging topics. Before he knew it, the bar had closed, and instead of having Trix take the tube, he'd driven her home. He'd stayed for breakfast the following morning.

A then recent graduate of Oxford University, Galen had just started an entry-level position at a marketing company in London while also helping his grandfather run Carmichael's Furniture—the family's mediocre-performing household furniture company.

He hadn't been looking for a romantic commitment, and neither had Trix. They'd both been content with a purely physical relationship—a friends with benefits deal. She worked at a small bank in London by day, and as a bartender by night. She was a fun-loving girl with no real plans in life. She went where the wind blew her—her very own words. Words, he knew, she would be regretting for the rest of her life.

"Galen, will you do that for me? Will you just tell our son that I'm dead? It's the least you can do."

Galen tried to mask his emotions with a deceptive calmness in his voice. "There's no need for Geoffrey to think that you're dead. I will bring him to see you from time to time. Despite your —" He waved his hand around as he tried to find the right words to describe her situation. "Your unfortunate circumstance, you *are* his mother. Nothing can ever change that."

"I gave up the right to motherhood when I killed Jacob Miner."

"Oh no, you gave it up long before that."

She averted her gaze and stared at the wall behind him for a few silent moments. "You're right, and that's why I don't want him to ever know where I am, or what I did. I don't want him to bear the burden of my shame. If he thinks I'm dead, he won't go looking for answers."

Impervious to her teary eyes and voice, it nevertheless pained him to think that his son would be growing up without his mother in his life. Yes, it would be a lot easier for him to tell Geoffrey that his mother was dead, and spare him the knowledge of her crimes and lifetime incarceration. It was the easy thing to do, but definitely not the right thing.

Galen felt suffocated and handicapped by the eight-month nightmare that had ended a few weeks ago when Scotland Yard and the National Crime Agency had finally taken down the organized crime ring that had totally destroyed his life.

"All he'll know is what you tell him," Trix said, "and I hope you'll paint a decent picture of me, the way you knew me before all this happened."

"I grew up thinking that my father was dead because that's what my mother told me," he said. "I won't lie to our son. For now, when he cries for you, I'll tell him that you are away on holiday. I'll figure something out for the next few years when he asks about his mummy. But when he's old enough to understand, I will tell him the whole truth."

"The truth will crush him."

"Perhaps, but the truth always has a way of coming out from hiding. It may take years, sometimes decades, but it eventually makes its presence known." He fisted his hands on his thighs as the memory of his own mother's deception raced through him. A deception he'd learned about from Massimo, the half brother Galen hadn't known existed until an out-of-the-blue telephone conversation, almost four years ago.

Galen had learned from Massimo that their father, Luciano, had died six years prior to that call, and not twenty-five years ago as Galen had previously been told. At that moment, it had become clear to Galen that his mother had lied to him. *The reasons?* Neither he nor Massimo knew at the time. One thing was clear, though—their father had had an illicit affair with Galen's mother.

It was ironic that Galen was now having the kind of conversation with the woman who'd given birth to his son that might be similar in nature to the one his parents might have had with each other, twenty-six years ago.

"What do I say when our child asks about his father?" his mother might have asked.

"Tell him I'm dead."

And that's exactly what his mother had told him.

"Your father is dead, Galen. He died before you were born."

"What was his name, and how did he die, Mummy?"

"It's best you don't ask questions about him. He wasn't a very nice man, you know."

That had been the extent of Galen's knowledge about his father until Massimo's phone call. The fact that Luciano had been alive for the first seventeen years of Galen's life, and hadn't bothered once to get in touch with him, had filled Galen with anger and resentment toward both his neglectful father and his lying mother, who'd taken the answers to all his questions to the grave with her. He never wanted his son to feel such resentment toward him for lying about his mother. He was determined to be a better father than his had been—an involved and present father, the kind of father he'd been to Mindy's children.

Mindy. A bolt of lightning shot through Galen's body as Mindy's alluring face appeared in his mind. Her seductive eyes beckoned to him, and his body responded with vigor. He longed for her soft touch, her warmth, her…

"Galen, please! I don't want my son to think that I'm a monster."

Mindy's image vanished with lightning speed into the ethers. Galen glanced around at the other inmates and their visitors, whose attention Trix's outburst had drawn. This was her life, and he was probably the only visitor she would have from this day forward. All her friends had deserted her after she'd confessed to killing the night watchman at her bank. She was alone. He could lie to her now, just so she would have peace of mind. But she didn't deserve that, not after the mess she'd made of his and Geoffrey's lives.

"Geoffrey should learn the truth from me rather than from someone else, who might not be delicate in the way they explain it to him," he said quietly, even as he fought the nauseating feeling that had crippled him when he'd learned the truth about his own mother's affair with a married man. If only she'd been honest with him from the beginning. "The day will come when he will ask questions about his mother." He shook his head. "I will not tell him lies that I will have to retract when he stumbles on the truth in some other way. I will not lie to *my* son," he reiterated with cold emphasis.

"*Your* son?" Trix asked, rancor sharpening her voice. "A moment ago, he was *our* son. Am I to believe now that you might poison him against me instead of just telling him that I'm dead? That's worse, Galen. How can you be so cruel? I thought you—"

Galen slammed his fist on the table as all the misery she'd caused him the past few months slammed into his gut like a ton of bricks. He was tired of holding back his anger, of pretending that what she'd done to him and Geoffrey could be easily forgiven and forgotten.

"Cruel? You call me cruel?" he hissed under his breath to keep the argument in their corner, and the guards from escorting him to the door before he spoke his mind. They were very strict in here about confrontation.

"This is what cruel is, Trix: you drugged me and then hopped on me. You got pregnant and never bothered to tell me. You gave birth to *my* son in this hellhole of a prison, and recorded another man's name on his birth certificate when you knew bloody well I was his father. He spent the first seventeen months of his life here. Was not telling me about Geoffrey payback because I told you that I'd met someone in America when I woke up in your bed the morning after you'd seduced me? Was this payback, Trix?"

"At first, yes. I was cross that you'd thrown the fact that you had a new life, a new girlfriend, and two children you were playing daddy to in my face. My parents are dead. I have no other relatives. He was all I had. And quite frankly, I didn't think you would want him since—"

"How could you think I wouldn't want my son when you

know the hell I went through after learning that my own father had deliberately ignored me? How could you think that I would want my son to grow up without ever knowing me?"

"Well—"

"If it wasn't for my grandfather's stroke bringing me back to England at the right time, I probably would never have known of Geoffrey's existence. And how did I find out?" he snapped as his anger reached fever point. "From your partners in crime. They banned me from coming here to meet my son with threats to his life. They threatened Granddad's, Mindy's, and her children's lives if I didn't go along with their program. My past association with you led them to my grandfather. He may have died thinking that I was a rotten scumbag, all because of you."

"I didn't know the Fraser family was in organized crime or I wouldn't have gotten involved with Basil. By the time I realized why he'd befriended me, it was too late for both me and Geoffrey." She pressed her lips together as tears streamed down her face. "I had to do everything they wanted to protect my unborn child. I killed for him. And that still wasn't enough for them. Even here in prison, we weren't safe. They had people in here watching me, listening to my conversations. I couldn't trust anybody. I couldn't call you. I couldn't warn your grandfather. I'm sorry that he died. He was such a nice old chap."

Grief ripped through Galen's gut at the thought of the way his grandfather had died. He should have been here to take care of him instead of off in Granite Falls fighting Massimo for half of Andretti Industries. He took no comfort in the fact that had he won the case, he would have used the money to revive Carmichael's Furniture. Now, because of the disgrace attached to his family's business, he couldn't use that name anymore. He was as much to blame for his grandfather's death as Trix and her gang of thugs.

And on top of all that, it was highly possible that he had lost the love and trust of the only woman he'd ever loved because he couldn't call to tell her that from the moment he'd stepped onto English soil, he'd been trapped in an eight-month-long season of *The Catch*.

The most terrifying thought had been that he might never see his son, much less get custody of him. Galen had been all alone in the world with the knowledge that he had a young son who needed him, but whom he might never have the opportunity of meeting if he'd made one wrong move. He'd had everything to lose if he didn't stick to their program.

"Galen, you can have a bit of pity for me, can't you?"

Galen recoiled as he felt her hand on his. *Pity?* She wanted pity? "All this could have been avoided if you'd only told me that you were pregnant with my child long before you met Basil. I spent seven months in England before I was able to see my son, hold him in my arms." He pushed back his chair, raking the legs against the floor as he stood up. At this moment, he did not care about Trix's situation or her feelings. She had placed his freedom, his reputation, and the well-being of Geoffrey, Mindy, and Mindy's children in danger. Her actions had caused his grandfather's death. She had brought this disaster upon herself. She was not his responsibility. Geoffrey was his priority, and so were Mindy, Kyle, and Brittany.

"Galen, I'm sorry. If I could go back—"

"You can't go back, Beatrix, and neither can I. It's done," he said with a resigned shrug of his shoulders. "I have to look toward my future and that of my son. I will bring Geoffrey by tomorrow so you can say goodbye before we leave. It's the last time you'll see him for a while. Make it count." He yanked his jacket from the back of the chair and sprinted toward the exit, ignoring Trix's frantic calls.

Once outside, Galen leaned against the building and took a moment to cool him temper as a mixture of conflicting emotions stormed his brain. Since the threat from the Frasers had been removed from their lives, he'd visited Trix often to bond with his son while he was still in his mother's care, and so she could teach Galen about Geoffrey's schedule, his favorite foods, his likes and dislikes, the way he liked being held—things that only Trix, the only person in Geoffrey's life up to that point, would know.

Today was the first time he'd lashed out at her. Maybe it was because he finally had custody of his son and didn't need to fear anyone threatening to take him away if Galen stepped out of bounds. He'd actually *had* to step out of bounds as Geoffrey's eighteen-month birthday had drawn closer and closer—the date upon which he would have been placed into foster care or adopted, since that was the cut-off age at which Bronzefield allowed children to stay with their mothers. It was frightening to think of his son being raised by strangers who might have mistreated him all his life, or taken by the Frasers who might have simply decided to kill him, or sell him.

Galen inhaled deeply, gathering up the remaining fury still lingering in his belly and blew it out through his mouth. His muscles relaxed as he watched the long puff of vapor dissipate into the cold English night.

The past eight months had been hell on earth for him, but the end results—knowing he had a son and had gained custody of him—had been worth it. His only regret was that his beloved grandfather had paid the ultimate price—his life. Galen could only hope that his granddaddy had believed him when he'd denied stealing his life's savings and destroying his legacy. He could only hope, and take comfort in the fact that the Carmichael name and genes would continue on through Baxter Geoffrey Carmichael's grandson and great-grandson.

More composed now, Galen strolled toward his car in the visitors' parking area. As angry as he was with Trix, a tiny part of him understood her need to keep the only family she had close to her for as long as she could. Everybody needed love and acceptance from their relatives. His own need for family connection had led him to accept Massimo's initial invitation to visit him in the States.

He'd spent months with Massimo and Shaina—his wife of one year—their infant daughter, Aria, Shaina's younger brother, Cameron, and his girlfriend, Monica. It had been a wonderful experience to get to know Massimo, to bond with him and his family, and to learn about his paternal heritage.

The fact that Massimo had inherited the family's multibillion-dollar company hadn't bothered Galen at that time. He'd been grateful that Massimo had reached out to him, had wanted to include him in his life and introduce him to his extended family, the Andreases—especially his cousin Adam—owners of the world-renowned establishments, Hotel Andreas and Ristorante Andreas.

In addition to Adam, Galen had met Mass' other two, billionaire friends. Dr. Erik LaCrosse was one of the best OB/GYN in the world and Bryce Fontaine was the founder of Fontaine Enterprises. Those four families were the most respected and prominent members of Granite Falls and the surrounding communities. Galen had been proud that the blood running through his veins had come from one of the most brilliant, shrewd minds in the business world. He'd never felt as strong a sense of belonging as he had those few months he'd spent at the Andretti estates in Granite Falls, New Hampshire. That visit had changed his life in ways he'd never imagined possible.

Galen unlocked his car and, once he was seated and buckled in, he opened the glove compartment and pulled out a photo. In order to protect it from any association with Bronzefield, and from being tainted by the guards' hands during the customary search, he'd left it in the car.

His heart pounded against his chest as he gazed into the eyes that stared back at him. During his first visit to Granite Falls, Galen had also met Mindy Marshall—a single mother of two young children. He'd been captivated by her sweet brown eyes from the moment he first stared into them at Arabella, the boutique at Hotel Andreas where she worked—still worked—as a clerk.

Her sense of humor, her spontaneity, and fun-loving, energetic personality had drawn him into her mesmerizing world. Mindy was different from any other woman Galen had ever met. Unlike his norm when it came to women, he'd wanted to take things slowly with her, especially because she was so young and had two fatherless children. Also, he hadn't yet, officially, broken things off with Trix.

Galen had had many meaningless short-lived affairs in his young life, and had only come to understand his own salacious nature after meeting Massimo. It was in his blood. Ironically, like Massimo, and unlike their father, Galen had always been faithful to the women he dated. He didn't want Mindy to ever be labeled "the other woman" when she'd become "the woman" from the moment he'd first met her.

Mindy had also been cautious and reluctant at first, but as the rising passion between them became undeniable, Galen had called Trix to tell her that they were over. As he'd expected, she didn't care one way or the other, and had told him that she was already seeing someone else.

Free to fall in love for the first time in his life, Galen had pulled out all the stops to win Mindy over, not that she needed any coercion. His mind drifted back to that moonlit Saturday night when they'd first made love in his villa on Crystal Lake. That had been the most amazing night of Galen's life up to that point, and he'd had many more with her since then.

His throat tightened with emotion as he traced the outline of her mouth with his fingertip. "I miss you, Mindy, so much, love. My only hope is that you'll understand and forgive me when I explain everything to you."

He was heartbroken over the pain he knew his absence and silence was causing her, but the Frasers had warned him that they could get to Mindy and her children anytime they wanted. And knowing how much Mindy loved him, Galen knew that she would have been on the next flight to London if she'd even sensed that he was in trouble.

Mindy was the kind of woman who stood by her man, as she'd so fearlessly demonstrated by taking his side in his fight with Massimo. But standing by her man this time would have definitely gotten her killed, or worse, kept as a sex slave like many of the young girls he'd heard his roommate and other members of the gang discussing in the most degrading manner.

To protect Mindy and avoid getting even more blood on his hands, Galen had had no choice but to keep the silence between them going.

He'd thought of calling her after the authorities had finally rounded up and indicted the last of the gang, but the debilitating truth was that since he'd never told Mindy that he'd slept with Trix after they'd been together, how could he explain Geoffrey's existence? It wasn't the kind of conversation one had over the phone. He needed to be standing in front of her so that she could slap his face or punch him in the gut for betraying her if that's what she wanted to.

"I promise to make it up to you, baby, even if it takes me the rest of my life. I will never give up on us." With tears in his eyes, Galen kissed Mindy's picture and then placed it into his shirt pocket, close to his heart.

As he eased into the flow of afternoon traffic en route to London and his suite at Hotel Andreas-London, Galen knew without a doubt that his first visit to Granite Falls had been a life-changing event. He'd gotten over the fact that his father had neglected him and had instead chosen to revel in the acceptance and affection from Massimo and his family, his friends and their families, and the new relationships that he'd made along the way. Spending time with Mindy and her children had been one of the few pinnacles of his life.

He'd been on a natural high for months. Then the floor had collapsed from under him when he'd returned to England for Christmas that same year.

CHAPTER THREE

On her dying bed, Galen's mother's older sister, Gertrude, had told Galen that his parents had been in love with each other before he was born. Massimo's then pregnant mother, Giuliana, had threatened to take Massimo and her unborn child away from Luciano if he didn't end his relationship with Judith. Giuliana had also ordered Judith not to ever reveal the paternity of her bastard child to anyone, not even the child, or else the financial support she'd set up for him would stop.

Since Andretti family business was structured so that only legitimate heirs could inherit, Luciano had buckled under his wife's demands and sent his pregnant lover back to England. He never spoke to her again, nor had he ever seen the child their love had created.

Galen had gone to the pub where Trix worked and over a few drinks, had bitched and moaned about his father's wife, who'd come between Galen's father and mother.

He'd awakened the following morning to a grinning Trix praising him for giving her the best shag of her life. She'd said that she missed him while he was away, and that she was ready to get serious and settle down. She'd even asked if he'd take her back to the States with him.

Galen had told her about Mindy, and that he loved her and her two kids. And then he'd hightailed it from Trix's flat with remorse, disgust, and self-loathing for betraying Mindy, cramming the space where anger and heartbreak had been the previous night. Up to this day, Galen still could not remember the alleged night of sex with Trix, but Geoffrey's birth nine months later was proof that he'd slept with her.

Galen floored the gas pedal as he merged onto M25 toward London. He was anxious to get home to his son—a son he'd known existed for eight months, but whom he hadn't seen or held in his arms until recently.

As Geoffrey's eighteen-month birthday had drawn closer and closer, Galen's fear of never meeting him had outweighed his fear of the Fraser family. He still had one ace up his sleeve, one chip to cash in even though it meant losing a little dignity.

He got his chance when Geoffrey was sixteen months old. Christmas, as it turned out, was a big deal for the Frasers, plus one of the young women in the family was getting married on Christmas Eve. Galen's roommate—the man who had stolen Galen's identity— was spending less time at the flat and more at the family's luxury compound in Ireland. The *faux* Galen's coconspirators' visits had dwindled also, much to Galen's relief.

In mid-December, Charles Fraser, the patriarch of the family, had called Galen on the cell phone they'd given him and told him that since he'd been such a good, obedient servant, he would have a break from the impromptu frisking, searching, and beatings for the holidays. He was still expected to make his scheduled deposits and transfers though, and he'd better not do anything stupid since someone could be watching him.

The moment he'd hung up from Charles, Galen left his flat and walked into the restaurant across the street, snagged a cell phone from a stranger's coat hanging on the back of her chair, walked into the bathroom, and called Massimo. The call had gone straight to voicemail. Galen had left as much details as he could about his situation, his address, his schedule, and the names of the banks where he made weekly deposits. He'd begged Mass not to make Geoffrey pay for his mistakes.

To Galen's utmost surprise, Mass was sitting behind the desk, posing as a clerk in the bank where Galen had gone to conduct business the next day. It had taken all of Galen's strength not to break down and cry when he'd realized that his big brother—the one he'd tried to destroy—had come to his aid without a moment's hesitation.

While they worked on the deposits and transfers, Mass had told him that he'd done some digging and had all the scoop on the Fraser family—their illegal operations, their compounds and homes, their bank accounts, and he'd even found some of the other young women who'd fallen victim to them. He was certain they would testify against the Frasers if called upon to do so.

When Galen had asked him how he'd managed to get all that information so quickly, Mass had smiled and said, "Little brother, when this is all over, I will sit you down and school you about the power and reach of the Andretti name. Perhaps then you will want to adopt it."

Mass had informed Galen that he had friends in both Her Majesty's Revenue and Customs Department and the National Crime Agency who, from now on, would be posing as employees at the banks where Galen would continue to make his deposits and transfers. And thus a sting operation was born.

Mass had also employed the Andreas' London-based attorney, a Mr. Cedric Peabody, who'd already set the ball rolling for a paternity test to make sure Galen was indeed Geoffrey's father before they moved forward. He'd promised Galen that it was all covert, and that as long as Galen kept up the charade, he should have Geoffrey and his life back very soon.

His brother had stayed for a week, meeting with him in the bank every day to keep him abreast of Geoffrey's case, and just to lend moral support. Mass had been his ray of hope.

Three weeks later, the entire Fraser family was behind bars, and Geoffrey was out of Bronzefield and in Galen's arms. Come tomorrow, his son would have a brand new birth certificate with Galen named as father, Luigi added as his middle name, and Carmichael as last name. Galen would be picking up a new birth certificate for himself, as well, with Luciano Luigi Andretti filling the box where *Father: Unknown* was once recorded. It was a new beginning for father and son. He hoped their relationship would grow in depth and strength as the years rolled by.

Galen's heart skipped a beat as he recalled the first time he'd seen Geoffrey strapped in a car seat in the back of the car that had brought him from Bronzefield. He remembered the river of hot tears he'd cried, and the instant sense of protectiveness that had washed over him when he'd held his son for the first time. It was the second pinnacle moment in Galen's life.

That was the power of the Andretti name, Galen thought, as his mind wandered back to a conversation he'd had with Mass before he'd returned to the States to spend Christmas with his family.

"Why?" he'd asked, as they faced each other across the desk in the bank. "Why, after what I did to you? I tried to break up Andretti Industries."

Massimo chuckled. "You're an Andretti, little brother, and when one Andretti gets cut, we all bleed. Plus," he added with a shrug, "I grew to respect you during the case."

"Respect me?" Galen frowned at his dark haired, blue-eyed half brother, with whom he'd been at war for the better part of their four-year relationship. "I thought you hated me. You were so cold and shrewd, and…awful to me."

"It was just a show. I was testing your stamina. Your fighting me showed me that you had guts, that you weren't afraid to take risks and fight for your cause even if you knew the odds were against you. You didn't shy away. You acted like an Andretti. And that's when I knew we could be a family. I've been waiting for you to call."

The war between him and his brother was over, and soon Galen would be able to start building a relationship with his son. He'd be free to go back to Granite Falls, and Mindy.

"I owe you so much, Mass," he said in a hoarse voice. "I've said it a thousand times since you came to my rescue, but I'll say it again. I'm sorry for the trouble I caused you. I will find a way to make it up to you. I'm in your debt. Anything you need, whatever it is, I'm here for you."

"Apology accepted, and let's not talk of it again. Andrettis don't grovel. All I need is for you to start being my brother. Sign this, Mr. Fredrick Fraser," he said, sliding a form toward Galen, reminding him that they were still keeping up appearances even though Galen's "bodyguard" hadn't accompanied him to the bank today.

Galen signed the form and slid it back to Mass. "I want that, too."

"Good to know we're on the same page." Mass gave him an encouraging smile and turned back to the computer."

As Mass typed rapidly on the keyboard, Galen was reminded that his brother, who owned *La Banca di Bianchi*, one of the biggest banks in Europe, knew exactly what he was doing. His posing as a bank employee was the perfect cover.

Galen's back went ramrod straight. If the Frasers had known he was related to the owner of *La Banca di Bianchi*, those bastards might have forced him to help them rip off the London branch.

Galen had no idea if that would have played in or out of his favor. It could have totally annihilated his relationship with Mass who already thought him a gold digger. On the other hand, it might have also raised suspicions of brewing trouble and propelled Mass to come to his aid much sooner. Galen would never know. All he knew was that he was grateful to have his brother here with him now.

Mass turned to Galen. "Want to hear something that would cheer you up?"

Galen slanted his eyes. "Cheer me up? I don't think that's possible. Not until I hold my son in my arms."

"*This* will help." Mass placed his elbows on the desk and leaned closer. "The day our arbitration began, I had my accountants reassess Andretti Industries' financial state from the day you were born to the day our father died. I had my attorneys set aside half of the earnings and assets of those seventeen years for you. You have more than enough money to start a new business of your own once this fiasco is over."

"Massimo." Galen fought back the tears and struggled against his instincts to leap over the desk and hug his brother with unmitigated gratitude. "You make me feel like such a fool for taking you to court." His voice cracked with emotion he could not display.

Massimo tossed him a professional smile. "Like I said, this would not have happened if you hadn't fought me. Next account."

Galen gave him the necessary information for the next transfer, then said, "You have no idea how scared I was to go up against you. But I had nothing to lose, and—"

"Everything to gain," Mass interjected. "And talking about gain, it would probably be an honor to your grandfather's memory if you reinvented Carmichael's Furniture. It was his life's work."

"If the judge had ruled in my favor, I would have done just that and left it in the hands of a trusted CEO. I've been helping Granddad in the store since I was a teenager, and he always spoke about me taking it over one day. I gently told him that running a furniture business wasn't my thing. He was disappointed, and since he had no other heirs, he liquidated the company and retired—the best thing he could have done actually. I just wish he'd had more time to enjoy his retirement. He'd worked so hard all his life, only to be robbed of…"

"You must not blame yourself for what happened to your grandfather," Mass said when Galen choked up. "But if you're still interested in the CEO plan, I have a long list of clients you can tap into."

Galen shook his head. "I can't. Carmichael's Furniture is now associated with high crime and money laundering." He spread his hands and smirked. "I mean, I'm sitting here transferring ill-gotten money from my family's company to the bank accounts of criminals across the continent. Once the story breaks, everyone will think me a heartless bastard who stole from my grandfather and caused his death. I appreciate all your help, and I look forward to being under your tutelage when I decide what I want to do with my life. But for right now, I just want to concentrate on bonding with my son once I get him, and to be available for whatever he needs, whenever he needs it." *That, and winning Mindy back.*

"Do you plan to stay in England?"

"After what those people did to my name, I wouldn't be able to get a job as a street cleaner in this country, anywhere in Europe for that matter."

"You're an Andretti. You don't need a job. You just need a company to run, a board to control, and employees to carry out your orders."

"You make it sound so fun."

"It is. Why not come back to Granite Falls? You and Geoffrey are welcome to stay with Shaina and me until you figure out your life. Aria, MJ, and Adam's son, Alex, will all be excited to have another little cousin around."

"Well, Alex isn't technically Geoffrey's cousin." Galen stated.

"It doesn't matter. We're all family. Both Adam and I want our kids to be as close as he and I were as children. We value family ties. You're my brother, so that includes your children, too."

"I should have known there was a heart beating under that hard shell you project to the world."

Massimo raised an eyebrow as he punched some numbers into a calculator. "Our father once told me that if people know you have a heart, they will try to break it. He was talking about the business world of course." He paused and glanced up at Galen. "We both have daddy issues. Even though it was for different reasons, like you, I was full of anger and resentment towards him, primarily because of the affair he had with your mother. It broke my mother's heart. You don't even know the half of it."

"Mass, I'm sorry. I—"

"No, no." Mass shook his head emphatically. "I'm not blaming you. I brought it up to explain that I wasn't always this nice. It took the love and trust of a good woman to change me. What you need is a good woman to love, and who loves you. I'm going out on a limb here and say that you've probably found that kind of love with Mindy. She's a good kid. Admirable in my eyes for sticking beside you even though she knew that it could have cost her her job and ended her friendship with Tashi. She loves you."

Galen swallowed the raw ache in his throat. "I knew she was special the moment I first saw her. But I screwed it up royally by not being honest with her, not telling her that I'd slept with Trix two and a half years ago. I'd be lucky if she ever speaks to me again. She will never forgive me."

Massimo hit a key, sending documents to the printer behind him. "If she loves you, she will forgive you anything. You know my story with Shaina, how for years she blamed me for her father's death and all the hardship she and Cameron encountered in the ensuing years. Once she heard my side of the story—the *truth*—she sided with me against her own brother, who wasn't as anxious to forgive."

"Shaina's conflict with you began years before you became a couple. I cheated on Mindy. You never cheated on Shaina."

Mass made a guttural sound in his throat. "If the thought even crosses my mind—not that it ever will—I won't be around to talk about it, or even to deny it. Listen, we are powerless to the women we love, and they know it, but they also know that we're not perfect, that we're downright stupid sometimes. When we humble ourselves, kneel in front of them, lay our heads in their laps like contrite little boys confessing our inadequacies, they are more likely to forgive us than when we act all machismo. You have to be humble and gentle, yet persistent when Mindy tries to put more distance between you."

"It wouldn't be easy telling her that I'd been with another woman while we were together."

"No. But you didn't sleep with Trix intentionally either. You were upset and vulnerable when you went to see her. She drugged you and then took advantage of you. Your only transgression was not telling Mindy."

"I chose not to believe anything happened that night because I couldn't remember anything happening."

Massimo reached behind him and collected the documents from the printer. He glanced them over judiciously signed them in the necessary places, and then handed them to Galen. "You couldn't remember because of the drugs. Geoffrey is proof that it happened," he said, while Galen signed his fake name on each one. "Mindy will think that you had no intention of ever telling her. Therein lies your ultimate betrayal. She will be crushed. Her heart will be broken even more than it already is. If you want her back, you will have to fight like a dog to prove that you deserve a second chance, that you deserve her heart, her trust, and her love. Don't downplay what you did wrong, which was not telling her, but do up-play the fact that it would not have happened if you weren't upset, inebriated, and drugged."

As Galen now thought about that night, *upset* was a far cry from what he'd felt when his aunt had fed him that despicable lie about his parents—the lie his mother had concocted to hide the real story behind her affair with a married man and explain away the pregnancy that resulted from it.

During the arbitration, when witness after witness came forward to attest to Massimo's mother's character, Galen had begun to doubt his mother's story. Giuliana Andretti was portrayed as a kind, sweet, soft-spoken woman, and there was not one shred of evidence that she'd ordered her husband to abandon his child. Moreover, legal documents had been presented that indubitably proved that it was Luciano's sole decision to order Judith and her unborn bastard back to England.

Former and current employees of Andretti Industries, including Mindy's mother, Pamela, had portrayed Judith Carmichael—the then personal secretary to Luciano Andretti— as a manipulative, delusional woman who wanted Giuliana's life. No wonder Pamela Marshall didn't like him, Galen thought, as he fought to temper the shame of his mother's actions that had been dumped upon him. When more character witnesses swore under oath that Luciano was indeed in love with his wife and was heartbroken when she died, Galen's faith in his mother's character took a quantum leap south.

If Luciano had truly loved Judith, after his wife's untimely death, he would surely have brought her back to America and made a life with her and his son. Why hadn't he connected the dots before he'd begun the arbitration and embarrassed himself in the eyes of the handful of people who now saw him as nothing but a gold-digging son of a bitch—just like his mother?

Galen pulled his car into the front entrance of Hotel Andreas, dropped a hefty tip into the valet tray and hopped out. He strode through the automatic doors, crossed the expansive elaborate foyer, and headed for the elevators. As he rode up to the penthouse suite, he wished he'd been more aggressive with questions about his father before his mother's death, five years ago. Now, he might never know the real story.

Perhaps he didn't want to know.

Galen opened the door to his suite and stepped inside. Intense happiness immediately filled him at the sight of Geoffrey sitting on the floor surrounded by building blocks, rubbery creatures, pop-up books, and his trains—his favorite toys—and Sybil, his nanny, making funny noises as she mimicked the choo-choo sounds of trains moving along a track.

Galen hated to interrupt his child's play, but he hadn't seen him for hours, which felt like months since he'd only had the opportunity to hold him for the first time a few weeks ago. And today Geoffrey had become his, only his. He walked over and picked up his son, hugging him tightly. "Geoffrey, my boy, my little baby boy. You're mine. You're all mine," he crooned as he buried his face in his neck and lost himself in his baby scent for a few loving moments. He would die a thousand deaths and kill ten thousand foes for his son.

He loosened his hug when Geoffrey began to whine and struggle. "How has he been?" he asked the twenty-two-year-old brunette who'd once worked in the hotel's nursery, but who had been assigned as Geoffrey's nanny since he'd been released from

Bronzefield. She was quite responsible for her age and both he and Geoffrey depended on her.

"He's been jolly good, actually. Ate his supper and enjoyed his bath."

"That's Daddy's boy," Galen said, kissing Geoffrey on his chubby cheeks.

His heart melted when his son wound his arms around his neck and said, "Daddy. Boy. Daddy. Good boy."

Galen closed his eyes as mounting joy flooded his being. "Yes, Geoffrey. You're Daddy's good boy. Always and forever."

"He's getting used to you. Didn't cry for his mum that much today. I still can't understand how his mum could just up and walk out on him, and you, Mr. Carmichael. You're both so sweet."

Galen stared at Sybil. She obviously had no idea what she was talking about when it came to Trix's and his relationship. Neither Geoffrey nor he needed anyone's pity for something neither of them had done, nor could change even if they wanted to. It was nobody's business that the mother of his child would spend the rest of her life in prison, and so to stave off questions and speculations about his personal life he'd simply told Sybil and everyone else who'd asked that Geoffrey's mother had abandoned him.

He couldn't very well be broadcasting the truth he wanted to stay hidden until Geoffrey was old enough to understand it. There was only one woman on this planet with whom Galen intended to share the gory details of his story, and she wasn't standing in front of him at the moment.

"Have you had supper? I can order up something from the restaurant. What do you fancy?"

Galen smiled at Sybil's concerns for him. Once he'd made up his mind to move back to the States, he'd asked her to accompany him—just for a few months. It would be good for Geoffrey to have at least one familiar face in a strange place when he himself couldn't be with him. Sybil had agreed, even before he was finished making his case. She had just broken up with her boyfriend and was looking for a change, a new start, she'd stated. "Didn't you tell me you had plans with friends later tonight?" he asked.

"I did, but—"

"You should spend as much time as possible with your friends and family before we leave." He hadn't had supper, and he wasn't hungry. He just wanted to be alone with his thoughts and his son. "It will be months before you see them again."

"I don't mind staying home and taking care of Geoffrey while you attend to business. It's my job." Sybil pointed at a desk across the room. "Your phone has been ringing off the hook. You have lots of messages."

Galen suspected that most of the calls were from the authorities and his solicitor as they worked to clear his name and wrap up loose ends concerning the Frasers. Now that the nightmare was over, Galen felt no pressure to immediately respond to the messages nor the many emails he knew were waiting in his inbox. Not tonight anyway since it has only been a few hours that Trix signed the papers giving him full custody of Geoffrey, and permission to take him out of the country. That was cause for celebration. "I insist you go out, Sybil. I'm taking the night off from work. Geoffrey and I will be fine."

"Alright, Mr. Carmichael. See you in the morning, then."

As Sybil headed for her bedroom, Galen thought of Mindy, who'd been twenty-one years old when he'd first met her. Unlike Sybil, she was already grown up and taking care of two children on her own. Pregnant the first time at sixteen, the poor girl never had a chance to enjoy her youth. When girls her age had been out partying, going to movies, concerts, and pubs, as Sybil was getting ready to do, Mindy had been at home changing diapers and rocking her babies to sleep.

Galen walked over to the side of the room overlooking the busy London street below, vowing in his heart to find a way to give Mindy the experience of recapturing her lost teenage years, to expose her to the thrill of being childfree and carefree for a while.

He was grateful to Mass for giving him the means to fight for her, to be the kind of man she deserves—a man who could provide for her, take care of her, and give her the world, the moon, and the stars if those were the things she wanted from him.

"Mummy. Bear. Mummy," Geoffrey cried, reaching for a brown teddy bear sitting on the sofa—a parting gift from his mother.

Galen walked over and picked it up. "Here you go, son. Here's your mummy's bear."

Geoffrey tossed the bear to the floor. "No. Mummy. Mummy." He began to cry and struggle.

Galen held him close. "I'm sorry, Geoff. You mummy is away on holiday." Galen's stomach burned with regret as he spoke the first of many lies about his mother his son would hear from him. "Daddy is here, little chap. Daddy will always be here for you." That was no lie.

Galen hugged Geoffrey close to his heart and sobbed quietly for a plethora of reasons.

CHAPTER FOUR

Mindy ripped off her gloves as she bolted through the front door of her mother's house and switched on the light. She dropped her gloves and her backpack on the floor and sprinted across the living room, paying little attention to the unstable floor rattling beneath her. She blew air into her palms and rubbed them together before holding them as close to the radiator as she possibly could. Her fingers were frozen numb, as were her toes, she realized, as she clumsily toed off her sneakers and brought her sock feet closer to the heat.

It was early February, two months since her heat had given out, and she didn't know how much more of that cold car she could take. Thank goodness, her mother's house sat across the street from the elementary school, so driving her kids around was limited to two times a week when she took Kyle to swimming lessons and Brittany to ballet.

Although they complained about the cold all during the drive, they nonetheless enjoyed attending their classes in the luxurious Granite Falls facilities she'd enrolled them in after she'd begun working at Arabella. She was grateful to still be able to afford to keep them there. Those classes were the highlights of their week.

Mindy's hopes for her children's future had risen to an all-time high when she'd moved into her own apartment in Granite Falls. For once, she'd felt in control of her life and proud that she was able to provide a home for her children and buy them decent clothes instead of dressing them in hand-me-downs from her friends.

For the first time in their lives, the kids had a bedroom to themselves—big enough to accommodate two twin beds—instead of sharing a small room with her. She'd promised them that they'd have their own individual bedrooms one day soon after Galen, who'd been living with her at the time, had assured her that they would be a real family once the trial was over.

Her cheeks burned with humiliation. Whatever had she, a girl from a trailer park, been thinking when she'd dared to dream so high, dared to believe that she could be as lucky as Tashi and move up into the ranks of high society by marrying a man from that circle? She'd been desperate for love, had longed to be accepted and appreciated, and wanted to find a father for her children so badly that she'd allowed herself to be sucked in by Galen's empty promises and outright lies.

Anger ate at Mindy as she recalled the difficult period immediately following Galen's departure. Every morning and every night for weeks on end, Kyle and Brittany had asked where he was and when was he coming back. She'd truthfully told them that she simply did not know. Eventually, she'd had to begin the odious task of trying to return all their lives to a pre-Galen state of existence and reinstating her kids' daily routine to a one-parent home. She'd had to reassure them that they could trust her to be a constant in their lives, that she would never leave them.

She'd promised them that they were safe and that nothing

else in their world would change. But she'd had to eat that promise when her mom was hospitalized for weeks after falling in her bathroom and ended up breaking her collarbone, dislocating a shoulder, and twisting her ankle. With her brother, Billy, married and living in the Midwest, Mindy had the responsibility of taking care of her mother, whom she thought would be back on her feet in a few weeks.

But when the weeks turned into months of running back and forth between the two towns—sometimes two and three times in one day—Mindy knew she was in over her head. Billy wasn't around to pick up Kyle and Brittany from school and take them to their extra-curricular activities while she worked, or to watch them while she attended night school. Something had to give, and since she lived on the third floor of her apartment complex with no elevator service, bringing her mother to live with her until she recovered was out of the question. She'd had no other choice but to give up her apartment in Granite Falls. Luckily, her lease was about to expire, so she was under no legal obligation to pay for a year.

As her bones began to thaw, Mindy unzipped her jacket and began picking up toys and books and clothes strewn around the room and placing them into a pile to take to her bedroom later. Her mother had bought the modest two-bedroom house with her lump sum pension from Andretti Industries, and since there was no mortgage, she didn't take rent from Mindy. It was a kind of quid pro quo for Mindy nursing her mother back to health. All she had to do was help with the utilities and of course buy food for her and her kids.

The storm door creaked. A moment later, a key rattled in the door before it swung open and her mother walked in carrying a black canvas tote in one hand and a white paper bag in the other. "Hey, Mom."

"What are you doing home? Weren't you supposed to go out tonight?" her mother asked.

Mindy dropped a Barbie doll on the pile and walked over to close and lock the door, and slide the security chain and the dead bolt into place. "The question should be, where have *you* been?" She turned to critically survey the *still* attractive, average-size sixty-six-year-old woman with soft brown eyes and thinning blonde hair, peppered with silvery gray strands.

Like Mindy, Pamela Marshall had been a single mother, who'd worked two jobs to take care of her children. When Billy and Mindy were young, Pamela had worked at Andretti Industries as a kitchen employee during the day and a custodian at night. They'd lived in a trailer park in Evergreen, and although things had been rough, Mindy had never heard her mother complain once. She was never overly affectionate with Billy and her, but she'd taken care of them.

When sixteen-year-old Mindy had gotten pregnant with Kyle, Pamela had thrown her out, forcing her and Kyle to move into an apartment with his friends. Looking back now, Mindy realized that her mother had expected better from her.

Every mother wanted her child to have a better and easier life than she had. Mindy's getting pregnant at sixteen was a huge disappointment for Pamela. But, truth be told, as hard as Mindy had had it—still had it—she would not trade Kyle nor Brittany for anything in this world. She refused to believe that she, or her children were mistakes. They were surprises! Serendipitous surprises. She felt blessed for giving birth to two of the world's smartest and most beautiful children, and she would never turn her back on them no matter what kind of trouble they got into, especially her sweet little Britt.

"*You* didn't tell me you were going out tonight." She scanned her mother's attire—a pair of black slacks and blue, turtleneck sweater under a charcoal sheepskin jacket that sported a fur-trimmed collar. Mindy had used her employee discount at Arabella to purchase the ensemble last Christmas—a gift her mother thoroughly loved.

"You were out with Phin, weren't you?" Phineas O'Henry was a therapist and co-owner of Optimum Result, the physical therapy center where Pamela had gone for healing after her fall. She and Phin had been "going steady" as Pamela called it, ever since. "I didn't even know you had a date," Mindy added, as she shrugged out of her jacket and laid it over the back of the sofa, the only place to sit in the tiny living room.

Pamela walked over to a card table that functioned as a dining table in the corner of the living room and placed her tote and the paper bag on it. "Since Virginia apologized for her past behavior toward you, I didn't have to watch the kids tonight," she said, unbuttoning her coat and laying it over one of the four folding chairs around the table. "So Phin and I made plans for takeout at his house."

"Where's Bacon?" Mindy asked, just realizing that the children's brown lab hadn't come out to greet her when she'd gotten home. She'd been too busy concentrating on getting warm.

"The kids took him to Virginia's. I wouldn't have minded taking him with me, though. Phin loves him."

"As do you," Mindy said with a gentle smile. That was another good thing that had grown out of moving in with her mom. Pamela, who hadn't been keen on dogs before, had learned to love Bacon. He'd been a constant companion during the months she'd been confined to her bed. And when she got better, the first thing she'd done was hire some neighborhood kids to rig a fence around her yard so Bacon could run free outside—something he hadn't been able to do when they'd lived with Billy and in her apartment in Granite Falls.

"I brought you back something." Pamela held up the doggie bag. "It's from Chopsticks."

"You got all dressed up just for takeout at Phin's?" Mindy asked, tongue in cheek.

"Mind your business. I'm a grown woman. I can do whatever I damn well please. You want the food or not?"

Mindy's smile turned into a huge grin at her mother's reddening cheeks. Pamela would never admit that she was having old-people sex, but Mindy knew the telltale signs—like the dreamy gleam in her mother's brown eyes that indicated she'd been intimate tonight, and the unkempt state of her hair. She'd probably been trying to sneak back into the house before Mindy got home from class. Nonetheless, Mindy was happy that her mom had found a man who cared about her. She'd waited sixty-six years for Phineas O'Henry to show up. It gave Mindy hope that perhaps she herself might still be able to attract a man when she was her mother's age.

She sneered inwardly. Who was she kidding? She was twenty-three years old and couldn't attract a man. Well, she could attract them, but she had trouble keeping them around.

"What happened to your plans with Safi?" Pamela asked of Mindy's best friend who also worked at Arabella and attended Evergreen Community College. "Shouldn't you be at a club or something?" Pamela eased down on one end of the sofa, reached for the remote control on the lamp table, and turned on the sixty-inch TV.

"I canceled," Mindy said, dropping her weight onto the other end, her eyes fixed to the screen as the images came into focus. *Charade*, she guessed instantly at the sight of Cary Grant and Audrey Hepburn in the funny bar scene where their characters Peter and Reggie were passing an orange from one person to the other without using their hands. Since living with her mother, Mindy had come to appreciate and love old classic movies, and it was doubly nice to sit on the posh sofa and watch them on the giant-screen TV—two of the expensive household items Tashi had given Mindy when the now Mrs. Andreas had moved from Temple Street to Mount Reservoir.

A year and a half ago, Mindy had finally learned why Tashi had been living in such a rundown apartment, and yet could afford top-of-the-line furniture and appliances. Mindy had been blown away at Tashi's story. She'd come to understand why the girl had been so paranoid and scared out of her wits.

"I would think you'd jump on the opportunity since Kyle and Britt are with Virginia."

"I can't afford to spent money frivolously. Kyle needs new sneakers and new swim gear, and I have to buy the costume for Britt's ballet performance coming up in a month, plus ballet shoes since she ripped the cheap ones I bought last month. Should have known the price was too good to be true," she added with a twist of her lips. "And then there's my car. I was hoping to wait on repairing it, and buy a better car when I had more money saved, but after I almost passed out from the cold while driving home tonight, I have to get it fixed. It needs new tires and the exhaust leak plugged. It barely passed inspection last year."

"I wish I could help you, but I'm on a fixed income, and I don't make that much as a school lunch lady at the high school."

"I know, Mom. I'm not asking for your help. I'll take the money out of my savings, which I only have because I don't have to pay rent."

"I was a single mother once. I know it's tough even with that decent job you have. This isn't much." She waved her hand around the small room. "But at least it's paid off. It's dry and clean and it's not in the trailer park. You and my grandkids will have a place to call your own once I move on. It's all I have to offer."

"It's a lot, Mom." Mindy's voice cracked at the thought that her mother had willed the house to her alone, and not to her and Billy. But she also felt a sense of disconcertion that her mother would think that this was all Mindy would ever accomplish in life. Mindy had big dreams, and living near the old railroad track on Center Street—one of the poorest sections of Evergreen—for the rest of her life wasn't part of it. "I appreciate all that you're doing for me and the kids," she told her mother.

"I appreciate you taking care of me. You didn't even think twice."

"Why would I think about it? You're my mom and you needed help." She couldn't bring herself to say that she appreciated anything that her mother had done for her in the past, because quite frankly, Pamela had practically abandoned her since she was sixteen. She guessed her mother was just trying to make up for turning her back on her daughter when she'd needed her most.

Her mother shrugged, and her face clouded with unease. "Well, you know—"

"I know we're even then," Mindy said, not having the appetite for melancholy tonight. Everyone deserved a second chance, and she wasn't going to let her mother grovel at her feet. "And I get free fancy dinners once in a while. Can't beat that." She opened up the bag and was instantly overpowered by the delicious smell of chicken Thai fried rice. "Oh, this smells so good. Thanks Mom," she said, unwrapping the chopsticks and breaking them apart before digging into the container.

"You working, studying, or have class tomorrow?" her mom asked.

My life in pieces. "I don't have Saturday classes this semester. I open in the morning and work until three." She already felt tired at the thought of being on her feet for six hours. "And after work, I plan to put a huge dent in my homework assignments before

Virginia brings the kids around. She said she'll drop them off around seven."

Pamela smiled and reached over to pat Mindy on the shoulder. "I'm proud of you for putting that bitch in her place."

"Mom!" Mindy almost choked on a mouthful of broccoli. She'd never heard her mom use bad language before.

"Don't tell me you never thought of calling her a bitch. I've known women like that all my life, thinking they're better than other people while they're whoring, lying, and cheating their way up the ladder, and teaching their children to be just like them. Can't stand them."

"Who are these women, Mom? Do I know them?"

Her mother shuddered on a deep sigh and looked blankly at the TV screen, her thin lips thinning even more. "You don't want to know them, Mindy."

"I don't think Virginia is doing any of those things. I've never seen her with another man since her husband died. And Kyle was a good boyfriend to me and loving father to his kids. It's the one thing Virginia did right. It was his goodness that got him killed."

"I don't know what that woman is or is not doing these days. All I know is that she hated you the moment you took up with her son. It used to kill me the way she treated you, especially when I knew she wasn't that much better off than us."

"Then why didn't you say something? I was still a kid."

Her mother did a double take. "A kid? You grew up the minute you made the decision to engaged in adult activities with that boy. I fought for you when you were a child, just as you as a mother have to fight for your children until they can defend themselves. Standing up to Virginia was the first step. I was beginning to think you were completely spineless. You can't let folks walk all over you, Mindy. If you can't fight them at their game, you bring your own game and pin them in a corner."

Mindy dropped her chopsticks in the container and stared openmouthed at her mother. "Mom, who did you have to pin in a corner?"

Her mother's cheeks turned red. "It doesn't matter now. She's dead and her good-for-nothing—" She stopped and cleared her throat. "I just wish—"

"You just wish what?" Mindy asked. "Who's dead, and who's good-for-nothing?"

"Nobody you have to worry about. They are long gone." Her mother abruptly stood up. "I'm tired. I'm going to bed." Just as abruptly, she bent over and planted a kiss on Mindy's forehead.

"Mom." Mindy gazed up at the slightly wrinkled face, tears stinging her eyes at the unexpected, yet tender motherly gesture.

"Good night, Mindy." Pamela hurried down the short hallway and disappeared into her bedroom.

Mindy's heart beat with a nascent gentle filial love as she settled further into the sofa, pulled her feet up under her, and continued enjoying her dinner as Grant and Hepburn went through their comedic motion of falling in love on the TV screen.

It had taken her mother's need for temporary live-in assistance to bring them closer. Mindy had noticed the first sign of change in their relationship when she and the kids moved in, and Pamela had given up her master bedroom for the smaller one on the opposite side of the kitchen. And more recently, when Mindy had told her that she'd threatened Virginia, her mom seemed to have developed a kind of respect for her that Mindy had never noticed before.

Pamela didn't have a post high school education. She didn't know fancy words, and probably didn't even know a salad fork from a dessert fork, but she was brutally honest and fair. And she didn't take crap from anybody, a trait Mindy had recently discovered that she herself also possessed.

It had been risky to confront Kyle's mother, because as much as she disliked that woman, Virginia had always been willing and happy to babysit her grandchildren. That support was a lot to gamble away, but she'd gambled and won. Telling off Virginia had freed her emotionally, redeemed her self-esteem, and restored her honor in her mother's eyes.

"I love you, Mom," Mindy whispered on a smile as the sound of her mother's snoring reached her ears. Mr. O'Henry must have really worn her out tonight, Mindy thought as her smile turned into a grin of utmost approval. At least one of them was happy and lucky in love. Even Reggie and the not-so-honest Peter-Alex-Adam-Brian, she thought, as the movie came to an end.

Mindy shut off the TV, went into the kitchen, dumped the empty food container into the trash, filled a glass of water from the tap, and gulped it down. She took a full glass into the bathroom and sat it on the sink while she cleaned off her makeup, grabbed her kids' strawberry-flavored toothpaste and brushed her teeth. Back in the living room, she placed the glass of water on the lamp table, picked up her backpack from the floor, and was just about to sit down and get started on her reading for next week, when she heard a knock on the door.

"Please don't tell me that Virginia decided to bring the kids home tonight," Mindy muttered, even as her heart skipped an unexpected beat. She loved her children, but she was totally looking forward to having a little peace and quiet. Plus, it would be nice to have the bed to herself—a few and far between delight —instead of having to share it with Britt, who tossed, turned, and kicked constantly throughout the night.

She wasn't in the mood for company either, so maybe if she remained really quiet, whoever had come calling would think the occupants of the home were already in bed. Her wishful thinking went south at the sound of another, more insistent knock that made her heart leap again.

Why am I so jumpy tonight? Mindy wondered as she dropped her backpack and walked to the door to unlock, unbolt, unchain, and open it.

She gasped at the sight of the handsome, six-foot-two athletic figure of the man standing on the small porch.

CHAPTER FIVE

Galen, her mind screamed as her body went numb.

"Hello, Mindy."

At the sound of her name in his smooth English accent, Mindy flopped against the doorframe as a rush of fear, anxiety, and yes, excitement spun in her mind. How could she not be excited about seeing him? How could her skin not tingle at the memory of his warm hands roaming up and down her damp flushed body, the heady scent of his masculinity causing her to salivate in expectation, the thrusting of his tongue deep into her mouth and his licking at her pulsing womanhood, causing shuttering contractions deep within her belly? How could she not recall the intensity of their passion, night after night and day after day for the two and a half years they'd been together?

During the last couple of months, it had been easy for Mindy to pretend that he'd never existed in her world, or that she'd wished him into being. But now that he was here in the flesh, gazing at her through his seductive hazel eyes, she couldn't pretend anymore. The little taste of heaven he'd given her had been real, not imagined. Now she understood her nervous behavior from the moment she'd heard the first knock. Her foolish heart had leaped from recognition, but her wise mind had refused to acknowledge the possibility that he had returned.

"Mindy?" he said again, his lips parted in a smile of expectation, his eyes shimmering with hope under the porch light.

Still unable—or too afraid—to speak Mindy scanned his ruggedly handsome face. He'd changed, she thought detecting a commanding strength to his square jawbone and sturdy chin, and a firmness in his full rosy lips that she hadn't noticed before. Even the outline of his broad shoulders beneath his black wool coat seemed to exude the kind of power and confidence she had come to recognize in the wealthy businessmen who frequented Hotel Andreas. His dark wavy hair, brushing the collar of his coat, along with the curl that was wont to fall casually onto his wide forehead, added to his astounding sex appeal.

He was definitely not the whipped puppy who had left Granite Falls eight months ago with his tail between his legs, nor was he the rebellious, hotheaded boy who'd fought his half-brother, physically and in court. The man standing in front of her manifested success and an inherent commanding power— just like an Andretti male—the kind of man who simultaneously thrilled and frightened a girl, and in whose hands she might be tempted to place her heart, her faith, and her love, if she didn't know him.

But Mindy knew him, and the one thing she'd learned from his eight-month silent absence was to never trust him again. She was no Reggie Lampert in *Charade*. She would not be fooled by *this* nascent air of superiority he'd picked up while he was gone.

"Mindy, let's go inside. It's cold out here and you're shivering, love."

She *was* shivering, but it wasn't only from the cold air seeping through the uneven storm windows surrounding the porch. Her entire being was responding to his gaze slowly sliding down her body. She held her breath as she felt her breasts swell, her nipples harden against the soft cups of her bra, and the treacherous spot at the apex of her thighs pulsate with fire and need for him.

Afraid that he might detect her stupid vulnerability, she dropped her gaze to his brown crocodile-leather monk shoes. *Stemar*, an expensive brand and style she'd seen his brother wearing. He looked out of place amidst the rusted and broken-down yard furniture and other junk piled up on one side of the porch. He'd been *Andrettinized*. But how? When? She felt so underdressed in her jeans, wool sweater, and white bobby socks —one with a hole. Embarrassment caused her to pull her foot with the peeping unpainted big toe behind the door.

"Mindy? Come on, love. You'll catch your death of a cold. Let me inside for a few minutes."

"No." Mindy tightened her hold on the doorknob, knowing that if she let him into her home, or her head for that matter, it would take too much effort to get him out, or worse, she might not be able to get him out at all. "Why are you here? What do you want?" she asked, surprised that her voice was calm.

He frowned and tilted his head slightly to one side, as if he found her question absurd. "I came to see you."

"Okay. You saw me."

He braced his hand against the door to stop her from shutting it in his face. "I'm not leaving until we talk."

Mindy was a bit taken aback at the level of depth and authority in his voice. The Galen she'd known had never asserted any kind of authority, especially with her. He was more of a sheepish complainer, always whining about the unfair way his father had treated him, and she had indulged him because she, too had been feeling the sting of rejection and unfair treatment from her mother, Virginia, and life in general. She and Galen had been two peas in a pod—feeding off each other's insecurities. Well, she had grown up, and apparently, so had he.

She released her hold on the door and folded her arms across her chest, determined not to be impressed with his display of maturity. "Okay. Talk. But you aren't coming inside. I can take a little cold."

"Alright." He gave her a smile, equally as charming as the one that had made Mindy's heart tremble when she'd first met him. "But first, I have to say that you're as beautiful as ever."

"You sound surprised. Did you think I would shrivel up and die when you dumped me? If that's what you thought, you don't know me, Galen Carmichael."

"I didn't dump you. I've thought about you every moment of every day for the past eight months. I've missed you so much, darling."

"Stop your lies, Galen. And don't call me *darling*. I am not your *darling*, or your *love*, or anything else to you."

"You couldn't be further from the truth. You mean everything to me, Mindy Marshall. You and Kyle and Britt."

Mindy was thankful her children weren't home. To raise their hopes about Galen's return, only to have them dashed to pieces when he decided to leave again, would be negligent of her. Nobody was playing yo-yo with her babies' hearts, or hers, ever again. "Well, you wasted good money on an airline ticket, and you're wasting your time now. I don't want you. Why don't you do us all a favor and catch the next flight back to London?" She felt a measure of triumph when he winced.

"You have every reason to hate me. I've hurt you terribly. But there is a good reason for my silence."

"What is it?" Mindy's curiosity got the better of her. It was every woman's right to know why she'd been dumped, especially from a man who'd claimed to love her. Perhaps none of it was love. Perhaps it was just infatuation built around both their needs to be wanted by someone else. She straightened her back, ready to reject any excuse he gave her. There was none for what he'd done. "Why couldn't you get in touch with me? Why couldn't you even call me once to let me know you were alive and well?" She tried to keep her heart as cold and still as the night, but it fluttered away at the mere fact that Galen was here in Evergreen and standing in front of her and telling her that he'd come back for her.

His chest rose and fell on a deep sigh. "It's complicated, and I—"

"Complicated? Is that the best you can do, man?"

"A lot has happened since I left, Mindy. A situation developed in London. It wasn't something that could be explained via a phone call or text or even an email. It needed to be done in person."

"You're here now. Explain away," she demanded with a shrug of her shoulder.

While he seemed to struggle for his explanation, he pushed back the curl of hair from his forehead, but it immediately bounced right back out of place.

Mindy's breath caught in her throat at the memory of the playful way he used to catch her hand and kiss her palms whenever she attempted to pat the errant strand into place. She killed that memory and all the others that had been building up inside her since she opened the door. She cleared her throat, hoping he couldn't hear her heartbeat thumping inside her chest. "I guess you have no explanation after all. You've wasted enough of my time, Galen. I have—"

"It's not something I can talk about right now. Not here. I'd like us to—"

"Then why did you bother coming to see me?"

"To tell you, in person, that I am back, that my feelings for you are still as real and strong as they ever were. Perhaps even more so."

"You're too late. I've already put you out of my heart and out of my mind. You're dead to me, Galen Carmichael, so this conversation isn't even happening. Just go back to London and leave me alone." Mindy stepped back and was about to close the door again, when he jammed his shoe against it.

The next instant, she was forced back inside and he was standing with his back against the closed door, sucking up the air and space in the small room.

"You can't just barge your way into my home, Galen. If you don't leave, I will call the police," she threatened through clenched teeth even as she fought to combat his dangerous proximity, his heat, and the sensual efficacy of his cologne.

"Go ahead. Call." Galen's stomach was in a knot as he gazed into the flashing, angry, yet mesmerizing brown eyes of the one and only woman he'd ever loved. He'd known that it wasn't going to be easy explaining away his silence. Ever since he'd gotten full custody of Geoffrey and had decided to return to Granite Falls, he'd been imagining his and Mindy's initial meeting, their first awkward conversation—perhaps over a cup of tea, or lunch, or even dinner, his foolish heart had dared to dream.

From the moment she'd opened the door, all Galen had wanted to do was take Mindy into his arms and kiss her senseless. The intense physical attraction they'd had for each other hadn't waned a bit, but he'd fought his desire to act on his impulses because he did not want her to ever think he was forcing himself on her.

He'd anticipated her anger, her pain, but not this ruthless hostility. She was staring at him with the same disdain her mother had stared at him the first time she'd met him. Had her mother finally managed to turn her completely against him during the time he'd been gone? If that was the case, the odds were stacked highly against him, but instead of feeling defeated, Galen was perversely motivated, empowered to fight for her—by any and all means necessary.

Like Massimo had pointed out, he was an Andretti, and Andrettis fought for what was theirs. Mindy was his, and nothing, not even her mother with whom she'd obviously made up, was standing in his way of winning her back.

However, tonight wasn't the night to start his fight. He had to get home in case Geoffrey woke up. The poor child had been fussy and calling out for his mother on the eight-hour flight from London. He'd finally fallen asleep an hour before they landed, so Galen had sent him on to the estate with Sybil while he'd made this slight detour to see Mindy.

Granite Falls was a small town, and word got around fast among Mass and his friends. It was one thing for his brother to keep the details of his troubles in London and even the fact that he was returning to the States to himself.

Shaina would know when Galen showed up at the mansion, and he was certain that she would immediately call the other wives. The last thing Galen wanted was for someone else to tell Mindy that he had returned. It was best she heard it from him. "I understand how you feel, Mindy," he said in a lowered voice. It was a small room, a small house and he had no desire to be confronted by her mother whom he knew was home because of her little yellow VW Bug under the carport at the side of the house. One hostile Marshall was all he could deal with tonight.

"You have no idea how I feel, Galen, or you wouldn't be here."

"You have every right to hate me."

"I don't hate you. Hate would indicate that I care. I don't care. I feel nothing for you."

Galen stiffened as her hurtful words sank deep into his heart, even though he knew they were all lies. She could deny it all she wanted, but the look in her eyes and the tremor in her body when she'd opened the door told him that she still loved him. "I was trying to protect you, Mindy. You, and Kyle, and Britt. How are they? I've missed them."

"They're over you, just like me. We don't need you."

Galen balled his fists as he fought the urge to reach out and pull her into his arms and make her take back her pack of lies. "It pains me to hear you say that, Mindy. When Mass came to see me in London, he—"

Bewilderment brightened her eyes. "Mass went to see you in London? Since when are you and Massimo talking? You were at each other's throats the last time you were in a room together."

Here was the other explanation he wasn't prepared to get into just yet. Why hadn't he thought this through before acting on his impulse to see her tonight? Why hadn't he slept on it and come to see her tomorrow? *Because you love her and couldn't wait one moment more to see her. You wouldn't have been able to sleep, knowing that she was only half an hour's drive away. That's why.*

"My brother and I have made up," he said, suddenly feeling the weight of the world returning to his shoulders. "We've put the past behind us. I'm staying at the Andretti Estate until—"

"Good for you. It's nice to know that you and your brother are buddies when I'm still suffering the consequences of siding with you against him. You and your brother are—" She flailed her hands as though she were at a loss for words.

"What? What are we?" Taking two giant steps, Galen stood mere inches in front of her. His body quivered from the heat of hers. His fingers itched to undo her ponytail and watch her long, blonde, floral-fragranced hair cascade off her shoulders and down to her tiny waist like strands of lustrous glass.

God, he'd missed her. He wanted to hold her, feel the softness of her exquisite body melt into the hardness of his. His pulse quickened as he recalled the rapid beating of her heart in his ears, the silky feel of her damp skin meshed with his, the delicious thrill of her smooth legs wrapped around his waist, her hips undulating beneath his deep thrusts as they labored together in love for hours upon hours.

"Mindy," Galen whispered as his desires overpowered his restraints. He reached out and cupped her chin, his body shivering at the crackling electricity in their touch. She stood in front of him, paralyzed yet shaking, and gazing up at him, her brown eyes shimmering in the ceiling light. "Mindy," he whispered again, raising her face and lowering his head until their lips were a hair's breadth apart. She smelled like strawberries, and it made him hungry for her.

She braced her hands against his chest as if to push him away, but didn't. She instead licked her lips, amplifying their fullness, their glow. Her breath became quick and shallow and her chest vibrated from the raucous beating of her heart.

So she felt nothing for him, huh? She was over him, she'd said.

"I'm going to kiss you." He touched his lips lightly, tentatively to hers, so as not to frighten her, but to ease her delicately into the natural ebb and flow they used to share. He ran his tongue along the outside surface of her mouth as dizzying currents raced through his body, and centered in his groin. She parted her lips, whether consciously or not, he did not know, but he took the opportunity to thrust his tongue a little deeper into her mouth and seek out her own. It flittered teasingly against his before abruptly retreating.

"No," she whispered, pushing at his chest. "No!"

Galen immediately released her and watched with mixed emotions as she turned her back to him. He adjusted his crotch to relieve the unbearable pain and stiffness brought on by eight long months of no sex. He was so tightly wound he swore he would have come in his briefs if Mindy hadn't pushed him away.

"You need to go." Her voice was weak. Breathless.

"Mindy, I'm prepared to fight to win you back. I don't care how long it takes. I'm not giving up on us. After what just happened, I'm convinced that it's not over, no matter how much you tell yourself that it is. I love you. It's just that simple."

She whipped around, her eyes flashing with hurt, anger, and humiliation. "That was just hormones, Galen. I won't say that I don't want you, that I'm not attracted to you, but know *this*. I don't love you. I don't trust you. You broke my heart." Her voice cracked terribly, and her eyes shone with unshed tears. "You broke my children's hearts. I would be a fool if I let you back in just so you can do it again."

Galen swallowed the lump in his throat. He had broken her heart in a far worse way than she even knew. If she was this hurt about his silence, she would be completely destroyed when she realized that Geoffrey was conceived when they were together.

Mass was right—not telling Mindy that he'd slept with Trix was the ultimate betrayal. "I'm sorry. My silence was never meant to hurt you, but to protect you. If I could go back and do it all over again, I would have called to let you know that I was alright, that I—"

"Well, you can't. And at this point, I don't care why you ignored me for eight long months." She looked him over from the top of his head to his Stemar shoes as if she were seeing him for the first time tonight. "I guess you're a true Andretti male now. You're dressing and acting just like them—using women and then tossing them aside when you've had enough. You're all despicable! You disgust me. Now get the hell out of my house."

"Mindy, please—"

"You heard my daughter. Get out before I have you arrested for trespassing."

Galen's eyes shifted to Pamela Marshall, who had suddenly appeared, waving her cell phone in the air as if she were ready to fling it at his head if he said another word. He gripped his chest as his gaze returned to Mindy standing there, glaring at him.

Knowing that he couldn't leave her like this, Galen took a step toward her, but stopped when his phone alerted him that he had a text message. He pulled it from his jacket pocket and, just as he'd feared, it was from Sybil. Geoffrey was awake and crying hysterically.

He had no choice. He had to go look after his son. With regret and responsibility heavy in his chest, Galen looked at Mindy. "I'm not giving up on us. I love you. Just remember that above all else. And I promise, I will tell you everything, the reason for my silence, and I hope—"

"Nothing, short of being so sick that I'm knocking on death's door, unable to speak or use my hands would have stopped me from getting in touch with you if the tables were turned. I would have found some way to let you know that I was alive and that I still loved you, even if I couldn't talk to you." She shook her head in despair. "Now, I just don't care. I don't want to see you again," she said with a cold calmness in both her eyes and voice.

"Well, there it is," Pamela said. "Don't make us take out a restraining order against you. Go away, and don't come back. Leave my daughter alone."

With his heart crushed between a rock and a hard place, Galen walked out the door. The tears had frozen on his cheeks by the time he reached his car.

As soon as the door closed, Mindy collapsed on the sofa and dropped her face into her hands as pleasure and pain fought for precedence in her mind. Pleasure won out as she shook from the aftermath of Galen's hands on her body, his hot firm lips pressed against hers, the taste and smell of Irish coffee on his breath. She took deep harsh intakes of air as she struggled to keep herself from diving into the pit that had just opened up in front of her. Her body had betrayed her in the space of a few minutes. How long would it take for her heart and her mind to follow suit?

"Mindy! Pull yourself together."

She raised her head to find her mother standing in front of her, a look of pure displeasure on her face. "How long have you been listening?" Mindy slowly rose to her feet as her mother's presence killed the remaining lingering pleasure of the kiss. Well, all except the dampness in her panties.

"Long enough." Pamela deftly tightened the belt to her bathrobe around her waist. "I hope you're not stupid enough to believe a word of what he said."

Needing to alleviate the burning persistence in her throat, Mindy grabbed the glass of water she'd brought from the kitchen —it seemed like hours ago. She gulped it down in one long swallow. "I don't need a lecture, Mom," she said, walking into the kitchen.

"I disagree."

The *chip, chip* of slippers on the carpet as her mother followed behind her grated on Mindy's nerves, but she held her peace and rinsed out the glass.

"I saw the way you reacted when he touched you and kissed you. I was young once. I remember how easy it is to cave under pressure."

"Did I cave?" Mindy placed the glass into the dish rack next to a collection of brightly colored plastic dishes before turning around. "Why are you walking around the house spying on me in the dark? I thought you were asleep. Whatever happened to 'you're a grown woman, you have to fight your own battles?'"

"Your mouth is saying one thing, but I know in your heart you're thinking that you want to hear his explanation. Don't give him the chance to hurt you again. He *will* hurt you again. It's in his—"

"It's in his what?" she asked when her mother clamped her mouth shut—something she'd been doing plenty of tonight. "What were you going to say about him? What horrible stories did you tell the court about Galen's mother? What did she do that makes you hate her and her son so much?"

Pamela shook her head. "Nothing, Mindy. Just don't let him use you again."

"You can go back to bed and sleep tight. I have no desire or intention to see him again." Mindy brushed past her mother and ran into her bedroom on the other side of the living room, closing and locking the door behind her.

She threw herself down on the bed and stared up at the ceiling. She was just like Reggie Lampert, incapable of saying no to a man even when she knew he was being less than honest with her.

Mindy frowned as she recalled Galen saying that he'd stayed away to protect her and Kyle and Britt. Twice, he'd said it. What the heck did he mean by that? Protect them from what?

Maybe he would have explained what he meant if you hadn't been so busy trying to convince him that you didn't care, didn't love him anymore.

CHAPTER SIX

"Here you go, Mrs. Weisz." Mindy handed the gold gift bag with the word *Arabella* sprawled across the front in a white fancy font to the elderly lady, a Massachusetts resident whose family were frequent guests of Hotel Andreas. It was rumored that the friendship between the Andreases and the Weiszes, owners of Weisz Foods Incorporated—a supermarket chain in the northeast—went back generations.

"I hope Rosalind enjoys her birthday gift," she added with a warm smile. Mindy had met Rosalind, the oldest of Mrs. Weisz's five children, who was just as nice and friendly as her mother. Unlike many of the rich and famous guests of the hotel, the Weisz family did not look down on the help, but treated them with respect and equality, perhaps because they understood the value of dedicated, trusted employees.

"Thank you, Mindy dear. I'm certain she will love the scarf, along with the pearl necklace and matching earrings I got from the jewelry store. She showed me pictures of exactly what she wanted."

"In that case, she will be ecstatic," Mindy replied with a soft chuckle.

Mrs. Weisz glanced at the diamond-studded watch on her age-spotted wrist. "Oh dear, look at the time. I'd better head on over to the restaurant. I'm meeting some friends for lunch, and then we're taking the grandchildren to the winter carnival."

"That sounds like a lot of fun. As a mat—" Mindy stopped short at mentioning that she was taking Kyle and Britt to the annual Granite Falls Ice Carnival tomorrow. Mrs. Weisz had no idea that Mindy was a mother—a single one at that. One of the policies at Andreas International was to never commingle with the guests. You were to be professionally cordial without divulging any personal information.

The policy had been put into place decades ago after a married Frenchman befriended one of the hotel maids—a single mother of three—and then coerced her into exchanging sex for cash each time he and his friends visited Granite Falls. Alessandro Andreas, Adam's father, then CEO of AI, had been very sympathetic toward the maid, but he'd banned the man and his friends from visiting any Andreas International establishment on the planet, with the threat of exposing their nefarious crimes.

Since then, anyone caught breaking the rules of nondisclosure and commingling with guests or patrons was immediately terminated. Since she'd actually met Galen at Arabella, Mindy had initially kept her relationship with him a secret. Tashi was the only person who'd known about them, and her friend had kept their secret, even from her husband. The risks were huge, but Mindy had fallen so hard for Galen, she'd been willing to take them. Now, she wished she'd…

"Goodbye, Mindy."

Mindy snapped out of her reverie. "Goodbye, Mrs. Weisz. Enjoy the carnival."

As Mrs. Weisz walked into the lobby and disappeared into the throng of guests, Mindy took a quick glance around the boutique. Safi was ringing up a young man in her checkout section. Two of the five salesclerks were consulting with customers in the glove and leggings sections, respectively, while the other three ran about tidying the tables and racks that were in disarray after the Saturday morning rush.

The constant bevy of customers at her register had kept Mindy's mind preoccupied and off the implications of Galen's return. Hoping to maintain that mental state of preoccupation, she left her cashier station and walked over to the disorganized scarf display table. But it was no use. Folding scarves into neat little piles could not deter the bittersweet details of the previous night from dashing to the forefront of her mind.

After a sleepless night, Mindy still had no idea how she'd been able to function this morning—beginning with getting out of bed, getting dressed, and then climbing into her cold car to make it to work on time. But here she was, going on with her day, with her life as if her world hadn't changed last night. For better or worse? She didn't know. The one thing she knew was that she had to stay strong, focused, and positive for her children's sake. That meant no wishful thinking or dreaming about getting back together with Galen Carmichael.

She couldn't deny that she still loved him, and since she couldn't trust her heart or her emotions not to succumb to his charms, she had to avoid him at all cost. She couldn't risk a repeat of last night, she thought, even as her lips began to burn and tremble from the memory of Galen's brief, but oh so tantalizing kiss. If only…

"Okay. I know the signs."

Only then realizing that she'd been rubbing the pad of her thumb across her tingling lips, Mindy dropped her hand. She glanced up at Safi, who was standing in front of her, her long braided hair brushing the sides of her flawless face, and her eyes lathered with curiosity. Mindy couldn't believe that she'd been so deeply in thought that she hadn't heard Safi approaching. She glanced around to find that the only people in the boutique were the employees. "What signs are you talking about?" She picked up a cashmere scarf and proceeded to fold it.

"You got a new boyfriend?"

"Boyfriend? Girl, please," she said with a swipe of her wrist. "A man is the last thing I need in my life." She placed the folded scarf on top of the neat pile she'd started.

"Mm hmm." Safi crossed her arms and taped a red-tipped finger to her chin. "Is that why you blew me off last night? I had to go to the club with boring Liza. Sheer torment!" she said, shaking her hands in the air. "The girl doesn't drink. She doesn't dance. I mean what's the point of getting all dressed up and going out? I swear working on my calculus homework would have been more exciting."

Mindy grinned. Safi had a flair for the dramatic. Even though Safi was a straight-A student in her second year at Evergreen Community College, in Mindy's opinion, her friend should be studying acting and making her way to Hollywood or Broadway instead of finance with plans for Wall Street. A foreign student from an island in the South Caribbean, Safi began working at Arabella around the same time as Mindy, and so the two had become best friends while helping each other learn their way around the boutique. Safi was the only employee who hadn't turned against Mindy for siding with Galen.

"Oh come on, Liza isn't that bad," Mindy said of the timid girl who worked in the children's playroom and who usually ate lunch or dinner alone in a corner of the cafeteria. Feeling sorry for her, Mindy had invited her to sit with her and Safi one day. Liza had taken her gesture as an ongoing invitation to sit with them whenever their lunch schedules synced. "She's just shy."

"Boor-ring," Safi repeated in her exotic singsong accent. "Anyway, back to the new boyfriend." She slapped her hands on the table and leaned in toward Mindy. "You looked kind of dreamy. And when you touched your lips, I knew you'd been kissed since the last time I saw you. It's the same look you used to have when you'd spent the night with Galen."

Mindy boxed in her lips as if she could hide the evidence.

"Oh my God. He's back, isn't he? When?" Safi ran around the table to hug Mindy.

Mindy inhaled deeply and gently pulled herself free. She could lie, but then Safi would pester her about the identity of a new nonexistence man, or she could tell the truth and put it all to bed. She folded her last scarf and set it down. "He's back," she said nodding her head. "He came by my mom's place last night."

"And?"

"And nothing. I told him that I had nothing to say to him, that I didn't want to see him, that what he'd done—how he'd treated me was unforgivable. I told him I was over him."

"Good for you for playing hard to get back." Safi poked Mindy on her arm. "What was his excuse for being a total jerk?"

"I don't know. We never got that far."

"So why the dreamy eyes? I would think *pissed off* would be in play this morning."

"He said that he loved me and that he would fight to win me back, no matter how long it took, and—and we kissed, but then—"

"Oh man, not now!" Safi threw her hands up in frustration as the phone at Mindy's cashier station began to ring.

Mindy ran to answer it. "Good Morning. This is Mindy at Arabella. How may I help you?"

"Miss Marshall."

Mindy stiffened at the sound of Adam's voice. Even though she was friends with Tashi, Mindy's relationship with her husband remained strictly professional. She was always Miss Marshall. She leaned against the alabaster cabinet. "Yes, Mr. Andreas."

"I'd like to see you in my office."

His office? He was never in his office on a Saturday, except when he had an important meeting. The fact that he was summoning her meant that he didn't have one. Or was she *it?* "Your—your office. Now?" she asked, as the hairs on the back of her neck tingled.

"Yes. Right away."

"But that leaves Miss Ingram as the only cashier in the store, and your policy is—"

"I'm well aware of my policy, Miss Marshall. I sent someone to take your place. Head on up as soon as she gets there, and bring your things with you."

"My—my things?" The tingling intensified and spread down her back.

"Yes, your personal belongings. You won't be returning." *Click.*

Mindy hung up the phone and pressed her hands into her stomach as she tried to combat the tingling that had engulfed the rest of her body.

"What did the boss want?"

Mindy turned around and almost bumped into Safi. "He wants to see me in his office."

"He's in-house? Why does he want to see you?"

"He didn't say."

"Maybe it's your second evaluation. You know we don't have any warnings about those one-on-ones with the boss."

"It's Saturday. He never conducts evaluations on the weekends." She trembled on a deep breath. "He told me to bring my personal things because I wouldn't be coming back."

Safi was taken aback. "Coming back today, or—like—for good?"

"I—I don't know. He didn't specify. But he sounded serious, almost cold and annoyed, which is so unlike him." Moving in slow motion, Mindy unlocked the cabinet under the register and retrieved her purse and her coat. "Suppose he's firing me because of what I said to Galen last night."

"Come on, you know the boss, girl. If he was going to fire you over Galen, he would have done it the minute you sided with him against Mr. Andretti. Telling Galen that you didn't want to see him again would be cause to celebrate in the boss' mind."

"Yeah, about that." Mindy placed her stuff on the counter and looked around to make sure none of the salesclerks were in earshot. "I didn't tell you what I said to Galen after he kissed me."

"What? What? Spill."

"Well, first off, he told me that he and Massimo have made up and that he's staying at the Andretti estate. And girl, you should have seen the way he was dressed. Rolex watch and all."

"That's nice. Maybe Massimo gave him a slice of the Andretti pie."

"A huge one, and it made me mad that he'd been inducted into the Andretti clan when I was still paying for siding with him against them. I told him that he and his brother and all Andretti males are despicable creatures who use women and then toss them aside when they've had enough. I told him he disgusted me, and to get the hell out of my house."

Safi gasped. "Whoa, girl. You need to muzzle that mouth. Massimo is the boss' cousin. You know they're tight."

Mindy shuddered as the enormity of what she'd said sunk into her brain. Telling off Virginia had empowered her, freed her to stand up to people who looked down on her, but Galen had never looked down on her. He'd never made her feel shame for being poor and a single mother. In fact when she'd first told him that she had two children and had never been married, he'd told her that his parents were never married to each other either. They'd laughed, and that's when Mindy had known that her heart would be safe with him. But then he'd broken it. "I just wanted to hurt him like he hurt me," she said, her voice rising a pitch in anger.

Safi shrugged. "I get that, but dissing his brother and the entire Andretti family to make your point?"

"You think I went too far." She felt nauseous with dismay. "Maybe I shouldn't have dragged the Andretti name into it. Suppose Galen told Massimo what I said, and Massimo told Adam."

"You could lose your job."

"I can get another job. I'm more worried about finishing school, you know. My degree is my ticket to financial independence. I'm so close, Safi, and to think I might lose it all because of him."

Safi placed comforting arms around her. "Mr. Andreas isn't going to fire you. Come on, you're friends with his wife and all. For crying out loud, you were her maid of honor, and Kyle and Britt were page boy and flower girl in that big group wedding he and his friends had." Safi squeezed her shoulder. "You're like family. Maybe he's planning to promote you or transfer you—"

"To Siberia to teach me a lesson, probably," Mindy mumbled, as she noticed a woman from women's formal dresses entering the boutique and heading for her register. There was no time to contemplate Safi's optimistic counsel. "I guess you're here to cover for me, Gail," Mindy said, glancing at the woman's name tag. She forced a smile. No need to let the world know trouble might be brewing for her.

"My supervisor just told me that the boss wanted me to head on straight over here." Gail looked around with a giddy smile on her freckled face. "I used to work in here, you know, and I miss it. So much more fun than dresses. I told HR that I wanted to return if there ever was a vacancy."

So I'm being fired. The bottom dropped out of Mindy's

stomach as she slid her purse strap over her shoulder and draped her coat over her arm. "I'd better not keep the boss waiting. Safi, catch you later," she said, walking toward the door.

"Good luck," Safi called after her.

Mindy keep her head high as she crossed the lobby and headed for the elevators. A few minutes later, she stepped off onto the fourteenth floor. On a weekday, she would have met a guard stationed near the elevator, and then checked in with Noelle Jenkins, Adam's personal assistant, who occupied the first office on the floor. Noelle would have buzzed Adam, and he in turn would have decided when Noelle would send Mindy down to his suite.

Today was Saturday. There was no guard and no Ms. Jenkins, which was great with Mindy since there would be no witnesses to her humiliation when she left in tears after being fired. She clutched the straps of her purse and rearranged her coat on her arm as she hesitantly made her way down the corridor, her black pumps clicking on the marble floor as she walked.

Mindy had been working at Hotel Andreas for almost three years and she'd only visited Adam's office once. He made it a priority to meet with his employees randomly, his way to get to know them, he claimed. Since the evaluations were impromptu, every employee made it their business to be prepared for the unscheduled, yet expected summons. Some were fired, and some promoted after those personal encounters with the boss.

Knowing that Adam never mixed business with pleasure, and that her friendship with his wife would not influence his opinions about her professional efficiency at AI, Mindy had been nervous about her first-year anniversary evaluation, which had taken place a few weeks before the big group wedding where Adam and Tashi, Massimo and Shaina, Bryce and Kaya, and Erik and Michelle had renewed their marriage vows.

Adam had questioned her about her aspirations, her career

plans for the future, her college experiences, and he'd even asked about her children. Since she'd been forewarned to be prepared, Mindy didn't have to dig too deeply for the right answers to his questions. She'd responded as truthfully and thoughtfully as she could, and when he'd asked if she'd knowingly broken any of AI's policies, Mindy had been honest about her relationship with Galen. She'd apologized for her insubordination, even stating that she was willing to suffer the consequences for love.

Adam had told her that he'd known for months that she'd been seeing Galen, and that even though his sweet wife had denied she knew anything about it, she had nonetheless advocated, "hypothetically" on Mindy's behalf. Love, he'd told her, was worth any risk. He'd wished her happiness, and given her a raise with a promise of a promotion once she gained her Bachelor's degree.

Mindy had left that meeting, high on love and life and grinning like a lizard because she and Galen were free to express their feelings for each other in public, and especially at the then upcoming group wedding where Galen served as Massimo's best man. That wedding day had been one of the most amazing days of Mindy's life. She and Galen had danced late into the night at the reception, right here at Hotel Andreas, and then they'd gone back to Massimo's lakeside villa where Galen had been living at the time, and made love until the sun came up over Crystal Lake.

They'd been so happy, and then things rapidly slid from best to worst when Galen filed his case against Massimo for half of Andretti Industries. In an effort not to allow the rivalry between her cousin-in-law and Mindy's boyfriend to affect their relationship, Tashi had stayed loyal to their friendship and continued inviting Mindy to lunch or brunch and to the estate, but Mindy kept finding excuses not to meet with her. It just felt awkward.

Eventually, Tashi had stopped asking, even though she was

always friendly when they ran into each other at the hotel. Awkward had turned into embarrassing when everyone realized that Galen had left her high and dry. The blatant stares and hushed whispers had become unbearable, but eventually they'd faded as new gossip and more exciting news made the headlines.

Why couldn't he have stayed away? His absence had created a rift between her and Tashi, and now his unexpected and unexplained return could cost her her job and her college scholarship. What if Adam had made a special trip to his office today to personally fire her after hearing that she'd insulted the Andretti family by calling them despicable creatures? Her mother was right all along. Galen Carmichael was bad news. How she wished she'd listened.

Mindy's steps slowed when she turned the corner and the one-way mirrored wall of glass that separated Adam's office from the waiting area came into view. It was too late to turn around and run back to the elevator, out of the hotel, and into her car and save him the trouble of firing her.

Suspecting that he was probably watching her approach, she took a deep breath and forced a spring into her step as she walked through the empty waiting area. If she was going out, she was doing it with dignity. She stopped at the door and tucked her white blouse into the waist of her black pinstriped skirt before knocking.

"Come in, Miss Marshall," Adam's deep voice came from inside.

Here goes everything. Mindy opened the door and walked into the spacious office suite that overlooked Crystal Lake and the Presidential Range of the White Mountains. Adam, wearing a sweater and jeans, was sitting at his desk, his head bent over a pile of papers, a platinum pen poised in one hand while he spoke into the telephone receiver on the desk. Mindy didn't speak a lick of French, but the tone of his voice, the scowl on his face, and the rigid manner in which he checked off items on a sheet of paper suggested his impatience with the woman on the other end.

A glimmer of hope took root in Mindy's heart. Maybe the irritation she'd detected in his voice when he'd called wasn't directed at her. Maybe he was already in a bad mood. *Don't get ahead of yourself. You still don't know why he summoned you*, the rational voice in her head cautioned.

Without even looking up or breaking his conversation, Adam motioned for her to take a seat in one of the four chairs on the opposite side of his desk.

Mindy sat down in the one nearest the door. At least she wouldn't have too far to go when it was all over. She laid her coat and purse on her lap and studied her boss' face as her mind unwittingly traveled back to the hot summer afternoon, almost three years ago, when she'd first laid eyes on Adam Andreas.

Mindy had been instantly attracted to the tall, dark, handsome man with deep blue eyes, and a thick mane of black hair that reached all the way to his waist. She'd been sitting on her porch when he'd pulled his Aston Martin to a stop in front of her apartment building and hopped out. Her heart had raced, and the customary *girl-sees-hot-boy, girl-wants-hot-boy* reaction that had started inside her body had abruptly stopped when he'd walked around to the other side of his car and Tashi had emerged from the passenger's seat.

At the time, Mindy had only known Tashi as the shy, emerald-eye, curly redhead girl who lived next door, and who occasionally babysat her kids when Billy wasn't available and Mindy had to work. Tashi had never invited Mindy into her apartment, but had always met her at the door when she dropped off and picked up Kyle and Brittany. Strange, Mindy thought now, that she'd never once felt scared about leaving her children with Tashi, even though Tashi had been tight-lipped with personal information, no matter how hard Mindy had tried to pull it out of her.

Mindy had had no idea if Tashi had any friends or family. She'd never even seen her talking to anyone except their landlord. So imagine her surprise when the Italian hunk had taken Tashi's hand and escorted her across the street and onto their porch.

A dazed and confused Mindy had asked Tashi, right in front of the stranger, if he was her boyfriend, to which Tashi had delivered an emphatic "No." She'd even looked offended by the question, or the mere suggestion that she would be associated with the likes of Adam. Nevertheless, two weeks later, Tashi and Adam were married, and nine months later, Tashi had given birth to their son Adamo Alessandro, Jr.—nicknamed Alex. Tashi had really struck gold when she married Adam and joined Granite Falls' elite society, but she never forgot her neighbor, turned friend, from the old neighborhood.

If Mindy were to be honest with herself, she would admit that she was a little jealousy of Tashi. Not the mean kind, but the *why-couldn't-that-have-been-me* kind of jealousy. Why couldn't she have fallen in love with an honest, respectful, and wealthy man who cherished her and adored her and would do anything to make her happy? She didn't need a mansion and billions of dollars. She just needed someone to share her heart and life with. But instead she'd fallen for a poor, miserable, dishonest bastard who…

"Miss Marshall."

Mindy jumped and stared at Adam, who was leaning forward with his arms folded across his desk that, except for one folder, showed no sign that it had been littered with piles of papers minutes ago. When had he finished his conversation? And how long had he been trying to get her attention? She straightened her back and held his gaze. "I'm sorry, I was deep in thought, sir."

He tilted his head and gave her a probing look. "Are you happy working here, Miss Marshall?"

Stunned by the unexpected question, Mindy shifted in her seat, her fingers curled around her coat. She wasn't really, not for a year now, but she wasn't going to tell him that. "Um, what do you mean?"

He sat back, pushed his chair away from his desk, and folded one long leg over the other knee. "I mean, do you get up in the morning excited about coming to work? Do you anticipate interacting with the customers, waiting on them, anxious to meet their needs?"

"It's my job, Mr. Andreas." She fingered the name tag on her blouse.

"Not anymore." His gaze followed her hand. "Take off your badge and hand it over, Miss Marshall."

CHAPTER SEVEN

M indy stared at Adam, dumbfounded that he could so coolly deliver the worst kind of news an employee could hear. Where was the likable boss who always greeted his staff with a nod and a smile? "Sir," she whispered in a teary voice. "Are you firing me?"

"Your name tag, Miss Marshall," he said, his gaze, still unreadable, holding hers.

With shaking fingers, Mindy removed the plate from her blouse and placed it on his desk. "Why?" *You know why*, that voice in her head replied. *Family means everything to these people. You insult one family member and you insult them all.* "Mr. Andreas. I—I've been an exceptional employee, so I—"

"Yes, you have, Miss Marshall. But the truth is, I feel that you've outgrown your position at Arabella."

Mindy grabbed onto that sliver of hope. At least he didn't say she'd outgrown her position at AI. If this meeting had anything to do with her rash insults about the male members of the Andretti family, Mindy was sure Adam would have already made that clear. He was not known for beating around the bush.

She watched with bated breath as he reached into the top

drawer of his desk and pulled out a folder, then began shifting through the papers inside it. Maybe she was being promoted like Safi had suggested. It would make sense that he'd ask her to remove her name tag since they were all department-specific. Adam was known to transfer his employees from one department to the next to see how they adapted to change. Maybe he was switching her and Gail around as Gail had hinted. Anxious for answers to the questions in her mind, Mindy asked in a cautious tremulous voice, "What does that mean, Mr. Andreas?"

"It means that I'm terminating your employment."

"You're firing me?"

His lips parted on a half smile. "I would like to think of it as an amicable separation, Miss Marshall."

Amicable? There was nothing amicable about being removed from your job. "Mr. An—"

Her raised a finger to silence her before pulling a sheet of paper from the folder and sliding it across the desk toward her. With dexterous grace and aplomb, he placed his platinum pen on the sheet of paper. "I would like you to sign on the highlighted areas, Miss Marshall."

Mindy fisted her hands and stared at the two highlighted places on the sheet of paper. "I'm sorry, Mr. Andreas," she said meeting his gaze again. "I can't. I won't sign anything until you explain why you're terminating my employment. As far as I know, I haven't broken any of AI policies."

"You dare to be insubordinate with me, Miss Marshall?" He stood to his six-foot, three-inch frame, walked around the desk, and pierced her with his eyes.

Mindy felt like a gnat in his towering presence, but she would not be intimidated or bullied. If she was going out, she was going out fighting, and with her dignity still intact. "I don't think I'm being insubordinate, Mr. Andreas," she said. She wanted to stand up, but despite the boldness in her tone, she knew her legs wouldn't support her weight.

She cleared her voice. "A moment ago, you agreed that I was an exceptional employee, but that I'd outgrown my position at Arabella, not at Andreas International. In my opinion, you should be offering me a promotion and a raise, not terminating my employment. And if this is about Galen," she added, deciding to address the elephant she didn't even know for sure was in the room, "that is personal, and you can't fire me for that. I know my rights, and right now you're infringing on them, sir."

To Mindy's astonishment, a smile spread across his face. He stared at her for a moment longer, returned to his chair, leaned back, and bunched his hair in his hands. "Brava, Miss Marshall. That was exactly the response I hoped for."

Mindy frowned as relief and confusion flooded her. His voice was deep and mellow, free of the irritation she'd detected when she'd first walked into his office. She felt like a yo-yo being coiled and uncoiled from one extreme to the other. "So you're not really firing me?"

"Actually, yes. It's imperative that I terminate your employment." He reached across the desk to tap his finger on the highlighted places. "Sign."

"But—"

"Mindy, you're here!"

Mindy turned as Tashi emerged from the private quarters of Adam's office suite, wearing a coral long-sleeve maternity dress that showed off her six-month baby bump. "Tashi?" she whispered in surprise.

"Adam, I told you to call me when she arrived."

Adam strode across the floor to meet her. "You were resting, sweetheart, so I decided to get the preliminaries out of the way." He bent his head to plant a kiss on her lips while his hand roamed tenderly over her swollen belly.

"So you already terminated her employment?"

"I'm having difficulty convincing her to sign." He took his wife's hand and walked her to the desk. "Maybe you'll have better luck."

"I don't know. She keeps avoiding me."

This was all Tashi's idea? Mindy stood up, all fears about losing her job were gone. "You asked your husband to fire me because I keep ignoring your invitations to dinner and lunch and hanging out with you? I was busy with work and school and taking care of my kids, and my sick mother, Tashi. As I told your husband, I know my rights, and I don't care how rich and powerful you are, you're not getting away with this."

"Mindy, don't be upset," Tashi said as Adam seated her in his big black chair that seemed to swallow up her petite frame. "It isn't what you think."

"It isn't?" Mindy cocked her head and squinted.

"No. Sit down. Please." She waited until Mindy was seated before continuing. "I treasure our friendship. You are the first real friend I made in Granite Falls, even before Michelle, Kaya, and Shaina," she said, speaking of the wives of her husband's closest and most trusted friends who'd adopted each other as sisters. "I've never treated you differently from the way I treat them. You know that."

Mindy glanced from Tashi to Adam. Both seemed amazed at her outburst. She felt like a jerk. "That's true, Tashi. I'm sorry. To both of you."

"Apology accepted, Miss Marshall." Adam turned to his wife. "I have to run downstairs. The ball's in your court now, *cara*," he said, then walked out into the corridor.

Mindy threw her hands in the air. "Oh my God. I'm so confused."

Tashi chuckled. "Your fault. You kept avoiding me, so I

figured that the only way to get your attention was to have Adam call you to his office. I knew you couldn't refuse him."

Mindy giggled. "You got me there. And I'm sorry I kept blowing you off, but you must have known that I was embarrassed about the whole Galen affair," she said, feeling a lot more relaxed now that Adam was gone.

"Speaking of Galen, when I spoke with Shaina this morning, she told me that he's back in Granite Falls. He's staying with them."

Mindy cursed herself inwardly for bringing up his name. "I know. He came to see me last night."

"Oh. So you guys made up?"

"No. He—um. We…"

"Did he tell you why he didn't get in touch with you all this time?" Tashi asked.

"He said it was complicated. Do *you* know?" Mindy's eyes widened with curiosity.

"I don't. But Shaina thinks that Massimo knows. She said Galen called Massimo back in December, and that Mass left for England the next day and didn't come back for a week."

"Last night he briefly mentioned that Mass visited him in London. It must be serious then."

"Maybe. Did you know his grandfather died?"

Mindy pressed her hands to her mouth. "No. I knew they were very close. He loved his grandfather a lot." She felt horrible for being so mean to him last night. "He had a heart attack last year. That's why Galen left in the middle of the arbitration." She was more puzzled now. "But that still doesn't explain his silence for eight months."

"It doesn't, but that's all Massimo told Shaina. How did he seem to you?"

"Different. He looked like an Andretti, rich and powerful. And I told him—"

"What?"

"I said some unkind things to him about the males in the Andretti family using women and tossing them aside." She spoke without hesitation, knowing that she could be honest and open with Tashi without fear of repercussions.

"I don't blame you. I would have done the same thing. They did have bad reputations when it came to women. If it wasn't for Shaina, Mass might still be jumping from one woman's bed to another. You were just speaking truth to power. It takes inner strength and self-confidence to do that."

When Mindy had spat the words at Galen, she was feeling neither strong nor self-confident. She'd been pissed and hurt and determined not to let him back into her heart and life. "I thought Galen had told Massimo what I said, and that he told Adam in turn. So when Adam called me to his office, I thought he was going to fire me."

Tashi's eyes glowed with what Mindy knew was love and admiration for her husband. "My husband is a romantic, Mindy. He believes in risking it all for love."

"I know. He said as much to me when I finally told him that I had been seeing Galen behind his back."

"See? Before we got married, he shut his father down for grilling me about my background, when he himself didn't even know me at all, or about the trouble I was mixed up in. He didn't fire you for breaking Andreas International's employee rules, or when you sided with Galen against his cousin, and he won't fire you for cursing Galen out. I think both he and Mass admire you for choosing love over everything else."

Mindy relaxed into her chair. "I should have known there was more going on with your husband's confusing line of questions. I forgot how he likes to test people." She gave Tashi a measured look. "So why am I being fired?"

"Ohhhh," Tashi exclaimed, placing both her hands on her stomach, a wide grin illuminating her face. "She's kicking."

"It's a girl?"

"Yes. We couldn't take the suspense any longer. The wait with Alex was pure torture. Now I can decorate my nursery ahead of time and drool over pretty little baby girls' stuff. Adam is elated to have a little girl to spoil, not that he hasn't been spoiling Alex already."

Mindy smiled, remembering the exhilarating experience of carrying a new life inside her, even though she'd been an unmarried teenager at the time. She mildly wondered if she would ever experience such joy again. "We'll both have a boy and a girl. Maybe Brittany can babysit for you one day," she added in jest, knowing that would never happen in a trillion years.

Tashi laughed. "Or maybe Kyle would fall in love with my daughter, or Alex with Brittany. Alex may take after his father in that regard."

"Which regard is that?"

"Adam once dated a woman almost twenty years older than him."

"Wow. I did not know that. I guess anything is possible, then." Even though she was enjoying the little girl-talk detour, Mindy was anxious to know why she'd been summoned to Adam's office. "Why is Adam firing me, Tashi?"

"Because we can't have a conflict of interest between our two companies. I want you to come work for me at Tashi's Photography."

Mindy stared at her, totally confused again. Andreas International spanned the globe while Tashi's Photography was comprised of one small studio on the ground floor of Fontaine Towers #2 in downtown Granite Falls. It was a one-woman operation, and she knew for a fact that Tashi spent little time there—only to meet with clients, actually. She did most of her work at her home office at the Andreas Estates.

"I don't get it," she said. "You don't really have a company." She spoke with caution, not wanting to insult her friend. "You're great at photography." She shifted as her uneasiness mounted. It was a good thing she hadn't signed that termination letter. "With all due respect, Tashi, you're asking me to give up this cushy job that pays my bills and my college tuition, to do what, clean your camera lenses?"

Tashi threw back her head and laughed. "Don't look so petrified, Mindy. Just hear me out. And then you can decide if you want to work for me."

"Okay." Still skeptical, Mindy decided to give her the benefit of the doubt.

"You know I got a big break last year when I did that piece on twins in *Glamorous*."

Mindy nodded. She'd seen the article in an issue of the magazine that was lying around in the employee cafeteria downstairs. "The pictures of Eli and Elyse Fontaine were simply lovely," she said. "They were the cutest kids of all the sets. I'm surprised you haven't had more assignments like that—you know, big time. I mean, the Andreas name should land you the biggest jobs on the planet."

"I told Adam that I wanted to do this on my own. I don't ever want anyone to say that I got an assignment because of my last name. I do business as Tashi Holland, and my studio is owned by Evelyn Incorporated, so it's far removed from the Andreas name."

"I get that, but—"

"But what does that have to do with you working for me?" Tashi finished her question for her. "Do you remember telling me that you switched your major from Accounting to Office

Management because you wanted to run a big company one day?"

"I've always been good with numbers, so I thought accounting was what I should do. But after I took that Human Relations in Administration course, I was more interested in leadership, motivation, and developing higher productivity—all the stuff that managers do. I wanted to learn those skills."

"You already have great management skills, Mindy. You're reliable, efficient, and dedicated, and you have excellent communication and customer relation aptitudes." She chuckled. "I remember how you won over Adam with your wit fifteen minutes after meeting him, and as you know, he isn't a man who is easily won over. If you ever doubt your worth, just take a good hard look at your two beautiful charming kids. Parenting, I'm learning is the hardest job in the entire world. You're doing it all by yourself. Kyle and Britt are the greatest testament to your capabilities, your dedication, and determination."

Mindy pressed a hand over her heart. "Wow, Tashi, I didn't know you thought that highly of me."

"I do. I admire you, and that's why I thought of you when Dave Saturn approached me about buying out Saturn Studios so he and his wife could retire."

"Saturn is closing? They do most of the high-end functions in the area, including your group wedding." The pictures they'd taken of her and Galen at the wedding were the best photos Mindy had ever sat for in her entire life. Too bad the pictures had already outlasted the relationship.

"Although their business strategies are a bit antiquated, their photographers and videographers are exceptionally brilliant. We need to keep our local talent local, so I went ahead and bought out Saturn Studios. But I need someone to run it. You, Mindy."

"Me?"

"Yes, you."

"Why not run it yourself?"

Tashi let out a skittish laugh. "I don't have a business head. Look at my so-called studio. I have one employee who comes in to help me set up when I have to do a shoot. I'm a photographer. I'd much rather be outdoors with my camera than indoors failing at running a business. Also, *time* is a problem, especially with another child on the way. We both know that you're not enthusiastic about working at Arabella anymore. I thought this would be a great opportunity for you to test your capabilities as Chief Operating Officer of Tashi Photography."

Mindy was completely floored, but she had to face reality. "I appreciate your confidence in me, Tashi, but I don't know anything about running a photography business, any kind of business for that matter. You should hire someone with experience, then after I graduate next year, I can do an internship and if you're happy with my work, we can talk then. That's the way it's done in the business world. Besides, I'm still in school. My grades look good on paper, but asking me to manage the operation of your company, now, without practical experience is asking for failure for both of us."

Tashi brushed away her excuses and concerns with a swipe of her wrist. "I've already taken everything you said into consideration, Mindy. As I stated, when I decided to buy out Saturn Studios, you were on my mind. Adam has a long list of qualified candidates for me to consider, but I'd rather have a dedicated, inexperienced person I can trust, and already know and like, than some boring overqualified pompous ass who takes life way too seriously, and who might try to elbow me out because he or she knows more than I do about running my own business. You took a chance on me and asked me to watch your kids when you didn't even know me back when we were neighbors."

"Babysitting and running a company are two different stories, Tashi. But I felt I could trust you with my kids."

"You probably wouldn't have trusted me if you'd known the danger I'd been in day in and day out."

"I knew you were afraid of something, or someone, but I felt in my gut that you wouldn't hurt my babies. I trusted you. Call it gut instinct."

"I have that gut instinct with you, too. I know I can trust you, and that's why I have no hesitation in offering you this position."

Mindy's heart was thumping from excitement, anticipation, and fear. What if she took the challenge, and failed? "I'm just afraid of letting you down."

"You won't. I'm giving you free reign to do whatever you want with the studio. It's your baby. One of my conditions of the buyout was that Mr. Saturn shows you the ropes about how to run a photography studio. The staff will stay on until you decide if you want to keep or replace any of them. You'll have all the help you need. All you have to do is say yes."

"You sure?" Mindy asked Tashi, giving her friend one last chance to change her mind.

Tashi nodded. "I'm sure."

"Okay then, yes. I would be a fool to pass up this opportunity. But—" She hesitated. "What are your terms—like benefits, vacation, continuing my scholarship, etcetera? And you have to beat my pay."

Tashi grinned. "You won't be unhappy." She opened the same drawer Adam had opened before and pulled out a fat white folder. She opened it and turned to the last page of two multipage documents and signed her name on both before handing the folder to Mindy. "These are identical contracts, one for you and one for me. Take your time and read them over carefully. They are in layman's terms, nothing confusing. Make any suggestions that you want and call me when you're done."

She struggled to her feet and walked to the door leading out into the corridor.

Mindy opened the folder and began reading the top sheet. Her heart beat rapidly and she became more and more shaken as she continued down the page. She would have a personal assistant. Tashi was tripling her salary and her vacation time. Her hours were from eight to four with an hour break for lunch—no more shifts and working at nights. She could be home with her kids to feed them, put them to bed, make them breakfast in the mornings and see them off to school.

Mindy paused when her cell phone rang. Fearing that it might be Virginia calling about her children, she pulled it from her purse and checked the display. It was Safi, probably wondering where the heck she was. Mindy dropped the phone on the desk and returned to her contract.

She had weekends off, except when an emergency arose. She had travel, wardrobe, and childcare expenses during working hours. But what made Mindy burst into tears was the picture of a beautiful five-bedroom, six-bath, two-story home with an in-law apartment located on two acres of land on the Evergreen side of Crystal Lake. The folder also contained a picture of a brand new Mercedes SUV. The deed to the house and the registration to the car were already in her name, and the keys to both were in a pocket of the folder, next to a cell phone with a label that read *TP Business*.

Mindy placed the folder on the desk, picked up Adam's platinum pen, and hastily signed his termination contract, and then the two employment contracts for Tashi's Photography before they expired into thin air. When she was done, she placed everything on the desk and covered her face with her hands to stifle the sobs that shook her. "This can't be real," she kept telling herself. "I must be dreaming. I must be dreaming. I don't want to wake up. This can't be real."

"You're not dreaming, Mindy. It's real."

Mindy stiffened as she felt Tashi's hand on her shoulder. She raised her face to Tashi. "Thank you. I won't let you down. I'll work my ass off to make sure Tashi's Photography is a success. But you didn't have to do the house and car and all that other stuff, not that I don't appreciate the gesture. Just the salary, my benefits, and my scholarship would have been enough."

Tashi sat in the chair next to Mindy. "The house and the car are from the Evelyn Holland Haven for Single Mothers."

"Your mother's foundation? The one you started with the money you got from her murder case?"

Tashi nodded. "That one."

Mindy wished she hadn't posed the question when Tashi's eyes misted and sadness clouded her face. From what she'd heard about Evelyn Holland, Mindy knew she'd been a devoted and loving mother to Tashi. Even though Mindy and her own mother had never been close, Mindy knew that she would be really sad if her mother was gone from her life. She could only imagine the devastation Tashi had experienced growing up without her mother, and then to learn about the horrible way in which she'd died.

"As you know, my mother was a single mother," Tashi said. "When she was pregnant with me, she started a support group for other single mothers. Since I formed the foundation, I've given away houses and cars and whatnot to hundreds of struggling single moms across the country, most of whom I'll never ever meet in this lifetime. You are my friend," she said, giving Mindy a wide smile that lit up her green eyes, "so how could I not give to you in my mother's memory? You're a great mom. You work hard to provide for your kids. You're going to school to make life better for them. You, Kyle, and Britt deserve this. Oh, and once Kyle and Britt are ready for college, they can apply for scholarships. And you know their very biased Aunt

Tashi will accept their applications," she added with a conspiratorial wink.

"Oh my God, Tashi. Thank you so, so much. I've dreamed often about providing a nice place for my kids to call home, and I've worried about being able to send them to college, but this…" She pressed her lips together and shook her head as words evaded her.

"The house is fully furnished, so you only have to move in your personal belongings. I know your mom watches Kyle and Britt after school and at nights when you're at school, so I had Chase include an in-law apartment just in case she wants to move with you. This way, you'll both have your privacy. And you'll see, you have the best spot on the lake."

Mindy's eyes widened to the point of pain. "You planned this last year when DC Designs began developing the areas around the lake?"

She nodded. "You once told me that your ideal place to live would be on a lake, so that was the easy part. And as I said earlier, you're the first friend I made in Granite Falls. And since I married Adam, I've wanted to do something special for you."

"You got me the job at Arabella."

"No. Adam did that. Remember? He was so appreciative that you'd looked out for me when we were living on Temple Street. I needed something of my own to give you—something that wasn't linked to the Andreas name. My mother's case settlement provided that avenue. I'm sure your mother and Kyle and Britt will love living on Crystal Lake as much as you."

"They will. We all will," was all Mindy could say as her emotions overwhelmed her. She threw her arms around Tashi's neck and the women hugged each other in joy and gratitude.

"I guess I've lost a valuable employee."

Mindy released Tashi and turned to see Adam holding her signed letter of resignation. She offered him her hand. "I guess you have. It was a pleasure working for you, Mr. Andreas. Thank you for taking a chance on me even before you knew me."

"You don't work for me anymore, Mindy, so we can dispense with the formalities. It's Adam now." He smiled as he shook her hand. "I enjoyed watching you transform and grow since I met you. Sorry about being so tough on you earlier. But since my wife refuses my help and the power behind the Andreas name, I needed to make sure that her COO has a spine, that she has someone who will protect her interests in her absence."

"That's me, Adam. I *will* take care of your wife's business." Mindy stared at Tashi. "Does this mean that I have to start calling you Mrs. Andreas?"

"Not if you want to keep your new job," Tashi warned with a chuckle.

"When can I move into my new house?" Mindy asked, excitement turning her face red. She didn't care.

"Whenever you're ready," Tashi replied. "Your moving expenses are covered. Just save the receipts. And, oh, your new SUV is waiting up front. We already transferred your personal belongings, blankets and all, to your new wheels, and towed your old jalopy away."

"Are you serious?"

"Very serious, Mindy," Adam said. "You have no idea how it pained me to see you drive up in that piece of junk, and knowing that I could do nothing about it. I couldn't curry favor with my employee on my wife's behalf. I also knew that your hourly pay was hardly enough to support you and your children, but there again, I had to remain within the parameters of AI's pay scale. Our wages aren't based on need or gender, but on education and experience."

"I get it. You're an honorable man," Mindy said, remembering the day in Tashi's bedroom in her rundown apartment on Temple Street when Adam had offered her a job at

Hotel Andreas. She'd thrown her arms around him to thank him, but he'd quickly and politely put her into her place. She'd been crushing on him, and hadn't known, then, that he was already hooked on Tashi. She turned her attention to Tashi. "When do I start work?"

"We're meeting at Saturn Studio at nine on Tuesday morning. Mr. Saturn and the rest of his staff will be there."

"Are you moving Tashi's Photography to that location?"

"No. We'll be moving into a bigger space at Fontaine Towers, but for now, we will operate from Saturn."

"My head is spinning with ideas already." In her excitement, Mindy waved her hand so frantically around that she sent the folder and other items lying on the edge of the desk crashing to the floor.

Adam immediately stooped down to help her pick them up. "I hope you know that I'm not always this clumsy," she said as she stood up with the pen in her hand.

Tashi laughed. "It's a lot to take in. I understand."

Mindy offered the pen to Adam. "Thanks for the loan of this lovely writing instrument," she said, knowing that it costs thousands of dollars. "I can say without a doubt that it's the best writing experience I've ever had."

"It's yours, Mindy. Look closely at it."

Mindy held the pen up to the light and read the two lines of text engraved along the barrel: *Mindy Marshall COO Tashi's Photography.* "Oh my gosh."

"It's my parting gift to you, along with the matching pencil, also engraved." Adam handed her a black velvet pouch. "Use them wisely for success," he admonished.

"I will." Mindy slid the pen into the pouch next to the pencil and placed it into her purse. "You guys are the best." She wanted to hug Adam, but knew it was too much too soon. They'd just gotten onto a first-name basis. She didn't want to overstep her bounds. "Thank you both for everything you've done for me."

"It is our pleasure. Not to rush, you," Tashi added, "but Adam and I are meeting my dad and Dafne for lunch."

"Say no more." Mindy collected her coat, purse, and the folder with her signed contract. She'd met Tashi's father—retired FBI Special Agent Paul Dawson—when he first moved to Granite Falls, shortly after Tashi married Adam. He was the force behind the hunt for the men who'd murdered Tashi's mother when Tashi was only four years old. Mindy had also met his fiancé, Dafne Bellini, at the group wedding almost two years ago. Dafne was Massimo's childhood friend back in Italy. "See you Tuesday," she said, edging toward the door as Adam opened it for her.

"Oh, Mindy," Tashi called. "Shaina is throwing me a baby shower tomorrow. Well, it's more like a pregnancy celebratory party for my closet friends—no gifts allowed. Michelle, Kaya, and Desire will be there, and Yasmine, too. She and Robert and their son are visiting Michelle and Erik for the weekend. You're one of my closest friends, Mindy, and I'd love it if you could join us for an afternoon of fun."

"I'm taking Kyle and Brittney to the winter carnival after church tomorrow."

"Can you take them later in the week? You have Monday off now."

There, she had no excuses. And why would she want an excuse after what Tashi has just done for her? "Of course. I'd love to come to your shower."

"Perfect." Tashi clapped her hands. "It starts at four. You can bring Kyle and Britt. I'm sure they would enjoy hanging out with Alex, Aria, and MJ. It'll be good to have you back in my life on a regular basis, Mindy."

"You, too, Tashi. I'll be at your gate at four sharp tomorrow."

"Actually, the party is at Shaina's."

The bottom fell out of Mindy's stomach as she fought to keep her composure. She felt like she was walking in wet cement as she pushed her way down the corridor. Her resolve to stay far away from Galen Carmichael had just been shot out of the water with the news that the shower she'd just agreed to attend was taking place inside the enemy's camp where Galen had taken up residence. There was no way she could avoid seeing him. And if she did see him, how would she react after that kiss they'd shared and after she'd told him she never wanted to see him again?

And then Tashi had gone and complicated the situation, adding to her confused feelings towards him, by telling her about Massimo's hush-hush visit to England to see Galen. What the hell was going on? Did it have anything to do with the danger that Galen had mentioned last night—the reason he'd cited for not being in touch with her for eight months?

Maybe it was best she heard his explanation so she could move on without him. The one thing she was certain of though, was that there was no way in hell she was taking Kyle and Britt to the shower with her. She didn't need their puppy-dog faces and their, "Please, can Galen come home with us?" requests to influence her decisions about taking him back.

Oh, so you're thinking about taking him back. Huh. When did that happen?

CHAPTER EIGHT

Thank God for family.

Galen tiptoed toward the crib and gazed at his son sleeping in the nursery of the second floor east wing suite of the Andretti mansion.

It had been a long and exhausting twenty hours—both mentally and physically, but he'd finally been able to breathe a sigh of relief when Geoffrey had settled into a sound sleep a little over an hour ago. Actually, the entire east wing was breathing sighs of relief.

On his way from seeing Mindy last night, Galen had received an urgent call from Mass. Geoffrey was running a fever of a hundred and two degrees. Mass wanted to know if Galen preferred Geoffrey be taken to the emergency room or be attended by Aria and MJ's pediatrician.

Galen had opted for the latter, and then had broken every traffic regulation between Evergreen and Granite Falls. He'd arrived home to find his screaming son being examined by Dr. Jennifer Stewart, who'd immediately begun questioning him about Geoffrey's medical history. To sever as many links as he could between Geoffrey and Bronzefield Prison, Galen had decided not to have Geoffrey's medical records forwarded to Dr. Lloyd, the pediatrician he'd taken Geoffrey to after Galen had gained custody. He did not want the embarrassment of raised eyebrows and questioning stares for Geoffrey having been attended by prison medical staff.

"Has he had a cold recently?" Dr. Stewart had asked as she'd placed Geoffrey into Galen's arms.

"Yes, about three weeks ago, but he's been over it. Dr. Lloyd gave him a good bill of health just before we left England. Maybe I should have asked if he was okay to travel. I'm sure flying aggravated the situation."

"Perhaps, but don't blame yourself. Sometimes it takes a while for the Eustachian tubes to unblock long after the runny nose and sniffles are gone. Parents are bound to make mistakes, especially with their first child. Is he your first?"

"Yes." Her consolation hadn't made Galen feel any better. He should have been more attentive.

Dr. Stewart had prescribed some antibiotics for the ear infection, acetaminophen, sponge baths, cool cloths on his forehead throughout the night for the pain and fever, and lots of fluids. On top of all that, she'd told him that Geoffrey was also cutting a new back tooth.

Galen felt like a failure. He'd thought that Geoffrey's reduced appetite, his irritability, and his inability to sleep on the plane were attributable to a simple case of separation anxiety from his mother. His son had been in pain from an ear infection and teething for days, and his father hadn't been smart enough to figure it out and get him help.

Last night, as he'd lain in bed with a whimpering Geoffrey lying on top of him, Galen had promised his son that he would never make that kind of mistake again. He would never take his crying for granted. And to make certain that he kept his promise, Galen had borrowed all of Shaina's books about babies.

He'd spent the day reading up on taking care of young children, in between taking care of Geoffrey, who, in spite of the acetaminophen, was still in a lot of discomfort. It wasn't easy trying to get a baby who hurt each time he swallowed, to take fluids or a spoonful of medicine. But tender loving care and patience from the entire household had won out in the end.

Galen glanced at the closed door to Sybil's bedroom located on the other side of the nursery, where she was sleeping. He was grateful for her, too. Even though, like him, she'd been suffering from jet lag, she'd been on call throughout the night, and then today to get poor little Geoffrey on his way to recovery. Once again, she'd proved her worth after Mass and his family left early this morning for a prescheduled visit to Boston to spend the day with Shaina's brother, Cameron and his fiancé, Monica, who were both studying engineering at MIT.

Galen touched the back of his hand to Geoffrey's forehead and was elated to find it cool. He straightened the blanket over his son's lower body, then tiptoed away. He walked through the master bedroom of his suite and into the adjoining study. He sat behind the desk and stared at his cell phone as a moment of déjà vu immobilized him.

Before he'd gotten the call from Massimo last night, he'd been formulating his next meeting with Mindy, despite her declaration that she didn't want to see him again. He'd called Arabella first thing this morning to get her working schedule for the day. His plan had been to show up just before her shift ended and try to convince her to accompany him to someplace private and quiet so he could explain his eight-month silence without them being interrupted by her mother or anyone else. He'd even been prepared to book a room at Hotel Andreas just for the occasion. He could afford such luxuries now.

But Geoffrey's illness had thrown a monkey wrench into his plans. As it was, he hadn't even had the time to call her. After

Geoffrey had fallen asleep, he himself had taken a much-needed shower and then a forty-minute nap to rejuvenate his brain. Even now he could still use another two hours or so of sleep.

He glanced at his watch. Yep, Mindy was probably at her mother's—the last place on earth where Galen wanted to approach her. Not that he would even attempt to leave the mansion tonight. He had to stay put until Geoffrey's health was at least ninety-nine percent restored. Hopefully that would be tomorrow.

Mindy had once told him that as much as she loved him, if she had to choose between him and her children, she would choose .her children. Only now did Galen understand the significance of that statement. Thoughts of Mindy and the kiss they'd shared last night, and also the way they'd parted, had been rising to the forefront of his mind all day, but Galen had had to push them away every time. He'd had to choose Geoffrey over Mindy. And if she'd known of Geoffrey's existence, Galen knew she would understand. But…

Nothing, short of being so sick that I was knocking on death's door, unable to speak or use my hands, would have stopped me from getting in touch with you if the tables were turned. I would have found some way to let you know that I was alive, and that I still loved you, even if I couldn't talk to you.

Galen picked up his phone and dialed Mindy's number. It rang five times before going to voice mail. His heart somersaulted in his chest as he listened to her greeting.

Hi, this is Mindy. I can't talk right now. Leave a message, and I'll call you back. Have a wonderful day. Bye.

Galen hung up, leaned back into the chair, and took deep breaths to slow his pulse. After a few minutes he dialed again, and got the same results. He waited another ten minutes before making another attempt.

He tapped a finger against his temple while he waited for her greeting to end. "Hi, Mindy, it's Galen. I'm calling to say—um—that it was lovely seeing you last night. I miss you. I love you." He paused as his voice trembled at uttering the words he'd only spoken to one woman in his lifetime—her. "We need to talk. There's so much I need to tell you. I'd love for us to meet soon in a place of your choice—just the two of us. Let me know where and when, and I'll be there."

He hesitated at the slyness of using reverse psychology on her. But at this rate, he had nothing else to lose. "Mindy, you at least owe it to yourself to know why I didn't get in touch with you while I was in England. After you hear my story, if you still decide that you want nothing to do with me, then I'll leave you alone. At least we'll both have closure." He swallowed. "Also, think about Kyle and Britt. I'm certain that we will run into each other at some point, so it's best we get our situation squared away before that happens. At least we can both be honest with our answers to their questions. In the meantime, I'd be forever grateful if you could find it in your heart to give them each a hug for me, because darling, I missed them too. Please say you'll see me. I'm not giving up on us. I will never stop loving you, Mindy."

Galen dropped his phone on the desk, threaded his fingers through his hair and growled. God, he felt like an awkward teenager who'd just called to ask the prettiest girl in high school to the prom—a girl on whom he'd had the longest and biggest crush. The only difference was that he hadn't yet broken that young girl's heart.

He began tapping his temple again as he sized up the recent turn of events in his life. Trix had seduced him and then given birth to a son he hadn't known about. He'd been kidnapped, held prisoner, beaten, forced to launder money, and cut off from all communication with the woman he loved. He'd had his identity stolen, and had been accused of stealing his grandfather's lifetime savings, and then lost his grandfather. It was a wonder he could still function.

He pushed out of his chair and walked to the window overlooking a forest of trees. He'd been tempted to give up so many times. The temptation to run was always more profound after the unexpected visits that always ended with two members of the gang holding him down while the third punched him repeatedly in the gut. They always took turns, but they never hit him in the face—only in the gut and chest. Sometimes they kicked him in the thighs and shin.

"You're lucky we need your pretty face at the bank, mate. Nobody trusts a beat-up businessman," Charles Fraser had said to him during the first beating. "When we have no more use of you, maybe we'll give your head a go-around. That would be a nice parting gift, eh?" he'd added, patting Galen on the cheek. "Give you something to remember us by every time you look in the mirror."

With each assault, Galen would conjure the faces of the most important people in the world to him—Geoffrey, Mindy, Kyle, Brittany. He would remind himself that he was taking it all to keep them alive. Their well-being had kept him from running.

He shivered outwardly as memories of the excruciating pain flooded his brain. After Mass had come to his rescue, the first thing Galen had done was see a doctor to make sure he hadn't suffered any damage to his internal organs. He hadn't. Thank God for small favors.

"Daddy. Up. Daddy."

Geoffrey's voice brought Galen back from the dismal dungeon of his recent past to a present he hoped, in time, would erase that pain. Turning from the window, he sprinted through his bedroom and into the nursery to find Geoffrey standing in his crib with his arms outstretched.

"Up, Daddy."

At least he hadn't called for his mummy. It was a step in the right direction. "Daddy's here, Geoffrey." He picked him up and squeezed him for a few glorious moments before smiling into his beautiful little face. "I told you I would always be here, didn't I? Feeling better?"

"Better. Eat. Daddy. Eat," Geoffrey said, rubbing his stomach.

Galen kissed his ruddy cheeks, elated that the worst was over. "Okay, champ, we'll go eat, but let's get you into a dry diaper first, shall we?" Potty training had been placed on hold for a while, as were many other things Galen had grown accustomed to. He'd only been a single parent for a couple months and he was already exhausted and petrified of screwing up much more than he already had.

As he laid Geoffrey on the changing table, Galen's thoughts rewound to the time when he and Mindy had initially begun dating. He'd wondered how the heck she'd been raising two children on her own with hardly enough money to take care of them. After Mass had kicked him out of the lake house, Mindy had invited him to move in with her. He could have gotten his own apartment, but the thought of falling asleep beside her every night and waking up next to her every morning was too delicious an offer to pass up.

Raised by a single mother who never had to worry about taking care of him because of the financial support from his father, Galen had gotten a rude awakening about the struggles Mindy faced on a daily basis.

He'd been liberal with his money from the trust fund his aunt Gertrude had left him, buying her and Kyle and Britt whatever they needed. He'd offered to buy Mindy a decent car, but she'd argued that the one she had served its purpose. Any other woman would have asked for a Mercedes, especially if she suspected he had money, but not Mindy. He'd admired her frugality and carefulness, and had fallen more deeply in love with her.

When he'd returned to England to find that the rest of his trust fund had been wiped out by the Fraser family, Galen's only regret was that he hadn't used more of that money on Mindy and her kids.

Mindy was the most amazing woman he'd ever known, and only an idiot would let a woman like her slip through his fingers without a fight. Galen didn't think he was an idiot.

𝆕

Mindy leaned against the railing of the second-floor balcony and gazed down on the first-floor open-concept living area that encompassed a small foyer with a domed skylight, and the kitchen, living, and dining rooms. A wall of French doors opened up to a lavish four-season porch that had steps leading down to an immaculate lawn bordered by evergreen trees and trimmed shrubbery. From there, a red brick winding path wound its way to a small building, close to the beach, that provided a changing room, a shower, and a toilet.

"Mommy. Mommy, come look at my room! There are ballerinas dancing on the wall, and my bed is so nice with pretty lace and fluffy pillows, and lots and lots of nice stuff."

"My room is cool, Mom. I have my own bed and closet, and dresser, and bathroom. Man, this is wicked awesome!"

"I've seen your rooms guys." Her children's joyful shouts coming from their bedrooms where they were unpacking was music to Mindy's ears. They, too, had been powerless to contain their excitement as they discovered one unexpected aspect of their new home after another. One of the other few times that Mindy had felt such accomplishment as a mother was when she'd held each of them in her arms for the first time and gazed into their little pink faces. Her children were happy, and since a mother was only as happy as her saddest child, Mindy was excessively happy today.

"Bacon, get out of there. Stop drinking from the toilet. Go drink from your bowl. Go!"

Bacon bounced out of Kyle's room, and down the hall toward Mindy. He circled her, wagging his tail enthusiastically before scampering down the stairs and heading straight for the bowls of water and food Mindy had put out for him in a corner of the kitchen.

"Did you win a million dollars, Mom?"

"Are we rich now, Mom?"

Mindy chuckled. "No, I didn't win a million dollars. But we are rich in blessings and the favor and generosity of a fairy godmother."

Thank you, Tashi, she said for the millionth time today.

After leaving Adam's office, instead of going back to the boutique to tell Safi about her unbelievable news, Mindy had gone to the parking lot and straight to her white Mercedes SUV. She'd just wanted to make sure that she hadn't been punk'd, or was hallucinating about her meeting with Tashi before she told anyone else. Then she'd headed to her new house to make sure that was real too.

As she'd moved from one room to another, Mindy had cried tears of joy and gratitude. She'd been awed at the details that had gone into the architecture, the intricate fixtures, hardwood floors, sophisticated decorations, elegant furniture, and modern, state-of-the-art *everything* that she had the luxury of controlling with voice command—her appliances, her lighting, her electronics, her gas fireplaces. She could even control them remotely with a smartphone.

Fine china, sterling silverware, and crystal glasses were neatly arranged in the kitchen cabinets and drawers, and both the pantry and the laundry room were completely stocked. When Tashi had said that all Mindy had to do was move in her clothes and personal things, she wasn't lying.

Anxious to do just that, Mindy had gone to her mother's house to share her news, and ask her to move to the lake with her. Her mother was thrilled for her. However, she'd opted to stay put.

"I love being the mistress of my own house," she'd told Mindy. "But I'll visit you and my grandchildren often. Can Phin stay over in the in-law apartment sometimes?"

"Of course," Mindy had said, giving her mother a tight hug. "It feels weird saying it, but your falling and needing my help brought us closer than we've ever been in our lives. I'm glad you fell, Mom."

"I'm glad I fell, too. Now let's get you packed. It would be nice to have my bedroom back. By the way, can I keep the TV, the stove, and the sofa?"

"They're all yours, Mom."

They had spent the afternoon packing, and after Virginia dropped off Kyle and Britt, Mindy had loaded as much as she could into her SUV and driven her children to their new home.

Mindy was still struggling with the fact that, today, she had a magnificent home with a master suite that included a fireplace, an en suite with a Jacuzzi, a spacious walk-in closet and dressing room, an office, and a seating area—all of which opened to a balcony overlooking the lake—when only last night, she'd been simply happy to have the bedroom she shared with her children and the bed she shared with Britt all to herself.

Never in a trillion years did she ever think that she would be so tremendously blessed, simply because she'd been kind to the timid, frightened girl who'd lived next door to her, two and a half years ago. Tashi Holland had indeed been an angel in disguise.

After inspecting the house, Mindy had decided to call and

thank Tashi again, but she couldn't find her phone. She'd searched the car and the entire house until she remembered taking it out in Adam's office and concluded that it had probably fallen under the desk when she'd knocked over the items. She'd called Tashi on the business phone, and Tashi had promised to give it to her at the shower tomorrow. Well, at least she had the business phone to use in an emergency. It wasn't as if she was expecting any important calls anyway.

"Can you help me put my books on the shelf, Mommy?"

Mindy walked toward Britt's room that was separated from Kyle's by a study—a quiet place for homework. They also had a sound proof playroom on the first floor where they could be as rambunctious as they wanted, especially when they had company —which Mindy was certain would be more often than ever now —and a play area with swings and slides at the back of the house.

Tashi had obviously thought of everything when she'd approached Chase Hunter with the planning of this house. Perhaps because she remembered how wild Kyle and Britt had been on Temple Street, she thought, as she walked into the children's study. She picked her way through boxes and heaps of books and other stuff to Brittany's side of the room.

"I want my Dr. Seuss books up there," Britt said, pointing to the top shelf of the built-in bookcase.

"Maybe you should put them on the bottom self and put your stuffed animals up there."

'I don't read them anymore and I like my animals and my drawing books down here so I can get them when I want."

"Okay, fine. You hand the books to me, and I'll stack."

"I definitely don't want to live with Grandma now," Kyle said, walking into the study with Bacon at his heels.

Mindy clenched her teeth. *Virginia*. "What's this about living with your grandma?" she asked, as lightly as she could.

Kyle sat down on a sofa under a window that overlooked the play area. "Grandma said that if we lived with her, we can have our own bedrooms. She said she's gonna talk to a lawyer 'cause we shouldn't be sleeping in the same room with each other and definitely not with our mother."

"She says it's unhealthy," Brittany added. "Why are we unhealthy, Mommy?"

Mindy could feel her face turning red with rage. "Really? When did your grandmother tell you all this?" she asked, trying to keep a lid on her fury.

"Last night when she was putting us to bed. We don't have to go live with her now, right, Mom? Our new house is bigger than hers. We have our own rooms and our own bathrooms, and she only has one bathroom in her whole house."

"Uh-huh. And our new house is prettier," Brittany added, nodding her head so furiously, Mindy was afraid it would fall off.

That bitch! Mindy was going to strangle her the next time she saw her. She'd known all along that it was only a matter of time before Virginia pulled a stunt like this.

"Did you ever tell your grandmother that you wanted to live with her?" she asked them, knowing full well the longing that developed in destitute children's hearts. *Damn*, when she was a kid living in the trailer park, she'd often dreamed about living in the nice houses of the few privileged classmates who'd invited her to their birthday parties.

Brittany wrapped her arms around Mindy's waist. "No, Mommy. I don't want to live with Grandma. I want to live with you. I love you, Mommy."

"I love you, too, Britt, my sunshine girl." She hugged her daughter and glanced at her son who'd dropped his head and his gaze to the action figure in his hands. "Kyle?" she prompted, walking over to stand in front of him with Britt still hanging on her.

"I might have said it once," he said, raising his head to give her an apologetic smile. "But I didn't mean it."

"Of course you didn't mean it."

"I was just mad that you'd made Galen leave. He was cool. I liked him a lot."

Mindy felt as if her heart would explode. "I didn't make Galen leave. He left because his grandfather was sick."

"Is he coming back? Why hasn't he called us? I miss him."

"I miss Galen, too, Mommy. He let me paint his toes and put blush and lipstick on him, even though he's a boy."

"Doesn't he care about us anymore?" Kyle asked.

Mindy swallowed. *Last night he'd said that he cared. He said that he missed them as much as he'd missed her.* And her heart had been hurting for him ever since Tashi told her that his grandfather had died. Mindy had wanted to call him, but what did you say to a man you'd called disgusting and told you never wanted to see again?

"Come here." She opened her arms wide, and when Kyle stood up, she closed her eyes and hugged her children as tightly as she could.

A week ago, she'd accused Virginia of not helping her grandchildren just so she could hurt their mother. Was *she* doing the same thing? Was she hurting Kyle and Britt by not letting Galen back into their lives, just because she was angry?

"Woof. Woof!"

At the sound of Bacon's bark, Kyle pulled out of her embrace and grabbed the lab's collar. "I think he needs a walk."

"He probably does after the food and water he just gobbled down," Mindy said, happy to have the subject changed. Or perhaps Bacon was also voicing his frustrations about Galen. He'd loved Galen too. "Come on, we'll all take Bacon for a walk, and then go back to Nana's for another car load."

"I like your new car, Mommy," Britt said. "It smells nice and it's warm and it doesn't go *Putup! Putup, Bang!*"

Mindy laughed at yesterday's struggles. For the first time since she'd given birth to her two little darlings, she did not have to wonder how she was going to feed or clothe them or provide a safe place for them to live. All of their basic needs would be met until they left the nest. That was a huge accomplishment.

She wished she could as easily heal the pain Galen's absence had left in their hearts.

You can. You'll ease their pain when you ease your own. Hear what the man has to say.

Mindy could not argue with that little voice this time.

She should have taken Safi's advice and not come to the party, Mindy thought as she drove up the steep private road that led to the Andretti mansion. Seeing Galen on neutral grounds, in a place where she wouldn't feel intimidated by him and his grandiose surroundings would have been a much better idea.

But if she went that route, she would be disappointing Tashi who'd placed so much faith in Mindy's ability to run her company, and who had shown unparalleled generosity towards her and her children. Nobody had ever put that much faith in Mindy before.

How could she even entertain the notion of standing up Tashi when she'd awakened in her own king-sized bed this morning, made breakfast for her children in her state-of-the art kitchen while she watched the news on her giant screen mounted TV, loaded her children into her Mercedes, and taken them to church and then for lunch at a real restaurant, instead of the burger and pizza joints they were accustomed to?

Tashi wasn't just a friend whose invitations she could refuse with a lame excuse anymore. She was Mindy's boss. And as a new employee, Mindy would be imprudent not to attend Tashi's baby shower. Reneging on her first promise to her new boss would suggest ingratitude. It wasn't like she had Arabella to run back to if Tashi changed her mind. Nope, she'd signed that job and all its benefits away. If she happened to see Galen today and he insisted on talking, she would hear what he had to say, and then deal with it. Whatever *it* was.

Mindy stopped at the bulletproof glass-encased gatehouse, the last of three checkpoints one had to go through before being able to access the Andretti mansion. There were no guards at the previous gates. To get this far, visitors had only to press the intercom at the previous two and state their names and reason for visiting—which Mindy knew was cross-referenced at this main gate where everyone was expected to present IDs before being allowed to advance to the house.

The security procedures were similar to those at the LaCrosse, Fontaine, and Andreas estates. The richest and most powerful families in the region weren't taking any chances, especially after the very bad people Tashi had been hiding out from when she'd lived on Temple Street had unwisely made two attempts to kidnap her. Adam had brought the wrath of the Andreases down on them, forever wiping out all threats from his wife's life.

Mindy rolled down her window and placed her driver's license and car registration into the retractable tray.

One of the four heavily armed guards cross-referenced her picture and her face, and then her name on the day's guest register. That was another thing with these folks. You couldn't just decide to not show up for an appointment one day and expect to get in the next.

The guard sent the tray back. "Good day, Miss Marshall," he said before raising the barrier.

"Good day to you." Mindy collected her pieces of identification and closed her window. She placed her registration into her glove compartment and her license into her clutch, but instead of quickly driving off as she'd done in the past, she turned and looked at the guards. There was no embarrassment, no avoiding eye contact, no wondering if they were laughing at her as she *Putuped, putuped, banged* her way to the mansion today.

She liked this new feeling of empowering self-worth and self-confidence that her new position was affording her. She'd gotten her big break—the one thing most people needed to make it in this difficult world, and she was going to work hard to keep it.

Mindy drove through the gate and followed the road until it ended inside the lavish courtyard. She pulled up behind two sports cars parked in the visitors' section. The clock on her dashboard read 4:15 p.m., but knowing from experience that many of the guests to parties such as this one were chauffeured back and forth, Mindy was certain that she wasn't among the first guests to arrive, which meant she could be making a grand entrance.

She checked her makeup in the rearview mirror, patted two errant strands of hair into place, and rearranged the spiral curls that extended from the loose bun onto her cheeks. Safi had done an exceptional job with her hair and makeup. Satisfied that she was ready to mingle with the rich, powerful, and sophisticated ladies of Granite Falls, Mindy draped her coat around her shoulders, tucked her clutch under her arm, and exited the car. The cold New England wind immediately lashed at her propelling her to dash across the courtyard. She ascended the steps to the front door as quickly as her four-inch, ankle-strap sandals would allow. The door opened before she had the chance to knock.

"Good afternoon, Miss Marshall. You look very lovely today," the elderly doorman said as she stepped inside the foyer.

"Thank you, Martin." From listening to conversations between Tashi and Shaina, Mindy knew that Martin had been with the Andretti family since Massimo was a little boy. He was one of the many faithful employees who'd returned to the household after Massimo married Shaina, who'd turned the deserted abode into one of the liveliest entertaining hotspots on Mount Reservoir. "How are you?" she asked Martin as she handed him her coat.

"I'm doing well, thank you. Just waiting for winter to be over."

Mindy shivered, shaking off the little bit of cold she'd just picked up. "Me and you alike." Mindy gave him a big smile and glanced around the elegant foyer. It didn't matter how many times she visited this home or any of the billionaires' mansions, she was always awed at the beauty.

"Oh, by the way, Mrs. Andreas asked me to give this to you." Martin opened the drawer of a marble table and handed Mindy her phone.

"Thank you very much." Mindy slipped the phone into her clutch, next to her new business phone—the one she'd told her mother and Safi to call if they needed to get in touch with her. She would check her messages later.

"Mrs. Andretti and company are waiting in the east wing parlor. Would you like me to escort you down?" Martin asked.

"No. I know where it is. You rest your bones," she said with a wide smile.

"Enjoy your visit, Miss Marshall." Martin shuffled off into his office that doubled as the coatroom where she suspected he'd resume his position on his comfortable recliner to monitor the security screens that covered the courtyard and the front of the main house.

He had a nice job, Mindy thought as she waltzed along the marbled corridor, smiling at servants in uniforms going about their business. She turned left at the grand double staircase, then passed a seating area in the vicinity of the kitchen. Her mouth watered as she picked up the delicious smell of Azi's cooking. Azi, the head household chef, was Massimo's distant relative from Kenya. She had become Mass' surrogate mother after his own mother died. She was family, and loved and respected by everyone who knew her.

Mindy turned another corner and the sounds of children's laughter from the playroom sent a shard of guilt through her. Kyle and Britt loved visiting the mansions—one of the very few highlights in their impoverished lives that they could boast about to their friends. She found comfort in knowing that today they were at home with Safi in a house they had fallen in love with at first sight. She imagined they would be bragging about their new house to their friends in school tomorrow. She was doubly certain that they would be inviting their friends for sleepovers by the end of the week. And they wouldn't be in any hurry to go visit Virginia anytime soon either. *That wicked…*

"Mindy? Is that you?"

Bolts of electricity ricocheted through Mindy's entire body. She stopped in mid-stride, closed her eyes, and took a few precious moments to gather her wits before turning around to see Galen coming toward her. He was dressed casually in jeans and a black long-sleeve jersey that outlined the contours of his athletic body. And that stride, that stalwart stride of his, made her knees weak.

"Hi", he said, coming to a stop in front of her, his eyes, filled with both surprise and delight, riveted on her face.

CHAPTER NINE

"Galen." Mindy took shallow breaths as she tried to subdue the growing dizzying currents in her body.

His smile deepened as his gaze roved to her neck, and then slowly down the entire length of her. "That's a lovely dress, Mindy," he said. "I love you in red."

Mindy had bought the long-sleeve, curve-hugging dress with a boat neckline yesterday, to have something special and appropriate to wear to Tashi's party. She wondered now if she'd unconsciously chosen red just in case she ran into Galen. Was she trying to impress him?

"You always look enchanting to me, no matter what you're wearing," he added in a husky tone that made her cheeks grow hot at the double-entendre in his tone—a tone that reminded her of the way things had once been between them.

With shaky fingers, she tucked her curls behind her ears. "Tashi told me about your grandfather. I'm sorry. I know how much you loved him."

A muscle clenched along his jaw. "Thank you."

"I hope you got to spend some time with him before he passed. I hope you got to say goodbye."

"I did. We had a few weeks together." Two deep lines appeared between his eyes. "I would have loved for you to meet him. In fact, I was thinking of bringing him to Granite Falls after the case with Massimo was over."

"I would have loved that." Mindy wished she had the courage to take the three steps that would place her close enough to loop her arms around his neck, give him the comfort she knew he was craving. She couldn't help but wonder how long it had been since he had had a good long hug from anyone. Galen had always craved intimacy. One of the many things Mindy loved about him was his habit of sneaking up behind her and drawing her tightly into his arms when she was cooking, folding laundry, and sometimes when she was studying for a test or just doing homework.

He had held her hands when they were out in public, and at home when they sat at the table, sharing a meal or just a cup of tea. When they watched TV alone, he would stretch his long body along the sofa and lay his head on her lap. She would comb her fingers through his silky hair and trace the contours of his face and chest until the teasing and tantalizing grew to a fever pitch, and they would make love. Galen was the most affectionate and attentive person Mindy had ever known.

Oh, how she missed the time when they'd been open and honest with each other, when there was no pretense between them. Her heart beat with longing for those good old days, those tender moments.

He cleared his throat as if he, too, had been cruising down that same memory lane with her, and then hooked his thumbs into the front pockets of his jeans. "Did you get my messages? Is that why you're here?" he asked, his eyes eager as they searched hers.

"No. Tashi invited me to her party. When did you leave the messages?" she asked with a puzzled frown.

"Yesterday, and today. I asked if we could meet someplace and talk. When I didn't hear back from you, I was afraid you might think I was harassing you. After the way my visit ended the other night, I was sort of waiting for the sheriff to show up with a restraining order."

"I didn't—" She paused as two maids walked by wheeling two trolleys loaded with covered dishes—no doubt en route to the parlor where the party was taking place. Part of her wanted to follow them and escape the *talk* Galen had just mentioned, but another part of her knew it was best if she dealt with it and then moved on with her life. "I didn't get your messages because I forgot my phone in Adam's office yesterday. Tashi left it with Martin and he just gave it to me. I haven't had time to check my messages."

A relieved smile cracked his lips. "I'm so happy to hear that, Mindy. I thought you were just ignoring me."

"I would have answered your calls, Galen. If for nothing else, at least to express my condolences about your grandfather." Shame at the insults she'd hurled at him in anger prompted her to say, "I'm sorry about my behavior the other night—the stuff I said about all Andretti men."

"There's no need to apologize. But since we ran into each other, do you think we can talk?"

Just get it over with. "Sure." She pointed to a couple of club chairs a few yards away.

"No. Somewhere private."

"Okay. But I should at least let Tashi know where I am. It would be rude of me to just not show up in the parlor. I'm sure she knows I'm here by now."

"I'll call her." With lightning speed, he fished his phone from his back pocket and stepped aside to chat with Tashi.

Mindy watched him from the corner of her eyes, her heart beating with fear and anticipation as she recalled what Tashi had told her about Galen calling Massimo back in December, and then Massimo taking off for England the next day. She'd initially thought that it was because of Galen's grandfather's death, but Galen had just told her that his grandfather died a few weeks after he got to England. Even though he and Galen had been at war with each other, Massimo had immediately gone to his aid. The Andrettis, and their close circle of friends, were fiercely loyal and protective when it came to their individual families, and the members of each other's as well—even the extended ones.

She'd witnessed the depth of their friendship and dedication to each other's family last year when she'd caught Nadine Brehna—Kaya's mother, who'd been staying in the hotel—shoplifting a pair of earring from Arabella. Instead of following protocol of alerting security, Mindy had called upstairs to Adam, who'd asked her to keep Mrs. Brehna in the store until he got there. The incident was never made public—not even the security team knew about it. But Mrs. Brehna's luxurious stay at Hotel Andreas had come to a sudden end. Bryce and Kaya had set her up in an apartment at Fontaine Towers and hired a live-in housekeeper to keep track of her. She wasn't allowed to go anywhere alone. They had thanked Mindy profusely.

Mindy had never been exposed to people who were so resolute about protecting and preserving their families' names and legacies. The folks she knew were always eager to curse each other out in public and air family laundry. Take Virginia for instance. That woman had been calling Mindy trash since the first time they met, telling her friends that she wasn't good enough for her son. Mindy had thought it would stop when she birthed the woman's only two grandchildren, but it had gotten worse. It had died down a bit while Mindy was dating Galen. She was probably afraid of the power of the Andretti name. But for the past months when it seemed that Galen wasn't coming back, Virginia began blabbing to everyone that he'd dumped Mindy.

Galen might not have the Andretti name, but Andretti blood ran through his veins. He was Massimo's little brother, and that was enough to send Massimo running to his aid when he was in trouble. Mindy was eager to know if that *trouble* was the reason Galen had cut off all communication with her. She also needed to know what Galen had meant the other night when he'd said that he hadn't called because he was protecting her and Kyle and Britt.

All your questions will be answered soon enough, she told herself as Galen ended the call and returned his phone to his pocket. "Tashi says she understands," he said, coming back to her. "She says she will have Azi send us something to eat and drink. I declined alcohol and opted for mint tea. Is that alright?"

"You know it's my favorite."

"Yes, I do know that. Come on," he said, placing his hand under her elbow.

Mindy's knees trembled at his touch, but she forced strength and determination into her system and let him steer her into the direction she'd been previously headed. Instead of bearing right toward the east wing parlor, he turned left and stopped at the second door on the right.

"We'll have privacy in here," he said, opening the door and ushering her into a cozy room with a Victorian-style-gold-and-beige wallpaper, and gold-toned drapes, two white satin divans on a Persian rug, facing each other with a dragonfly-motif glass top coffee table between them. A slow fire burned in a white marble fireplace on an interior wall.

Mindy placed her purse on the coffee table and walked over to a slider that opened onto a portico with steps leading down to a garden she was certain bloomed and attracted butterflies during the short summer months. The Andretti mansion was so huge that even though she'd visited it several times, there were many areas that were still a secret to her. The same could be said for the Andreas, Fontaine, and LaCrosse mansions.

"This is nice. I've never been in this room before," she said, turning to look at Galen who was standing next to the fireplace, his expression a dichotomy of wonder—she supposed at finally having his wish of being alone with her—and wistfulness for being apart from her for so long. At least she hoped that was true. She wanted that to be true.

"It's called the *Nora* after Mass' and my great-grandmother, Nora Minnetti."

"Is that her over the fireplace?" she asked, pointing to an oil painting of a dark haired, brown-eyed, delicate-looking woman in a fashionable blue and gold dress, perching on a windowsill that overlooked an old cobbled street.

"Yes," he said, turning to stare up at the painting. "That portrait was painted just before she sailed from Napoli for America. She met our great-grandfather, Bruno Andretti, in New York, and after they were married he moved Andretti Industries to Granite Falls and began building his empire here. According to our family history, this room used to be a nursery. My grandfather, Piero, was born in here. It is where Nora spent most of her time. She loved butterflies," he added, staring past Mindy to the nets hanging just below the Evergreen tree lines of the garden below.

"It's very warm and welcoming in here."

"It is. The room has a somewhat therapeutic aura about it. Mass and I were in here earlier talking about our family's future. He was extremely close to our grandfather, so this room holds a special place in his heart."

Mindy didn't miss the pride and ease with which Galen used the pronouns *my* and *our* when he spoke of his ancestors. Her heart warmed with affection that he was sharing it with her. "You don't think Massimo would mind you bringing me in here?"

He walked over to her. "Mass likes you, Mindy. As a matter of fact, he—"

A knock at the door caused them both to turn their heads in that direction. Upon Galen's command, Mrs. Riley, the head housekeeper, entered the room. A younger household employee with a cart, laden with a pitcher of water, a pot of tea, glasses, cups, dishes, utensils, and two covered serving plates, followed behind her.

"Mrs. Andretti thought you would like some appetizers until dinner is served," Mrs. Riley said, leading the way across the Brazilian wood floor to the coffee table.

Mindy exchanged a faint smile with Galen as the women worked quietly and quickly, spreading a linen tablecloth on the table and then setting out the appetizers and dishes.

"Thank you, ladies," Galen said when they were done.

They nodded and smiled before departing, taking the cart with them.

"The food smells good," Mindy said, sitting down on one of the divans. She uncovered the serving dishes and stared at the assortment of grilled oysters, prosciutto-wrapped pears, oven-roasted tomato bruschetta, and kale-and-white-bean crostini. "Wow, these are some kind of hors d'oeuvres."

"*Horse de ovaries*, as Britt calls them." Galen chuckled as he filled their water glasses from the pitcher. "How are she and Kyle?" he asked as he eased his weight down on the divan opposite her.

"They're fine." Mindy kept her gaze low as she filled two plates with the hors d'oeuvres and placed one on his side of the table, at the same time he placed a saucer and teacup with mint tea on her side.

They simultaneously met each other's gaze and said, "Thanks."

At least they still had some form of synergy, Mindy thought. She bit into a crostini then took a sip of tea. She'd had a filling lunch with her kids and wasn't really hungry, but she wasn't going to pass up treats like these. Dinner, Tashi had told her, would be served at six. She should be ready to gorge herself again by then. And who knew how long she and Galen would be in here anyway? "Aren't you going to eat?" she asked on her second bite when she noticed that he hadn't touched his plate, but was instead sipping his tea and watching her with a guarded expression on his face.

He shook his head and, for the first time since running into him, Mindy detected a sense of hesitation—or was it fear—animating from him. For a moment, Mindy forgot that she was angry as her love for him, her concern for his well-being, slammed into her gut. She set down her crostini and wiped her hands and mouth on her napkin. "Talk to me, Galen. That's why we're here, right?"

His lips thinned into a forced smile. "Yes." He took a deep breath as his eyes scanned her face. "There's so much that it's hard to decide where to begin."

Mindy straightened her back, her stomach in knots. "Why don't you pick up from the last time we spoke? You know, when you called to tell me that you were on your way to see your grandfather? That was the last time I heard from you until last Friday night."

Galen leaned forward and placed his empty teacup into its saucer. "I guess that's a good place to start." His eyes traveled the length of Mindy, sending his heart leaping in his chest and his stomach fluttering. She looked enticing in her body-hugging red

ANA E ROSS

dress that emphasized the voluptuous rise of her breasts, her narrow waist and tight belly. He'd love to remove each piece of clothing slowly, kissing and caressing every inch of her ivory body as it was exposed to his eyes and his hands—every piece but her black stilettos that showed off her dainty red-painted toes.

He missed burying his face in her shimmering blonde hair whether it was cascading down her back or up in a bun like it was now. He envied those two curly strands that brushed her cheeks and the creamy contours of her neck every time she moved her head. He missed all of her.

He wondered if this would be the last time they would share such an amiable setting after he bared his heart and soul to her. Part of him argued against telling her now, and instead told him to pick her up into his arms, take her upstairs to his suite, and make passionate love to her for the balance of the evening.

He wanted to extend these warmhearted moments, keep talking about nonessential issues for as long as he could, but time was of the essence. Geoffrey had been asleep for half an hour, and since his sleep pattern and schedule were off balance from jet lag and the lingering effects of his ear infection, he could awaken at any moment and start crying for his daddy. It was time to start talking.

He picked up his glass of water and leaned back against the cushions. "After I hung up from you, I took a car to the hospital. I almost had a heart attack when I saw Granddaddy hooked up to machines with tubes in his arms and—" His mind burned with the grisly memory, but he forced himself to go on. "He looked as if he'd aged twenty years from the last time I'd seen him. He couldn't speak, and could barely move. All he could do was stare at his surroundings. But as I began to talk to him, his eyes focused on me, and at that moment I felt like he knew that I was there."

Galen blinked away the image of his grandfather's frail body, his thinning silver hair matted to his scalp, and his gaunt face—an image that would haunt him for the rest of his life. His mother had died in her sleep from deep vein thrombosis, and his aunt Gertrude who'd battled Type 2 diabetes most of her life had quickly succumbed to a deadly strain of pneumonia. His last images of them were pleasant. Not so with his Granddaddy.

"What caused his heart attack?" Mindy asked. "Was he sick before?"

Galen shifted his weight on the divan. "No. I mean, he was eighty-five years old. He was enjoying his retirement, traveling across Europe with other seniors and doing whatever people his age do to keep themselves active and happy. Everything in his life was perfect until last June when his mortgage company tried to make the monthly withdrawal from his bank. There wasn't enough money. That immediately sent up a red flag because Granddaddy had close to a million pounds in that account the last time I visited him."

"Which was just after the group wedding," she interjected.

"Yes. How could that much money disappear in the space of a year? Granddaddy was never a big spender. He was always frugal, even when I was a kid." A neighbor drove him to the bank, where they showed him documentation that I, who had power of attorney over all aspects of his life, had visited the bank and transferred large sums of money over the course of several months into several accounts in Ireland and Switzerland. Granddaddy just fell to the floor. He had a heart attack right there in the bank. I know he was shocked, mortified that his trusted, loving grandson had wiped him out. It was all the money he had, his retirement nest egg after he liquidated Carmichael's Furniture."

"Oh, Galen I'm sorry. We know it wasn't you because you were in Granite Falls the entire time."

Her voice was soft and caring, so different from the other

night. This was the Mindy he knew. "Exactly. Someone had been impersonating me."

"Did you know all this before you left?"

"No. I learned about it from his neighbor who'd accompanied him to the bank, the same one who'd called me. He was in Granddaddy's room when I got to the hospital. He told me everything as I sat holding my grandfather's hand." He wiped at a tear that had slid from the corner of his eye.

She shook her head slowly. "I can see now that you had your hands full and probably couldn't think of anything else."

"That's not the reason for my silence, Mindy," he said, as the gloom rose inside him. "I needed you more than ever then. Just hearing your voice would have helped me deal with the horror. But that was just the tip of the iceberg I was about to crash into."

"What do you mean?" Her face clouded with worry.

Galen took a sip of water and struggled with the best way to tell her about the physical torture he had endured almost on a daily basis. There was no *good*, *better*, or *best* way in this situation. It was all bad. *Should he even tell her?*

"I left the hospital, intending to go straight to the bank to figure out the mess, and begin the process of fixing it, hoping to get my grandfather's money back. But four men were waiting outside at the main entrance for me. They surrounded me, and one jammed a gun into my back, and—"

"Oh my God, Galen." Her hands flew to her mouth as she stared at him.

"They forced me into a van, blindfolded me, and drove to an abandoned building. They took me to the basement, took off my blindfold, tied me to a chair, and informed me that they were the ones who'd stolen my identity and my grandfather's money. They'd even wiped out the trust fund my aunt had left me."

"But why? Identity thieves don't usually kidnap their victims. Most of them don't even know them, don't want to meet them."

"They don't. But these men obviously didn't bank on my grandfather suffering a heart attack. When that happened, they knew it was only a matter of time before I showed up and figured out that my identity had been stolen. Now, if all they wanted was my personal information in order to steal my grandfather's money, they would have been long gone. But it wasn't. A much more sinister plan was afoot."

As Galen watched Mindy sitting still as a log, clutching her hands so tightly that her knuckles had turned as white as her face, he wished he could spare her the frightening details. "The men were members of the Fraser family—a crime family," he continued. "Charles Fraser, the patriarch, ruled the clan, in-laws included. They robbed banks, wealthy homes, and institutions. They fenced stolen art, trafficked drugs and humans. They had a number of shell corporations scattered across the UK to launder their money across Europe. They'd revived Carmichael's Furniture months before I got there, and had been laundering money through it."

"Oh my God."

"They couldn't have me going to the authorities and causing trouble, so they informed me that from there on out, I would be laundering money for them. I told them to go jump into the deepest part of the Thames. That's when the beatings began."

A soft gasp escaped her. "They beat you?" she whispered in a faint voice.

He nodded as the pain echoed in the black stillness of his mind. "They took my phone. Miraculously it was locked and when I refused to give them the password, they continued to beat me." He shook his head slowly. "You see darling, there was too much sensitive information about you and Kyle and Britt, too many racy photos of you, and delicate texts messages between us on that phone. I would have died a thousand deaths before I let them have it."

Tears dampened her long dark lashes. "That's what you meant the other night about protecting us?"

"Yes." If only that was all there was to tell. "They took a hammer to my phone and then set it on fire. It was backed up to iCloud so I wasn't worried about losing my data. They also burned the luggage I'd brought with me and they threatened to go to the hospital and finish off my grandfather if I didn't do what they asked. When I still refused to cooperate, they pulled out a photo of you, Kyle, and Britt, and threatened to harm all three of you."

She jumped forward. "What? Where did they get a picture? Were they in Granite Falls watching us?" Her voice shook from astonishment and fear.

Galen's heart began to pound as he got closer and closer to the edge of the precipice he was about to tumble from. There was no saving him from the disgrace, only perhaps rescue, and if he were lucky, nurtured back to emotional and psychological health. He wanted to get up and stretch his legs, but he knew if he moved, he would chicken out. He had to go the distance, finish it and put it behind him. This was the last time he would speak of those seven harrowing months of his life.

He leaned forward and rested his elbows on his knees. "I told you about Beatrix."

Her eyes narrowed. "The woman you were buying the gift for when we first met in Arabella."

"Yes, that woman. *She* gave them the pictures."

Deep lines appeared on her forehead. "You broke up with her before we were together. So how could she have pictures of me and my kids? Did you send them to her?"

Galen could almost hear the cranking of the wheels turning in her head as she tried to fathom how Beatrix figured into the equation. "She stole them off my phone when I saw her."

Her hands unclasped and her body retreated into the back of

the divan in very slow motion. Her voice was low, almost inaudible. "When—um—did you—you—see her?"

Galen clenched his teeth as he felt the constriction in his lungs begin to build. He couldn't pretend that night never happened, not when he had an eighteen-month old son to prove it. "When I went home for Christmas the year you and I started dating."

She folded her arms and began to twitch while red blotches appeared on her neck. Galen was well aware of her telltale signs of distress.

"You're aware of the lie my aunt Gertrude told me about my mother's relationship with Massimo's and my father," he continued. "You knew how angry I was when I learned that Massimo's mother had robbed me and my mother of the life we should have had with my father. I needed to vent, so I went to the bar where Trix worked. And—um—"

Unable to hold her gaze, he shifted his to the window above her head and the fading daylight beyond it. When the members of the Fraser family had finally been apprehended, Galen had thought that the darkest days of his life were behind him. But he was wrong. So wrong. Could he survive Mindy leaving him for good?

"Galen?"

He returned his gaze to her face and wiped his hands down his cheeks. "Oh, Mindy. You will hate me, my love. I know it."

"Galen?" Her voice cracked, and torment and fear glittered in her eyes. "What did you do?"

He shook his head, tears brimming over now. "I don't know, Mindy." *But you do know.* "All I know is that I awoke in her bed the next morning. I don't know how I got there."

She froze for a split second, then said in a sinking tone, "You hooked up with your old girlfriend?"

"Mindy, no. I—"

She dropped her face into her hands, crying, "Oh my God. Oh my God, Oh my God," over and over again.

Galen wanted to sit beside her and cradle her in his arms until her sobs subdued, but touching her now would only make her angry. She needed space to absorb the shock of his confession of waking up in another woman's bed, even though he'd told her that he didn't remember how he got there. He'd shattered her heart. As he silently and helplessly watched the woman he loved reel from his betrayal, Galen knew that her agony would only intensify when he finally let her in on the secret of Geoffrey.

"I didn't *hook up* with her, Mindy," he said, knowing that vocabulary didn't matter. *Slept with, hooked up with, had sex with.* In a different situation, they would mean nothing, but in this one, they meant everything. A slice of pie was a slice of pie, no matter which part of the whole pie you cut it from.

She raised her head. Her eyes were red and puffy, and her face that was perfectly flawless moments ago, was now streaked with her ruined makeup. "Then why would I hate you?" she asked warily, as if she didn't really want to know the answer.

"It wasn't intentional."

"What the hell does that mean?" She slammed her fists into the seat of divan, her eyes flashing with frustration and confusion. "Did you sleep with her or not?"

"She admitted to drugging me, Mindy. That's why I can't remembering anything about that night." He needed to get his non-participation of that night out before he dropped the bombshell. "She claims that she thought I would do something stupid and that she just wanted to calm me down."

"So you're not sure that anything happened?" Her eyes narrowed incredulously, but he could see hope in their depth too.

"*She* said it did. I told myself that if I couldn't remember, it didn't really happen. She could have been lying for all I knew."

"Why would she lie about something like that?"

"Because she wanted me back."

Her eyelashes fluttered. "If you think nothing happened, and that she was lying, why are we talking about it?"

Galen pressed his fingers against his temples as he searched for the right response. There was only one. "I know she wasn't lying because we have a son. Geoffrey is eighteen months old. He was conceived that night. I'm so sorry, Mindy. I'm so sorry, love."

CHAPTER TEN

Mindy jabbed her fists into her stomach and doubled over as excruciating pain ripped apart her insides—pain she'd only felt twice in her lifetime when she'd been in labor. Never in a trillion years would she have thought she'd ever hear Galen say the words, "We have a son," when referring to another woman. She'd thought that line had been reserved for the two of them one day in the future.

"Mindy. I'm sorry. I never meant to hurt you like this."

Mindy shot off the divan, her startled hurt turning into white-hot anger. "Would you please stop saying that you're sorry? It doesn't matter if you meant to hurt me or not. You *did*, when you slept with another woman while we were together. You made a baby with her, and you didn't tell me." Fresh tears poured down her face.

"I didn't know about Geoffrey until eight months ago when I arrived in London."

She stamped her foot and balled her fists, wanting to hit something. "I'm not talking about him. I'm talking about two years ago when you got into bed with his mother. You should have told me about it when you came home, whether you thought it had happened or not. Telling me, *now*, that she drugged you and then seduced you is not an excuse."

"You're right. It's not an excuse."

"You shouldn't have gone to see her!" She punched the air with her fists as her nose burned and her eyes stung with fresh tears. "You should have called me." She slammed her hand into her chest. "I was your woman, your lover, your confidant, and best friend. You are supposed to call me when you're hurt and upset."

He leaped to his feet. "Right again. I should *not* have gone to see her. I *should* have called you. I made a horrible mistake."

"No, Galen. No! Your mistake was not telling me when you returned to Granite Falls. You had unprotected sex with another woman and then came back here and made love to me. You knew that Kyle was the only other man I'd ever been with. I told you that I didn't sleep around because I was afraid of catching STDs and not being able to take care of my kids. You knew I am all they have. Yet you carelessly and recklessly put my health in jeopardy."

"I thought about that, Mindy. I remembered that you were allergic to latex, and since condoms weren't an option, I had myself tested before I came back. I was clean. I haven't been with anyone but you since."

"So you believed her enough to have yourself tested, but not enough to tell me that you might have slept with her? You lied to me by omission, Galen." Her mind reeled with disgust. Everything she'd said to him the other night when he showed up at her door had been well deserved.

He hung his head, staring at the table of food as his face flushed with apparent shame. After a few silent moments, he raised his head and spoke in a miserably broken voice. "Yes. I lied. I didn't tell you because I couldn't bear to hurt you. I was a coward. I was afraid of losing you, to see the look of disdain and loathing in your eyes. The look I'm seeing right now."

He gulped hard, and tears rolled down his cheeks. "Our relationship was new, as were the feelings I had for you. I'd never been in love before. I was afraid you wouldn't understand, wouldn't forgive me. I didn't want to take the chance of saying something if nothing really happened. I do regret it now."

Mindy bit into her bottom lip and gazed into the dying fire in the hearth behind Galen. *Another relationship, another love, down the tubes.* "You should have trusted me, Galen. You told me that you loved me. You can't have love without trust. Even I knew that at fifteen when I fell in love with Kyle. We never lied to each other, either outright or by omission." Mindy's throat ached with the one regret she would carry for the rest of her life—her inability to lie to Kyle. She should have waited until the next day to tell him what Danny had done to her. He would be alive today, and she wouldn't be standing here in front of a man with her heart ripped to shreds.

"I know I have no business to ask, Mindy, but I hope that someday you will find it in your heart to forgive me for making the two most horrible mistakes of my life—seeing Trix, and not telling you."

Mindy forced herself to look at him, to take in the tears and obvious regret in his eyes. No parent should ever say that the act that brought his child into the world was a mistake. Her mother had called her a mistake several times, even though Mindy had no idea why. As hard as Mindy's life had been raising her children on her own, she'd never thought they were mistakes, much less utter the words aloud. But she wasn't about to tell Galen any of that. She wasn't in any mood to ease his guilt. She had no sympathy for him.

She glanced down at her purse lying on the edge of the table. The temptation to pick it up and walk out of the room was strong, but she wanted all the facts. She deserved to known why she and her children's lives had been in danger, why they'd been used as pawns by these Fraser people, and if she needed to protect herself from potential future harm from them.

She dropped wearily down on the edge of the divan and eyed her glass of water. Her throat was parched from crying, but she didn't even have the energy to pick up the glass. She felt numb and weak and nauseous.

She met Galen's puppy-dog gaze. "I want to hear the rest of it, then I'm going to leave. I don't want to hear any more apologies, no begging me to forgive you. Just tell me what happened in the last eight months you've been gone."

He nodded and then perched on the edge of his seat.

She thought the two of them looked like flighty birds about to take off in different directions. "When did you find out that you had a son?" she asked to get the conversation moving. The sooner he was done, the sooner she could leave.

"The day I arrived in London."

"Did you see his mother? Did *she* tell you about him?"

"No. My son was on the list of people I loved and needed to protect. The Frasers showed me his picture, but I was forbidden to go near him, or his mother."

Mindy winced. She was a parent, so in that regard, she understood how petrified he must have been to have his son's life threatened. She would do anything to protect her children, even if it meant killing someone in self-defense. "How did they know you had a son when you didn't?"

"This is where Beatrix comes in. The morning after she did whatever she did to me, she told me that she wanted me back. I told her that I was in love with you, that I wanted to make a life with you and Kyle and Britt, and then I got out of her flat as fast as I could, not realizing that she'd broken into my phone and sent the pictures to hers. That was the last time I saw her until I visited her in prison about a month ago."

Mindy frowned. "Why is she in prison?"

"She killed a night guard at the bank where she worked during the day."

She pressed her hands against her ears. This was getting weirder and weirder. "She's one of them? She's a Fraser?"

Galen's thoughts were jagged and painful. He wished he didn't have to recount Trix's story, but he knew it was vital for Mindy to know the details. If he ever became so lucky that one day she would forgive him, and welcome him and Geoffrey into her heart, she needed to know that Trix would never pose a threat to her. "No. She was pregnant with Geoffrey when she began dating Charles Fraser's oldest son, Basil. She thought nothing of it when he began asking her questions about the father of her unborn child. She told him everything about me and my grandfather. They broke into my grandfather's flat and stole vital personal information about both of us."

"So they could steal your identity."

"Yes. And then they told her what they'd done." Having Mindy question him helped to get the details out.

"Why didn't she report them?"

"They threatened to cut her child out of her."

She flinched and crossed her arms over her stomach as if she were protecting a child in her womb, but she said nothing.

Only a mother could understand that kind of threat, he thought. "Their *modus aperandi* was to target women who were single and alone with an absentee father-to-be. It was easier to steal identities of people who aren't around. Beatrix was also targeted because she worked in a bank. It was a small bank, and she had access and codes to the security system and the vault. It was supposed to be an easy in-and-out heist. She knew it would happen, but she didn't know when.

"One day, when she was six months pregnant, she got a call to leave her laptop and her cell phone in her desk and to walk outside at the end of the day. Basil was waiting for her. They blindfolded her and took her to an unfamiliar location. At midnight, they had her call the night guard to ask if she could pick up the items she'd left on her desk. Of course he agreed. They gave her a gun and told her that it was loaded with blanks, and that she was to fire a warning shot if the guard reached for his weapon. Basil, one of his younger brothers, and a cousin donned masks, and waited out of sight. When the guard opened to let her into the bank, they forced their way in. She shot at him when he reached for his weapon.

"When he fell to the floor with blood pouring from his chest, she realized that she'd been tricked. But the guard wasn't dead, and while they were on their way to the vault, he fired a fatal shot into Basil's back. The other men grabbed the security tape, dragged Basil away and left Beatrix to take the fall. She was arrested, charged with murder, and sent to Bronzefield, a women's prison in Surrey."

"Surely she could have explained all that to the authorities," Mindy said in a suffocated whisper.

"Nobody would believe her, not without proof she had accomplices. Her fingerprints were on the gun that shot the guard."

"These people think of everything. They cover every angle."

"They'd been at it for years. They'd learned from other criminals' mistakes."

"So your son was born in prison."

He rubbed his hands slowly along his thighs. "Yes."

"Well at least she'd saved the boy's life. I would have done the same thing to protect my children. Her son was safe from them."

"Not so fast. They'd threatened to have both of them killed in prison if she snitched. They also made her name Basil as his father."

"Why? He was dead. Wouldn't that have connected her with the family?"

"Not really. Fraser is a very common surname in England. Plus Basil's death wasn't public knowledge. They'd buried him in Ireland. Another thing—this family had never been on the National Crime Agency's radar, so there was no cause for suspicion. Having Trix name Basil as Geoffrey's father was insurance to keep her from talking when he turned eighteen months old."

"What would have happened then?"

"He would have aged out of Bronzefield and been placed into foster care, or adopted. Naming Basil as his father gave the Frasers first rights to him as next-of-kin. Knowing that they had him and that they could do anything to him, anytime they wanted, was insurance to seal her lips forever." Galen balled his fists and clenched his jaws to keep from swearing out loud. Every time he thought of the possibility of his son being raised by a gang of hoodlums and being inducted into a life of crime, his blood boiled.

"Oh, Galen. That's what you've been dealing with for the past eight months?"

"Seven actually. I knew my son existed for eight months, but it wasn't until last month when the nightmare came to an end that I had the opportunity to meet him. I have full custody of him now."

"That is a horrific story, but I still don't understand why you didn't reach out to me, let me know what was going on. I could have helped."

"How could I have called you and laid all this on your shoulders? Remember, they'd threatened your life as well. If I'd called you, you would have jumped on a plane and walked right into the lion's den. No, sweetheart. This is what I meant the other night when I told you that my silence was to protect you."

"Now I understand," she said quietly.

Galen took that as a good thing. "I couldn't call, even if I wanted to. After they beat me into agreeing to launder their money, they gave me a new identity. I was Freddy Fraser, Charles' nephew—the name and National Identification Number I later learned belonged to a child that was born of another one of their victims. They had also used Geoffrey's NIN to make wire transfers."

"These people have no limits. Only the most wretched minds would sit around and devise such evil plots to steal from others."

She had no idea. "They forced me to live in a flat with the man who'd stolen my identity. So, there I was, Freddy Fraser, living with my impersonator. I was given a cell phone with a tracker, and was not allowed to leave the flat unaccompanied. Someone was always with me, even when I went to the banks to make the deposits and transfers."

"You were in prison."

"A prison with no locks or bars. I got a good understanding of the emotional and psychological horror victims of human trafficking live with on an hourly and daily basis." He saw no reason to tell her about his daily beatings. She'd heard enough for one day. Perhaps another time—if she gave him another chance. "They would have known if I'd called you. The phone was strictly for them to reach me when they wanted to give an order, which wasn't often since I was living with my impersonator, and to track me if I ever decided to detour from their narrow path."

"Tashi told me that Massimo went to see you just before Christmas. Did you call him?"

Galen marveled that she could so calmly show interest when

he'd just admitted to betraying their love and their trust. She was really a gem. He would be the luckiest man alive if she forgave him and gave him a second chance. "I had no one else. My grandfather had passed away, not that he could have helped me from his hospital bed. I had to get Geoffrey out of Bronzefield before he turned eighteen months old and ended up in the clutches of those criminals. I had no choice but to swallow my pride and call Massimo. I left him a message, not even knowing if he would come. I mean, the last time I saw him he'd called me a conniving little usurper. But lo and behold, he showed up the very next day."

"It didn't matter that you and Massimo weren't on speaking terms. You're his little brother. That's all that matters to him."

She spoke as if she had some inside scoop about his brother's state of mind regarding family.

"So you used their phone to call Massimo, knowing that that they would find out? I guess at that point you had nothing else to lose. Geoffrey would have left the prison one way or the other."

His heart trembled when she spoke his son's name for the first time. It seemed so natural that he was sure she wasn't even aware that she had done so. "I still had you and Kyle and Britt to lose. So, no I couldn't take *any* chance."

Her eyes sparkled with what he hoped was the first sign of forgiveness and understanding. "So how did you call him? You borrowed someone's phone when they weren't looking?"

"Something like that." He spent the next few minutes giving her a short version about the events that finally brought down the house of Fraser, starting with the Christmas gift phone call from Charles Fraser to the moment Galen had shown up at Mindy's door two nights ago.

When he was done talking, Mindy's hands were thrust against her mouth, and tears were streaming down her face, making a wet mess of her red dress. Her entire body was shaking like a dry leaf in the autumn wind. She's apparently kept calm as long as she could so he could get though his story. But now that she'd heard it all, her sea of pain and sorrow had broken through her defenses.

Without even thinking, Galen stepped over the coffee table and sat beside Mindy. She made no protest when he gathered her into his arms, but seemed to soak up the comfort instead. God, it felt so good to hold her, even if she was crying from pain that he had unintentionally caused her.

We are powerless to the women we love. They know we're not perfect. When we humble ourselves, kneel at their feet, and confess our inadequacies, they are more likely to forgive us even if they don't understand us.

As Mass's words rang in his ears, Galen fell to the floor in front of Mindy and gently tugged her hands from her face, holding them tightly in his own. "Look at me," he pleaded when she turned and looked across the room.

His heart rocked when she met his gaze, her beautiful brown eyes filled with the love he knew she still had for him but couldn't give him at the moment. He would wait an eternity for her.

"You told me not to say that I'm sorry, not to ask for forgiveness, but I'm going to do just that, Mindy. I *am* sorry that I lied to you, that I hurt you, that I caused you pain that will probably take a while to heal. But while you're doing that, remember that I love you with everything inside of me. It was stupid and coward of me not to tell you about that night. But I promise that from this day on I will never hide anything from you again. Give me another chance. Please."

She pulled her hands from his and clasped his cheeks. "I know you're sorry, Galen, and I'm sorry about the nightmare that you went through these past few months. But the fact is, if you hadn't reached out to Trix instead of me, none of this would have happened."

She spoke the truth. The problem hadn't started with the

Frasers targeting Trix, stealing his identity, causing his Grandfather's death or ultimately threatening Geoffrey's life. It started when he'd made the conscious decision to go to Trix's bar that night when he should have gotten on the phone and called Mindy. That, in itself was a case of blatant rejection of her love and her faith in him. He had trampled on her love for him.

"Maybe some time in the future I'll be able to forgive you, but not now, not today, or tomorrow." She shook her head and dropped her hands from his face, causing him to shiver as if he'd been sprayed with ice-cold water.

"And when that day comes, I hope we can somehow move past this."

Her eyes were filled with pity, defeat, and brokenness. "You have an eighteen-month-old son, Galen. We've been together for two and a half years. It's only a matter of time before the entire world knows that you made a fool out of me. There's no moving past this. I can't—I can't be around you. I can't look at you. I'm sorry."

She inched away from him and picked up her purse. "If you respect me, please don't call me again. I don't want to talk to you." She turned and walked across the floor.

Galen closed his eyes, unable to watch her leave. Each click of her stilettos heels against the hardwood floor was a nail being hammered into Galen's heart. His existence seemed to fade as her footsteps got fainter taking her farther and farther away. The door opened and closed.

And then everything went quiet.

Galen strolled into the nursery to find Geoffrey, fully dressed in a pair of corduroys and a fleece sweater. He was sitting on a bench with Sybil kneeling in front of him.

As he approached them, Galen realized that he lacked much of the excitement he'd come to welcome at seeing his son first thing in the morning. He'd read in one of Shaina's baby books that children, even those as young as Geoffrey, were equipped with powerful sixth sense which gave them the ability to pick up on the moods of those around them.

So in an effort not to project his sour disposition and the stark reality of his darkest fears onto his son, Galen had stayed away all yesterday afternoon and last night, allowing Sybil to attend to Geoffrey's needs, which thankfully were minimal. He'd only heard him cry out once during the night, and by the time Galen had donned his robe and walked to the door leading into the nursery, Sybil was already there. She was a lifesaver, and he had to find a way to reward her hard work and dedication.

He stood behind the bench and asked in as stable a voice as he could, "Is he ready?"

"Almost. I just have to finish tying his shoelaces. And—one two, three, we're done." Sybil picked up his son and placed him into Galen's arms. "Here you go, little fellow, all bathed and dressed and ready for the day with Daddy."

Galen kissed his son's cheeks, then hugged him close to his heart, a heart that had been hurting for the past fifteen hours straight. "Daddy loves you, Geoffrey. Daddy loves you so much."

Geoffrey wrapped his arms around his neck and squeezed him back. "Daddy loves Geoffy. Geoffy loves Daddy."

"Yes, my boy, yes." Happy chuckles burst from Galen's throat as tears misted his eyes. *Daddy loves you, Geoffrey* had been Galen's daily mantra to his son from the moment he'd first held him. Even when Geoffrey pushed him away and cried for his mummy, Galen had stayed the course, breaking down Geoffrey's walls of resistance with patience and tender loving care. And finally, he'd been rewarded with the words he'd been longing to hear. *Geoffy loves Daddy.* Galen closed his eyes and pressed his cheeks against

Geoffrey's. This right here was what he'd spent the last eight months of his life fighting for.

And just as he'd fought for his son, he would stay the course and fight for the woman of his dreams. Mindy loved him. He'd seen it in her eyes, heard it in her voice, and felt it when he'd held her in his arms for a brief moment yesterday. She'd pushed him away because she was hurt and angry. She wouldn't be human if she hadn't acted in that manner.

All he could do now was give her time to digest what he'd laid on her, time to be angry, and time to grieve, but he would not give her time to get over him, to forget him, to completely wipe out what they'd shared from her memory. He needed her and she needed him. And he would make damn sure they both got what they needed from each other.

And then there were Kyle and Brittany, he thought as an intense feeling of failure overcame him. He loved those kids as much as he loved his own son. Living with them, taking care of them had given him a taste of what it would be like to be a father. He'd promised them that he would always be there, be the father they never had. When he'd kissed them goodbye eight months ago, he'd told them that he would be back, never thinking in a million years that he would unintentionally break that promise.

He'd failed them, and he had to make it right, mend his broken promises, make new ones and keep them this time around. But in order to heal the hurt he'd caused Kyle and Brittany, and be a devoted and attentive father to them and to Geoffrey, he first had to convince their mother to give him another chance.

Mindy had to forgive him. He could not, would not take *no* for an answer.

"Perhaps after his doctor's visit, we can take a drive into town together, you, me, and Geoffrey. I haven't had a chance to explore the city yet. What do you think, Galen?"

Galen stared at Sybil. She'd called him Galen, *and* here she was stroking his arm in a very inappropriate manner while she smiled sweetly at him. He took a step back from her, breaking the contact. "What are you doing?"

She thrust her hands behind her back. "I'm sorry, Mr. Carmichael. You've been down in the dumps since yesterday evening. I just thought…" She dropped her gaze and her voice trailed off.

He cocked his head. "You just thought what?"

"That you might need a bit of cheering up, a little comforting."

"And you thought you could provide that cheer and comfort? Have I ever indicated that I was interested in that kind of relationship with you?" *Dear God, had he?*

She raised her head. "No, sir. You haven't. I have overstepped my bounds. I'm sorry. It won't happen again."

Bloody hell it wouldn't. Why hadn't he seen this coming? Back in London, Sybil had been at his beck and call, choosing to stay at home rather than hang out with her friends and family, even when he was there. She'd been caring and responsible with Geoffrey when he wasn't around.

He took another step back as her previous subtle batting eyelashes, her demure smiles, her comments that he was a wonderful man and fine dad took on a meaning of their own. *Huh*! He'd been caught up in his own world, too preoccupied with survivor's happiness and striving to gain custody of his son to think her kindness was anything more than genuine concern.

Perhaps he should have paid more attention to the fact that Sybil had shown no regret, remorse, or even sadness when she'd abruptly ended her two-year relationship with her boyfriend a week after becoming Geoffrey's full-time nanny. Was Galen the reason she had made herself available, and had accepted his offer to come to Granite Falls with him, even before the question was fully out of his mouth? Did she hope that he would one day look at her *that* way?

Disturbing images of Sybil's scantily clad body walking around the London suite flashed across Galen's mind. He wouldn't deny that she was an attractive girl, and that if he'd met her under different circumstance, he probably would have shown some interest. But for the past two years and counting, Mindy Marshall was the only woman Galen had ever wanted, would ever want for the rest of his life. That fact, he realized now, had saved him from succumbing to Sybil's subtle attempts at seduction. She'd been offering the kind of TLC any red-blooded English bloke in his position would have jumped on in a heartbeat. It was his quest for that kind of comfort that had gotten him into a hotbed of mess with Trix—the result of which he was holding in his arms.

"Sybil," he stated in a voice he hoped left no doubt in her mind about the role she played in his life, "you are my employee. You're Geoffrey's nanny. Your duty is to take care of his needs, and his alone. I will forgive you this one blunder, but if you ever cross this line again, I *will* let you go. Are we clear?"

CHAPTER ELEVEN

Sybil's cheeks were red with apparent embarrassment. "Yes, Mr. Carmichael. We are clear," she said, regret in her eyes and voice.

Satisfied that she would not make that mistake again, Galen softened his stance. "How are you and Reese getting along?" he asked of the Andretti children's nanny.

"We seem to like each other."

"Jolly. Aria and MJ are spending the day with the Andreases, and I overheard Reese discussing spending the day in town with Alex's nanny, and having lunch at the country club. It would be a good way for you to make some new friends. I'll ask if she minds you tagging along. Do you have the credit card I gave you before we left London?"

"Yes."

"Lovely. Treat yourself to whatever you want. Perhaps a new wardrobe. Reese will know where to take you shopping."

"Thank you, Mr. Carmichael."

With their roles back in place, he turned to his son. "Geoffrey, say goodbye to Sybil."

"Bye, bye, *Bilbil*," Geoffrey said with a wave and a grin.

"Bye, Geoffrey." She brushed back a curl from his forehead. "Have a good day with your dad. I love you, little chap."

Galen walked out of the nursery, his mind filled with new concerns as he made his way toward the first-floor common areas of the mansion.

The bond between Sybil and Geoffrey grew stronger every day, every minute that they were together. She was the only constant and reliable female caregiver in his life. He'd also read in Shaina's books that, over a period of time, a young child could mistake a nanny for a mother, especially if that mother wasn't on the scene. Trix would be spending the rest of her life in prison, and the only other woman Galen wanted to play the role of Mommy in his son's life was Mindy. And who knew how long it would be before he was even able to introduce them—if ever. As unthinkable as it was, he still had to deal with the fact that Mindy might never forgive him.

In the meantime, Geoffrey was becoming more and more dependent on Sybil. It would be a setback for Geoffrey if Galen was forced to end Sybil's employment. But end it he would, if she ever pulled a stunt like that again. He hoped she used the day to reflect on her behavior and understand that she would not be given another chance.

Five minutes later, Galen walked through the informal dining room and onto a porch where the family sometimes ate breakfast together. One would know how many members would be attending by the number of settings. This morning there were three chairs for adults, and three highchairs with bibs folded across them, so the entire family was expected for breakfast.

"Eat, Daddy." Geoffrey pointed at a buffet table with fresh fruits, yogurt, fragrant breads, bagels, and pastries, a variety of cheeses and a delicious looking charcuterie board. Coffee, espresso, and cappuccino machines were stationed on a smaller table. The tempting aromas coming from the kitchen next door reminded Galen that he hadn't eaten since lunch yesterday.

He glanced at his watch. It would be precisely thirty minutes before the servants would promptly bring in the breakfast orders that had been placed the night before. "Would you like some melon and banana slices and juice while we wait for Uncle Mass and Aunt Shaina and Aria and MJ?"

"Memon and 'nana, Daddy." Geoffrey nodded as he named his favorite fruits.

"Coming right up, mate." Galen secured him in a highchair and tied a bib around his neck. He poured some orange juice into a kiddie cup from one of the pitchers on the table, then went to the buffet. He returned with Geoffrey's order, as well as a cup of black coffee and a bowl of fruit, yogurt, and nuts, and some meats from the charcuterie board for himself.

"Leave some room for your scrambled eggs and oatmeal," he said on a chuckle as Geoffrey grabbed a handful of melon chunks and stuffed them into his mouth.

As Galen watched his son, he was taken back to breakfasts and lunches and dinners in Mindy's apartment where he, Mindy, Kyle, and Britt would all cram around a tiny table in her tiny kitchen. This spacious patio was probably bigger than Mindy's entire apartment had been, but he would trade it in for her place any day.

Yes, he'd inherited the genes of the powerful and super rich Andrettis, but his DNA also included those of a simple English family. He was raised in a two-bedroom flat where from his cozy bedroom, he could hear his mother moving around in the kitchen and smell the aromas from her cooking. Living in a mansion with servants running around—bringing him meals at assigned hours of the day and night, making his bed, cleaning his bathroom, and doing his laundry—wasn't a lifestyle he'd ever imagined possible. And now that it was within his reach, Galen wasn't sure he wanted it. He liked simple and cozy.

He pushed his empty dishes away and, with coffee cup in hand, walked to the wall of glass that overlooked well-kept grounds with a fountain garden, and downtown Granite Falls and Crystal Lake in the distance.

Mass' financial generosity was overwhelming—far beyond Galen's dreams or expectations. Yesterday he, Mass, and Steven Lynd—Mass' attorney—had gathered in the Nora Room to transfer the funds from Andretti Industries into Galen's newly established personal accounts and trust funds.

When Mass had told him that he was splitting seventeen years of Andretti Industries' assets and profits with him, Galen had figured he'd be a multimillionaire, at least. He would have enough money to take care of his son, send him to the best schools, and secure a promising and successful future for him. But when he'd seen the figures yesterday, he'd been paralyzed with both shock. He'd known that Andretti Industries was worth billions of dollars. He just hadn't realized just how deep and multilayered those billions were.

In effect, without lifting one finger, Galen had become a billionaire overnight. Well, he'd lifted eight fingers and two thumbs when he'd sued Massimo for half of AI. As Galen had expected, Massimo's generosity came with some heavy stipulations. Neither Galen nor any of his progeny would ever try to sue Andretti Industries for any reason ever again. They could never work at, sit on the board, or own stock in the company.

The list went on and on, but Galen wasn't upset about Mass' attempt to secure his own descendants' future. He understood that even though he and Mass were getting along well now, it didn't mean their children or their children's children would build congenial relationships down the road. It was best to keep the two families apart in that respect.

"What in God's name am I to do with this money?" he'd asked Mass after Steven had left.

"Whatever you want," his brother had said with a grin. "I'd love it if you lived on Mount Reservoir so our families could visit often."

But Mindy is a lakeside girl.

"Now that Geoffrey is feeling better, he and MJ seem to be developing a friendship. And Aria definitely enjoys having another little person to boss around."

"She's bossy like her mother, isn't she?"

Massimo laughed. "That she is, and I wouldn't have either of them any other way."

When Mass had mentioned *our families*, Galen's thoughts had gone directly to Mindy. During the first weeks of their relationship when he'd watched her interact with Tashi and the other wives, he'd often wondered if she fantasized about being the lady of a luxurious mansion of her own, ordering staff around and planning elaborate dinners and parties like her rich friends.

But as he'd gotten to know her better, he'd discovered that like him, Mindy was an ambitious dreamer who enjoyed the simple and moderate things in life. Walking five minutes from his bedroom to the dining room wasn't something Galen wished to do every morning for the rest of his life, and he would bet his life that it wasn't something Mindy wanted either.

She was a hardworking woman who believed in the rewards of a full day's work. She probably would have been better off if she'd stayed at home and collected government assistance for her kids. But she hadn't done that. She'd gone to work to provide for them, and now she was earning an education to enhance their future. While she'd sat across from him in the Nora Room yesterday, Galen had wondered at her reaction if he'd told her that only hours before, he'd attained the means to buy her her own mansion and to staff it with devoted servants to be at her beck and call. For all he knew, Mindy might have changed in the eight months they'd been separated. *He* had. Perhaps pleasing Mindy wasn't as simple as it used to be, he thought, placing his cup on a corner table.

Galen smiled, knowing in his heart that his billions wouldn't impress her one bit, especially since that money had been handed to him. Mindy had been encouraging when he'd shared his plan to invest in Carmichael's Furniture if he'd won the case against Massimo. But now that Carmichael's was a nonissue, he needed to start thinking of launching his own company.

After all, he was half Andretti, and Andrettis built powerful and successful empires. He just needed to figure out what kind of empire he wanted to build. It had to be something that would bring him great joy and satisfaction in creating and maintaining. And since he was a dreamer, it had to be the type of business that would help others obtain their own professional dreams. *That*, would impress Mindy, he thought, tapping his finger against his temple.

"Dad used to do that, you know."

Galen dropped his hand as Massimo walked onto the patio, dressed for the office in a white shirt, a black and gray striped tie, and dark slacks. He carried a matching suit jacket that he draped over the back of his chair before going over to give Geoffrey a little attention.

"Dad used to do what?" Galen asked, as he watched his brother interact with his nephew.

"Tap his fingers against his temple when he was weighing propositions," Mass replied as he made his way to the espresso machine.

"I should kill that habit, then." Galen pushed his hand into the pocket of his jeans as if to prevent his fingers from committing that appalling act again.

With a steaming cup of espresso in his hand, Mass joined Galen at the lookout. "He wasn't a monster, Galen. He was a cheating whore who broke his wife's heart, disappointed one son, and neglected the other. But we *are* his children, and we are bound to have inherited some of his mannerisms and characteristics."

I guess you're a true Andretti male, now. You're dressing and acting just like them—using women and then tossing them aside when you've had enough. You're all despicable! You disgust me. Galen shook his head, trying to block out the repugnance in Mindy's voice and eyes when she'd thrown those vile words at him a few nights ago. He'd proved her right yesterday when he'd admitted to cheating on her. "Apart from being a shrewd businessman and a redeemed man-whore, what have you inherited?" he asked with a slice of humor.

Massimo set his cup down, folded his arms, and stroked his lower lip with the pad of his thumb as he gazed thoughtfully at Galen.

"You do that when you're deep in thought," Galen said, casually amused.

"*Si.*" Mass picked up his cup and sipped his espresso. "Aside from being a crappy father and an unfaithful husband, Luciano did a lot of good for a lot of people. He positively impacted many lives, locally and globally. Those are the attributes I dwell on and try to emulate when I think of him." He shrugged. "Bryce's success as a businessman is a constant reminder of the positive contributions Dad made to the world."

"Because he mentored him," Galen said, remembering the story about Luciano taking a very young Bryce Fontaine under his wings after Bryce had inherited a small fortune from his grandmother.

"Dad was all too happy to have a prodigy to worship him and

hang on his every word since I wasn't paying much attention to Andretti Industries at the time."

"You were still in your rebellious stage," Galen said.

"You can say that. He was even trying to marry me off to the right woman or, more precisely, into the right Italian family."

At least you had a father to meddle in your life, as unwelcome and annoying as it might have been, Galen thought, as he recalled the numerous times he'd wished for a father to teach him *anything* about life. His grandfather had tried to fill that void, but it wasn't the same as having a man who lived under the same roof with him—a man he called Dad instead of Granddad. Since discovering that his father had been alive for most of his life, Galen had often wondered if Luciano even knew what his other son looked like. Would he have recognized him if he'd passed him on the street? *Had he passed him on the streets of London?* Had he thought about him daily, weekly, monthly, yearly? At all? Had he even known his birth date, and had he cared?

Galen's throat tightened when he felt Massimo's hand on his shoulder.

"I can tell you that you were better off without ever having him in your life, but that would be a lie." Mass dropped his hand and stated with a hint of irony in his voice, "The truth is that there were times when he was a caring and devoted dad. He loved my mother. He was gentle and kind with her. Our relationship started to deteriorate after I found out he'd been cheating on her."

Galen sensed a pensive forbearance in Massimo's tone. They had never really discussed the minute details of that period in their parents' lives. During the arbitration last year, Galen had heard a lot about Luciano's love for his wife, but he had yet to hear his brother's story. Mass was only ten years old when his mother died. "How old were you when you found out he'd been cheating on your mother? Was it with my mother? Did your mother know?" The questions gushed out of Galen like water from a fire hose.

A painful shimmer appeared in Mass' eyes. He crossed his arms and stared blindly through the glass. "It was a long time ago, Galen. The bottom line is that my father broke my mother's heart. I have no desire to dwell on that painful period of my life. Rehashing the past isn't going to change what happened. We need to accept it and move on."

Galen took a swift look across the room at Geoffrey, who was still working on his fruits. Juice was dripping off his chin and his elbows, but that was quite okay. Galen turned back to Mass. "There are still so many questions that remain unanswered."

"Perhaps. But the future is what's important. Having a family who depends on you changes your perspective about life in general. You're a father now, and your focus should be on building a successful future for Geoffrey and any other children you might have down the road. Not looking backwards at things you cannot change."

Galen detected guardedness in Massimo's voice that had developed and grown in depth ever since they'd begun discussing Luciano's affair with Galen's mother. He felt as if there was something his brother wasn't telling him, but he also knew him well enough to know that when Mass changed a subject, whether overtly or cunningly, the subject was changed.

Mass was a master conversation manipulator but, as far as Galen was concerned, his big brother could bloody well assert his manipulative skills in the boardroom, not in the family breakfast room.

"I've been doing a lot of thinking and computing," Galen said, needing to get to the bottom of the story once and for all. "When you came to my aid in London, you drew a comparison between my grandfather receiving bad news and suffering a heart attack in the bank, and your mother collapsing in the music room after receiving a phone call. You said that it was the breach of trust in those they loved that broke their hearts."

"And?" Mass shrugged.

"The timeline of events suggests that your mother died the same day Luciano found out that my mother was pregnant with me and had ordered her to leave the country. Your mother went into premature labor immediately following that phone call. After the horrible things I learned about my mother during the arbitration last year, I have to wonder if she was the one who'd called your mother."

Mass' brows knitted and his lips drew into a thin firm line.

"Mass, I need to know. I have the right to know." Galen prompted when he said nothing.

"Sometimes we think we want answers until we get them, little brother."

"So there are answers to be gotten. I knew it!" He cocked his head to one side as he stared up at Mass. "It was my mother who called your mother, wasn't it? What did she say to have caused your mother such stress that she and her unborn child died?"

"Daddy."

Both Galen and Mass turned to see three-year-old Aria racing toward them.

"How's Papa's beautiful baby girl?" Mass asked, as she flew into his arms with the fluidity and grace of a ballerina.

"I'm excited," she said, her brown eyes beaming as she wound her small hands around his neck.

"What are you excited about?" Galen stroked her soft curly black hair that reached down to her waist. She was such a beautiful little girl.

Aria let go of Mass' neck and played with his tie. "MJ and I are going to spend the day with Alex and Aunt Tashi and Uncle Adam and Grandma Arabella and Grandpa Alessandro," she rattled off in one breath. "It's gonna be lots of fun."

"I'm sure it will be. And I will miss you while I slave away in the office," Mass said, kissing her nose and cheeks.

She turned her attention to Galen. "Can Geoffrey come with us, Uncle Galen?"

"Another time, sweetheart. Geoffrey has a doctor's appointment today."

"Is he gonna have shots? I don't like shots. They hurt." She pouted while rubbing her upper arm as if she were in pain. Then in the next breath, she asked, "Can I please have some fruit, Daddy? Please?" while rocking back and forth in her father's arms.

"*Certamente, cara, mia.*"

While Mass moved on to the buffet table with his daughter, Galen went over to his son. "You have made quite a mess of yourself, haven't you?" he asked, wiping Geoffrey's face and hands with a napkin. "I might have to change you before we leave for the doctor."

"More. Memon and 'nana." Geoffrey pointed to his empty plate and then to the side table. "More."

Galen glanced at his watch. Breakfast would be served in eight minutes, but he nevertheless got the boy a couple more slices of fruit since the other children would be eating in front of him anyway.

"Oh good. Everyone's here."

Galen looked up as Shaina joined the breakfast party, carrying thirteen-month-old MJ on her hip. MJ was the spitting image of his father—olive complexion, just a tad darker, ocean-blue eyes, black wavy hair, strong chin and wide forehead. He was definitely Massimo Junior, while Aria had inherited her mother's fine exotic features and brown eyes.

Galen had developed a special kind of respect for Shaina when he'd heard that she'd raised her younger brother, Cameron, after their father's death when Shaina was seventeen years old. Galen was sure that his fondness for his sister-in-law stemmed from the fact that, like Mindy, Shaina had experienced the struggles of being a broke, single mother. When he'd first met her, Galen had told Massimo that Shaina was too good for him, to which Mass had replied, "I tell myself that every day."

"Shaina, you look absolutely lovely as usual," Galen said, admiring his brother's slender, dark and lovely wife dressed in tailored cream slacks and a fashionable hot pink blouse. He skipped morning greetings since he, Shaina, and Mass had bumped into each other in the home gym earlier.

"Flattery will get you everywhere, Galen." She tossed him a big grin as she settled MJ into the chair beside Geoffrey.

The toddlers immediately began kicking their legs in enthusiasm and reaching toward each other with big grins on their faces.

"Isn't that darling?" Shaina said, as she struggled to velcro MJ's bib into place.

"It is. Indeed," Galen replied, elated that the boys were getting along. It was too late for Galen to form the kind of special bond that Mass and Adam enjoyed growing up, but there was hope for Geoffrey and MJ yet. And Aria, too, he realized as she ran up and squeezed between her brother and her cousin, trying to get in on the action.

With melon juice dripping off his elbows, Geoffrey pointed at the youngest member of the family and said, "MJ," then, "Aya." Then seemingly proud of himself, he pointed to the adults in turn and said, "Aun Sana, Uncu Mass, Daddy." Then he jabbed his chest and said, "Geoffy!" which made them all laugh.

"Good job, Geoffrey," Mass said. "You are indeed an Andretti who understands the first order of business is to know your family history."

Shaina chuckled. "We all know how important family history

is to anyone with the name Andretti." She poured some milk into MJ's kiddie cup before taking her seat at the table.

"Not just Andrettis, pussycat, but Norwoods and Carmichaels too," Mass stated as he helped Aria into her booster seat and placed a plate of fruit in front of her.

Shaina eyed Galen as Mass returned to the buffet table. "Have you spoken to Mindy since yesterday?" she asked.

Galen sat down, his heart pounding with angst. He'd known it was only a matter of time before either she or Mass asked that question. He waited to respond while Mass set coffee, a bowl of fruit and yogurt, and a plate filled with pastries, cheese, and meats in front of his wife. He felt a flush of envy when Mass kissed her lovingly and lingeringly on the lips, then whispered something in her ear that made her blush.

"No, I haven't spoken to Mindy," he said to tone down the heat between his brother and his wife, who seemed to be in a world of their own. They made him miss Mindy all the more. "She told me not to call her if I respect her."

"And I hope you're not planning on following that order, little brother. Respect isn't going to get you anywhere. You need to fight for her. Let her know that you're not giving in that easily. I looked for Shaina for seven years, and when I did finally find her, I fought like crazy to keep her, even though she hated my guts. I just made sure that all her needs were taken care of. Women love men who take care of them."

"Even when the woman tells the man to go bugger off?"

"Especially then," Shaina responded with a deep laugh. "I actually told Mass to take a flying leap off Mount Washington into Crystal Lake."

"Several times, actually," Mass said, joining in her laughter and their walk down memory lane.

"He wore me down so badly that I had no energy left in me to fight anymore. I just had to submit and commit."

"There's hope for me and Mindy then." Galen said, his spirits soaring a notch. "I'll just wear her down with love and kindness until she submits and commits. I want to take care of her and Kyle and Brittany. Provide for them, give them everything their hearts desire."

Mass gave him a daunting look. "Shaina and I learned last night that Mindy has a new job, or should I say a promising career, and a new home on Crystal Lake. She might not think that she needs you as much. She doesn't need rescuing. She's an independent woman now and independent women are the hardest to win over."

Galen dropped the piece of bread he was about to eat. "Mindy has a new job and a new home on Crystal Lake? When did this come about?"

"I thought she would have mentioned it yesterday," Shaina said, as she buttered her scone.

"We didn't have time to talk about her." HIs voice dropped in volume as the image of Mindy sobbing weakly pierced his heart.

"Tashi bought Saturn Photography and hired Mindy as COO after Adam dragged her over the coals to make sure she was fit for the job." Shaina was clearly amused. "She didn't get it just because she and Tashi are friends. She got it because Tashi believes she will do an excellent job."

"That's lovely of her." Pride swelled in his heart. Mindy was intelligent and determined, but sometimes it took more to make it in this world. A chance, a break, a favor, and knowing the right contact were what most people needed to bring their dreams to fruition. He'd gotten his break from Massimo, and Mindy had gotten hers from Tashi. "And the house on Crystal Lake?"

"It was a gift from Tashi's mother's foundation, that and a new Mercedes SUV. She's already moved into her home," Massimo said over his espresso cup.

"When did all this happen? She was at her mother's when I saw her on Friday night."

"Saturday," Shaina said.

"Wow," was all Galen could say because the servants chose that precise time to deliver their breakfasts. Mindy didn't need him to rescue her from poverty. She'd done it all on her own.

When Mass had walked in earlier, Galen had been thinking of surprising Mindy with a new house on the lake. He remembered how much she loved it from the times they'd spent at Massimo's villa. He'd been wondering what kind of car to buy her to replace the old one he'd seen at her mother's place the other night.

His generosity wasn't intended to win her back. It was to show her that he cared deeply about her and her children. He wanted them to have the best of everything life had to offer. It broke his heart that she'd had to struggle through life, and he just wanted to ease her burden, show her a different kind of life.

Even if she never forgave him, nor took him back, Galen would spend the rest of his life making sure that Mindy, Kyle, and Britt were comfortable.

His happiness depended on hers, whether or not they were together.

Could this day get any worse? Could his life get any worse?

Rage and despair vied for dominance in Galen's heart and mind as he turned off the recorder and removed his headphones, effectively silencing his mother cursing out Massimo's mother, calling her the most vile names that Galen had ever heard, telling her that her husband didn't love her, that he was divorcing her, taking her children away from her, and putting her out of her home.

"You've had your goodbye fuck. Now start packing, bitch!" was the last thing Judith barked before the line went dead.

Galen trembled as he sat upright on the edge of his chair trying to absorb the nauseating truth about his mother's cruelty, how her actions had caused the deaths of Giuliana Andretti and her prematurely born child who'd lived only for a few precious moments after she was taken from her mother's womb.

How could Galen ever get over what she'd done? Her selfish, immoral, and malevolent behavior had caused the deaths of two innocent people, and robbed a ten-year-old boy of a life of happiness with his mother. He had no sympathy for Luciano losing his wife, because as far as Galen was concerned, his father was equally to blame for the years of dark grief that had descended upon his family. Cheating on his wife made him just as guilty as Judith.

Galen's gut coiled with regret as he recalled the day, two summers ago, when Mass had caught him in the music room sitting at his mother's piano playing *Für Elise* from the music sheet on the stand.

Just before he'd given him the tape tonight, Massimo had told Galen that he had been sitting next to his mother listening to her play *Für Elise*, when the phone rang. Mass said that seconds after his mother picked up the receiver, she'd turned as white as a ghost and then collapsed onto the floor. The piano room was the last place in the mansion where Mass had happy memories of his mother, and ironically the worst, as well. Mass' happy memories had become tainted with bitterness and sadness after learning that Judith Carmichael had made that call and had, in his opinion, murdered his mother and his baby sister.

Fury choked Galen as he thought of the lies his mother had told his aunt, and who in turn had passed them on to him. He hung his head in profound revulsion as he thought of his role in sullying that sacred room, merely by crossing the threshold, and then adding insult to Massimo's injury by ignorantly throwing the lies his aunt Gertrude had told him about Luciano and Judith's love for each other into Massimo's face.

Massimo had had every right to have gone into a rage and thrown Galen out of the room, and then beaten the crap out of him in the hallway while the servants looked on, probably with glee since many of them had been with the family for years and had loved Giuliana. If Shaina hadn't pulled Massimo off him, Galen knew his brother would have choked him to death that day. Maybe Shaina should have let Massimo kill him since he was a constant reminder of their father's betrayal and Judith's vindictiveness.

Was that the way Mindy would always think of Geoffrey? He shivered at the bone-chilling comparison between Luciano and himself, and Trix and his mother.

Galen swallowed the bile in his throat and raised his head to look at Mass, who was quietly sitting behind the desk in his home office, probably waiting for Galen to break the morbid silence that had been heavy in the room since they entered it. Tears of empathy for his older brother, who'd suffered irreparable and unimaginable sorrow all these years, burned Galen's eyes.

He glanced at the tape recorder on Mass' desk. He wanted to smash it into tiny little pieces, pour gasoline on it and burn it. But even so, he would never be able to kill the sound of his mother's hateful voice, nor forget the disgusting words that came out of her mouth.

"How could one woman do this to another, especially a pregnant woman who'd never done anything to her? She knew all those years that she'd caused your mother's and the baby's deaths, and yet she had the audacity to make up a deplorable lie to cover her behavior. My mother was a vile human being," he said as the last shred of respect and love he had for her fled into the cold darkness of her grave.

Massimo's Adam's Apple vibrated as he swallowed. "You understand now why I was reluctant to talk about it at breakfast this morning? I told you sometimes it's best if you don't get answers to your questions. For twenty-five years I wanted to know who had called my mother and what he or she had said to have caused her to collapse. I always suspected that it was Judith, but I didn't have the proof. When I finally got it, I wished for the mystery of not knowing."

"How long have you had the tape?"

"A week before the group wedding, someone sent me a note stating that they knew that my mother had received a call just hours before she died and that they knew the identity of the caller. We met, and I was handed the tapes. Actually, it was just before I came to see you at the villa and told you that our relationship was over until you decided to grow up."

Galen took a moment to let the fact that Massimo had restrained himself, even when he must have been livid, sink into his brain. "You knew then and didn't say anything. You could have thrown that information into my face while I was standing there still harping on my mother's lie and threatening to sue you for half of Andretti Industries. You could have shut me up once and for all by playing that tape, Mass. Why didn't you?"

"Those aren't words a son should hear coming from his mother's mouth."

"Nor should they be the words a son should hear entering his mother's ears."

Mass's nostrils flared and his blue eyes went as cold as the arctic. "I chose not to listen to the tape. I didn't need the sound of your mother's hateful voice in my head, nor to know the last cruel words my mother might have heard before she departed this world. I chose to remember the sound of *Für Elise* floating up from the piano, the sweet warm smile on her face, and her soft voice telling me that she loved me."

"If you didn't listen to the tape, how do you know what's on it?" Galen asked quietly.

"I asked the person who recorded it to give me a short version."

Galen frowned. "Earlier you said you got the *tapes*, not the *tape*. Are there more concerning my mother?"

Massimo left his chair and walked around his desk to stand in front of Galen. "Yes, there were more, but I destroyed them."

"Why did you keep this one?"

"I don't know." He chuckled cynically. "Maybe part of me wanted to hold on to the evidence that caused my mother's death. I had put it out of my mind and had decided not to talk about it again. But when you brought the subject up this morning and then again after dinner tonight, I needed to put it to bed once and for all. Now you know the whole sordid story. I've dealt with it in my way. You have to deal with it in yours."

"May I ask who gave you the tape?"

"You may ask, but I won't tell you."

"Fair enough." Galen stood up and put his arms around Mass. "I'm sorry, Massimo. I'm sorry for everything."

"There's no need for you to be sorry. You didn't do anything," Mass said, hugging him back. "I will never forgive your mother for what she did to mine and my sister. But I refuse to be her victim any longer. I've decided to be happy, instead."

Galen held him tightly, and for the first time since they'd met almost four years ago on that cool March evening, Galen felt a deep sense of love and peace coming from his brother's embrace.

"It's time to move into the future and find happiness with the ones you love, Galen," Mass said, breaking the hug, way too quickly for Galen.

"Yes."

After I have the last piece of the puzzle.

171

CHAPTER TWELVE

"Thanks for meeting me at home."

"No problem," Mindy said, as Tashi, with Alex in her arms, ushered her into the elegant white foyer with marble floors and curving marble staircases in full view.

"I was too tired to drive back to town after spending half the day at Michelle's Children's Foundation." Tashi placed Alex on the floor and pointed him toward her home studio on the first floor. "I volunteer once a week, as you know. I took Alex with me today which made it extra exhausting."

"It's nice you volunteer your time," Mindy said, walking beside her. "You, Michelle, Kaya, and Shaina have been valuable assets since you moved to Granite Falls. Your husbands have always been the most affluent and philanthropic members of our community. You could have simply donated money and stayed in your mansions on the hill chilling by your pools all day drinking wine and eating caviar and—"

Tashi laughed. "I don't even like caviar."

"You know what I mean," Mindy said, chuckling. "Instead you rolled up your sleeves, got to work and started charities to make life better for so many people. Me included," she added. "I wouldn't be where I am—here—if you hadn't moved to Granite Falls."

"Our philanthropy is somewhat selfish, I think," Tashi said, clearly refusing to be held in high esteem for contributing to her community. "We have to raise our families here so we work hard to make sure that our children would want to stay here when they grow up. But at the same time, we try to teach them the value of humanitarianism by getting them directly involved in all sides of society. And we do that by taking them with us when we serve at the soup kitchens, the homeless shelters, or wherever," she added, ruffling Alex's curly dark hair, as he toddled along with them. "We teach them that just because they were born into wealth, it doesn't mean they're better than those who weren't. Alex has made some great friends at Michelle's Foundation, and they're all invited to his birthday party next month."

"My party, Mommy," Alex said, staring up at his mother.

"How old will you be?" Mindy asked Alex.

"Two," he said, holding up two fingers, and giving her a blue-eyed smile.

"You are getting so big. Can I come to your party?"

"Uh-huh." He nodded his head vigorously. "I want lots of presents and cake and balloons."

"Of course. It wouldn't be a party without any of those things. Who are you inviting?"

His forehead furrowed and his lips curled as he tried to concentrate. "Me and Mommy and Daddy, and Nonno and Nonna and—and—Aria and MJ, and EJ, Matt, and Fiona and Tiffany, and Eli, and Stacia, Ronnie, Mary, and—and Elyse. She's my *gurfriend*," he said, nodding his head.

Mindy and Tashi burst out laughing, then Mindy said, "Good choice. Elyse is a sweet little girl. I'm sure Uncle Bryce will be happy to have you as a son-in-law."

"I told you he might like older women," Tashi said as they

neared the door of her office to find Alex's nanny waiting for them. She bent down as far as her pregnant belly would allow. "Mommy has to work for a little bit, okay, baby? Can you be a good boy for Joya?"

"Yes, Mommy."

"Say bye-bye to Aunt Mindy," Tashi said as she handed him over to his nanny.

"Bye-bye, Aun' Mindy." Alex waved before his nanny led him away.

"Bye, Alex. Love you." She blew him a kiss before following Tashi into the office.

Tashi closed the door and pulled Mindy down beside her on a sofa facing a window. "Before we get down to business, you have to tell me what happened with you and Galen on Sunday. I know it must have been a shocker to find out that he has an eighteen-month-old son. I didn't even know until I showed up Saturday to spend the night with Shaina. She said she didn't tell me because she was afraid I'd let it slip when you and I talked. I still don't even know the whole story about Geoffrey's mother and all that. But he is so adorable, isn't he?" She tapped Mindy's arm.

I wouldn't know if he's adorable. I haven't met him, yet.

Mindy's pulse quickened as she set her briefcase, filled with a week's worth of work, on the floor—her ideas for the new and improved Tashi's Photography that she needed to confirm with Tashi before making final decisions.

After the litany of shockers on Sunday evening, she was grateful to have more than ringing up sales and tidying display tables at Arabella to keep her mind occupied. She'd worked tirelessly with Mr. Saturn and his staff for the past four days, listening and taking notes as she tried to learn the art of running a photography studio, while at the same time coming up with creative ways to enhance all aspects of the company. It would be a long, difficult task, but to her surprise, Mindy had found herself enjoying the responsibilities and the challenges her new job brought, not to mention the perks.

Then every night for the past four, after she'd helped her kids with their homework, fed them, and put them to bed, she had closed the door to her suite, lain across her bed and cried for the pain Galen had suffered at the hands of the Frasers. She'd cursed him for turning to Trix instead of her and putting them in this situation. She'd grieved for the love that had once burned in their hearts for each other. And then she'd cried some more out of pity until she'd turned her insides into an empty hollow shell.

She'd skipped classes on Monday and Wednesday nights, and was skipping the one tonight because she'd been unable to concentrate on reading and homework. She had a lot of catching up to do this weekend while the kids spent it with her mother and Phin.

After a week of that destructive, self-pitying behavior, Mindy had told herself this morning that enough was enough. She'd survived Kyle's death. She would surely survive Galen's betrayal and the death of their love. It was the last brooding-over-a-man party she would ever have since she had no intentions of making herself vulnerable to one ever again. From here on in, her son would be the only man in her life. Her children were her priority.

"So are you guys going to work it out?" Tashi's voice penetrated Mindy's thoughts.

Mindy leaned back against the sofa cushions and stared out the window. Perhaps it wouldn't hurt to hear another woman's opinion about her situation. When she had returned home last Sunday night, Mindy had told Safi that she'd seen Galen, but that she didn't want to talk about it at the time. Safi had respected her wishes and not pressed for more, and she'd called Mindy every day to let her know that she was there when Mindy was ready to talk. Mindy had finally called her back midweek, but had used the excuse that work was keeping her too busy to visit or chat. She couldn't bring herself to tell her friend that Galen had cheated on her. Mindy hadn't told her mother either since she had a darn good idea how that conversation would go. She didn't need to hear, "I told you so," again.

Tashi was a different story, though. Since she already knew about Geoffrey, Mindy's embarrassment wouldn't be as severe as it would be when she explained Galen's absence to Safi.

Mindy turned sideways to face Tashi. "How would you have felt if Adam had shown up with a child you knew was conceived after you were married?"

"I would cut off his balls and feed them to him," Tashi said without blinking.

"Even if the woman had drugged him and he couldn't remember having sex with her?"

Tashi grabbed Mindy's arm. "Galen was drugged and raped?"

"Well, I wouldn't call it rape."

"Because he's a man?" She released Mindy and sat back with a forlorn expression on her face. "Men get raped too, Mindy, and it's just as devastating for them as it is for us women. It's a violation of one's body, one's privacy. Those people who targeted me when I was living in New York targeted boys too. Boys are drugged and raped every single day, just like girls."

"You're right," Mindy said after clearing the frog from her throat. "But that's not why Galen and I can't work it out. I'm mad at him for not telling me after it happened."

"But you said he didn't remember."

"Trix—" Mindy pressed her lips together. It pained her to speak that woman's name. "Geoffrey's mother told him the morning after, but he said that he didn't tell me because he didn't know if she was lying just to get him back. I don't think he would have said anything if she hadn't gotten pregnant. He only came clean because he had to explain Geoffrey."

"Oh boy. Now that would be hard for me to forgive and forget."

"So you get my point."

"I do, but if it were Adam, I would have found some way to forgive him because I love him. My mom never told my dad about me. He found out after she was dead and I was a grown woman, but he didn't hate her. He still loved her, and he forgave her. Nobody is perfect, Mindy. We all screw up at some point. I believe that Galen genuinely loves you. He was scared of losing you."

"That's what he said."

"Do you still love him?"

"I do, but sometimes love isn't enough."

"Sometimes love is all there is. Mass has forgiven him."

"Well that's obvious, or else he wouldn't be living at the Andretti mansion."

"No, I mean *really* forgiven him. He gave him half of seventeen years' worth of Andretti Industries. Galen is a multibillionaire."

"Shut up!" Mindy stared, openmouthed, at Tashi.

"He didn't tell you, huh?" Tashi said with a wicked grin.

"No, but it doesn't change anything," she said as the shock of the man she loved becoming a billionaire overnight quickly wore off—perhaps because she was constantly in the company of billionaires and understood that the only thing that separated them from her was the size of their bank accounts. They were just people. They hurt and bled and worried, just like her and everybody else. "I was never with Galen for money. Neither of us had any when we were together. I was with him for love."

"Then forgive him for love, Mindy! Don't deny yourself the chance to be loved because he made a cowardly decision two years ago. He could have stayed in England with Geoffrey's mother, or moved to any other country in the world, kept Geoffrey a secret, and made a great life for himself. But he didn't do that. He came back to Granite Falls and confessed, knowing that he might very well lose you forever. That took a lot of guts. It shows that he's sincerely remorseful about lying to you. Take your time to be angry and then forgive him. You must know he's hurting too. But know that while you're hell-bent on punishing him for his mistakes, you'll just end up punishing yourself. Heal together instead of apart. Live the life you've always fantasized with him."

Mindy was touched by Tashi's insightfulness. *Well, isn't that why you posed your what-would-you-do question to her? To make sure that you weren't acting irrationally by refusing to forgive him and accept the love he wants desperately to give you? You have your answer.* "When did you get so wise?" she asked Tashi.

"When I realized that I had been carrying an unconscious resentment toward my mother for not telling my father about me, and consequently robbing us of twenty-two years of a father-daughter relationship. But here's the reality: if my father had known of my existence, my life would have taken a completely different turn. Dad would not have been on an FBI assignment in Europe to meet Adam all those years ago, and I wouldn't be Adam's wife today. I wouldn't have met you, and you wouldn't have been working at Arabella the morning that Galen walked into the boutique. I came to forgive my mother because, in the end, it all turned out perfectly. I would go through all the pain again just to have Adam, Alex, and this little girl I'm carrying, in my life. I have an amazing life and I thank God for it everyday." She took a deep breath and caressed her stomach.

"That is some deep stuff, Tashi."

"Well, I didn't get here overnight, nor by myself. It's not just silliness and fun and games when Shaina, Michelle, Kaya, and now Yasmine and Desire and I get together. We talk about our charities and organizations and plan events to raise money and awareness about the issues that make this world a crazy place. We discuss important issues surrounding our spouses and children, too. We help each other to see situations from different angles and from our husbands' and children's point of view. No marriage, no relationship is without strife, Mindy. Even billionaires are tested sometimes." She placed her hand on Mindy's and gave her a comforting smile. "Once you and Galen get back together and settle down, you will be part of our circle, as I'm sure Galen will be part of our husbands'. The men need each other just as much as we, women, need each other to help iron out the wrinkles in our marriages." She took a deep breath and leaned back. "Now, show me what you have in mind for Tashi's Photography."

Mindy opened her briefcase, grateful for the topic change but also realizing that Tashi wasn't privy to the trouble Galen had run into in England with Trix and the Fraser crime family, or that Trix would be spending the rest of her life in prison, making it impossible for Galen to have run off into the sunset with the mother of his child.

Galen had shared the entire painful and sordid story with Mindy because he wanted her back in his life. But apparently, he hadn't shared it with anyone else but Massimo. It wasn't as if one could search the Internet to get the scoop of what he'd been up to in London for the past eight months. She hadn't found anything when she'd Googled his name, but her search for the Fraser family had returned quite a bit about their crimes. Nothing about Trix or Geoffrey, either.

The far-reaching power of the Andretti name had kept Galen out of the very public investigation. As close as the four families were, it seemed that certain pieces of information were still kept hidden deep inside the walls of their respective mansions. The level of loyalty, respect, and honor they shared within and among themselves was simply amazing.

What Tashi had said about her own life's path affected Mindy deeply. Tashi's journey to happiness had brought her into contact with Mindy, which in effect had changed Mindy's path, placing her directly into Galen's, not to mention the opportunity to attend college, start a promising career, and provide a bright and prosperous future for her children. It was the one thing all good mothers wanted more than anything in the world. Well, that and love for herself and her kids.

Galen had willingly suffered severe pain for her and her children in the name of love.

Would she willingly suffer humiliation for him and his son in the name of that same love?

That was the billion-dollar question.

Galen turned off Crystal Lake Road and drove along a paved private driveway, when Mindy's house, surrounded by evergreen trees, shrubs and a huge lawn, with the clear blue waters of Crystal Lake in the background suddenly burst into view.

The exterior architecture was as sleek, elegant, and stylish as he had expected from self-made billionaire Chase Hunter, founder of DC Architectural Designs. Chase had made his mark around the globe, and then returned to Evergreen last year to settle down with his childhood sweetheart, Desire Summers. A long-time friend of Bryce Fontaine, Chase had designed the Fontaines' billion-dollar estate on Mount Reservoir, Fontaine Enterprises Headquarters, and Fontaine Towers #1 and #2 in downtown Granite Falls, years ago. He was steadily adding to his list of magnificent buildings since his return.

This morning, during his short-lived fantasy about building a surprise home for Mindy, Galen had thought of hiring Chase to design it. It would have been similar to this one, just much bigger on the most prime piece of real estate on the Evergreen side of Crystal Lake. As a matter of fact, knowing how much Mindy loved being on the lake, Galen had been prepared to approach the new owners of the prime properties and make them offers they could not refuse, just to have a place where he and Mindy and their children could call home until they designed and built their own lakeside mansion.

He'd stayed away too long, giving Tashi the opportunity to offer Mindy the very luxuries he'd intended to provide.

Galen brought his Aston Martin to a stop in front of the three-car garage and killed the engine. The garage doors were closed, so he had no idea if Mindy was home. She wasn't at Saturn's Studio or Tashi's Photography when he'd gone by looking for her, so he'd figured that she must be at home in her new house.

He glanced at the wall of tinted windows that encased the large front porch—an extension of the house—and a vision of he and Mindy reclining on the porch, watching the sun set over the lake while they sipped tea, flashed in his mind. He'd promised to give her time to adjust to the news he'd laid on her five days ago, but he wasn't willing to let another day go by without seeing her, without making an effort to bring all his fantasies about them to life.

Determined to win back his woman, Galen exited his car and ascended the steps to the porch. Finding the door unlocked, he stepped inside, his heart pounding against his chest in anticipation of coming face-to-face with Mindy again.

But before he was halfway across the tastefully decorated porch, the front door suddenly opened and Pamela Marshall walked out and closed it quietly behind her as if she didn't want the other occupants of the house to know they had company. A

mixture of irritation and impatience thundered through Galen at
her brazen attempt to once again run interference between him
and Mindy.

She could huff and she could puff until she was purple in the
face, but since he had the goods on her now, this would be the
very last time Galen would ever go through her to get to Mindy.
Knowledge was indeed power, and he was taking hers away from
her once and for all. "Is Mindy at home, Mrs. Marshall," he
asked, rather politely despite his suspicion of her intention to
derail him before he even got back on the track.

"My daughter told you to leave her alone a week ago."

Galen's lips parted on a secretive smile. So Mindy hadn't told
her mother about their conversation on Sunday. It was a bit of
relief since he had neither the intention nor the desire to discuss
his son with Pamela Marshall, or anyone else, until he'd fixed the
rift between him and Mindy.

"What is it with you people?" Pamela grated under her
breath, clearly to keep their voices from carrying inside. "Can't
you take a hint when you're told to get lost? 'It's over,' means it's
over."

"You people?" he asked with a raised brow.

Her eyes were like daggers in the fading afternoon light. "You
and your worthless, detestable mother!"

Ah, there it was—the last piece of the puzzle falling into place.

As soon as Mass had laid out the timeline of his possession of
the tapes—just before the wedding when Galen and Mindy were
becoming a hot item—and then refused to say who had given
them to him, Galen had suspected that it was Pamela Marshall.
There was no other reason for Mass to protect the identity of the
person who'd given them to him, other than that he didn't want
to cause further conflict between Galen and his potential, future
mother-in-law.

The knowledge had hit Galen hard: the mother of the

woman with whom he was planning to spend the rest of his life knew that his mother had caused the death of Giuliana Andretti and her infant daughter.

During the arbitration, Pamela had stated that she was the only cleaner who was allowed in Luciano's and his assistant's offices after hours. That, Galen was sure had given her the perfect opportunity to plant her bugs. Her degree of disgust for his mother had far exceeded the other former employees who'd been called as witnesses. No wonder she'd shown dislike for him since the day she'd found out that he was Luciano's and Judith's son. "It was you, wasn't it?"

"It was me, what?"

"I know why you hate me so much."

"I doubt that," she replied on a defiant shrug.

"You bugged Luciano's and Judith's offices while he was having his affair with her. I haven't put my finger on the reason you would do that yet. But I know it had to be more than you concluding that Judith was a vindictive woman who would do anything to get what she wanted."

"*Vindictive* is too kind a word for your mother. What she did to that family was criminal. I prefer to call her a nasty, evil bit—"

"Be careful of what you say about my mother to my face, Mrs. Marshall," he warned, even though he himself had reached the same conclusion about Judith after listening to the tape. He could think or say whatever he wanted about the woman who'd carried him, at whose breasts he'd nursed, whose hands had bandaged his bruised knees and wiped the tears from his eyes. But he would not allow anyone else to speak unkindly of her to his face. Ugly or not, she *was* his mother. She'd loved him and taken good care of him, and together with his grandfather had molded him into the man he was today. Yes, he'd had hiccups along the way, but everybody needed room to grow and improve. *He* was the *one* good thing Judith

ANA E ROSS

had done in her entire life. And he had to give her credit for that.

Galen stepped back, putting much needed space between Pamela and himself. "You aren't as solicitous as you pretend to be, lady," he said in a critical tone. "You could have given my father the tapes so he would have known why his wife and infant daughter died. But you were afraid of what he would do to you for violating his privacy. After he died, you could have destroyed the evidence, or at least handed it over to Massimo so he could get some closure. But you held on to the tapes for two decades until your maternal instinct to protect your young kicked in. You gave my brother those tapes only after Mindy and I became a couple and you heard that I was about to sue him for half of Andretti Industries. You blame me as much as you blame Judith for what happened to Giuliana Andretti."

"Yes. I blame you. You shouldn't be here, in this world. If your mother hadn't gotten pregnant, Giuliana Andretti and her daughter would be alive today, and perhaps Mr. Andretti too. His life would have been different."

Galen turned away, closed his eyes, and clenched and unclenched his hands. Her logic was spot on. He'd reached the same conclusion after listening to the tapes. If his mother hadn't gotten pregnant, there would have been no need for Luciano to end the relationship when he did. Giuliana would have carried her baby to term and they both would be here today.

"Too many people suffered and died because your whore of a mother chased after a married man and deliberately got herself knocked up. Why did her baby survive when other mothers had to bury theirs?"

Galen spun back to find Pamela's eyes glowing with a tortured dullness. "Other *mothers*? I thought Giuliana was the only one. What other mothers lost their babies because of my mother's behavior, Mrs. Marshall?"

184

She folded her arms and dropped her gaze to the Asian rug covering the granite-tiled floor.

As he observed her silence and stiff posture, Galen became quite certain that there was more to Pamela's hatred for Judith than merely her affair with Luciano. There was no doubt in his mind that his mother had done something personal to make this woman hate her. "What did my mother do to you, Pamela?" he asked in a conciliatory voice.

She pressed her lips together and after a long silence, she raised her head. "We're done here. You need to leave before my daughter comes home." She placed her hand on the doorknob.

"No," Galen said. "We're not done. After today, I do not intend to spend another minute of my time and energy dealing with your attitude. I love your daughter, and nothing you do or say will ever change that. Mindy and I *will* get back together because I know in my heart that she loves me, just as much as I love her. I saw it, I heard it, and I felt it when we were together on Sunday."

That gave her a jolt. "Mindy saw you on Sunday? She told me she was going out with friends."

"There," he drawled with a triumphant smile. "I guess she never told you about our long talk. The fact that she kept it from you is proof that she doesn't want you influencing her decision about *us*."

"Or maybe it isn't as important to her as you think it is. Perhaps you don't mean anything to her anymore. You're nothing to talk about."

Galen knew that Mindy's silence stemmed from the humiliation she would feel once the world knew he'd cheated on her. That bitter acknowledgement was the reason he had been cooped up at the mansion all week, the reason he hadn't taken Geoffrey out in public. He'd been giving Mindy the time she needed to come to terms with their situation. But he would not sit around any longer and let her mind be distanced further and further away from him as time ticked by.

He refused to hide their love any longer. He hadn't returned to Granite Falls to pine away on Mount Reservoir. He could've done that in London. He'd returned for Mindy, and he was having Mindy, even if he had to plow down her mother to get to her.

He met Pamela's cold-eyed stare with a benign smile. "I *will* be part of your family, whether or not you want me, *Mommy. Nana*," he said derisively. "Get used to having me around. Things would run smoothly for both us if you ended your hostility toward me, right here, right now. Tell me what my mother did to you, and then literally and figuratively step aside and let me love Mindy."

Her response, if she'd intended to deliver one, was delayed at the sound of a vehicle coming up the driveway. Galen turned his head, and his heart stopped when he spotted Mindy behind the wheel of her Mercedes SUV. Boy, Tashi had gone all out for her friend. He turned back at the soft thud of the front door closing to find that Pamela had fled the scene.

With his heart racing with excitement and trepidation, Galen descended the steps of the porch as the SUV came to a stop beside his car. He rushed to open the door and stood back with fire surging in his veins as Mindy climbed down from the vehicle. She looked sophisticated in black pumps, and an unbuttoned beige double-breasted thigh-length wool coat over a multicolored dress that showed off her soft curves and toned legs. Her lustrous blond hair fell across her shoulders, the ends spilling on to the soft mounds of her breasts—those creamy firm breasts with pink-cherry nipples that used to taste like candy in his mouth.

They stood silently looking at each other as the undeniable passions they had once shared began to resurface. He could feel the heat rising from their bodies, streaming outward and upward like invisible coils of fire and light wrapping around each other to combat the cold, late February breeze swirling around them. The sultry aura was so potent, it created the illusion of standing on a sandy Caribbean beach or in the middle of a hot African dessert while the noonday sun beat relentlessly down.

Galen's cock tightened and pulsed against his jeans with longing as the sweetly intoxicating scent of her body overwhelmed him. It was the first time since his return that he'd allowed himself to succumb to the sexual effects she had on him.

As his heart raced, his mind filled with doubt. Was he setting himself up for an even harsher rejection than the one on Sunday when Mindy had been in shock after hearing about Trix and Geoffrey? Had the time spent apart since then softened her heart enough to forgive him, or had it hardened it to the point where she was certain that she absolutely wanted nothing to do with him?

It was time he found out his fate. "Hello," he said, not in the least embarrassed at the tremor in his voice.

CHAPTER THIRTEEN

"Hello," she replied in a voice as unsteady as his.

At least she hadn't told him to get lost, he thought as his eyes raked over her, taking in her stiff posture that indicated an internal war. One bold step would bring her into his arms where she would find peace and comfort from the storms of emotions rioting inside her—the same storms that were wreaking unbearable havoc on his insides—spinning, churning, jabbing.

Tired of waiting, he took the forward step, his arms open. "Mindy—"

She drew back, pressing her body against the interior of the car door. "No. I can't. I'm sorry. I—I have these—these images in my head of you and—and her," she said in a broken whisper.

Panic stabbed through Galen's stomach. He knew those images would haunt her for a very long time. Had he come by too soon? Should he have given her more time? Relentlessly pursuing her and making a nuisance of himself was not the right approach, but neither was sitting idly by and doing nothing. He was damned if he did and damned if he didn't. And now he had to face his biggest fear that he might never be able to win Mindy back when she was in daily contact with her mother, the one person in the world whose sole ambition was to tear them further apart.

Galen took a swift glance at the house, certain that Pamela was watching them from inside and gloating at Mindy's rejection of him. He sucked air into his lungs, surprised at how much it hurt to even breathe. "I wish I could erase those images, but I can't. I never intended for them to ever exist. Believe me, the thought makes me sick to my stomach."

Her eyes searched his face. "I know you didn't cheat on me. But I told you not to call me."

"I didn't call. I came," he said with quiet emphasis.

"Which is even worse." She glanced warily at the house. "I asked you for time."

"And I gave you time."

"A few days isn't enough, Galen," she said in a voice spiced with exasperation.

"A few days is too long when you love someone as much as I love you. The night I came back to Granite Falls, I told you that I would never give up on us. Nothing has changed, except that I'm more determined now," he said, deciding then and there that he would take the relentless pursuing approach. She had to know how he felt. "I want to share my life with you—the good, the bad, and the ugly. You've seen my ugly and I promise that you'll never see it again. *Ever*. I want all of you, darling, and I want you to want all of me. So I will continue to show up at your house, your work, and stalk you around town if I need to. I want to be *there*, *here*, *present* when you finally decide to forgive me and take me back. Only one thing in this world will keep me away from you, Mindy Marshall."

"What's that?" she asked with a skeptic twist of her lips.

"A restraining order. I would have to obey the law to avoid going to jail, but only because I have a son who depends on me to look after him. Geoffrey needs me."

She winced at the mention of his son, the one constant reminder that he'd broken faith and trust in her, and had ultimately tainted their love. She'd told him that he should never think of Geoffrey as a mistake, but the fact remained that if he hadn't gone to see Trix that night, his grandfather wouldn't have had a heart attack. He would not have gone to England and been detained and separated from Mindy for so long. He would have become a billionaire eight months ago, and he and Mindy would be married by now, and she would probably be carrying their child in her belly in this very time and space. He couldn't change the past, but he could try to convince her to give their future a chance.

"You look beautiful," he said, hoping to sway her thoughts from Geoffrey and Trix and everything else that might distract her from focusing on the perfect life they used to have, and could have again.

A small smile ruffled her lips. "You say that every time you see me."

"And I mean it every time I see you. You didn't tell me about your new career, your new home and wheels when we saw each other on Sunday." He nudged his head at the house and SUV as he mentioned them.

"And you didn't tell me that you are a billionaire. A multibillionaire," she said with a wry smirk.

"I had more important matters to discuss with you." When a soft breeze whipped a few strands of hair against her cheeks, Galen was powerless to resist the temptation to brush them away.

He felt her quiver as the electricity shot through his own system. Their eyes locked, but she didn't pull away this time. The power of their touch was as strong as ever, he thought as his skin tingled. It was only a matter of time before he would be undressing her slowly, kissing every inch of her silky creamy body, watching the passion light her eyes as he laid her under him and entered her hot, wet sex. It had been too long since he'd experienced that kind of connection with a woman—his woman.

She turned her neck, breaking the physical contact and forcing him to drop his hand. "What were you and my mother talking about?" she asked, raising fine, arched eyebrows.

Galen balled his hand into a fist, trying to trap the lingering tingles from the warmth of her skin. "We were talking about you. I was telling her that I would be in her life so she might as well start trying to like me."

Her soft giggle sent prickles zinging up and down Galen's spine and set his pulse pounding. But that tiny euphoric moment was interrupted, or perhaps it was elongated as the porch door burst open and Kyle and Brittany raced down the steps calling his name.

Galen's heart swelled beyond imagination as he dropped to his knees, opened his arms wide, and wrapped them tightly around the two precious children.

"You came back. You came back!" they screamed in unison, kissing his face and squeezing him so tightly he thought he would pass out from lack of oxygen.

"It is so good to see you. Both of you," he said, tears streaming from his eyes as he pushed them a little away so he could see their faces. "I missed you so much. You have no idea."

"We missed you too, Galen." Brittany hugged him again as if she didn't want to let him go.

"When did you get back?" Kyle asked.

"Are you going to stay forever?" Britt followed up without giving him time to respond to Kyle's question.

"Mommy was sad when she didn't hear from you. Why didn't you call us?"

. . .

That last question jumpstarted Mindy's heart, which had become paralyzed with a plethora of emotions and scenarios from the moment she'd driven up her driveway and spotted the Aston Martin in front of her garage. She'd never seen that car before, but she knew only wealthy men owned Aston Martins. Since she'd just learned that Galen had become a billionaire, she'd known instantly that he was at her house. She'd thought about turning around and waiting until he left, but then she remembered that her mother was watching the kids, and leaving her and Galen alone for too long was not a good idea. She had to save them both from themselves and each other. She was just happy that no one had been strangled before she arrived.

"Kyle, Britt," she called to her kids who'd run out without their coats, "get back inside before you catch your death of cold."

"Okay, Mommy."

"Come on, Galen."

Knowing that it was pointless to even suggest that Galen should leave, she climbed back into her car, pressed the garage door button, and eased into her spot.

As the garage door closed behind her, Mindy shut off the engine and laid her head on the steering wheel, thankful for the few moments of peace and quiet to compose herself.

On her way home from the Andreas estate, Tashi's admonishments had run through Mindy's head. *Sometimes love is all there is. Don't deny yourself the chance to be loved because he made a cowardly decision two years ago. While you're punishing him for his mistakes, you'll end up punishing yourself. Live the life you've always imagined with him. .*

By the time she'd exited Route 80 East and turned on to Crystal Lake Road, Mindy had made the decision to forgive Galen. She'd figured she would have time to erase the images of him and Trix from her mind, time to tell her kids that he was back, get them ready to see him again, and to muster up her courage to call him since she'd told him not to call her if he respected her.

But there he was, in the flesh, at her home, looking as appetizing as she could ever imagine, touching her, awakening her desires for him, and then hugging and kissing her children with tears in his eyes as if they were his own whom he'd missed while he was away.

That wasn't the scene she'd expected to come home to today, but it was the scene Mindy longed to come home to every day for the rest of her life. Galen was the man she would be comparing all other men to—always—whether or not she had a romantic interest in them.

Live the life you've imagined with him. There was no need for Mindy to fantasize about that life anymore. The fact that Galen was here meant that she could have that life. All she had to do was open her heart, reach out her hand, and grab it. Was she strong enough to make herself vulnerable again, though?

Knowing that she wouldn't be able to function properly—either personally or professionally—if she was constantly angry and harboring resentment in her heart, Mindy had decided to forgive Galen for her own peace of mind. But getting back together with him wasn't a decision she was ready to tackle, yet.

Mindy raised her head at the sound of the garage door opening and a car engine turning over. "Mom." She jumped out of her SUV, ran to her mother's car, and knocked on the driver's window. "You gonna just sneak out of here without saying hello or goodbye to me? I haven't seen you all week," she said, when her mother rolled down the window.

"You don't need me anymore, Mindy."

"Today, or ever?" Mindy asked at the look of dejection in her mother's eyes and tone.

"That depends on you."

Mindy felt momentarily saddened that if she ever decided to

take Galen back, she might have to choose between him and her mother again. It had been a no-brainer to choose Galen the first time around. It wouldn't be as easy now since she and her mother had been trying to form a healthy relationship for the first time since Mindy was sixteen years old. She didn't want to lose that mother-daughter connection. She bent over and kissed her mom on the cheek. "I shouldn't have to choose between you and any one else, except my children."

Her mother's brow pulled into an affronted frown. "I think you already chose. You told me you were going to see friends on Sunday. I guess *he* was the friend."

Mindy lamented inwardly that she hadn't trusted her mother enough to tell her the truth of her whereabouts. Maybe her mother was right that she'd already chosen—consciously or not—when she'd gotten dressed up in her red dress and gone to the Andretti mansion, knowing there was a ninety-nine percent chance that she would see Galen. "Galen told you?"

"With pride and triumph, knowing he had one over on me."

"I would have eventually told you, Mom."

Her mother stared at her incredulously.

At the sound of the garage door closing, Mindy pushed to her full height. "Did Galen tell you what we talked about?"

"No, but that's not the point. The point is that my daughter lied to me to protect a man who broke her heart."

"I didn't lie, Mom, and I'm not protecting anyone. Tashi invited me to her baby shower, and I just happened to run into Galen. We just talked," she said, with a nonchalant shrug as she tried to minimize the enormity of that run-in.

"Where was the shower?"

Mindy grimaced. "At the Andretti mansion."

Her mother's laugh was laced with scorn and indignation. "Oh, Mindy. You walked right into the lion's den, and gave that man exactly what he wanted without him having to work for it.

And now he's with your children who are over the moon to have him back in their lives. Is he the reason I haven't seen you all week? You've been *making up* with him?"

"Come on, Mom, you know I was busy with my new job. This is the first time I've seen Galen since Sunday. I haven't even spoken to him on the phone. I didn't expect him to show up. I didn't invite him here." *And what if she had? She was a big girl. She could invite whomever she pleased to her home without having to explain her actions to anyone, her mother included.*

Pamela's eyes brightened with the tiniest speck of hope. "So you're still undecided about him?"

She nodded.

"Did he tell you why he wasn't in touch with you for eight months?"

Mindy nodded again.

"What was his excuse?"

"I can't share any of it with you yet. I promise you'll know soon." *You, and the rest of the world.* "Thanks for bringing the kids home," she continued in an attempt to preempt further questions about Galen. "I'll bring them by after breakfast tomorrow." Her mother was supposed to take Kyle and Britt with her tonight and keep them for the weekend so Mindy could catch up on her schoolwork. But they both knew that plan had died the moment the kids saw Galen. "You are their favorite grandmother, you know that, right?" she said with a grin.

"Well, duh!" Pamela smiled back, taking the hint. She gave Mindy's attire a quick once-over. "You look really nice, Mindy. I'm proud of you. I'm happy about the direction your professional life is going, but not so much about your personal one. Just keep your head on. Don't forget who you are. Don't let them change you."

Mindy frowned. That was a different attitude. Where was the *You-stay-away-from-my-daughter-or-I'll-have-you-arrested*, mother from a week ago? What had Galen said to her to temper her hostility toward him?

Pamela pressed the garage door opener that was clipped to her sun visor and put her car into reverse. "I'll see you when you drop the kids off in the morning," she said, and backed her car out of the garage.

Mindy remained in that spot for a long time, just staring at the garage door. It was new and white and clean, but one day it would be covered with scratches, dents, and stains, and it might not open and close as quickly and quietly as it did now. And one morning when she came out, it might not open at all. But instead of tearing it down and tossing it out, she would give it a chance, call someone to repair or replace the motor or the springs. And then it would start working again. She might even wash it down, patch the scratches, and paint over the stains to make it look good again. That was the cycle of life for her garage door.

Her relationship with Galen had been new, bright, and exciting once. But during their cycle it had picked up fears and doubts, distrust and mistrust, secrets and lies, pain and despair. It wasn't working as well as it used to. It was broken. Should she walk away from it out of fear and her inability to forget, or should she give it a fighting chance like she would give her garage door when it became temporarily inoperable? Should she trust Galen and take the chance of being hurt, or in all fairness, blissfully happy again? She wanted to be happy and in love again. She wanted to keep the same grin on her children's faces as when they'd seen Galen a while ago.

By punishing him, you'll end up punishing yourself. As Tashi's words rang in her ears, Mindy realized that she wouldn't just be punishing Galen and herself. She would be punishing her children, too.

She went back to her SUV to retrieved her briefcase and her

purse when the door to the mudroom opened and Britt ran into the garage with a tail-wagging Bacon following behind her.

"Hey, you." She hugged her daughter, happy to be getting some attention finally.

"Can Galen stay for dinner, Mommy? He said it was up to you."

Oh, so it was still about Galen. How nice of him to leave it up to her. He could have simply told her kids that he had to leave. Didn't he have a child he had to go take care of? "Well—"

"Please, Mommy, please!" Kyle appeared at the door with Galen, their arms about each other and both giving her a puppy-dog face. Even Bacon, with his head angled to one side and his tongue hanging out, seemed to have come to a consensus with her children.

Heal together instead of apart.

Mindy sighed. She'd had a long day. She didn't want to deal with Galen, nor did she desire to argue with her children, but the former was definitely more palatable of her two options. "Okay, Galen can stay for dinner, but only—"

"Yippee! Thanks, Mom!"

"You're the best mommy ever."

"Not so fast," she said, as they jumped up and down with excitement. She still had an out that would prevent them from arguing with her. "Did you pick up your bedrooms and your study? This morning you promised to clean up when you got home."

"We already did," Kyle said.

"Nana made us," Brittany added.

"What about homework?" she asked, grasping at straws.

"It's the weekend, Mom. We don't have homework. So can Galen stay?" Kyle stared at her, daring her to come up with another excuse to say no.

Mindy looked at her daughter, whose expression mirrored her

brother's. She had none. Surprisingly, she was almost happy she didn't as she reflected on their delight when they'd discovered that Galen was back. She wanted their faces brimming with joy, not apprehension. She owed them, especially Kyle whom she knew had missed him more than Britt. Perhaps this was her day to hand out second chances. "Okay, Galen can stay if you do something for me."

"What?" they blurted together, their faces scrunched in agitation.

"Take these inside." She handed her briefcase to Kyle and her purse to Britt. "And stay there. Galen and I need to talk for a few minutes."

"Thanks, Mom." They raced inside, almost mowing Galen down as they fought to get through the door.

"Wow." Galen walked into the garage. "I forgot how much energy your kids have. I've been with them for barely fifteen minutes and I'm ready for a nap."

His hearty chuckle made butterflies flutter in Mindy's belly. "They're models of what's in store for you when Geoffrey gets older." Mindy knitted her brows at the ease with which she'd spoken his son's name. Even more alarming was that the apprehension and resentment she'd been feeling all week when she thought of the situation surrounding his conception was mostly gone. Had the healing begun?

A faint light twinkled in the depths of his hazel eyes. "I really appreciate you letting me stay and reconnect with Kyle and Brittany. I love your kids as much as I love Geoffrey. I hope you believe that. Being a surrogate father to them prepared me for fatherhood." He searched her face. "I know it's a lot to ask so soon, but I hope that one day you'll be able to open your heart and love my child as much as I love your children."

Mindy swallowed the lump that threatened to choke her, but she could do nothing about the tears that escaped the corners of her eyes as she recalled the day, two and a half years ago, when she'd invited Galen to dinner in her apartment to meet her children.

Even though he'd questioned her incessantly about them prior to the meeting, asking about their interests, their likes and dislikes, she had still been a bit wary of his reaction when he would finally meet them. She'd also been worried about Kyle and Brittany's reaction to him since Galen was the first man she had ever brought home. Up until that day, they'd never had to share her with anyone else. She was their whole world, theirs alone.

Her fears had been for nothing, though. Galen had walked boldly into her apartment and, after giving her a lingering kiss, had immediately settled down on the floor with her kids and joined them in play with trucks, action heroes, puzzles, and dolls. He'd engaged them in conversation about their favorite cartoons, TV shows, and foods, winning them over with his charm and interest in their little worlds, while they'd won him over with their sweetness.

While she'd watched from the kitchenette where she'd been cooking a dinner of baked chicken, mashed potatoes, and a salad, Mindy had known then that she had chosen well. She had found a man who was comfortable with a ready-made family and who loved her children and her unconditionally. How had she ever gotten that lucky? she had wondered.

"Mindy?"

"Yes, Galen," she said, over her rapidly beating heart. "I can love Geoffrey."

"Even though you've never met him?"

"You loved my children even before you met them. It shouldn't be so hard for you to understand how I can love him. He's your son. That's all that matters."

A cry of relief broke from his lips. "I never thought I'd hear you say these words this soon."

"I never thought I'd say them this soon." She bit into her bottom lip as she gazed into his eyes. "When can I meet Geoffrey?"

"In a few minutes."

She gawked. "He's here?"

"Close by," he said, his mood becoming suddenly buoyant. "He's in a limo with his nanny and a driver on Crystal Lake Road. I just have to call them." He flashed his phone.

She smiled wryly. "I passed that limo on my way home. Well, you may as well call."

He speed dialed a number, and said, "You can bring him," and then pushed his phone in his jeans pocket.

The lust and love glimmering in his hazel eyes and the visibly beating pulse at the corners of his mouth lit a torch in Mindy's belly. "How long?" she asked.

"Five minutes or so," he replied, his expression suddenly going serious.

Mindy made no protest when he pulled her into his arms, pressed her face against his chest, buried his face into her hair, and inhaled deep gulps of air as if he were trying to suck her into his system. She clung to him, her heart hammering loudly, matching the rhythm of his beating beneath her ears. God, it felt so good to be held by him, to feel the heat and strength of his body and to succumb to his arousing manly scent.

She trembled as his hands roamed freely up her back, over her shoulders, and found their way inside the collar of her coat. She quivered at the teasing brush of his warm fingers against the sides of her neck as he raised her head from his chest and clasped her face in his hands.

"You pulled away from me earlier, so if you're still not ready for this, tell me now."

"I want it," she said, licking the dryness from her lips, getting them ready for contact with his mouth, the mouth that had brought her so much pleasure in the past. Even though she was still upset with him, disappointed in him for lying to her, her heart hurt for the beatings, the pain he'd suffered to protect her and her children. He needed healing for his physical pain just as she needed healing for her emotional and psychological pain. *Heal together.* Healing was what Mindy sought as she clasped her hands to the back of Galen's head and pulled him down.

She closed her eyes and groaned when his mouth covered hers hungrily, passionately, sending bolts of fire throbbing through her blood as their mouths opened and their tongues collided in a firestorm of passion, twirling around each other, thrusting and licking and sucking in turn.

This kiss was in stark contrast to the tentative kiss of a week ago. Then, he'd been testing her, daring her to prove her contempt for him, to back up her claim that she felt nothing for him, that she didn't love him anymore. But this kiss was a testament to the passion, the trust, the love and lust they once shared, and now desired to share again.

As if to prove her point, Galen picked her up and pulled her firmly against his hard swollen shaft, causing the soft moistness between her thighs to pulsate with need and heat at the salacious contact.

"God, I missed you," he whispered against her neck, his hot breath on her skin spurting shivers of need through her system.

"I missed you too," she whispered into his ear, before running her tongue over his lobe.

He groaned heavily, placed her on the hood of her SUV, settled himself between her thighs and locked his hands against her spine. His hazel eyes were ablaze with lust as his pulsing mouth captured hers again. He slid his tongue back and forth inside her mouth, gently and teasingly, matching the tantalizing rhythm of his hips as he thrust his hard shaft against her softness through their clothes, the friction and desire consuming her, drawing out the pent-up sexual tension that had been building up inside her for eight long months.

"Galen! Mommy! Where you guys at?"

They froze, mouth-to-mouth, groin to groin. Then at the sound of approach feet, they jumped apart.

Galen helped her off the hood and turned around while she pulled down her dress and combed her fingers through her hair just as Kyle appeared at the door.

"What are you still doing out there?" he asked, looking at them with what seemed like a scowl on his face.

Mindy cleared her throat, trying desperately to calm her heart and cool the fires still burning inside her. "Talk—talking." On unsteady legs, she sauntered past Kyle into the house. "Why were you yelling for us? What's wrong?"

"The doorbell was ringing. Didn't you hear it?"

"He got here a lot sooner than I expected," Galen said.

Mindy's stomach clenched as Galen strolled through the kitchen and took a shortcut to the front door.

"Who is it, Mom?" Kyle asked, following Galen.

Mindy held his arm and walked him toward the stairs. Perhaps she shouldn't have allowed Galen to bring Geoffrey to her house before she'd had a chance to tell her kids about him. It was one thing for her to be ready to meet and accept Galen's son, but forcing him on her children only minutes after he'd come back into their lives could be a mistake. Sharing their mother's love and attention with a man they thought of as a father was one thing. Asking them to split the attention and love they received from her with yet another child was something completely different. "Where's your sister?" she asked Kyle.

"Upstairs. In the bathroom."

"Okay. Go up to your room and I don't want you or your

sister to come down until I call you," she warned, as voices gushed in from the porch.

"Why?"

"It's a surprise." *Boy was it a surprise.* "You don't want to spoil it, do you?" she asked in a firm voice. "Now, scoot." She waited until he disappeared around the corner of the second-floor balcony before she headed to the front door, her heart beating erratically.

She walked out onto the porch to find Galen sitting on a chaise longue with Geoffrey on his lap.

He glanced up as she approached them. "I stayed out here because I thought it would be better if you met him before Kyle and Britt did."

With uncertainty and trepidation quickening her pulse, Mindy stared at the little boy with dark curly hair and big hazel eyes. At least she wouldn't have to wonder if he had his mother's eyes every time she looked at him. "I was thinking the same thing. I sent Kyle upstairs and told him to stay there until I called them down." She sat warily down beside Galen, but her eyes were fixed on Geoffrey. "He's adorable, Galen. Beautiful," she said, finally voicing her initial reaction to his son.

His face broke into a sunny smile. "Thank you." He rubbed his hands up and down the little boy's arms and kissed the top of his head. "Geoffrey, this lovely lady is Mindy. Can you say, hello?"

CHAPTER FOURTEEN

Geoffrey stared at Mindy for a long tense moment then said, "*Ello.*"

"Hello, Geoffrey." Mindy couldn't resist reaching out to caress his chubby rosy cheeks. "It's nice to meet you."

"Meet you," Geoffrey said, giving her a big grin.

"He likes you," Galen said. "Would you like to hold him?" Before she could answer, he placed Geoffrey on her lap.

Instant love flooded her as the little boy wrapped his arms around her neck. She held him close, as the thought that from this moment on she would be acting the role of mother in this child's life registered in her mind. She welcomed him into her heart, just as Galen had welcomed her children into his. "Oh my, you are a sweet and precious little boy," she said, pressing her cheek against his.

Her eyes met Galen's. They were bright with love, affection, and thankfulness. "I forgive you," she said, knowing that he needed to hear the words. "I'm giving you a second chance, but if you ever lie to me again either deliberately or by omission, it will be the end of us. We have to be able to trust each other."

He nodded as tears glittered in his eyes. "I will never hurt you again, Mindy. I swear it." He leaned over and placed his lips against hers, sealing his promise with a tender kiss. He drew back and searched her face. "There is one thing I feel that I should tell you though, or else it would be a lie of omission if it ever becomes a problem down the road."

A surge of misgivings swept through Mindy as her mind jumped to the worst possible scenario. Had some other woman drugged him and he'd just discovered that he had another child to be claimed in England? "What do you need to tell me?" she asked as she placed Geoffrey on her lap, using him as a barrier between them just in case she was tempted to slap Galen's face.

"Don't look so glum," he said, running a finger along her cheekbone, causing flashes of electricity to whip through her, reminding her of the heated passion they'd shared not too long ago.

"It's hard not to, when I'm holding—" She paused and wrapped her arms about Geoffrey. "Just tell me."

He waited a moment before speaking. "After I got custody of Geoffrey, Mass hired a nanny to take care of him until I was able to move into Hotel Andreas. Her name is Sybil. I brought her to Granite Falls with me, solely because I thought it was imperative to maintain some form of consistency in Geoffrey's life. He'd just been taken from his mother, his sole caregiver up to that point, and I didn't want him to go through another change so quickly."

"That's understandable." She shrugged. "I don't get why Sybil would be a problem down the road, though. She's obviously doing a great job or else you wouldn't have brought her with you."

He held her gaze. "She came on to me."

Mindy's arms tightened around Geoffrey. "When? Back in London?"

He shook his head while he appeared to be holding his breath. "At the mansion."

"What did she do? Kiss you?"

"She caressed my arm and suggested that she could lift my spirits. It was the morning after you and I talked. I was an emotional wreck."

"What did you do?"

"I told her I was not interested in her. I warned her that she would be fired if she ever overstepped her bounds again. The only reason she isn't back in London already is that Geoffrey needs her. She's the only other constant in his life. But if you want her gone, she's gone. Geoffrey will adjust in time. I don't ever want you to worry about me falling prey to another crazy love-struck woman again. I can find another nanny, but I would never find another you, Mindy." He laid his hand over hers, laced together on Geoffrey's tummy. "Tell me what you want, love," he said, caressing her wrist with the pad of his thumb.

Mindy closed her eyes, rested her chin on Geoffrey's head, and soaked up the affection in Galen's gentle touch. *What did she want?* She wanted to drive up to the Andretti mansion and scratch Sybil's eyes out, but that was childish, except… She opened her eyes and stared at him. "Did Sybil know about me when she came on to you?"

"She only learned about you today. I thought I owed her an explanation for having her sitting in a car by the side of the road. I don't discuss my personal life with her. She doesn't even know the real story about Trix. Sybil thinks Trix just abandoned Geoffrey and me."

"Well, I can't fault her for coming on to you when she didn't know you were involved. You're a hunk, a billionaire hunk. I can't stop women from trying. Geoffrey needs her for now, so—"

His chuckle made her heart turn over in her chest. "So we *are* involved?" he asked with a raised brow.

"I still have things to figure out, Galen. I think we got carried away in the garage. It's obvious that our physical desire for each other is just as intense as it used to be. But when we do make love again, my heart, my soul, my mind, and my spirit have to be completely engaged."

He put his arms about her and drew her head down onto his shoulder. "I'll hold on to *when we do make love again*. Those words say a bloody lot."

"Juice, Daddy," Geoffrey said, reaching for his father. "*Tursty*."

Mindy handed him to his father and stood up. "Why don't we go inside? It's getting late and I know my kids must be hungry. It's time they meet Geoffrey, anyway."

Galen picked up a baby bag from the floor and pushed to his feet. "I hope they like him."

"I'm sure they will." She reached up and brushed back the curl from his forehead and, just as he'd done in the past, he caught her hand and kissed her wrist, sending a hot flush straight to the apex of her thighs. Her panties, which had somewhat dried out since the garage, were instantly soaked again.

She tugged her hand away and walked on unsteady legs into her house. She watched from the bottom of the stairs as Galen sat on the sofa, placed Geoffrey on the floor between his feet, and gave him a sippy cup, that he immediately stuck into his mouth.

"Kyle, Britt, you can come down now," she called to her kids.

Moments later a clatter of feet sounded above before her children raced each other down the stairs.

"Who's that?" Kyle dropped to the floor at Galen's feet.

"This is Geoffrey," Galen answered.

"Where'd he come from?" Brittany joined her brother on the floor.

"From sex, silly. I told you babies come from sex." Kyle shot his sister an impatient glance before returning his attention to the newest member of their little circle.

Mindy met Galen's gaze over the children's heads and a soft light passed between them.

"Where's his mommy?" Brittany asked.

Geoffrey pulled his cup from his mouth, glanced up at his father, and said, "Mummy."

"Are you his dad?" Kyle asked the most important question. "He kind of looks like you."

"Yes, Kyle, I'm Geoffrey's father." Galen got down on the floor with them, and pulled Geoffrey into his lap. "Geoffrey, this is Kyle, and this is Britt. Can you say, Hello?"

"*Ello*," Geoffrey said around his cup.

Such a darling boy. Mindy joined them on the floor and laced her arms around her children. It felt good to have Galen back, and to have her children accept his son, like Galen had accepted them.

"Can I hold him?" Without waiting for an answer, Britt took Geoffrey by the arm and pulled him down onto her lap.

Mindy's heart trembled at the ease and comfort with which Geoffrey laid his head against her daughter's shoulder and wrapped his free hand around her neck.

"Are you and Geoffrey going to live with us?" Kyle asked.

"He can be our baby brother," Britt added.

Mindy shot to her feet. "Who's hungry?"

"I am," her kids and Galen said in unison.

Geoffrey sat his cup on the floor, patted his stomach, and said, "*Ungry*," which made everyone laugh.

"Since you asked if Galen could stay for dinner, it's only fair that you help me make it, right?" Mindy looked at her kids.

"I'll help you." Galen got up and stood beside Mindy. "Kyle, why don't you and Britt take Geoffrey to the playroom?"

"You sure?" Mindy stared up at him, shocked that he would trust his eighteen-month old son with her seven-and six-year-old children who'd met the child only a few minutes ago.

"They'll be just fine. I trust them," he said, planting a kiss on her forehead

"Come on, Geoffrey." Kyle pulled him gently out of Britt's arms to his feet. "We have a slide, and cars and trucks big enough for you to sit on."

"And a doll house so we can play house," Brittany added, jumping up to hold his other hand.

"He's a boy," Kyle chastised her as they led Geoffrey off to the playroom. "Boys don't play house."

"Uh-huh, they do. Galen plays house with me sometimes."

"Can't argue with that." Galen pulled Mindy fully into the circle of his arms. "I love playing house with Britt, but I love the reality of making a home with her mother even more. What do you say?"

Mindy wrapped her arms around his waist and smiled up at him. "Let's see how dinner goes first."

"By the way, what does Kyle know about sex?"

"Nothing. Nothing at all." Mindy smiled. She'd had that "sex talk" with her son. He was still her innocent little baby for a bit longer. *Thank God*. "He thinks sex is when a man and a woman sleep together," she said, as she and Galen washed their hands at the sink and dried them with paper towels.

"He is right, you know. *Sleeping together* is just a delicate euphemism for what really goes on between a man and a woman in bed."

Mindy tossed the paper towels in the trash bin under the sink. "I mean really *sleeping together.* Falling asleep in the same bed. He asked me why you and I didn't have a baby since we used to sleep together."

"What did you tell him?"

"I told him that babies only come if the mommy and daddy want them."

Galen dipped his head to one side. "Really, Mindy? You can't possibly allow him to go on believing *that*. It's not bloody healthy."

"I know. It's embarrassing talking about sex with my seven-year-old son. I was going to ask Phin—"

He stiffened. "Who's Phin?"

"He's my mom's boyfriend." She was tickled that he was jealous of the possibility that another man might have moved in on her while he was away.

"Your mom has a boyfriend? That's interesting."

"A lot has happened since you left. Do you know how I ended up living with her?"

"Mass told me you moved in to take care of her after she fell and hurt herself. I'm sorry I wasn't around to help. It must have been difficult for you."

"It was, but nothing compared to what you went through."

"Is she fully recovered from her injuries?"

"She is, thanks to physical therapy. That's how she met Phin. He was one of the therapist at the medical center where she got her treatment."

"That's lovely. Does he treat her well?"

"Yeah. Phin's a wonderful man. They are very much in love." Mindy turned on the oven and, opening the fridge, she pulled out the roasting pan with the four pieces of chicken breasts she'd seasoned this morning. Galen would have her Mom's share since Pamela had decided not to have dinner with them after all. "He treats us all well. He immediately and eagerly assumed the role of grandpa for Kyle and Britt," she said, leaning against the counter. "And since there's no other man in his life, I—"

With one step, Galen was standing so close his breath fanned her eyelashes. "I'm here now. *I* want to be the *man* in Kyle's life. I want to be the *man* in all your lives, if you'll let me in." He held her hand to his lips and kissed her palms as he gazed into her eyes.

Affection welled up in Mindy's throat and her body tingled from his kisses. There was still so much to be sorted out. She smiled up into his eyes. "Kyle would love that so much. He has always looked up to you. He'd been angry with me, thinking it was my fault you'd left. I'm scared of what would happen if—"

"Shh." He pulled her into his arms. "I'll make it all right. I'm not going anywhere, Mindy, ever again. I'm yours. Forever. You know that. You believe me, right?" He squeezed her tightly against his chest.

I know. I believe you. But she was still afraid even as she drew comfort from him.

Thanks to Tashi, she was finally at a point in her life where she didn't need anyone. She was financially independent. She could take care of her children. They were happy. She'd been somewhat emotionally independent since the moment she'd accepted the fact that Galen wasn't coming back. But he did come back, carrying a truckload of baggage. She believed him when he said that he was hers forever. But what if something went wrong and she and her children were left alone again?

If you live your life in fear of the unknown, all you'll have in your life is fear, nothing more, nothing less, nothing better, nothing worse, her little voice of reason whispered.

"I know. I believe you," Mindy whispered into his chest. It was the best she could do for now.

❧

"One more to go." Mindy hit the *return* button on her laptop, sending off her second five-page essay to yet another professor, both of whom would deduct ten percent of her grade for turning in late work.

She stared at the textbooks and the pages of notes she'd copied from a classmate, strewn across the dining table. She rotated her neck from side to side while massaging her muscles with her fingers. Sitting for almost eight hours straight had done a number on her.

In need of a break before she read the required chapters and notes for her last essay, Mindy grabbed her mug and the plate with her half-eaten turkey sandwich and went into the kitchen. She lit the burner under the kettle and dropped a new mint teabag into her mug, and then walked over to the sliders overlooking the lake.

It was only four o'clock in the afternoon, but it would be dark soon and she would be spending her first night alone in her new home. She missed her kids, but she was happy to have the day to herself.

Her mother had called early this morning, and upon learning that Galen hadn't spent the night, she and Phin had come by and taken the kids out to breakfast, then to the Winter Carnival as was previously planned. Phin had texted her a while ago to let her know that they were back at his house and that the kids were watching movies in his home theatre. Although she felt a little guilty that she wasn't the one to take them to the carnival this year, Mindy was happy that her kids weren't missing out on the annual tradition that had been in motion since Kyle was born.

They'd been jumping with excitement when they'd left with Phin and her mom this morning. She guessed they didn't care who was taking them, just as long as they were going. They probably preferred going with their nana, anyway, since Pamela let them eat as much candy and junk food as they wanted. Well, their bellyaches were her mom's bellyache, tonight. Not Mindy's.

At the sound of the kettle whistling, Mindy went back to the kitchen and made her new cup of tea. As she settled into her seat at the dining table, she spotted Galen's brown-leather glove sitting on the windowsill. Her mother had found it in the driveway this morning.

Mindy wrapped her hand around her mug to squish the temptation to slide the glove on, as she'd done this morning, and imagine that it was Galen's large, warm hands caressing her. Her heart rate accelerated as she thought of her short phone conversation with him after the kids had left.

She'd called to tell him that she'd found his glove. He'd chuckled and confessed that he'd dropped it deliberately so he would have an excuse to stop by today. Mindy had begged him not to so she could concentrate on her schoolwork. He'd offered to help her since he too had studied marketing and management, but she'd insisted that he stay away. She would have loved to see him, but she didn't have the strength to fight him and her body at the same time. Not after the passionate moments they'd shared on the porch last night.

Her body spasmed as she recalled Galen's tongue strumming her mouth as his hands moved up her legs, and crept under her dress to explore the soft tingling flesh of her thighs while she sat across his lap, riding the ridge of his erection through their clothes.

Higher and higher, his fingers had inched tantalizingly on their way to the heat of her womanhood. She'd whimpered with desire as his other hand crawled along her back to unzip her dress and unhook her bra. Mindy had shivered with longing when he'd pulled the dress and her bra straps off her shoulders and arms, baring her oh so swollen, aching breasts to him.

"I want you so badly, Mindy. Let me please you, baby," he'd whispered. Then his hot mouth had closed over one of her mounds, sucking ravenously, while his fingers stroked her soaked crotch, sending electrical currants spiraling in the deepest parts of Mindy's body.

Even as her body had cried out for release, Mindy had known that she wasn't emotionally or psychologically ready to be with Galen. "No. No," she'd gasped between deep soul-drenching breaths. "Galen, no." Somehow, she'd found the strength to untangle herself from him, hop off his lap, and move to the other side of the porch. "I'm not ready," she'd said as she pulled her clothes back on.

"I'm sorry, love. You just make me so crazy."

"You make me crazy, too." She'd turned, happy to be standing in the shadows so he couldn't read the longing in her eyes—longing mixed with uncertainty. She'd told him that she forgave him and that she was giving him a second chance, but she wasn't ready to jump back into bed with him, not until she'd completely accepted and processed all that had happened to him in England. "I think you should leave, Galen. It's late and—"

"Mindy."

The panic in his voice nipped at her, but in her heart Mindy knew that making love with him tonight would be wrong for both of them. She didn't doubt his love and renewed commitment to her, but she doubted her mind's ability not to bring up the images of him and Trix in bed. "It's not forever. I just need more time. I'll come around soon. I promise."

"How soon?"

"I don't know, Galen." *When my mind is ready*.

Mindy took a deep breath and sipped her tea. She had no idea when "soon" would come, but she knew it wasn't today. She placed her mug on the table, opened her Human Resource Management textbook, and forced her mind off Galen Carmichael and back to the educating of Mindy Marshall. She was halfway through the second of the three chapters she needed to read when her cell phone rang.

She glanced at the screen and dropped her highlighter when she saw the photo of Safi's smiling face. Feeling that she'd kept her friend in the dark long enough, Mindy hit the *accept* and the *speaker* buttons on her phone. "Hey," she said in a guilt-ridden voice.

"*Hey*, my ass. Where the hell have you been all week? I stopped by your place twice and you weren't there."

"Working. I've been burning the midnight lamp over at Saturn. I meant to call you."

"Mhm."

"Honest. I was going to call you last night."

"What stopped you?"

"Galen."

"*He's* what you've been *working* on?"

Why was everyone assuming that she would be back with Galen already? *Perhaps because they don't know the details of the events that kept him away*. "I was with Galen last night."

"You guys did it last night?" Safi's voice was ripe with sultry curiosity.

"Absolutely not. Last night was the first time I've seen him since Sunday. I really have been too busy, even for him," Mindy said, twisting a strand of hair around her finger. "He stopped by uninvited and we talked some more. Kyle and Brit were happy to see him, as expected." She wasn't ready to tell anyone that she'd gotten hot and heavy with Galen.

"So why was he gone so long without even a phone call to you?" Safi asked.

Since there was no point for Mindy to continue to dodge the question, she gave Safi a watered down version of Galen's absence, using his grandfather's stroke as the primary reason for his extended stay in London.

"I still don't get it," Safi said when she stopped talking. "If Galen's grandfather died a month after he left Granite Falls, why didn't he call you? It just doesn't make sense."

Damn! She was such a terrible liar. Mindy picked up her cell phone from the table and went to sit on the window sill overlooking the porch, but when the memories from last night surged into her mind, she got up and began to pace the floor.

ANA E ROSS

Besides Galen, only two people in Granite Falls knew the real reason for his absence and silence—her and Massimo. Without being told, Mindy knew that she was not at liberty to talk about the Frasers and the nightmare they'd inflicted on Galen. One thing she could talk about though, was Geoffrey. She wanted her best friend to hear about him from her instead of from gossip or reading about it in the local newspaper.

"Hey, are you still there?"

Mindy plopped down on the sofa in the living room and set her phone down on the coffee table. "There's something I haven't told you."

"What?" Safi asked eagerly.

"Galen has a son."

"Galen has a *son*?" Safi's shock reverberated around the room.

"Yes. I was shocked, too."

"How old is he?"

"Eighteen months."

"Eighteen months?" There was a long pause as Safi obviously did the math. "So that means he…"

"Slept with another woman after we were together," Mindy said, finishing the sentence when Safi's voice trailed off.

"Oh, Mindy. And you forgave him? Girl, I would have kicked him in the balls, and never spoken to him again. You were right to tell him that he was a disgusting Andretti the other night. I really didn't expect this from him. But you never know what people will do. Such a jerk! I can't believe you're even talking to him after that."

Mindy winced. "He didn't sleep with her willingly. She drugged him, and took advantage of him."

Safi scoffed. "Girl, you believe that BS?"

"Galen wouldn't lie to me."

"He lied when he didn't tell you he had a kid. Come on,

216

Mindy. You're smarter than this. How can you forgive him that kind of betrayal?"

"He didn't know about Geoffrey. He only learned about him when he went home to see his grandfather."

"So where's the kid's mother?"

"Back in England." Safi remained quiet, waiting for more, so Mindy gave her the short version surrounding Geoffrey's conception. "It's the woman he was seeing when he first came to Granite Falls. He broke up with her to be with me. When he went back home for Christmas that year, he got some disturbing family news and ended up at the bar where she worked. She wanted him back, and so she slipped something into his drink and took him back to her apartment. He still doesn't remember what happened that night, and that's why he never told me. When he found out about Geoffrey and confronted her, she admitted it."

"Holy crap. This sounds like a freaking Lifetime movie."

"You're telling me. Anyway," she said with a shrug of self-preservation, "Geoffrey is proof that something happened that night. Galen couldn't deny it anymore. It wasn't something he could explain over the phone and that's why he didn't call me. He had to stay in England until he got full custody of his son."

"His mother just gave him up like that?"

"She was in a situation and didn't have a choice." And that was all she was going to say about the matter.

"Well, if that's the case, I take back everything I just said about Galen. But that's some serious crap."

It was nice to have her friend on her side. Now, her mother would be a different story when Mindy finally told her everything.

"Have you met the kid?" Safi asked.

"Galen brought Geoffrey here last night. He's so adorable, Safi." Mindy couldn't stop the smile that curved her lips. "Kyle and Britt took to him like cold on snow, and he took to them too."

"That's nice. But shouldn't you have waited until you knew for sure that you and Galen will work out before you got all caught up in his kid? And what about your kids bonding with Galen again? They see him as a father, Mindy. Are you ready to disappoint them again if it doesn't work out?"

At Safi's perceptive question, Mindy wrapped her arms around her middle and stared at the flames in the fireplace. "I had those concerns, but Galen ambushed me in my driveway yesterday, then the kids came outside before I could make him leave." *Did you want to make him leave?* her little voice asked.

"Mhm. I think he played you, girl."

Maybe, Mindy thought as she recalled Galen admitting to dropping his glove last night so that he had a reason to come by today.

"Gotta hand it to him. He's one smart Brit." Safi chuckled.

Mindy's phone buzzed, alerting her of an incoming call. Relief at the opportunity to dodge Safi's questions washed over her, but just as quickly she was filled with dread when she realized that the other caller was her mother. She couldn't decide between the two critics of her life's situation.

"Mindy?" Safi said.

Mindy placed her feet on the floor. "Sorry, Safi. I have to go. My mom's calling, and she has my kids."

"Okay. We'll continue this convo later. I miss you at the boutique, girl. Envious tongues have been wagging at your good fortunes."

"I bet they have," Mindy said with a giggle. "And they'll keep wagging when they hear about Geoffrey, I'm sure."

"Haters gotta hate, lady. When can we get together for some real fun?"

"Soon. I'll call you," Mindy promised, before switching to

her mother's call. "Hi, Mom. Are the kids okay?" She asked that question of anyone who called while watching her kids.

"Kyle and Britt are fine."

Then why are you calling me?

"Are you at home?" Pamela asked.

"Where else would I be, Mom?" Mindy fought to keep the irritation from her voice as she picked up her phone, walked back to the dining table and sat down. "You and Phin took the kids so I can catch up on schoolwork. Remember?" she said, grabbing a highlighter.

"Are you alone?"

"Yes, Mom. Galen isn't here."

"That's not what I was asking."

"Wasn't it?" She tapped the highlighter on her textbook. "Why did you call?"

"I need to talk to you. Can you come over?"

"To Phin's?"

"To my place."

"What are you doing at your place? Are the kids with you?"

"They are still at Phin's."

Mindy was confused, but not alarmed. She knew her kids were safe with Phin, but… "Did you and Phin have a fight?"

"No. No! I just need to talk to you."

"Right now? I still have a lot of work to make up. Can't it wait until tomorrow afternoon when you bring the kids home?"

"It can't."

"Is this talk about Galen? 'Cause I already told you—"

"It *is* about Galen, but it's not about you and him. It's about him and his mother. There are things you need to know. Just come, okay. I'll put on some coffee." Pamela hung up before Mindy could say anymore.

219

CHAPTER FIFTEEN

Mindy sat stunned, appalled and too scared to move or interrupt her mother's recount of Judith Carmichael's sinister plot to seduce and trap Luciano Andretti by telling him that she was on the pill so they could have unprotected sex after the STD tests he'd ordered her to take came back negative.

The most disturbing part of the story was the details of the skanky phone call Judith had made to Mrs. Andretti after Luciano had told Judith that he wanted no part of the bastard child she was carrying. He'd fired her, told her to pack her bags and leave the country never to return or else the financial support he was about to set up for the child would never happen. That malicious, retaliatory phone call had sent the lovely young Giuliana Andretti into premature labor and ultimately caused her death and that of her baby girl.

"So do you understand now why I didn't, couldn't take to her son? He was a reminder of everything that was evil in that woman. And as far as I'm concerned, she was *all* evil," Pamela said, spreading her lips in disgust.

Mindy's stomach was in turmoil, her ears were ringing, her eyes were stinging, and her heart was lodged inside her throat, but she managed to push the question through her parched lips. "Does Galen know? Did you tell him?"

"I didn't tell him, and I wasn't sure until yesterday, but yes, I'm quite sure he knows."

Mindy was trembling as she tried to grapple with the pain and shame Galen must have felt after hearing such a deplorable story about the woman who had brought him into the world. His mother had lied to her family when she'd told them that she and Luciano were in love and would have been together if it hadn't been for Luciano's wife. She had lied to Galen when she'd told him that his father was dead. Was this the dirt he'd heard about his mother during the arbitration? Was it shame that had kept him from speaking about it when she'd asked? "How long has Galen known? Who told him?"

"Well, he knew his mother was a vindictive manipulator who seduced his father, but I don't think he knew about the phone call until very recently. I suppose his brother finally told him."

Mindy folded her arms across the card table. "Massimo was a child when his mother and baby sister died. How would he know the details about something that happened almost thirty years ago? How do *you* know all this information?"

Her mother took a deep breath, then a sip of her instant coffee. "I bugged Judith's and Mr. Andretti's offices. I gave the tapes to Massimo just before that big group wedding."

Mindy jumped back. "Why? What had she done to you to make you even think of bugging her office, and to take the risk of bugging Mr. Andretti's? From what I've heard about that man, he wasn't someone to mess with."

Pamela flinched and glanced out the window behind Mindy for a few tense moments before bringing her gaze back to her daughter. "Galen asked me that same question yesterday, but I wasn't ready to answer it. Judith did a lot of things to make me not like her, but she did *one* that was unforgivable."

Mindy was shaken from the hate she heard in her mother's voice.

"I first met Judith when she moved into my apartment building on Keller Avenue."

"I thought you'd lived in the trailer park all your life."

"There are a lot of things neither you nor your brother know about me, Mindy. I asked you to come over so I could finally get it all off my chest."

Mindy took a sip of water from her glass and waited for her mother to begin speaking again.

"Judith moved into Pine Forest with her American boyfriend —a boy she'd met while he was studying in London. She seemed nice, so we struck up a friendship. Her boyfriend eventually dumped her, leaving her without money to pay her rent or even buy food. I felt sorry for her, so I asked my cousin Amos, who owned the cleaning company I worked for, if he could give her a job. She didn't have any papers so he paid her under the table. She soon got a roommate to split the rent. Things had begun looking up for her, but I had the feeling this girl was not satisfied. She wanted more. Nothing's wrong with that, mind you. There is a big difference between greed and ambition. Judith Carmichael was not ambitious. She was greedy and envious. It was obvious in the way she looked at people and things. I just knew."

Her mother sighed and took another sip of coffee. "After some time, she asked to be on my cleaning crew at Andretti Industries. My cousin refused because anyone who worked at AI had to be fully vetted with background and criminal checks. Since she was here illegally, that wasn't possible. So Judith did what Judith always did to get her way."

"She slept with Amos," Mindy said.

Her mother nodded. "She videotaped it and threatened to show it to his wife."

"God, she was really...something." Mindy wanted to call her

a bitch, but she couldn't bring herself to use *that* word to describe the mother of the man she loved.

Her mother snorted. "She got into AI as a day cleaner, and then the next thing I know Mr. Andretti's personal assistant had retired and Judith had taken her place."

"How the heck did she do that?" Mindy asked, dumbfounded.

"I later found out that she'd slept with some sleazebag in exchange for falsified working papers."

"Oh my God, Mom. No wonder you hated her."

"I wanted to tell Mr. Andretti what she'd done, but I was afraid that Amos would lose his contract and maybe his marriage, and probably be sued for breach of contract if anyone found out how Judith had gotten into AI. She used to treat me like crap, thinking that she was better than me because she'd schemed her way into becoming the personal assistant to one of the richest men in the area. She had a lot on us to keep us quiet. I feel responsible for Giuliana and her baby's death. If I'd only spoken up before it got that far…" She shook her head slowly.

As she took in the mixture of regret and hostility in her mother's voice and expression, Mindy's mind rewound to the conversation they'd had a week ago when her mother had exhibited bitterness and hate for women who thought they were better than other people while they themselves whored and lied and cheated their way up the ladder. She'd even said that these women taught their children how to lie and cheat like them. Now, Mindy knew that Judith Carmichael was the woman her mother had been talking about. "Is that when you started bugging Judith's office to get dirt on her?" Mindy asked.

Her mother shivered, folded her arms over her stomach, and for a brief moment she stared off into space as if she was watching another story unfold in front of her eyes. "Yes, I needed to get rid of her before she destroyed that family, but even more so after I discovered that she'd slept with another man to get her way." She swallowed, and her face went pale.

Mindy reached across the table and touched her mother on the shoulder. "Who was it, Mom? Who was the other man Judith Carmichael slept with?"

Pamela's chest rose and fell on a deep sigh. "He was my fiancé."

Surprise siphoned heat to Mindy's cheeks. "You—you were engaged?"

"Yes, Mindy, I was engaged to be married. This time it was for love and not out of fear."

Shortly after she'd moved back in with her, Pamela had told Mindy about being forced into marrying her abusive boyfriend when she was eighteen years old. After he was killed in a freak accident in the New Haven, Connecticut auto-body shop where he worked, having no one else to turn to or anywhere else to go, she had packed up a six-month-old Billy and moved to Evergreen to live with her cousin, Amos.

After hearing that story, Mindy had been astonished that her mother had thrown her out when she was pregnant with Kyle. Pamela should have been more understanding and supportive since she too had gone through a similar experience. "Who were you engaged to, Mom?" she asked eagerly. "What was his name?"

"His name was—" Pamela swallowed again, her face scrunching up as though it was painful for saliva to pass through her windpipe. "I haven't spoken his name in over twenty-eight years, but it was Darren Cushman." She let out her breath as if she'd been holding it while she spoke.

The name was unfamiliar to Mindy. "Where is he? Does he live around here?"

"He's dead, as is the baby I was carrying at the time."

Mindy shot to her feet as a different kind of shock resonated through her. "You lost a baby and never told me nor Billy? Mom?"

Her mother's eyes were misted when she raised her head. "I was the only cleaner who had a key to Mr. Andretti's office," she continued, ignoring Mindy's question about her miscarried baby. "Judith needed to get in there. For what? I have no idea." Her mother shrugged. "Anyway, Darren, Billy and I were all living together at the time. I was three months pregnant when she slept with him and then blackmailed him into stealing the key off my ring so she could copy it. The problem was that you couldn't make a copy of that key. It was coded. I caught him trying to put it back. He just broke down and confessed everything. If it was any other woman, I might have found it in my heart to forgive him because I truly loved him, but I couldn't bear to look at him, much less have him touch me after knowing he'd been with *her*. The thought made me sick to my stomach. I immediately threw him out. But the shock and pain of betrayal, and the broken heart were too much. I lost my baby."

"Oh, Mom." Mindy rushed around the table to wrap her arms about her mother. "I'm sorry. I can't imagine how I would have felt if I'd miscarried Kyle or Brittany. Judith was an awful person. You have every right to hate her as much as you do. Her baby lived and yours and Mrs. Andretti's died. It's not fair. I understand now why you hate Galen. He reminds you of the baby you lost. I'm sorry that my relationship with her son brought those terrible memories back to life."

Mindy paused as she contemplated asking the impossible. If she'd known two and a half years ago what she now knew, she would have listened to her mother and not gotten involved with Galen. She would not have deliberately aided in resurrecting her mother's ghosts, even though their relationship had been strained at the time. How could she hurt the woman who'd given birth to her when she now understood the pain she had suffered at

Galen's mother's hands. She licked her dry lips? "Do you want me to cut Galen out of my life for good, Mom? Is that why you told me what Judith Carmichael did?"

Pamela raised Mindy's head from her chest and dabbed at her tears with the edge of the tablecloth, spinning Mindy's mind back to when she was a little girl. "No, baby. I don't want you to leave Galen. I want you to love him. He obviously makes you and my grandkids happy."

"You mean that?" Mindy's heart trembled with love and affection.

"Of course. Judith Carmichael wrecked my life and filled me with so much hate and distrust for men that for twenty-eight years I closed my heart to any possibility of love. I chased men away even before giving them a chance to hurt me."

"What about my father?"

"He was a drunken one-night stand."

"Your mistake," Mindy said dolefully.

"That's what I told myself to keep my emotions detached. I didn't want my heart to be broken again, not even by my child. I've met mothers whose hearts had been broken by the children they loved. I didn't want any more disappointments. But deep down inside I always thought of you as a blessing, Mindy. A blessing and a joy to have in my life. You were such a smart, curious child, much more intelligent and sociable than your brother. Everybody loved you as a baby, and a child. You were special." She placed her cool lips against Mindy's forehead. "When you got pregnant at sixteen, I was disappointed. I felt betrayed, like you'd crushed all the dreams and plans I had for my little girl."

"I'm sorry you *felt* disappointed, Mom." For Mindy to say she was sorry to have disappointed her mother would be admitting that Kyle was a mistake. *He wasn't.* She would do it again to have him and his sister in her life. Her children were the only proof that Kyle Grainger had walked the face of this earth. A man as gentle, as kind, and as loving as he had been, should leave a legacy. Kyle and Brittany were his legacy.

"I felt as if I'd failed you," her mom continued. "I couldn't deal with my own failure. That's why I threw you out of the house. I'm sorry for not being there when you needed me most. Forgive me, baby. Please forgive me."

Mindy wrapped her arms about her mother's waist and laid her head in her lap. She'd waited twenty-three years to hear her mother tell her that she was a blessing and that she was happy to have her in her life.

Her mother stroked her hair as they both wept for the pain and disappointments they'd suffered at each other's hands, and from those of others over the years.

Finally Pamela raised her head and gazed into her daughter's eyes. "I got a second chance at love with Phin. It's because of him that I can tell you without hesitation that you must give Galen a second chance. This cycle of single parenting and disenfranchisement has plagued both our families for three generations. It's time to break that dysfunctional wheel and start something new."

Mindy badly wanted that *something new*. She was tired of being a single parent. She was never more sure about it than last night when they'd sat around the dinner table and she'd listened to her children bring Galen up to date about the events in their little lives. The love she'd detected in his eyes when he smiled at her children was no less when he smiled at his own son. He loved them equally, and as she thought about it now, she knew that she could love Geoffrey as much as she loved her own children.

Perhaps Safi was right when she'd said that Galen had played Mindy when he'd brought Geoffrey to her house to meet her and her kids before Mindy was sure she wanted to resume their lives together. But the truth was that Kyle and Britt needed a dad, and Geoffrey needed a mom.

They would all make such a wonderful happy family if she would only give them a chance. She could see them now each morning having breakfast around the dining table and dinner each night. She envisioned them huddled together in the playroom frolicking with their kids, and then each night after the children were tucked into bed, she and Galen would make love and then fall asleep in each other's arms.

"You're at the beginning of a wonderful career." Her mother's voice broke into her musings. "You have a magnificent house on the best lake in the area, and two amazing children. All you need is the love of a man to make your life complete. That man for you is Galen Carmichael, Judith's bastard son. She never knew it, but she gave birth to him so he could love you, and heal some of the pain that she caused me. I still don't know why he abandoned you for eight months, but I saw love for you in his eyes and I heard it in his voice when we spoke yesterday. Whatever it is, forgive him and let him love you, or you will end up an old bitter bat like me."

"You're not a bitter bat, Mom. You were deeply hurt." She reached up and caressed her mother's cheeks and, as she gazed into her eyes, Mindy realized that for the first time in her life, she felt loved by her mother. What she felt coming from her mother's heart was tantamount to what Mindy felt for her own children— a bond that was only recognizable, only felt between a mother and the child she had given birth to.

Heal together.

Who would have known that those two words would extend beyond her and Galen's relationship to include her and her mother's? Mindy smiled as more pleasant images of her future with Galen and their children danced around in her mind. Her mother's confession had made that future possible, a future that was free of doubt and hostility. "Thanks for giving me hope, Mom."

"Thank you for giving me back my life, Mindy. If you hadn't been born, I would not have had a reason to forgive Judith, and I wouldn't have been able to accept Phin's proposal."

Mindy's mouth dropped open. "Phin asked you to marry him? When?"

"Two nights ago when he came over for dinner. And of course I said yes."

"You've been engaged for forty-eight hours and you didn't tell me?"

"I didn't want to flaunt my happiness in your face while you were going through a difficult time with Galen."

"Oh, Mom, that is sweet of you. Did he give you a ring?" she asked, grinning.

Pamela reached into her bosom and pulled out a diamond ring. "I've been keeping it close to my heart," she said as she slid it on her finger and held it out to Mindy. "Isn't it beautiful? Phin is definitely a keeper. I'm so glad I fell down in my bathroom."

For the first time in her life, Mindy saw a twinkle in her mother's eyes—the kind of twinkle she had come to detect in the eyes of women who were truly in love with their men, she included. "It *is* beautiful, Mom. I'm so happy for you. You deserve a man like Phin to love you and look after you."

"And you deserve a man like Galen who has loved and been taking care of you since you met him. I know he helped you financially when you were living together. He was providing for you and you weren't even married. He cares about you. You and my grandchildren are happiest when he is around. I want you to get back to that place of peace and joy."

Knowing now that she could tell her mother anything, especially about Galen without fear of condemnation and ridicule, Mindy held her mother's gaze. "Mom, Galen has an eighteen-month old son he didn't know about until eight months ago. His name is Geoffrey. I met him last night. He's adorable and beautiful, and Kyle and Britt love him to pieces already. They're already calling him their little brother."

Her mother cupped her chin. "Kyle and Brit told me about him."

Of course. They are children. They can't keep secrets, not that she'd told them that Geoffrey was a secret.

"Is that why he hadn't called you?" her mom asked.

"That's part of it. How do you feel about it?" she asked, giving her mom a guarded look.

"It doesn't matter how I feel about it."

An hour ago, Mindy would have been confused at her mother's response.

"I suppose Galen told you how Geoffrey came about," Pamela said.

"Yes."

"Have you forgiven him? Are you at peace with it?"

"Yes," she said on a choked whisper.

"Then that's all that matters, Mindy. Leave the past in the past and look to the future."

Mindy hugged her mother as her heart thumped with a kind of love she never knew a daughter could have for her mother— the kind of love that Mindy received from her own daughter every single day.

It was wonderful, beautiful, unconditional, and it was nice to be the giver instead of the receiver for once. She never ever wanted to lose that feeling.

Galen got out of his car, walked around to the driver's side, and retrieved four paper bags from the footwell. He kicked the door shut and strode toward the house, smiling as he anticipated the look of surprise on Mindy's face when she opened the door. She'd been adamant about him staying away to give her time and space to catch up on her schoolwork. Galen had respected her wishes for as long as he could.

As he'd fallen asleep last night he'd promised himself that as long as they were within a hundred miles of each other, never a day would go by without him gazing upon her gorgeous face, kissing her tempting lips, and running his hands up and down her warm slender body. "Feeling trapped, buddy?" he asked his cock as it stirred against his silk boxers.

After Kyle and Britt had been put to bed, and Geoffrey had been corralled by cushions on the bed in the guest room last night, he and Mindy had retired to the porch for some much needed R&R—which had steadily turned into touching and stroking, and moaning and groaning into each other's mouths.

She hadn't had time to change so the dress she'd worn all day had made it easy for him to slide his hands up her smooth thighs and brush his fingers against the hot, soaking wet crotch of her lacy panties while his tongue had been doing the tango with hers. It had been too much, too soon for her, and she'd pulled away, bringing their heated session to an abrupt halt.

Back at the mansion, Galen had stood under the cold shower sprays for a long time, but when that didn't help, he'd had no other choice but to bring himself to release. He wouldn't have been able to sleep otherwise. It was the first time in eight months that he had buffed the banana, and maybe it was a good thing Mindy had put the brakes on, or else he would have embarrassed himself by coming after only one or two deep thrusts into her. He'd buffed his banana again before leaving home tonight—just to be on the safe side. He was hoping to hit a couple home runs tonight, but if she said no, at lease the pain in his groin won't be so intensive.

He needed her. This time his cock stirred vigorously in anticipation of being buried inside her tightness tonight.

The porch was unlocked. "I must speak to her about safety," he murmured as he glanced through the wall of window from the porch. The lights were dimmed and a low fire burned in the gas fireplace. The dining table was covered with textbooks and notebooks, and her open laptop sat on a chair that was pulled away from the table. She was home.

Butterflies fluttered away in Galen's stomach as he rang the doorbell. It seemed like an eternity ticked by before it finally opened and the lady of the lakeside manor stood in front of him, wrapped in a white towel. Her wet blonde hair cascaded from her crown framing her lovely face, the dripping ends clinging to her shoulders and the hillocks of her breasts, partially exposed by the towel. She stared at him with wide brown eyes, stormy with need and passion, and love—*perhaps*.

Galen swallowed as his senses immediately skidded into a frenzy from the mixture of tea tree and lemon shampoo and the rosy aromas of her bath oils, and the fact that she might be buck naked under that towel. Oh, the sweet memories of breathing in her essence as she lay beneath him, sated and exhausted.

Galen's cock came fully awake and thumped against his jeans with the force of a sledgehammer trying to break through the ice of a frozen lake when, all of a sudden, Mindy slowly unwound the towel and dropped it on the floor. The bags, filled with tasty dishes from *Ristorante Andreas*, dropped to the floor as Galen's body went limp.

Upon arriving at Mindy's house, he had planned to send her upstairs to take a long soak in her Jacuzzi while he busied himself creating the scene from their first date—a table set with the same dishes he'd ordered to the lakeside villa the night he and Mindy first made love—wine, candles, and soft music. During dinner, he'd planned to slowly and tantalizingly woo his way back into her bed.

But with Mindy standing before him in all her heart-stopping, naked sexiness, he could only conclude that some time today, she'd obviously made a decision to get back together with him. Whether or not this was a preconceived plan for their reunion, he loved hers much, much more than he liked his own.

His heart pounded so vigorously it shook his entire body, jumpstarting his brain again. Saliva backed up into his throat as his eyes feasted on her slender flawless body. Her breasts—oh God, how wonderful they had tasted in his mouth last night—were high, firm, and tight on her chest. Her erect nipples, surrounded by puffy areolas, begged to be licked, sucked, and nibbled upon, and her taut belly heaved with each breath she took. Galen's eyes skidded lower to the neatly trimmed mass of blonde hair covering her Venus mound. Fire spread through him at the sight of the tip of her woman's powerhouse peeking shyly through her slick wet folds. A thick rivulet of overflow trickled down the insides of her thighs.

"Fuck!" Galen's harsh cry pierced the electrified air that had trapped them inside its fiery vortex, and sent her into motion licking her lips provocatively and smiling wickedly as she fluttered backward like a ballerina on the edge of a dream, silently inviting him to come on stage with her.

Galen stepped inside and kicked the door shut behind him. He immediately heeled off his sneakers and shrugged out of his jacket before dragging his sweater and T-shirt over his head in one full swoop. He dropped them on the floor and then stripped his jeans, boxers, and socks off in a record moment.

He stood straight and tall in front of her gaping eyes that were glued to his cock pressing against his belly, a drip of pre-cum coating its tip. They moved at the same time as if a choreographer had given a cue to begin the mating dance. With a harsh groan, he picked her up, sat her on the ridge of his pulsing cock, and captured her mouth as she locked her legs around his waist.

Gasps of ecstasy sprang from deep inside them both, only to be pushed back down each other's throats as wet hot silk glided over and then settled sensationally against hard hot muscle, her soft folds spreading to coat his girth with her love juices. Her arms wound around his neck, pulling him closer as his palms glided erotically up her back to close over her shoulders, holding her steady and secure as she rubbed against him, urgently and tantalizingly.

"Please me," she whispered into his mouth before capturing his tongue and sucking on it so ravenously his knees buckled, sending him tumbling back against the door.

"Yes, love." His breath came out harsh and labored. He closed his eyes and willed his brain to stay the explosion he knew would soon come. Forcing strength into his legs, Galen stumbled toward the dining table, sat her on an open textbook lying on its edge, and then pressed her back down on top of her notebooks, notepads, and loose papers.

Homework was about to take on a whole other meaning.

CHAPTER SIXTEEN

With their mouths still locked in a combative and passionate kiss, Galen reached between them and, taking hold of his cock, he pulled back his British foreskin and pressed the broad tip along her slick heat, starting from her swollen clit and working his way slowly and enticingly down to her tight opening.

She moaned and arched her back as he pushed the head gently inside, testing to make sure she was indeed ready for him. He was a large man. She was a tight woman, and without asking Galen knew she hadn't had a cock inside her since the day he left. He wanted to take his time and nibble and taste every inch of her soft skin as he'd envisioned every day and night for the past eight months, but this was not the time for that kind of loving.

From the moment Mindy had dropped that towel, exposing her beguiling body to him, they'd both known that their reunion would be a raw and frenzied tumble, neither giving, but both taking what they needed from each other without apology or regret.

As if reading his mind, she pulled her mouth from his and

whispered, "Fuck me hard. Bring me back to life," before tightening her arms around his neck and her legs around his waist. She dug her heels into his buttocks, brazenly urging him to take his best shot.

Fire blazed through every cell in Galen's body. Needing to witness his plunder, he raised his head and gazed into Mindy's eyes as he pulled his cock head back then launched forward, forcing his entire length inside her body. Oh, yes, this table was the perfect height for some deep fucking.

Piercing, broken cries erupted from both of them as the soft walls of her sex parted and stretched to welcome his foray deeper and deeper and deeper, until he hit her cervix and his head lodged itself inside. He grabbed the edges of the table on either side of her head and, flexing his buttocks, he locked his groin to hers on a deep grunt and pulsed his shaft inside her, claiming her as his own.

"Oh God, I'm co-o-oming…" And just like that, her back arched off the table and her groin gyrated around his as her mouth opened in shock and pleasure. Her head thrashed around on the table, causing her damp hair to stick to her face—flushed with the color of love—while her irises rolled back into their sockets to transform her eyes into white spheres. She was the perfect picture of carnal delight.

Her soft walls quivered like an earthquake around him and her eyes closed completely as the boisterous waves of her passion coursed through her body over and over again. She milked him, drawing him deeper still into her wet tunnel where a roaring fire blazed so hot he felt as if his cock head would disintegrate into tiny fleshy pieces. Her sharp nails raked down his back and dug deeply into his flesh, but the delicious sensation of her hard nipples grazing his chest, her trembling thighs clamped against his hips and her heat gripping and pumping him—excruciatingly, amazingly—turned the stinging pain in Galen's back into whitewashed pleasure.

She screamed out his name as a river of scalding woman's cum gushed from her contracting walls and coated the hard pulsing length of his shaft, sending sharp electrical shocks to every nerve in his body. Galen trembled on his feet, gritted his teeth, and called on all his willpower to stop the flood of cum that threatened to burst from inside him. When her storm passed, she fell weakly back onto the table, gasping harshly between a series of sexy little moans as she fought to catch her breath and calm her racing heart.

Knowing from experience that Mindy needed time to desensitize her nerves, Galen raised his body from her and waited patiently, but wholly empowered by the knowledge that he'd made her come with only one powerful thrust, and the fact that he'd managed to stay his own release.

His heart thundered as he took in the erotic scene of her flushed damp body spread out over her schoolwork while he was still buried, hard and deep inside, her blonde pubic hair mingling with his dark black. If only her professors could see her now, if they could have heard her licentious request, they would surely forgive her for missing classes all week and for turning in late work, he thought with a wicked grin. *Damn*, he'd forgive her *anything* for this. She already had an A-plus and the course hadn't even begun yet.

It was the first time either of them had used that four-letter word. Perhaps they were changing, for better or worse—either way Galen didn't care. There was a certain erotic *je ne sais quoi* about a woman making such a command to her man. It had nothing to do with love, but everything to do with hunger and self-serving gratification. They'd been together countless times in the past. They knew how to arouse each other with lingering kisses and tender caresses. They'd watched the play of emotion in each other's eyes, and teased and tempted each other with foreplay until their passions had built and blazed out of control.

Foreplay would come later tonight when they eventually made it upstairs to the bedroom. For right now, Mindy had given an order. He was a man who did what he was told when it came to his woman. *What Mindy wants, Mindy gets.*

Galen drew in a deep breath as she licked her rosy lips on a smile of satisfaction and wrapped her legs around his waist again. *Sensuous.* Her eyes remained closed and he could only guess that she didn't want to send them down a gentler road by allowing them to gaze into each other's eyes. She'd asked to be fucked hard, not for tender lovemaking. In this moment, she was a female in heat and he was a male who'd picked up her scent. There was only one outcome.

Eager to please, Galen stationed his feet on the hardwood floor. His hands closed around her breasts. He squeezed their fullness and pinched her pebbled nipples between his fingers as he began to rock his hips from side to side and around and around, giving her time to get used to having him moving inside her after his long absence.

Her sighs of ecstasy and the delightful grazing of her heels against his buttocks sent shivers racing up and down his spine. Tightening his hold on Mindy's voluptuous breasts, he dragged his cock slowly out of her until he could feel her tight hot entrance squeeze the head. He caught his breath on the divine sensations zipping through his entire body, but only for a moment before he slammed back in with power and might, groaning with ecstasy as her softness fisted around him, possessively, womanly. She emitted a guttural sound from deep inside her throat, her stomach and pelvis undulating as she ground her groin against his.

He drew back, but her succulent walls pulsed around his cock as if forbidding him to leave. When he slammed back in they yielded to his strength, coaxing him deeper and deeper into their secret labyrinth. She bit down on her lower lip when he slowly withdrew, and when he slammed into her for the third time, she groaned aloud and grabbed the edges of the table, sending papers, books, and pens flying to the floor. Her back arched completely off the table and her legs tightened around his waist in a death lock as she came again, her body writhing and twisting beneath him as another hot burst of love juices coated him.

Determined to ride the tide with her, Galen splayed his hands down her body, over her taut belly, her hips, and along her silky thighs. He raised her legs in the air and placed them over his shoulders, leaving her completely vulnerable.

He began to ride her steadily with long slow rhythmic strokes, each one butting her cervix and leaving no room for doubt that she'd gotten what she'd asked for. Her moans were music to his ears and the sight of her body rolling and bucking under him fueled his own arousal. She gasped, and he groaned each time he rammed into her. They sucked in their breaths each time he withdrew, and before long they were moving in time and in rhythm to an erotic symphony composed from the bottom of their lust-filled hearts.

Sweat poured off his chin and dripped onto her chest, rolling down her sides to the books and papers under her. As their passion grew in depth and hunger and as the delicious friction of flesh grazing flesh mounted, Galen lost control. His hips slammed into her faster and faster, rocking the table and spilling more of its contents to the floor.

She clutched the table, using it as an anchor against his delightful assault on her body. Her groans grew louder and higher and her writhing became increasingly erratic as the fire spread to them both. He knew the signs well. It was only a matter of time before she tumbled off the edge of bliss again, this time pulling him into the fiery currents with her.

Galen felt the familiar tingling along his spine, the pressure building up in his cock as her hot velvet walls clamped around him like a bloodthirsty parasite. There was no more yielding or expanding to give him access. She was one constricting ball of fire wrapped around him as they sped along the delirious path with only one satisfying outcome. Her body sheathed him, sheltered him, bathed him in her hot honey and offered him comfort and refuge from the cold and the pain he'd endured these past eight months.

Mindy was his everything—his hope, his joy, his salvation, his life. This feeling of utter bliss, complete surrender, and total helplessness inside her body was the reason he'd fought so hard to stay alive, why he'd taken the beatings to keep *her* safe and secure and alive. He'd come back for her, for this chance of resurrection, to feel, and love, and live again. Tears stung Galen's eyes and rolled down his cheeks as he gripped her hips, pulling her into him and holding her in place as he fucked her fast and hard.

She arched upward and tightened her legs around his neck, almost choking the life out of him. She clawed at his belly and chest, wailing and screaming as her entire body went stiff as a board and the walls of her sex locked his cock in place. A hot tide rippled through Galen's body, down his spine, and settled into his groin in a fiery ball of bliss. He threw back his head and roared as he thrust forward and poured his cum deep into Mindy's waiting womb before collapsing on her, twitching as if he'd been shocked.

Their cries of pleasure ricocheted off the walls of the commodious room as they surrendered to the passion they had awakened and now slaked in each other.

A long while afterward, when their breaths had quieted and their bodies had relaxed, Galen felt Mindy stir beneath him. He lifted his head with a groan of exhaustion and gazed into her beautiful brown eyes glittering with the love and warmth of their aftermath.

"Hello," she whispered on a shaky breath.

"Hello." He supported his weight on his arms and dipped his head to plant a lingering kiss on her lips. "Feel better? Were you pleased? Are you back to life?"

She nodded on each of his questions. "Totally. I needed you." Her voice broke with emotion and her eyes glittered with tears.

Galen's heart sang with love and enchantment. "I needed you, too, love. I was hoping to have you tonight, but not like this. Not that I'm complaining," he added hastily on a grin. "I loved every minute of what we just shared, but I was thinking of a much slower dance." He kissed her lips again. "What were you doing answering the door in your towel anyway? It could have been anyone there."

"I knew it was you." She reached up to twist her finger around the errant lock of hair on his forehead. "I saw your car coming up my driveway." She tipped her head to one side and pouted. "Didn't I tell you not to come by today?"

"Yes, m'lady, but you said nothing about tonight," he countered, brushing back her hair from her face. "I guess you came around, huh?"

"Wise guy." She slapped his arm playfully and chuckled, forcing his limp shaft from inside her.

He dropped a kiss in the damp valley between her breasts, pushed off her with a groan, and helped her up.

Her knees buckled the minute her feet hit the floor, but his hand under her arm kept her from falling. "Oh my, you did a number on me," she said, clinging to him.

"You did ask for it hard," he said running his hands up and down her back, loving the feel of their warm bare skin, sticky with love juices, melding into each other. Then to his utmost surprise, his shaft sprang to life and pumped against her belly.

She pushed out of his arms with a dreamy look in her eyes. "So soon?"

"That's what you do to me, love. I've been without you for too long, but I'm a gentleman, so I'll give you some time to recover from that assault before I take you again." He felt energized, as the remnants of his anxieties over getting back with her melted away.

"You mean before I let you have me again," she stated in a testy tone.

"Hey, you're the boss of you, and me."

"And don't you forget it."

"Like I could."

She glanced at the table and then at the floor. "We made a real mess, didn't we? My books and notes are in ruins."

He helped her pick them up. "I'll buy you new ones. I can afford it now," he said, grabbing his boxers and her towel from the floor, as well.

"So can I," she declared, depositing a handful of papers on the table.

"Excuse me, Miss Independent You."

"Bet your sweet ass."

"You know it's sweet." He grinned as he handed her the towel, then pulled his boxers carefully over his semi-erection. Warmth spread through his heart as he watched Mindy wrap the towel around her body while smiling at him.

At long last they were on their way back to normal, back to the kind of life and relationship they'd shared before he left for England. He wondered mildly just what had changed her mind and made her so open and eager to take this giant step. But at this point, he was just grateful.

He pulled her into his arms and buried his face in her hair. "I love you so much, Mindy Marshall."

She pressed her face into his chest. "I love you, too, Galen Carmichael, much more than you can imagine."

"Oh, I can imagine anything after the past half hour we shared." When she began to tremble, he raised her head from his chest and gazed into her eyes. "What is it, love?"

She hesitated before answering. "I learned something about your mother's past today. I intended to tell you before we made love again. But when I saw you standing at my door, all I wanted was to be with you, love you and have you love me."

"Oh dear. Your last words are the sweetest I've heard since I returned," he said, deliberately ignoring the ones about his mother.

"What I have to tell you isn't pleasant at all."

Galen wasn't overly concerned since he guessed that her mother had probably told her about the tape. What other *something* could there possibly be to tell about Judith Carmichael? He'd heard it all, he was sure. "You can tell me now."

She pulled away and tightened the towel around her body. "Let's eat first. I'm hungry, and I can smell the food you brought from *Ristorante Andreas*. But give me a minute to go upstairs and freshen up."

"Good idea." His gaze dropped to the apex of her thighs— the sweetest spot on her body and the place where he'd love to bury his face right now. "Or we will be eating each other for dinner and dessert."

"Boy, you do have a dirty mind, Mr. Carmichael."

"Says the wench who said, 'Fuck me hard.'" He cupped her chin. "I didn't hurt you too much, did I?"

She bit into her bottom lip and gave him an exquisite smile. "A strange time to ask, but no. I loved every second of it. I can still feel you pounding away inside me. I think I will feel you for days to come."

"That's the kind of talk a man loves to hear from his woman.

Now, hurry upstairs and get dressed. The sooner we get through dinner, the sooner we can get to dessert."

"What's for dessert?"

"A hot, succulent, and ultimately pleasing little tart called Mindy Marshall."

"In that case, do you consider slipping on a robe getting dressed?" Her eyes twinkled with wickedness. "It would make getting to dessert much easier."

His cock pulsed at the notion of her sitting in front of him with only a robe between them. He would love for her to dine in her silky alabaster birthday suit, but they both knew where that would lead. "I love the way you think." He delivered a light slap to her derrière, then pointed her toward the stairs. "Go, before we both faint from hunger."

She giggled like a little girl and ran upstairs. Galen collected the rest of his clothes and headed for the bathroom off the kitchen. A few minutes later he emerged and retrieved the bags of food from the porch. He was thankful that the covers had remained in tact inside the padded thermal cases and that the century-old bottle of Chateau Lafite Rothschild he'd swiped from the Andretti wine cellar hadn't broken when he'd dropped the bags.

In the kitchen, Galen opened the wine to let it breathe while he busied himself collecting plates and utensils from the cupboards and drawers. He laid them out on a three-tier cart along with the four-course meal that included antipasti of diamond-shaped cheesy tomato bruschetta, roasted bell pepper salad, and sautéed mussels with garlic. The main course consisted of roasted lamb with herbs, seasoned steamed vegetables, and tagliatelle with hazelnut pesto. For dessert, he'd brought Mindy's favorite—tiramisu.

The sight and smell of the food made his stomach growl, forcing him to steal a couple bites of a bruschetta. He was reaching for the wine when a sharp realization hit him in the gut. He and Mindy had just had unprotected sex. His hand trembled as he poured the wine into the glasses.

Mindy hadn't been on the pill when they first started dating, and since she was allergic to latex, condoms wasn't an option. Young, horny, in love, and yes, irresponsible, they had chosen *coitus interruptus*. But after the first incident of his inability to leave her, they'd realized the urgency of using another method to avoid a pregnancy neither of them was ready for.

Mindy had gone on the pill. But her mood and hormonal balance were so severely affected, after a year they'd eventually decided that she should stop taking it. They'd been seeking out other birth control methods when he left for England eight months ago, and he was almost certain that she'd stopped taking it while he was away. *What would be the point to continue?*

An hour ago when Mindy had dropped her towel in the doorway, birth control had been the furthest thing from Galen's mind. She hadn't voiced any concerns about it, so he had to assume that she was okay with the possibility of them making a baby together. *And why not?* They were both financially secure and clearly back together.

A smile touched Galen's lips and spread to his heart. When he'd walked into Arabella thirty-one months ago and laid eyes on Mindy Marshall, his soul had instantly recognized its life mate. He'd wanted her, not just physically, but emotionally and spiritually. The uncontrolled thumping of his heart, the shortness of his breath, the prickly feeling in his stomach, and the weakening of his knees at that moment were feelings Galen had never experienced with any other woman before. It was the feeling he wanted to experience every day for the rest of his life.

In his mind's eye, he'd envisioned Mindy running across a lawn giggling with excitement as little children with blonde or dark hair chased after her. He'd felt vulnerable and scared, but delightful and complete, but he'd known, without a doubt, that what he'd felt for the *then* strange girl was pure, unadulterated love.

Galen wheeled the cart out of the kitchen. As he passed the dining table where he had just deposited his sperm inside Mindy's womb, his pulse quickened at the possibility of her giving birth to his child in as little as nine months. Yes, that would be a colossal rate of return on his deposit. *Lovely*. Lovely indeed, he thought, grabbing his jacket from the floor and continuing to the living room. He parked the cart next to the glass-top coffee table and placed his jacket over the back of the sofa.

He lit the pillar candles around the living room area and turned off all the lights, then gave an order to Alexa to play Peter Gabriel's "Secret World" album—the album to which he and Mindy had often made love in the past. As "Come Talk To Me" filled the room, Galen fished his cell phone from his jacket and sat down on the sofa.

He might as well make good use of the time while he waited for Mindy to join him.

Mindy pushed her empty plate aside. "That was simply delicious, Galen. Thank you." She smiled at him over her water glass.

"You know me. I live to please you, Mindy."

His devastatingly handsome grin made her heart jolt. "You've pleased me twice tonight already."

"And I plan to please you again and again," he said as he gathered their empty dishes and placed them on the mobile cart. "Ready for dessert?"

"I thought *I* was dessert." She gave him a false look of disappointment.

"Thanks for reminding me," he teased, leaning across the coffee table to stick a finger inside her robe and look inside.

"Hey!" She slapped his hand away. "No peeking at the goodies until after—"

"Until after what?"

Until after we talk about your wicked mother. "Dessert. We never got to dessert on our first date."

"We didn't finish dinner, either." Mischief flashed in his hazel eyes.

"Then I'll say we're making good progress." She pointed at their empty dinner plates. "Good things come to those who wait," she added, smiling seductively at him.

"In that case, let's get dessert going. It's tiramisu—your favorite—so I know we'll get through it quickly," he said, reaching for the covered dish on the bottom tier of the cart.

"I can't wait," Mindy said with more excitement than she actually felt. How could she feel excited about telling the man she loved that his mother was even more egregious than he already knew?

When she'd come downstairs, she'd intended to dive right into the story about Judith during dinner. But when she'd seen the romantic transformation of the living room and smelled the delicious dinner Galen had set out on the coffee table, she hadn't had the heart to spoil the mood. Instead of talking about his mother, they'd sat on cushions on the floor and discussed her new job as Chief Operating Office of Tashi's Photography while they ate. Galen had showered her with praise, especially at the fact that Tashi had put her trust and faith in her, even though Mindy was still in school.

"Here you go, love."

"Thanks," she said, staring at the plate of tiramisu Galen placed in front of her. She waited until he'd cut a slice for himself before taking her first bite. "Mmm, this is so good." She moaned as her tongue wrapped around the rich, creamy, cheesy texture and her taste buds sprung to life at the bittersweet combination of cocoa and liquor. "Mind-blowing loving, delicious food, and scrumptious dessert. I can die now and go to heaven without regrets."

Galen chuckled around his first bite. "At least I know how to get back on your good side when I mess up. Good thing I can afford to buy tiramisu by the truckload now. There was a time when we could only afford it once a week. Remember, love?"

"I do," Mindy said as her heart bubbled with warm memories of her and Galen splitting a takeout slice between them in her apartment. They used to take their time eating it, savoring every bite. "Those were some good times even though we were struggling financially."

"It's nice not to have to worry about money," he said, taking a sip from his wine glass.

"Speaking of… what are you going to do with your inheritance?" Mindy asked. "I know you'd once thought of rebuilding Carmichael Furniture. Are you still doing that?"

"No. Not after—" A painful shadow clouded his eyes, making Mindy feel like a toad for bringing it up. "As a matter of fact, I filed papers with the town to start my own company."

"Really? What kind of business are you considering? Something related to Andretti Industries?"

"No. Can't touch that, remember?"

"Oh yeah, neither you nor your progeny can ever work at Andretti Industries."

"So I'm starting a marketing consultant company—Carmichael Initiative."

"I love that name. Has a catch to it. Will you be focusing on new or already established companies?"

"Both. During my preliminary research, I came across a few local businesses that are interested in expanding across the country. Some are even thinking globally. I'll have to convince the CEOs to put their trust in me, considering that I'm fairly new to the field."

"You're not that new. You worked as a market research analyst in London after you graduated from Oxford University."

"True, but I've been out of the game for three years. Experience goes a long way in this field." He took a bite of his dessert. "I'll have to start small and work my way up to the bigger companies, I suppose. But that's alright, I'm in no hurry. I'm still learning how to be a father—a good one—and you and I are learning to trust each other again. You, Kyle, Britt, and Geoffrey are my priority."

"That's sweet of you, Galen." Mindy rested her hand on his lying on the table. "But I think you can handle your personal and professional lives simultaneously."

His eyes shimmered like emerald glass in the firelight. "I appreciate your vote of confidence, sweetie. But, as you know, starting a business entails a lot of hard work and long hours. I prefer to work on our family first and then—"

"You should add Weisz Foods to your list of potentials," Mindy said, determined to erase all doubts from his mind. Although she didn't think he'd ever met Mrs. Weisz personally, he must be aware of the friendship between the Andreas and Weisz families.

"Why Weisz? I'm sure a corporation that large already has marketing consultants in place. They may not be interested in expanding beyond the Northeast."

"I guarantee they are." Mindy swallowed her last piece of dessert and washed it down with wine.

"You guarantee?" He quirked an eyebrow.

"Last month, while I was ringing up her purchase at the register, I overheard Mrs. Weisz tell a shopping companion that her eldest son, who took over the business after her husband died, wanted to expand beyond the northeast. She said that her husband had been content to stay local, but that her son has ideas for the southeast that he wants to explore."

"As I said, my dear, I'm sure that a well-established company as Weisz Incorporated have their own marketing team in place."

Mindy shrugged. "Maybe, maybe not. I can talk to Mrs. Weisz for you. She likes me, and it wasn't as if she was trying to keep her conversation private. A huge company like Weisz Foods would put the wind in Carmichael Initiative's sails. That is, if you're up to the challenge," she added, daringly teasing him into action.

He whipped around the table, pushed her gently to the floor, and settled his body between her thighs. "Do you think I'm up for it?" he asked, rubbing his hard shaft against her softness.

"Oh yes, you are up to it, Mr. Carmichael Initiative." Mindy laughed as she wound her arms around his neck and opened her mouth to receive the thrust of his tongue. She drank in the comfort of his nearness, the sweetness of his mouth, and moaned as the wine, his persuasive kisses, and the arousing pressure of his erection began to take effect on her senses.

"I want you again," he whispered against her neck as his mouth traveled lower to her chest and breasts. "Let's stop talking now, go upstairs, and make love all night long."

Mindy gathered all her strength and stilled his hand as it crept inside her robe. "Galen, we have to talk about your mother."

"I'm sure I already know what you are about to tell me. Your mother must have told you about the tape recording of my mother's call to Giuliana Andretti the day she died. It's disgusting to say the least, and frankly, I don't wish to hear anymore about it."

"It's not about the tape. It's about why the tape exists in the first place. It explains why my mother was driven to bug your parents' offices in order to protect herself."

His eyes narrowed. "Do I really need to know?"

"Probably not. I wish my mother hadn't told me, but she did. She wanted to let me know why she disliked you. Taking about it is the only way to put it all behind us. I need it out of my head so that when we wake up in the morning, you and I can start the day—our life together—without any of our old baggage hanging around. Don't you want that, baby?" she asked, clasping his face in her hands.

"Just when I thought the worse was over." With a groan, he eased off her and sat down, resting his back against the sofa.

Mindy pulled herself into a sitting position. Even though they were only a few feet away from the fire, a chill ran down her spine. "I'm sorry, Galen," she said, placing her hand on his arm. He was stiff. Tense.

"Get on with it, then." He raked his fingers through his hair and leaned forward, turning completely away from her as if to keep himself detached from the information she was about to disclose.

CHAPTER SEVENTEEN

Mindy's misgivings mounted by the minute as she relayed the story her mother had told her about Judith Carmichael to Judith's son—information Mindy knew Galen would never hear from anyone else. She didn't hold anything back. Her gut cramped each time he winced at a disturbing revelation, each time she named yet another man Judith had seduced to get what she wanted.

When Mindy left her mother's house this afternoon, she'd been undecided about whether or not to tell Galen what she'd learned about his mother. But as the hours ticked by and the likelihood of resuming her relationship with him became more real, she'd decided to tell him, just in case Pamela brought up the subject weeks, months, or years down the road. If Galen found out that she'd known all along and not said anything, he might take it as a form of betrayal, just as she'd taken his failure to tell her about Trix a betrayal. She couldn't take that risk. She never wanted them to be in that place of distrust again.

Fresh from the shower, she'd been wondering how to go about calling to tell him that they needed to talk without sounding ominous when she'd spotted Galen's car coming up her driveway. She'd contemplated taking the time to dress and make herself pretty before receiving him, but the thought of Galen assuming that she wasn't home and leaving before they could talk propelled her downstairs. When Mindy had opened the door and gazed into Galen's eyes, all thoughts of adding to the pain his mother, her mother, his father, his brother, Trix, and the Frasers had already inflicted upon him vanished from her mind.

She had wanted nothing more than to spare him from the embarrassment and heartbreak of his mother's past, at least until after he'd had a moment of bliss that only she alone could give him. Asking him to fuck her hard was her attempt to help him unleash the hurt he'd suffered in the past eight months. Mindy wanted to share his anguish, but she'd failed when he'd brought her nothing but ecstasy, over and over again on her dining table —filling her with with himself and his love.

Mindy slowly stroked her hand up and down Galen's back. "I'm sorry I had to tell you more awful stuff about your mother. My mom only told me because she needed to explain why she threw me out when I got pregnant with Kyle, and also why she'd been hostile to you from the get-go. I could have kept this information to myself for fear of hurting you, but we're starting to trust each other again, and I don't want any secrets between us. If we're going to work, we can't lie to each other, either deliberately or by omission."

With his back still to her, he turned his head and gazed into the fireplace. Tense moments ticked by before he spoke. "Your mother lost her fiancé and her child. Luciano lost his wife and child. Mass lost his mother and his sister, all because *my* mother was a contemptuous human being who shagged every bloke who would get her what she wanted. She didn't give a damn about the lives she destroyed along the way. God only knows how many more men she'd seduced to get her way. Why was she like that? Why?"

"I don't know," Mindy answered even though she knew it was a rhetorical question. "Maybe somebody did something to her when she was a child to have made her so miserable."

"She *was* miserable. As her offspring I feel so guilty for what she did, all the people she hurt. I feel as if I need to make amends for her." Shame and pain were livid in his eyes and voice.

Mindy slid across the floor to sit in front of him. She placed her hands over his fists and caressed them until he relaxed his fingers and allowed her to lace them with hers. "You aren't guilty of anything. You can't blame or punish yourself for your mother's sins, Galen."

"Part of me wishes that your mother had given those tapes to Luciano so he could have taken revenge on Judith for killing his wife and child. He probably would have strangled her with his bare hands." His eyes flashed dangerously. "It's what I would have done if someone had hurt you like that."

"If Luciano had killed Judith, you wouldn't have been born, Galen. Think about that."

"I have thought about it, and I'm torn, Mindy!" His fingers tightened around hers as he apparently fought the amalgam of emotions the new information had generated.

"I know, baby."

He suddenly uttered a sarcastic laugh. "Judith and Trix. What a pair! What cruel irony that my mother and the mother of my child are so much alike. I already have to worry about what to tell my son about his mother. Now I have to be concerned about his grandmother's past, too?"

"You tell him what you know about her, not what other people have told you. You said she was a good mother to you."

"Good mothers don't lie to their children. You taught me that. My whole life has been a lie. I'm the product of evil! Suppose there is some of her in me just waiting for the right time to come out? I might be just as nefarious as she was." He pulled his hands from hers, pushed to his feet, and walked to the window overlooking the lake—invisible now under the darkness of night.

Determined not to allow him to put distance—emotional or physical—between them at this crucial time, Mindy followed him and, lacing her arms around him from behind, she pressed her cheek against his back. "You're not a lie, Galen, nor are you nefarious. You're a good man. Don't let anybody or anything make you feel otherwise." When he said nothing, she continued. "I know your heart, and so do Kyle and Britt and Geoffrey. Even Bacon knows you're genuine. You have people who love you, who want you in our lives, and you don't have to cheat or lie or whore for our love. We give it freely and abundantly. You're nothing like your mother. And as much as we might hate her, we have to realize that if she hadn't done what she did to gain access to Luciano, you wouldn't exist, and neither would I."

"Why wouldn't you exist?"

With her arms still circling his waist, Mindy eased around to gaze up at him. "My mother would have married Darren. She wouldn't have had a miscarriage, and she would never have had that one-night stand with my father."

"Bloody hell." He raked his fingers furiously through his hair, then placed his hands on her shoulders. "Judith destroyed lives, entire families. She killed dreams. How can we be happy knowing that we were born because she hurt so many people, that lives were sacrificed for our existence, Mindy?"

"We are innocent. We deserve to be happy. If we let her destroy us, too, we will just be adding to her long list of casualties. We can't let her actions dictate how we live our lives, or make us feel guilty for being happy. If we do, she will continue winning. We have to get over Judith and start working on our own perception of our future."

His eyes softened as he brushed his knuckle against her cheeks. "You're very wise and philosophical. Two of the many qualities I love about you. Massimo expressed the same feelings about refusing to be Judith's victim any longer and choosing to concentrate on the future with Shaina and his kids."

"My mom has moved on, too. She and Phin just got engaged."

He cocked his head. "Didn't they just start dating a few months ago?"

"I guess when you know, you know."

"Phin sounds like a smart guy with the right idea," he said, gazing at her with compelling and magnetic eyes. "I've *known* for two years, seven months, and two weeks, but I was in no shape to ask you to trust me with your heart and life." He sighed deeply. "Now that I know everything about Judith, perhaps I too should make an effort to find peace and happiness. We're the last outliers in this heinous affair, but we can fix that by deciding to forget the past and move into the future. Are you ready, Mindy?" His voice cracked.

Mindy swallowed. "Yes, Galen. I'm ready."

He kissed her forehead. "Don't move," he said, before walking to the sofa to take something from his jacket pocket.

Mindy's heart lurched madly when he walked back, knelt in front of her, and flipped the cover of a small velvet box. "Oh my God, Galen," she whispered as the enormous diamond sparkled in the light from the fire.

He took her left hand and gazed up at her. "Mindy Marshall, will you be my wife, my lover, my best friend, and mother of my child as I pledge to be your husband, your lover, your best friend, and father to your children?"

"Yes. Yes." She dropped to the floor as joy and love bubbled in her heart. "I'll be your everything, Galen. It's what I've wanted ever since I met you."

He slid the ring on her finger and then gathered her into his arms. "I want to begin our lives together immediately. No long engagement. No waiting."

"I want that, too," she said, lifting her mouth to meet his kiss, sealing their commitment to each other, to the children they already had, and those they would have in the future.

All too soon, he lifted his head and smiled at her. "How's next Saturday? I called Mass tonight and he said we can honeymoon on *Baia degli Amanti,* as long as we're off the island by the following Saturday when he and his gang arrive for their winter getaway. We can leave right after we say, 'I do.'"

"That would be wonderful." She reveled in the fact he'd been so certain she would accept his proposal that he'd gone ahead and made honeymoon plans before he popped the question. Well, to be fair, she could see how he would feel confident after that raunchy encounter on her dining table. "But—"

"But what?"

"I want to get married in Evergreen Community Church, but I don't know if my pastor is available at such short notice."

Galen's smile was priceless as he stood to his feet and pulled her up with him. "Pastor Dixon is available. I already spoke to him."

"When?"

"I called both him and Mass while I was waiting for you to come back downstairs."

"Boy, you work fast."

"Actually, I'm pretty slow. I should have married you two years ago."

"Yeah, you should have," she said, holding up her hand to the firelight and smiling with complete happiness. "But if you had, you wouldn't have Geoffrey," she said on a more serious note.

His eyes darkened with emotion as he brushed the pad of his

thumb across her lips. "How can you say that, knowing how he was conceived, and that I lied to you? Not to mention the—"

Mindy placed a finger over his lips. "I believe that every child that comes into this world is here for a reason. You may not yet know Geoffrey's purpose, but he wouldn't be here if he wasn't supposed to be. We're back together in spite of it all. So let's put that behind us too."

"You're the most amazing woman I've ever met, Mindy Marshall. I plan to spoil you and show you how much I love you every single day for the rest of our lives, starting right now," he added, lifting her into his arms so suddenly she gasped from surprise.

Mindy wrapped her arms around his neck and buried her face in his throat. The musky smell of his aftershave mixed with his masculine body scent sent her heart racing. "And how do you mean to spoil me, Mr. Carmichael?" she asked in a sexy voice.

"In every way imaginable." He cradled her snugly to his chest as he snuffed out the candles and instructed Alexa to turn off the lights and the gas fireplace. "Now, up to bed," he said, planting a very persuasive kiss on her lips before taking the steps two at a time.

In the bedroom, lit only by the fire Mindy had left burning in the fireplace, Galen placed Mindy's feet on the floor beside her king-sized bed and stepped back to gaze at her, his hazel eyes already ablaze with licentious promises. Eager to drown herself in the ecstasy of his touch, Mindy held his gaze while she slowly untied her robe, slid it off her shoulders, and let it fall in a silky pool at her feet.

She felt a jerk of excitement in anticipation of making love with him, having his large warm hands roam her body, his soft lips brush her skin, his tongue lick her, awakening the pleasures that had been lying dormant in her for eight uncertain long months.

His eyes glowed as his gaze raked down her body, leaving a hot invisible trail on her skin. "God, you're lovely," he said in a tremulous voice, reaching out to brush away the strands of hair that had fallen across her breasts.

The touch of his fingertips on her skin sent her heart racing and a sharp pulse throbbing between her legs. "I want to see you," she whispered, reaching for the tail of his sweater and causing him to tremble when her fingers grazed his stomach.

"Then see me," he said on a shaky breath as he helped her lift the sweater over his head. A spurt of hunger flooded Mindy's being at the light pink streaks faintly visible through the mat of dark hair running along his powerful chest—streaks she'd made with her nails as Galen had kept her locked inside a fiery cyclone of ecstasy on the dining table. But as her gaze dropped to his washboard stomach, her heart ached as she thought of the beatings he'd taken to keep her and their children safe. Instinctively she stepped closer, placed her hands on his arms, and planted a series of light kisses across his chest. "I love you so much, Galen," she said as her lips traveled lower toward the hard span of his stomach where she pressed her mouth against his belly button and kissed him repeatedly.

He inhaled sharply but he made no attempt to help or stop her when she fumbled with the button of his jeans and then pulled the zipper slowly and carefully down over his erection. As blood rushed to her head, Mindy knelt in front of him, hooked her fingers into the waist of his boxers and pulled them and his jeans down to his knees. She gasped when his turgid shaft slapped her in the face. She brushed her nose against him, loving the musky smell of his man flesh.

He moaned at the contact, but when her hand closed around his hot flesh and she aimed the tip toward her mouth, he clutched her face in his hands. "Not so fast, love," he said in a tremulous voice, even as he bent over her to completely remove his jeans and boxers. He placed his hand under her chin and gazed at her with so much love, desire blazed through her. "I want to please you by taking my time kissing every inch of your sweet, little body. I've fantasized about it every day these past eight months."

"Let me do this first. I want to do this for you and for me," Mindy said, gazing up at him while she pumped him slowly and methodically. Without waiting for a response, she ran her tongue across her lips in preparation to devour him as thoroughly as she knew he would devour her when his time came. Satisfied that he would allow her this pleasure, she pressed her mouth to the root of his cock and began a slow steady climb upward, kissing and nipping him gently on her journey to the tip.

He trembled on a deep groan and then stiffened on a sharp intake of air when she pursed her lips over the mushroom head and flicked her tongue across the broad smooth expanse of his man flesh.

"You like that?" she asked, pausing to smile up at him.

"Yes. Oh God, yes, baby," he murmured huskily, placing his hands on her head and tangling his fingers in her hair.

Emboldened by his tremulous response and the tangy taste of pre-cum on her tongue, Mindy began to suck him gently while she stroked her hands along his length. It excited her to give him something special, something she knew he loved receiving from her. Over the years she'd learned how to inflame him with her mouth and hands by controlling the velocity and pressure of her suctions, and the rate and tempo of her stroking. She knew the pleasure points on his body that drove him wild.

Her yearning to please him in every way possible was just as strong and compelling as his to please her, especially tonight after he'd learned even more unpleasant truths about his mother. She was determined to make him forget all the ugliness, and concentrate on the love she was lavishing on him, even if it was just for a while.

As his groans grew deeper and harsher and he began to thrust back and forth pushing more and more of his cock into her mouth, Mindy wrapped her arms around his hips and squeezed his ass cheeks while she bobbed her head up and down. Stepping up her game, she relaxed her mouth, just a fraction when she thrust forward, and clamped down as he drew back. It drove him into a frenzy and he grew hotter and harder with each dive.

"Deeper," he groaned, tightening his hands around her head to better control the speed and depth in which he pumped into her mouth.

She opened wide on a thrust, and a forceful tremor coursed down her body and settled in her sex when the tip made contact with the back of her throat, triggering a copious amount of lubricant inside her mouth. Skillfully, she used the moisture to work her tongue up and down his length, sucking and squeezing while he filled her mouth. She reached one hand under him and gently caressed his balls while she smiled up at him with what she knew was carnal intent in her eyes.

His groans became deep and guttural. His body trembled and jerked. He grew thicker and hotter, and when he began to spasm uncontrollably, Mindy tightened her hold on his buttocks and clamped her mouth around him. It was a sweet thrill to watch his head roll back, his face contort, and his mouth open and close in ecstasy. As his passion rolled through him, she raked her nails along his thighs, across his hips, and up the heaving muscles of his stomach and chest, spiking him on to his finish line.

Knowing that his knees would soon buckle, without interrupting their connection, Mindy pushed him down onto the edge of the bed and leaned into him. A second later, he called out her name, went stiff as a board, then poured his climax down her throat.

Mindy wrapped her hands around his hips and held him tightly as he rocked from the force of his orgasm, and when the pressure of his hand on her head eased, she raised her head and let him fall from her mouth onto his thigh. With a smile of contentment, she dropped soft kisses along his semi-hard length, making it twitch in response. "No mess this time," she drawled as she crawled up his body and kissed him on the lips, giving him a taste of himself.

He drew her hard against his damp, warm body and caressed her shoulders and back and the swell of her buttocks, causing shivers to rush across her skin. "You're a very naughty girl, Mindy Marshall. I have no choice but to punish you for what you just did. I would say a good licking and then a sound pounding would be appropriate."

A pulse vibrated in the core of Mindy's sex. God, she was so hot and wet from blowing him and at the thought of him pounding away deep inside her while she lay trembling beneath him. The blaze of passion in his eyes told her that she'd done her job. She'd made him forget about the dark ugliness of the past and brought him into the light and laughter that presently cloaked them from the rest of the world.

"Bring it on, babe." She taunted him by dragging her breasts across his lips. "Oh God!" she cried in the next breath when his hand closed over one breast while his mouth engulfed the other. He sucked her ravenously into his mouth, taking her deep as his tongue caressed her taut, sensitive nipple, suckling her like an infant who'd been starved to near death.

His erotic gratifying groans sparked a renewed flame in Mindy's veins. She rubbed her lower body against Galen's, sliding her thighs against his shaft until she felt it growing with weight and heat again. "I want you inside me," she whispered as her hand closed around him and she shifted her body to guide him to her pleasure spot.

He stiffened and released her breast, causing them to ache in protest. "Oh, no. You've had your fun, love. It's time I had mine." He flipped her over onto her back and, supporting his weight on his arms and knees, he dipped his head and dropped tantalizing kisses on her forehead before moving to her eyes, and then her cheek, fluttering over the bridge of her nose, like an uncertain butterfly, to the other side, heightening her senses by the mere fact that his lips were now the only part of his body touching hers.

Mindy quivered as his teasing shifted to the corner of her mouth then, as light as a whisper, sidled across her lips to the other quivering corner. He tickled her with his tongue, causing fiery sensations to crawl along her skin, rousing her appetite, fanning her ardor to be loved. When she parted her lips on a sigh of delight, he groaned and settled his mouth possessively over hers, thrusting deep.

A hot ache ripped through Mindy's belly and she moaned as she gave herself over to the drugging effect of Galen's tongue flicking erotically against hers, thrusting back and forth, stroking the insides of her cheeks and the sensitive roof. As the thrilling sensations whipped through her, she closed her eyes and arched her body, trying to connect their sexes, but he shifted his body, placing his right thigh between her legs and pinning his growing erection against her left one.

"You will not make a liar out of me tonight, Mindy," he said on a sensuous chuckle that echoed around and inside her. "I promised to kiss every inch of your sweet sexy body tonight, and that's exactly what I plan to do." His warm lips brushed the sensitive skin of her neck before sliding down to her chest.

Mindy's heart pounded out an erotic rhythm when he went back to her breasts—palming, tweaking, kneading, licking the marbled nipples and then sucking the aching mounds into his mouth, sending a line of fire blazing from her breasts to her belly and into her pulsing sex. As the fire grew, Mindy began to hump against the thigh Galen had stationed between her legs, and before long she was panting and writhing and raking her nails up and down his back as she came in a firestorm of surrender.

"Beautiful," he whispered as he released the breast in his mouth and, while his hands moved restlessly over her body, he dragged his lips across her ribcage, kissing and nibbling his way south, telling her how much he loved her silky, sexy body, how much she turned him on, how much he wanted to taste her, and how anxious he was to feel her love juices flowing into his waiting mouth.

Galen's sensual chant in his sexy British accent sang through Mindy's veins, working such titillating magic on her senses that by the time his hot roaming lips brushed the triangle of curls at the top of her Venus mound and the tip of his tongue grazed her swollen clit, she was writhing on the mattress as a series of powerful electrical shocks ripped through her.

"Lovely, simply lovely," he murmured. Spreading her thighs wider, he settled himself between them and blew his hot breath on her, making her quiver in response. "Now for your punishment as promised." A second later, his mouth closed over the most private, most erotic part of Mindy's anatomy.

She fisted her hands around the sheet and groaned her pleasure out loud as Galen teased her, licked her, ate her, caressed her with his fingers and his tongue, moving up and down, left and right, around and around until her mind went numb and she began to drown in the steaming sensations of his deep tonguing. Unable to do anything else, she began to pant and shake as Galen pushed her toward the peak of her arousal and kept her there, poised at the edge of the abyss for a blissful second, before he eased the pressure and brought her back down to earth.

As she lay on the mattress with electricity arching through her veins, he pressed the heel of one hand into the region just above her groin and began his taunting again—arousing her, teasing her, flicking her until her heart began to thump in her ears and the fire in her body deepened and strengthened. He pushed a finger inside her while lavishing her clit with his lips and tongue, and just when she was about to reach the brink of release, he switched his strategy, delving his tongue deep inside her while grazing her sensitive clit with his magic fingertips.

The combination of tantalizing sensations sent Mindy's heart jackknifing into her throat and her senses reeling with confusion as she bucked and writhed on the bed. Before long, she found herself back on that dangerously spine-tingling, breathtaking precipice of euphoria. He held her there. Suspended. Animated. Her pleasure kept building, swelling to the point where only two choices were available—relief or insanity from the continuous barrage of sweet agony that felt so, so, so, so-o-o good.

Feeling as if her heart would explode from the inside out, Mindy grabbed hold of Galen's head, pushing him deeper and holding him there as she hurled her hips into his face. She groaned out her rapture again and again as the raging fire coiled inside her. "Galen—"

"Come," he said against her. "Come to me, love."

His tongue and his fingers worked their British magic and soon white-hot pleasure was coursing through her in powerful waves, her body undulating with each one, and just as she was about to crash to shore, Galen rose above her, covered her mouth with his and buried his hard cock so deep inside her that she immediately exploded in an awesome downpour of shuddering sensations.

Galen held and kissed her through her orgasm and only when she stopped trembling and her flesh relaxed around him did he turn onto his left side, bringing her onto her right, and arranging her left leg over his hips. This was one of their favorite positions—face-to-face with their hands free to roam and explore each other's bodies—a position in which they had sometimes stayed for long periods, loving and enjoying each other with no hurry for release, just a continuous giving and taking from each other for as long as they could both endure the bliss.

"Now, we make sweet, slow love," he said in a husky voice, his eyes gleaming with passion and promises and love as he began to move slowly inside her.

"Slowly," Mindy agreed as she began to move with him, their faces mere inches apart and with the musky intoxicating smell of male and female love juices lingering on their hot breaths, fanning their need and desire for more of each other.

With their gazes locked, their hands caressed each other lovingly, methodically, sending tingles zinging through each other's veins as their sexual dance created a hypnotic field of indescribable delight that bound their bodies, minds, and souls in a fissure of seraphic joy.

Mindy moaned as she felt Galen grow bigger, longer, stronger inside her, the turgid veins running the length of him generating a delectable friction to the inside of her sizzling sex. Joining her mouth to his for a deeply passionate kiss, she matched him thrust for thrust of hip and tongue.

He shifted his angle just a fraction so that each time the tip of his cock butted her cervix, his pelvis ground into her clit, causing rhapsodic shockwaves of sweet agony to reverberate through her veins. Again and again.

This was lovemaking, she thought, comparing the golden waves of passion that now flowed between them to the frenzied romp on the dining table earlier tonight. In that encounter, they'd been blowing off the steam that had been building up inside them since the night he'd shown up at her mother's house. But this roaming of hands over each other's damp bodies, this swaying together, this dancing to the rhythm of their hearts, this melding of their flesh for an endless period of time, bathed in the fountain of each other's presence and essence—was lovemaking. Electrifying. Galvanizing. Intoxicating. Born from love.

As their moans of pleasure and the speed of their thrusts intensified, Mindy pulled Galen closer, holding him so securely, the heat from his body coursed down the entire length of hers, seeping through the pores of her skin, feeding her hunger, pushing her closer to that flame that would ultimately incinerate her, turning her into an ash pile of desire.

"Oh love, I'm sorry, but I can't dance much longer."

"Neither can I," Mindy confessed as the fire licked at her skin, causing her muscles to contract around him, pump him, massage him, caress him, as she reveled in the delirious enjoyment of his heat and his power.

With a hoarse groan, Galen flipped her onto her back and wrapped her legs around his waist. He laid his body flat against hers, slid his hands beneath her and, clasping her buttocks, he pulled her into him and began to ride her hard and fast like an English jockey spurring his American thoroughbred to the finish line.

Fire blazed through Mindy as he pumped faster and deeper into her tingling, writhing body, pounding her zealously as their moans and groans of ecstasy and their orgasms built. Their damp bodies slapped together in a mating song, and when she started to vibrate from the electrical charges whipping through her, Mindy wrapped her arms around Galen and abandoned herself to the pleasure, the euphoria, the sweetness, the love, and the raw sensuousness of the beautiful man on top of her, his thickness filling her, exciting her, grazing the walls of her sex until their bodies melded into one giant orb of sensitivity.

"Now," he groaned, slamming into her one last time and locking the head of his cock against her cervix.

Mindy's body tightened and she cried out in ecstasy as the sensations of Galen's hot cum pushed her off her pinnacle of desire into a sizzling free-fall of pulsating pleasure.

They came together in a quivering, screaming chorus of love.

Love had returned to Mindy's heart, and passion to Evergreen, at last.

❧

Mindy smiled at her daughter as she hopped out of the SUV parked by the curbside of Evergreen Elementary School. "Have a good day at school, okay? Listen to your teacher and play nice." She pulled Britt's hat down over her ears then handed her her lunchbox.

"Okay. Bye, Mommy. Hey Callie, wait up," she called to one of her friends who'd hopped out of the car ahead of them.

"I didn't know that was you. You got a new car?" Callie asked as she and Britt walked toward the entrance of the school.

"Yeah, it's wicked cool, right?"

"Did you win the lottery or something?"

"My mommy got a new job, and we got a new house with a gigantic playroom. You should come over. And my mom and Galen are getting married, and my nana…"

Mindy grinned as the girls moved out of earshot. *Oh, how the tides had turned.*

"Our friends aren't laughing anymore," Kyle said.

"No, they're not. They're green with envy now."

Kyle glanced across the street to his grandmother's house. "Are you picking us up or are we going to Nana's after school?"

"I'm picking you up. Nana and Phin are leaving for Philly today. Remember he's taking her to meet his family?"

"Oh yeah, I forgot. I'm glad Mr. Phin's going to be our

grandpa. He says we can call him Grandpa even before he and Nana get married. I like him. Do you like him, Mom?"

"Of course. I would like any man who makes my mother happy." Mindy drew the collar of his coat tighter around his neck to keep out the chill.

"If we're not staying at Nana's, who's watching us when you're in school tonight?"

"Galen."

"Is he bringing Geoffrey?" he asked, his eyes wide with excitement.

"Yes. They're spending the night."

"Cool. Galen can help me with my science project. It's neat we're going to have a grandpa and two grandmas, and a daddy and a little brother when you and Galen get married. Our family is growing, Mommy."

Mindy smiled. "Yes, it is. By leaps and bounds."

"Can I be your pageboy like I was for Auntie Tashi in that big wedding?"

"Even better, I want you to give me away to Galen. You have been the only constant man in my life for the past seven years, Kyle Mateus Marshall. Will you do me that honor, baby? That is, if you think Galen deserves me?"

"He deserves you, Mommy, and you deserve him. I love you and Galen so much." He wrapped his arms around her waist and squeezed her tightly.

Blissfully happy and fully alive once again, Mindy pressed his cheek into her belly. "And we love you and your sister and your brother very, very much."

He gazed up at her. "Are you and Nana going to have a double wedding like Auntie Tashi and her friends?"

As much as Mindy loved her mother, there was no way in hell she was sharing her wedding day with her. "No, baby. I want my own special day."

"Are you going to invite Grandma to your wedding?"

"Do you think I should?" she asked.

His nose twitched in thought. "I don't like it when she says bad things about you, Mommy. I want to tell her to stop, but I'm scared. I don't want to go to her house tomorrow night, 'cause she's gonna ask us if we want to live with her again. I don't want to live with her, but I don't want to lie to her 'cause you tell us not to ever lie. Are you going to make us go, Mommy?"

She kissed the worry from his face. "No, son. I will never force you to do anything that makes you uncomfortable." Virginia got the kids one weekend a month and one day out of each week. She was scheduled for tomorrow night, but that was not going to happen. Virginia had to pay the price for trying to turn her children against her and for attempting to take them away from her. She'd warned her last week, and instead of backing off, she'd escalated the war between them. Well, it was payday. "You don't have to see your grandma until you're ready. Now, go on. I have to get to work."

"Bye, Mom! See you later."

"See you, Kyle." Mindy waited until he disappeared into the throng of kids on the playground before she climbed into her car.

An amalgam of emotions battled inside Mindy as she pulled away from the curb. She'd hoped that it wouldn't have to come to this, but Virginia was giving her no choice. The sad thing about the whole affair was that she knew without a doubt that Virginia loved her grandchildren and that they loved her.

A part of Mindy wanted to think that, in Virginia's head, she was doing what she thought was best for her grandchildren. But the other part of her knew that the old bat was on a mission to make Mindy suffer the pain of losing her children, as she herself had suffered—was still suffering—from losing Kyle.

Virginia could have chosen to deal with her pain in a more

productive manner by opening her heart to the mother of the only grandchildren she would ever have. Instead, she'd chosen to try to destroy Mindy through her grandchildren. Mindy's hands tightened around the steering wheel as she drove around Pearl Circle toward the Mannis River Bridge.

She'd kept quiet in the past and allowed Virginia to walk all over her, perhaps because Kyle and Britt were too young to understand what was going on. But they were older now, and their little minds had caught up to Virginia's hatred for their mother.

What kind of message would she be sending to Kyle and Britt if she continued to act as if it was okay for anyone to disrespect her?

Not a good message at all.

It was her job as their mother to protect them from evil, even, or especially, if that evil was their grandmother.

CHAPTER EIGHTEEN

At Mindy's knock, Virginia appeared at the door with a coffee mug in her hand. She cracked the storm door just enough for their voices to carry through.

"Virginia." Mindy had no need to grovel for babysitting favors. She would have her own full-time nanny once Sybil moved into the in-law apartment as she and Galen had discussed yesterday afternoon.

Virginia frowned as she eyed the SUV parked in front of her house. "I didn't hear your old jalopy sputtering to a stop. You borrowed somebody's car?"

"Something like that."

She brought her scornful eyes back to Mindy. "You're wasting my heat," she said, stepping away from the door.

Mindy went inside and immediately felt as if she were being swallowed up by the past when she saw the pictures of Kyle and his father hanging on the walls and on table tops. Virginia had made a shrine of her house. She pressed her hands against her belly as her nerves tensed. She'd once loved Kyle as much as she now loved Galen, and she still missed the father of her children. She would always miss him.

"Why are you at my house this early in the morning, Mindy? What do you want?"

Mindy took a deep audible breath as she slid back into the present to find Virginia looking her up and down. Mindy was tempted to remove her coat so that Virginia could see her tailored dress, and the diamond necklace around her neck that Galen had given her yesterday—a necklace he'd brought from London. But she wasn't here to rub her happiness in Virginia's face. She was here to set her straight.

"Are my grandkids okay?" Virginia asked.

"Your grandchildren are perfect. In fact they couldn't be more perfect. I plan to keep them that way. You're not going to fill their minds with poison anymore."

"What is that supposed to mean?" Virginia set her cup down on the coffee table and placed her hands on her hips, ready to fight.

But Mindy didn't have to fight. She just had to lay down the ground rules. "You asked my children if they wanted to live with you. You told them that sleeping in the same bed and room with me is unhealthy. You made them feel as if they were less than human. You told them that you were going to talk to a lawyer to see if you could take them away from me. Do you have any idea how much you scared them?"

"They didn't seem scared when I brought it up. They said they would like to have their own bedrooms. I have room to spare, so—"

"I don't give a hoot what you have, Virginia. What makes you think they would choose you over me, their mother, who's been there for them since the moment they were born, just to have their own bedroom?"

"Why don't you ask them?" she asked, jutting her chin with a confidence Mindy knew she shouldn't be feeling.

"Kyle just told me that he doesn't want to see you anymore because you're always saying bad things about me."

"I only speak the truth, Mindy. If Child Services knew that—"

"Here's a truth you should chew on, Virginia. Perhaps if you'd been a better mother to your son, he would be alive today. Like you said, you have room to spare and yet you didn't offer us shelter. If you'd taken us in, I wouldn't have needed a ride from the supermarket that day when Danny tried to rape me, and Kyle wouldn't have gone after him. So if you want to blame somebody for his death, blame yourself."

"You little bitch!"

Mindy ducked and jumped aside as Virginia swung her fist at her, only to end up banging her knuckles into the door.

"See, that there?" Mindy barked, wielding her hands in the air. "That right there is why I'm cutting off your access to my kids. I warned you. You will not see them until you respect me. You don't have to like me, but you will respect me, damn it."

"You can't do that. I have rights."

"Actually, you don't have any rights. My children's last name is Marshall. You didn't want them to have your family name if Kyle and I weren't married. Remember the big fight you and Kyle had right here in this living room? That broke his heart, but he respected you and wanted to honor you over his own children's birthright."

It had hurt Mindy when Kyle had caved in to his mother, but he'd assured her that it was just to keep the peace since they were still minors. He'd promised her that as soon as they got married he would change Kyle's birth certificate. He died before he could keep his promise.

Virginia's nostrils flared as she nursed her red bruised knuckles. "My son's name is on their birth certificates. You can't deny me visiting rights."

"I *can*, and I *am*. And just in case you think I have no one in my corner to fight for me, think again." She ripped off her glove and shoved her engagement ring under Virginia's nose. "Galen is back. We are engaged. I will be an Andretti soon. You know they have a ton of power around here. Try anything, *anything* at all, and they'll crush you like a cricket first, and then ask questions later."

She loved the helpless expression on Virginia's face. "You and I will schedule visiting time, right here in this house you've kept off-limits to me for eight years. Until I'm satisfied that you're over whatever it is you have against me, Kyle and Britt will remain off limits to you. Don't call me. I'll call you when I'm damn good and ready."

Mindy walked out of Virginia's house and headed for Evergreen Cemetery.

A short while later, she stood at Kyle's grave with tears rolling down her face. "I'm sorry for the way I spoke to your mother, Kyle, but she has gone way too far. I took as much as I could, but I can't keep quiet any longer now that her hate for me is affecting our children. Kyle is scared that she would force him to live with her, and he's distraught about the things she says about me. You loved me, and you loved our children, and I know for certain that you would not approve of your mother trying to take them from me."

She sniffled and swiped her hand across her nose. "Both of our mothers turned their backs on us when I got pregnant, but our love for each other and for our kids was stronger than their disappointment in us. My mother has finally come around, and I pray to God that yours will soon, because for your sake, I want her to have a relationship with your children. But if she doesn't…" Mindy pressed her lips together, unable to finish her sentence. She was sure Kyle knew what she would have to do.

She pulled off her gloves and held up her hand with her

engagement ring. "You know I will always love you. You were my first, my one and only love until Galen Carmichael came along. He reminded me what it felt like to be loved, desired, appreciated. He screwed up," she said, "but after understanding why, I forgave him, and now we're engaged to be married."

She inhaled deeply. "The best thing of all is that he loves Kyle and Britt as if they were his own children. And I know this might be hard for you to hear, baby, but they love him, too. If you were here, I know you would have been the best dad to them. Galen is the best alternative to you. He is the father they need. I promise to never let them forget you, Kyle. They will always know that our love created them, and that you loved them more than anything in this world." She wiped her cheeks as more tears rolled down her face. "We can't live in the past any longer, baby. We have to move forward, but we will take you with us. You will be in our hearts, always and forever."

Mindy stood at the foot of Kyle's grave, doubled over as the sobs racked her body—sobs for the past filled with loss, pain, regret, and sorrow, and then sobs for a future filled with happiness, light, and peace.

When a deep profound calm finally settled on her, she raised her head and stared at the headstone. *Kyle Grainger. Loving Son and Father. Gone Too Soon. 1993 - 2013.*

She moved to the headstone and, pressing her fingers to her lips, she kissed them three times and traced them along Kyle's name. "So long for now from me, Kyle Mateus, and Brittany Angelica," she said, before turning to head back to her car.

She couldn't say goodbye. There could never be goodbye when she would see him every day in the smiles on her children's faces and feel him in the warmth of their hugs and kisses.

❧

"Come on in, Galen."

Galen had been dating Mindy for almost three years, yet this was only the third time, and the second in two weeks that he had set foot into Pamela Marshall's house. The first—when Mindy had brought him here to introduce him to her mother—had begun amicably until Pamela had learned that he was Luciano's and Judith's bastard son. He did not blame her one bit now that he knew the root cause of her hatred for him and his mother. He hoped for a different outcome this time.

He glanced at the card table covered with a cream table cloth, and set for four. Pamela had called yesterday to invite him and Mindy to lunch with her and Phin so they could celebrate their engagements. They were having takeout since she and Phin were leaving for Philadelphia this afternoon. But this morning, Pamela had called and asked him to arrive an hour before Phin and Mindy.

Even though he'd known that he and Pamela were due a private face-o-face to talk about his mother, and about their non-relationship, Galen was a bit apprehensive about what he would learn from the only person in this world who knew the true Judith Carmichael, who knew that the image she had projected to the rest of the world was a farce. It was damn ironic that Pamela Marshall was *that* person.

"May I take your jacket?"

"Of course. Thank you." Galen unzipped his jacket and handed it to his future-mother-in-law.

"Have a seat," she said as she hung it on the coatrack near the door.

A sweet thrill nipped Galen in the gut as he eased down on the sofa on which he and Mindy had committed numerous acts of carnal debauchery when it used to take up space in her Granite Falls apartment. Acts that were similar in heat and intensity to the ones committed on the new sofa in her lake house yesterday afternoon.

"Would you like something to drink?" Mrs. Marshall asked.

"No thank you. I'm good. I can wait until Phin and Mindy get here."

Mrs. Marshall sat on the opposite end of the sofa and eyed him circumspectly. "Thanks for coming by earlier. I hope I didn't pull you away from anything too important," she said, stretching her legs out and crossing her ankles.

Galen mimicked her by stretching his legs out in front of him. It was a treat to feel comfortable in her presence instead of being on edge. "Nothing that I can't jump right back into," he stated with a warm smile.

She looked away for a few tense moments. "I'm sure Mindy told you everything I told her about your mother."

"She did. We are learning not to keep anything from each other. Keeping secrets is what got us in trouble in the first place." Mindy had also admitted to him that she'd told her mother about Geoffrey. *Half the story at least.* Mindy had astutely not divulged any information about Trix's crimes and incarceration, or about the Frasers. Not that he didn't trust Mrs. Marshall, who'd kept her secrets for over twenty-five years, but the fewer people who knew about his trouble in England, the better. He didn't need anyone slipping up and telling Geoffrey about his mother sometime in the future. It was his job, and his alone to be the bearer of that bad news to his son. "She told me you know about Geoffrey and the circumstances surrounding his conception."

"Yes. I probably wouldn't have believed how low some women would stoop to get what they want if I hadn't seen your mother in action. I'm glad you and Mindy were able to work it out. That girl loves you. She stood by you even though I warned her against you."

"And I love her for loving me when everyone else was against me. But I give you the credit for us being able to move forward this quickly, Mrs. Marshall. You advised Mindy to forgive me, and to let me love her."

"Too bad I didn't do that two years ago, or even before then. I had the power to stop your mother, but I didn't exercise it. It would have saved us all a lot of heartache."

It definitely would have made a difference two years ago since he would have known that Aunt Gertrude's story was a big fat lie the moment she'd opened her mouth. He would not have been consumed by rage and gone to Trix's club that night. She wouldn't have had the chance to drug and seduce him. There would have been no need for him to sue Mass, and their relationship would have been on the right track years ago. He and Mindy might be married by now and have at least one child already. His grandfather would be alive. Trix wouldn't be in prison for the rest of her life. Galen wouldn't have been kidnapped and beaten for eight months.

And Geoffrey wouldn't have been born.

Galen trembled on the latter hypothetical, even as his mind reeled with one even more significant thought. *If* Pamela had stopped Judith when she'd first started down her destructive path, Giuliana, Aria, and Pamela's child would be alive today, and neither he nor Mindy would have been conceived. Others had been sacrificed for their existence. Galen suspected that that conflicting truism would plague him for the rest of his life.

"Yes, it would have saved us all a lot of heartaches, but you were in a different place, Mrs. Marshall." There was no need to list the facts that would make her feel worse than she already did. "You were a young single mother, worried about losing your job and about causing trouble for your family. From what I've heard about my father, I know he would have put your cousin out of business for hiring Judith. You were thinking about your own survival which was the right thing to do."

"It doesn't ease my guilt for not stopping the train before it left the station, but thanks for understanding, Galen." She looked away for a moment. "I should have known you were nothing like your mother from the way you took care of my daughter and my grandchildren. I apologize for the way I've been treating you. I hope you can forgive me."

"There's nothing to forgive, Mrs. Marshall. In fact, I'm the one who needs to apologize for all the horrible things Judith did to you. She was a monster. I'm convinced of that now. We are all victims of Judith's diabolical world." Galen reached across and placed his hands on Pamela's resting on her lap.

She jumped at his touch, the first meaningful and deliberate physical connection between them. But after a few strained seconds ticked by, she relaxed and patted his hand. "You're marrying my daughter. You can drop the 'Mrs. Marshall' and call me Pamela."

Galen sat back as they broke the affectionate contact. "Okay, Pamela." He wondered mildly if she would ever suggest that he call her "Mom." He hoped not, mainly because of the nature of her relationship with his mother. That would be eerie.

"There's another reason I asked you to come early," Pamela said. "Your mother wrote a letter to your father about a year after you were born."

"And how would you know? Did he share it with you?"

"I found it in the trashcan under his desk. He obviously didn't care about anything she had to say. He was still grieving for his wife and baby daughter, while trying to comfort his heartbroken little boy who'd lost his mother." Pamela picked up an envelope from the lamp table and handed it to him.

Galen stared at his mother's beautiful flowery handwriting. It might have been the only beautiful thing about her. "You never opened it," he said, turning it over in his hand.

"It wasn't mine to open."

"Why did you take it?"

"Maybe I hoped it would be another nail in her coffin," she said in a neutral tone.

"Why didn't you give it to Mass when you gave him the tapes?"

"I'd forgotten all about it until Saturday night after Mindy went home. I tore my house apart until I found it in the bottom of a box in the back of my closet. From the weight and thickness, I would guess she sent him pictures of you. Pictures he never saw, didn't want to see."

Galen was unable to comment on his father's decision to not open the letter. "Thank you, Pamela." He folded the envelope and tucked it into the back pocket of his jeans, not certain if he himself wanted to open in. At least the many questions he'd had about his father when he'd discovered he'd been alive for the first seventeen years of his life were now answered. His father had never wondered about him. Never thought about him. He'd never seen a picture of him. He hadn't known his birthdate. He just hadn't given a damn about him.

His mother, on the other hand, had cared about him. She'd loved him. At least he had her filial love to hold on to. He was just glad that his childhood memories of her were pleasant ones. He glanced at Pamela. "Mindy said there was a time when you and my mother were friends—when she first came to Evergreen. During that time, did she ever tell you about her life in London? All my family is gone and I'm trying to make sense of her life, figure out why she was the way she was. Did she ever talk of some trauma in her childhood? Mistreatment from someone, anyone?"

Pamela shook her head. "She didn't talk much about her childhood, or any aspect of her life, for that matter. Except…" Her forehead furrowed and the corners of her eyes crinkled.

"Yes? Are you recalling something?" He sat forward.

"I um—I remember asking her how she ended up in Evergreen."

"She followed an American boy here when his semester abroad ended. I know that much."

"I meant the reason she decided to leave England in the first place."

"What did she say?"

"She told me that she was dating an aristocrat who attended her university."

"King's College. That's where she studied."

"She was head-over-heels in love with him." Pamela snorted derisively. "Knowing Judith, I'd say it was his status in society and his money that she was in love with. Anyway, the week before graduation, she caught him with her roommate."

"Oh dear. That must have ripped her apart."

"I think she was more angry than hurt. Judith wasn't grieving for a lost love or from a broken heart. She was like a child whose sister had walked into her room and taken one of her dolls. She was angry and she wanted revenge."

"And so she went on a rampage hurting other women the same way she'd been hurt."

"Just imagine what the world would be like if we all reacted to hurt that way."

"It would be a horrible place."

"We have much to be grateful for." Her eyes twinkled with warmth as she smiled at him.

"Yes, we do, Pamela." Galen reveled in the first authentic smile Pamela Marshall had ever bestowed upon him. He hoped it was the first of many to come. Anxiety to read his mother's letter to his father was ripe within him, but he felt as if he and Pamela had both reached their *Judith* limit for the day. So he chose to steer the conversation to a more present and pleasant topic. "Thank you for convincing Mindy to give me a second chance."

She chuckled. "I didn't convince that girl of anything. She was going to take you back the minute she opened the door and found you standing on my porch a week ago. It was just a matter of time."

"Perhaps, but your finding happiness a second time and encouraging her to move out of the past expedited our reunion." His body reacted vigorously as the images of that reunion on Mindy's dining table, in her bed, on her couch, and on her four-season bedroom balcony all weekend long, flashed before his eyes. He crossed his legs. "Congratulations on your engagement, Pamela. I can't wait to meet Phin. Mindy speaks very highly of him."

Her eyes lit up even more as she gazed at her ring. "He's a keeper. I'm one very lucky woman, for sure. And speaking of—I think he's here," she added at the sound of a car door slamming out front.

"I'll help him. You go freshen up," he stated with a smile as Pamela patted down her curly hair and pinched some color into her cheeks.

"Thanks, Galen." She disappeared around a corner.

Galen chuckled at the fact that, even at her age, Pamela's number-one concern was to look the best for her man. He understood why when the door opened and a tall, handsome, lean jock with a full head of salt-and-pepper hair and dark brown eyes entered, his hands loaded with bags.

Galen rushed to assist him. "You must be Mr. O'Henry," he said, taking a couple of the bags and leading the way to the dining area.

"It's Phin. Everyone calls me Phin," he said as they set the bags on the table.

"It's a pleasure, Phin," Galen said, as the men exchanged a hearty handshake.

"It's nice to finally meet you, Galen. But I feel like I've known you ever since I met Pamela."

"How so?" Galen asked as they began to unpack the food from Meat & Green—a local farm-to-table restaurant.

"Kyle wouldn't shut up about you. If I didn't know the truth, I would have thought you were the boy's father. That kid loves you to pieces."

"And I love him and Brittany as if they were my own children."

"That goes without saying." Phin stopped what he was doing and met Galen's stare. "I knew your father personally."

The world was indeed small. "Did you once work at Andretti Industries?"

"Good Lord, no. I've been a therapist all my life." He resumed unpacking his bag. "Thirty-seven years ago when my partner and I were looking for funding for Optimum Results, your father was the only one who responded to our proposals. He promised to fund us as long as we made our services affordable to low-income families, and free to those who were uninsured and or couldn't pay at all."

"Not a promising way to start a business."

"That's exactly how Chip and I felt. We were fresh out of school and buried to our eyeballs in student loans. But we thought, you know, this man is one of the richest in the world, so he must know something that we green tomatoes don't. We signed. He funded. And after a few years of struggle, we began receiving some high-paying clients that included famous athletes vacationing in the area who'd heard about us through family, acquaintances, friends, and friends of friends. Before long, we were catering to millionaires and homeless alike, sometimes together in the same group therapy sessions. We had more patients than we could handle in care and space. We bought a bigger building and hired more staff. Huh!" he uttered on a chuckle. "It finally dawned on Chip and me that it wasn't about the money up front, but about the care and the services we provided. If you provided something better than your competitors, your demand would soon outweigh your supply. That's when the money start rolling in. Your father taught us that very valuable lesson."

"Sounds like him, from stories I've heard from my brother." Luciano had cared about his immediate community and was always striving to make it better. Too bad he hadn't felt the same way about his other son. Even though his father had provided for him financially, that dull ache of abandonment he knew he would never be able to shake, settled deep inside Galen's soul.

Totally oblivious to Galen's inner struggles, Phin continued. "I'm not a millionaire, but I make a very good living and I was able to give my late wife a spectacular life. We traveled all over the world." His voice faded to a gentle murmur.

"I didn't know you were a widower."

"It was a while ago that she passed."

"I'm sorry. Did you have children?"

"No. She suffered from leukemia." A faraway look appeared in his eyes. "But my sister and my brother's kids filled the void, somewhat." Then as if to shut the door on the past, he said in a livelier voice, "Hard to believe that both Pam and I knew your father, and that we lived within ten miles of each other for decades and yet our paths never crossed until she, a low-income patient in need of therapy, walked into my center five months ago." He wagged his head. "After Maureen, I never thought I would find another woman who would make my heart tremble."

"Lucky for you, I came along," Pamela said, sneaking up beside Phin.

"Luckier for me, darling."

Galen's heart beat with tenderness as he watched the older couple embrace and kiss as if they were nineteen years old. He hoped he and Mindy would be that in love with each other when they themselves were old and gray.

"Luckiest for me," Galen stated as the storm door rattled. In a record minute, he was on the porch enveloping Mindy in his arms and kissing her as if he hadn't seen her in ages. "I missed you, baby," he said, finally coming up for air, while keeping her locked in his arms.

"I can tell," she said, rubbing her belly against his growing erection.

"Don't tempt me," he stated, easing a little away from her.

"How did your talk with my mom go?" she asked, reaching up to brush his curl from his forehead.

"Very well." He caught her hand and kissed her palm before lacing their fingers together. "She said I could call her Pamela."

"That's better than very well. That's extremely well," she said with a giggle. "And Phin?"

"He's a peach."

"Isn't he? My mom is so blessed." Her eyes narrowed. "You can ask, Galen."

"What?"

"You know *what*. You want to know why I didn't tell you that Phin was African-American."

"Not at all. I've accepted the fact that jungle fever runs rampant in these twin town and within both our families."

"It does, doesn't it?" She grinned.

"What I want to know is why you didn't tell me Phin was so bloody handsome and strong and fit."

Her eyes lit up with laughter. "He is all that, and more. I don't see Phin as an African-American man, no more that I see you as a Caucasian English man. He's simply a man—a good-hearted, kind, and gentle man who loves my mother and makes her happy. We're just people, no matter our ethnic makeup."

"Amen to that," a deep voice said behind them.

"Phin!" Mindy broke away from Galen and ran straight into Phin's arms.

Galen went back into the house and closed the door, shutting out the cold and the rest of the world.

"You hungry, baby girl?" Phin smiled down at Mindy.

"Starving," she answered.

"Okay then, but before we sit down to eat, I feel a family hug coming on. Get in here, Pammy. You, too, son," he added, winking at Galen.

Galen choked up as he joined the circle and felt Pamela's and Phin's arms lock around him. It was the first time in his life that a man, other than his grandfather, had called him *son*.

"Let's eat." Phin led Mindy to the table. "You sit here little angel."

"Galen." Pamela took his hand in hers as if she'd been doing it for ages. "Have you and Mindy set a date yet?"

"Yes. Next Saturday." Galen's heart leaped with happiness as he felt the acceptance flowing from Pamela's heart to his.

"So soon?" Phin asked, as he walked back from the kitchen with a pitcher of iced tea, and filled their glasses.

Galen seated Pamela and then took his seat across from Mindy while Phin sat across from Pamela.

"Galen and I don't see the sense in waiting." Mindy reached across the table and threaded her fingers through his. "We love each other and we want to start growing our family right away."

"Then next Saturday it is," Pamela said. "You are young and we don't want another child being born out of wedlock in this family, even though one may already have been conceived. Let's say grace," she added, putting the matter to bed.

Galen took Pamela's hand in his left and squeezed her

daughter's in his right. *This was what family felt like.* He loved this family that lived next to the old railroad tracks in Evergreen just as much as he loved the one residing on Mount Reservoir in Granite Falls.

❧

Galen sat hunched over on the sofa in the bedroom, staring at the unopened letter in his hand. Part of him wanted to toss it into the trash as his father had done twenty-odd years ago, but another part of him needed to know what his mother had written to his father. He and Mindy had pledged to put the past behind them and concentrate on the future, but that was before he knew about the letter.

He could have lived the rest of his life and never known about it and he would have been okay, but he knew that if he destroyed it without opening it, he would be wondering for the rest of his life. Mass had said that sometimes it was best not to know the answers to troubling questions; however, he'd also said that he'd only been able to find peace after he'd found the answer to the one question that had plagued him for two decades. Galen needed to know if his mother had somehow grown a conscience and had apologized to Luciano for destroying his life.

Nobody was perfect, but it was every child's wish that his or her parents were basically good, decent people, and that they at least would show remorse for bad behavior. From what Galen had heard from others, including Massimo *and* from Phin today, Luciano was a decent man who had helped others succeed in life. Massimo had called him a loving and compassionate father and husband, with one great sin—infidelity—which Luciano had spent the last eighteen years of his life regretting.

Galen turned the envelope over in his hand, running his fingers around what he suspected to be the outline of photos inside. He told himself that it might have been guilt that had kept his father from reaching out to him, that perhaps getting to know Galen would have been a constant reminder of how badly he'd screwed up. Perhaps not knowing anything about his illegitimate son had been Luciano's penance for his one great sin, or perhaps he'd simply been trying to protect Massimo—his legitimate heir —from more shame and scandal.

On the other hand, Galen had yet to hear one good word about his mother from anyone who'd known her. Deep in his heart he wanted to believe that she'd felt at least one ounce of guilt for tearing the Andretti family apart. He hoped she'd expressed some remorse in her letter to his father.

"I'm so tired. I could sleep for a whole week."

Galen glanced up as Mindy walked out of the ensuite, wearing a white satin nightgown.

"That's not surprising, love," he said, going over to help her remove the decorative pillows from the bed and toss them on the floor. "You've had a tough week, physically and emotionally. Dealing with my betrayal, learning the ropes of a new job, and catching up on schoolwork all weekend would have worn out even the most fit person."

"Don't forget catching up on us." She smiled with beautiful candor as she got under the covers and rested her back against the padded white headboard.

"That too." He felt a sweeping pull in his groin as he thought of the numerous times they'd made love over the weekend, especially yesterday when they'd spent the entire day in bed. "At least you don't have to plan our wedding," he said, kicking off his slippers. He sat on top of the covers and leaned his back against the headboard. "Weddings by Desire is taking care of everything and you've already picked out your dress. You'll have me and a full-time live-in nanny to take care of the kids. All you need to do is concentrate on work and school."

ANA E ROSS

"It was a treat to come home and be able to relax with a glass of wine over a hot meal while you got the kids ready for bed. I haven't had that luxury since you left. Thanks for taking care of our kids. You're a good dad."

"You don't need to thank me, love." Galen stroked her cheek. "I learned how to be a good parent from watching you."

Her eyes shifted to the envelope in his other hand. "What's that? Something concerning Carmichael's Initiative?"

"I wish. Unfortunately, my mother's ghost is still haunting me." He shook the envelope. "She sent this to my father about a year after I was born."

"But it's unopened," she said, taking the envelope and inspecting it closely. "Where'd you get it?"

"Your mother gave it to me today before you and Phin arrived for lunch."

Her lips puckered. "My mother? Where did *she* get it? Or should I even ask?" She handed it back to him.

"She fished it out of my father's trash. He'd really meant it when he told Judith that he wanted nothing to do with her, or me."

She scooted over and laid her head on his chest. "Galen, I'm sure if Luciano had met you, he would have loved you. Maybe he was afraid of betraying the memories of his wife and the child he'd lost because of what he'd done."

Galen kissed her forehead. "I tell myself that, too, to ease my pain of abandonment. But since I've had the letter, I've been wondering if my mother had grown a conscience and admitted to calling Giuliana hours before she died. If that's the case, I'm somewhat relieved that my father hadn't read it."

Mindy sat up and stared at him. "Oh my God, you're right. To think of what Luciano might have done if he'd known Judith was directly responsible for his wife's and baby's deaths. He might have had her killed."

"I don't think he would have killed her, but he probably would have cut off all financial support, or worse, taken me away from her and sent me to Timbuktu, just to make her feel the same kind of pain he was feeling."

"If she confessed, then I'm glad he didn't read it," Mindy said. "Your life would have turned out differently and we might not have met. I can't imagine living my life without you."

"Nor I you, love," he said, squeezing her tightly.

"Let's find out and then put it behind us like we've done with everything else," she said.

Sweat coated Galen's brow as he ripped open the envelope. There were three photos of him inside—one of the day he was born, one of him at six months old, and one of him at his first year's birthday party. He handed them to Mindy.

"You were so cute. Geoffrey looks just like you," she said softly.

"Yes, he does."

"Is there a letter?"

Galen reached into the envelope and pulled out a folded sheet of paper. His fingers shook as he unfolded it and held it up so both he and Mindy could read it together.

My Dearest, Sweetest Luciano,

I'm sorry to hear about the deaths of your wife and child, but perhaps it was God's will to take them out of this world to make room for you and me and our darling son to be together. I would have written before, but I thought I should give you a little time to get over them. Here are a few pictures of our son, Galen. I think he looks a lot like you. All you have to do is say the word and we will both be in your arms in a matter of hours. I will always love you, Luke.

Yours Forever,

Judith.

Galen's thoughts tasted like gall as disappointment tunneled through him. He crumbled the letter into a ball.

"Oh Galen. I'm so sorry," Mindy whispered.

"I'm not surprised." He rose from the bed, walked across the room, and tossed the letter into the fireplace. Surprisingly, he experienced a huge wave of relief as he watched all hopes for his mother's redemption turn to ashes in the flames. She was who she was and nothing and no one could ever change that.

Galen strode back to the bed and shrugged out of his robe before getting under the covers. He gathered Mindy into his arms, delighted to find her naked. "It's over," he said.

She caressed his face and traced her fingers along the high bridge of his nose and the strong contours of his chin. "It's just beginning, my love."

Their lips met and their hands roamed, seeking out the pleasure points on each other's bodies until their breathing became labored and moans of pleasure filtered through the room.

"I thought you were tired," Galen said as Mindy straddled his hips and reached behind her to close her hands around his erection.

"Never too tired for you, love," she whispered, rising up slightly to place his tip at the wet hot mouth of her body. "Never too tired," she reiterated as she dropped her hips, taking him deep inside her.

"Oh yes," Galen moaned as he felt his cock burrow deep inside her succulent sex. He held her hips as he began to rock up inside her, groaning, as her muscles clamped around him, loving him, appreciating him like no other woman had ever done, would ever do.

"Please me," she whispered, throwing her head back as desire built inside her.

His hands closed over her taut swollen breasts and he gave himself over to her loving, knowing that all the hope he needed in this world came from pleasing Mindy.

EPILOGUE

"Close your eyes and tilt your head back a little, Mindy."

"You're the boss, Riah," Mindy quipped, following the directions of her makeup specialist who'd taken over from Marcy, Mindy's hair stylist forty-five minutes ago.

Riah and Marcy had worked in the salon at Granite Falls Country Club for twelve years until a years ago, when they'd taken the entrepreneurial leap and started their own hair and makeup salon in downtown Evergreen, not far from the street where they'd grown up.

Instead of patronizing the country club like most of the upperclass did, Mindy had decided to support the local establishment and had hired the women to do her hair and makeup for her wedding last year, and her mother's as well. Then tonight, Mindy had summoned Elegant-U Hair and Beauty Salon to the third-floor private salon of her lakeside mansion to prepare her for her very first official socialite event.

"You ready to see the results?" Riah asked.

Mindy opened her eyes and smiled. "Well, yeah."

Riah placed a small mirror in Mindy's hand and swiveled the beauty chair around.

Mindy turned her head from side to side to inspect both her hairdo and her makeup and then caught Riah's gaze in the vanity mirror. "Oh my gosh, Riah, you guys have really outdone yourselves. I look like a…"

"Goddess." Riah grinned as she unsnapped and removed a white cape from around Mindy. "Those other women at that gala tonight will have nothing on you, girl. Thanks for trusting me and Marcy. Once folks found out that we did a billionaire wedding party, our business has boomed." She began to put away the makeup, brushes, and other apparatus she'd used to transform Mindy.

Mindy got up from the beauty chair, reached into the pocket of her robe and pulled out a wad of bills. "There's no doubt that networking helps to grow a business, but all the credit belongs to you and Marcy. Your work speaks for itself," she said, placing the tip into Riah's hand.

"Thanks, Mindy. Speaking of, we're thinking of opening up salon number-two in Vermont. We would really like some marketing research help from Carmichael Initiative. You think your husband would be interested in working with such a small company?" she asked as she picked up a tote from the counter and shoved the tip inside it.

"Of course," Mindy said without hesitation. Carmichael Initiative had landed a few big corporations in the past months, Weisz Foods Incorporated included—thanks to her—but Galen also had a strong desire to work with smaller businesses. "I'll make sure Galen gives you a huge discount," Mindy said as she walked Riah to the stairs that led to the first floor. "Expect a call from him soon."

"Thanks, Mindy." She gave Mindy a quick hug. "Remember, do not put the dress on over your head. Step into it. Can't have you messing up our work."

"I will. And thanks so much," Mindy called as Riah descended the stairs.

With butterflies fluttering in her belly she walked next door to her dressing room and over to three life-size fiberglass mannequins.

She surveyed the one displaying the dress her husband had bought for her to wear tonight—a fully sequined silk Valentino gown with a sweetheart neckline, ruffled shoulder straps, and a seamed high waist with an A-line skirt. And of course it was red, Mindy thought with a smile as her gaze continued to the floor where the hem of the dress partially hid a pair of Christian Louboutin gold metallic sandals. The dress was complemented with a GIA ruby and diamond platinum pendant and a matching pair of earrings that Galen had given Mindy when their first child was born. A gold Kate Spade clutch—a birthday gift from Shaina last year—swayed from the extended arm.

It was hard to believe that it was only one year and four months ago that Mindy's life had been going in a completely different direction—not a totally bad direction, mind you, just one that would have been far less exciting than this one. It was even harder to believe that she'd accomplished so many goals and reached as many milestones in such a short time.

Well, it really isn't that hard to believe since love, happiness, diligence, and an abundance of support were the driving catalysts behind your achievements.

"True," Mindy said out loud as she slid out of her robe and then removed the matching black silk and lace bra and panties, and a pair of garters from the lingerie mannequin.

Just last month, she'd graduated with honors from Evergreen Community College with a Bachelor's degree in Marketing and Management. Prior to that achievement, she'd launched the opening of TP Studios, formerly known as Tashi's Photography.

And now with the help of Carmichael Initiative—her husband's nationally and soon-to-be internationally recognized marketing research company—TP Studios would be opening its second location in Boston in eight months.

As she'd become more comfortable in her leadership role, Mindy had talked Tashi into offering internships to photography technology students from Evergreen Community College, and from both Evergreen and Granite Falls high schools. The program had worked so well last year that they had opened it up to the surrounding areas for the upcoming school year with plans to expand to the neighboring states. TP Studios was garnering so much attention that Mindy knew that it was only a matter of time before they branched out across the country.

Mindy unfolded a pair of thigh-high, lace-top silk stockings from the arm of the lingerie mannequin and sat down on her vanity chair. There was one event in the past year that had brought her a mixture of joy and sadness.

Last summer, Safi was discovered in the lobby of Hotel Andreas by a guest, Fabien Chaput, who worked for one of the biggest modeling agencies in Europe. Fabien had been smitten by Safi's exotic looks and had offered her a contract, on the spot, to become a runway model. With her flair for the dramatic, Safi hadn't needed too much training on how to work the runway and by October last year she'd been booked solid for shows in Paris, Milan, London, Tokyo, and Berlin. She was scheduled for shows in Rome, Sao Paulo, Barcelona, Los Angeles and New York City for this year. Mindy had promised to meet her in New York City for a couple days of fun, and also for Safi to spend time with her goddaughter.

Even though she and Safi talked often on the phone and texted every single day, sometimes just to say, *Hey girl, thinking of you,* they missed each other terribly. They'd hung out in

December when Safi had come home for Christmas, and then again in Milan during Easter school break when the Carmichaels and the Andrettis had visited the family's home in Bellagio. Now that she was done with school, Mindy hoped to visit with Safi as often as both their busy lives would allow.

Mindy attached the last suspender clip to her lace-top stockings, stood to her feet, and took her dress off the mannequin. As she stepped into it, and then slid her feet into her sandals, she wondered what Tashi, Michelle, Yasmine, Kaya, Shaina, and Desire would be wearing to the five-thousand-dollar-a-plate fundraiser at the Fontaine Center in Granite Falls tonight.

She unclasped the necklace and the earrings from the mannequin and walked over to the wall of mirrors on one side of her dressing room as she thought of the day last March when she'd been officially inducted into the billionaires brides club. Mindy felt closer to those six wonderful women, who treated each other like sisters, than she'd ever thought possible. But being a part of that circle came with commitments. Each member had to either join an already established charity organization or start one of her own. *Opportunity for All* was their motto.

Michelle had been the first philanthropist among them when she founded her Children of the Future Foundation that catered to disadvantaged children around the globe. Kaya's One Spoonful at a Time fed the homeless and stocked homeless shelters. Shaina, a former math teacher, founded the Adopt a Teacher Project and donated funds for supplies and improvement for low-income schools. Yasmine's Lawyer Up provided free legal advice and representation for the poor. And just last year, Desire formed You're Invited, an organization that hosted birthday parties for kids whose parents can't afford to. Scouts and agents roamed the country in search of benefactors for the charities. Since Mindy was the only wife with a career, she'd been offered exemption. She'd declined and had instead joined Tashi in running the Evelyn Holland Haven for Single Mothers.

It gave Mindy a sense of completion to be a part of something much larger than herself. Tonight's fundraiser was the first to be hosted by the joint effort of the billionaire brides' clubs, and all the proceeds were going to the islands in the Caribbean that were destroyed by Hurricanes Irma and Maria last year.

Fontaine Constructions, along with DC Designs, and Fonandt Energy that was owned by Bryce and Massimo were already on the islands volunteering their services to rebuilding the infrastructure. Ristorante Andreas was providing food to the schools, hospitals, and the shelters that had been set up on the islands, and the Erik LaCrosse Doctor's Abroad Foundation along with Carter Dentals were offering medical services and supplies. Carmichael Initiative had done its part in soliciting some of the richest, most influential donors in the world—including some famous Hollywood stars.

They'd all worked hard to make this event a success—some from their maternity beds. Yep, their families were growing like wild weed, she thought as she reached behind her to zip up her dress.

Last February, Desire and Chase became first-time parents when their daughter, Hope, was born. Tashi and Adam were blessed with baby Evelyn Arabella in May. And three months ago, Michelle and Erik welcomed their second biological son, Christian Nicholas, into the family. Michelle's pregnancy had been a surprise to everyone, even her and Erik.

Mindy's heart fluttered as she thought of the most amazing addition to her own family five months ago when she'd given birth to a beautiful baby…

"Oh my dear Lord. You look absolutely stunning, extraordinarily amazing, incredibly gorgeous."

Mindy chuckled as she turned to see her husband, dressed to the nines in a black and white tux, approaching her. Her nipples tingled, her breasts tightened, and a definite pulsing between her legs began to mount as she recalled their phenomenal lovemaking session in their bedroom and then in the shower earlier this evening.

After Sybil had taken all four kids to visit Mindy's mom and stepfather, Mindy and Galen had grasped the opportunity to enjoy each other. Even with full-time household help and a nanny, it had been somewhat difficult for them to give undivided attention to each other in their own home since their daughter Gia was born. They'd sneaked off to Hotel Andreas a few times since her gynecologist had given them the green light to resume their sexual life, but today it had been nice to relax in the privacy of their own bed.

"You know all those words have the same meaning, right?" she said as Galen came to a stop in front of her, his eyes boring into hers with the love and devotion she'd come to appreciate.

"There aren't enough words to express my awe at seeing you, love. I'll be the envy of every man at the gala tonight." He traced a finger lightly along her cheek, making her quiver at his touch.

"And I will be the envy of every woman," Mindy responded in a shaky voice. She'd become the envy of the town last year when Galen had bought out their abutting neighbors' properties, bulldozed the houses and expanded Mindy's house into a three-story, eight-bedroom mansion, complete with an indoor swimming pool, a fully equipped gym, a state-of-the-art sauna, and commodious adjoining home offices for each of them. Of course it came with a man cave for Galen to entertain the husbands of the billionaire husbands' club. He spared no expense when it came to trying to please her.

"How much did you spend on this dress and jewelry?" she asked, narrowing her eyes at him. "I told you that I don't need

ANA E ROSS

expensive clothes and jewelry to make me happy," she said, even as she turned so he could finish zipping her up.

He engaged the hook and eye at the top of the zipper then spun her around. "Ah, but it makes me happy to buy them for you, love. Especially when you wear them so well—astonishingly beautifully." His eyes swept the length of her.

"There you go with the adjectives and adverbs again." Her heart skipped a wild beat at his admiration.

"Punish me," he begged on a wicked grin.

"Later," she promised. "You look very smart, yourself—dashing and debonair."

He pressed his warm lips to her forehead as he pulled her closer. "You think we have time for a quickie?" he asked, running his hands along her back and down to her buttocks, pulling her into his pulsing erection. "I can just hike up your dress, bend you over your vanity table, and take you, love."

Galen's husky, salacious suggestion fired off a series of electrical shocks deep inside Mindy's womb and sent fluids gushing from her sex. Bending her over her vanity was something they'd never tried before, and the thought of doing it with her expensive Valentino dress tossed over her head fed her desire, her lust for her husband. "Galen," she whispered, clutching the lapels of his jacket as her entire body flushed and tightened in excitement.

"Mom! Dad! We're back."

Mindy let out a frustrated moan at the sound of Kyle's voice in the master bedroom next door.

"To be continued after the party," Galen said, sneaking in a quick wet kiss before releasing her.

"Definitely," Mindy whispered, forcing her heart to settle down as she tried to retreat from the role of lover to that of mother.

300

"Mommy, Daddy, where are you guys?"

Britt's call was followed by Geoffrey, "Mommy. Daddy."

When Mindy opened her mouth to respond, Galen placed a finger on her lips. "Let's see if Gia calls for us too."

"Don't be silly. She's only five months old. All she does is gurgle."

"Kids, you know you shouldn't burst into your parents' bedroom unannounced. You'll get me into trouble. Come on, let's go back downstairs and wait for them."

"No!" Geoffrey yelled.

Mindy smiled as she imagined his arms folded across his chest and his little ruddy face twisted into a stubborn frown. He was as headstrong as his older brother. "It's fine, Sybil," she called, pulling Galen into the corridor that led into their bedroom to see the children racing in their direction with Bacon bringing up the rear.

Both she and Galen opened their arms as the children and their dog flocked to them. There was never an occasion when their hugs wouldn't be welcomed.

"Mommy, you look like a princess," Brittany said.

"Better than a princess. She looks like a queen." Kyle gazed at Mindy with pride and admiration. "You're really beautiful, Mommy. You too, Dad, you look really nice," he added, grinning at Galen.

"Thank you, son." Galen ruffled Kyle's hair then scooped Geoffrey up into his arm. "What about you, little man? What do you have to say about your mommy and daddy?"

"Say they look beautiful," Britt prompted, pulling Geoffrey's leg.

"No!" Geoffrey belted out his favorite word and laced one arm around Mindy's neck while holding onto his father's with the other. "Mommy's lovely," he said, smiling at her.

Mindy chuckled. "You're a true English gentleman, Geoffrey, and I love you so much." She kissed his cheek.

"He's right. You do look lovely," Sybil said. "Both of you."

"Bacon. Come here, boy." Geoffrey wiggled his way to the floor to play with the family dog he'd grown to love.

With a joyful, beating heart, Mindy picked up a blanket from the foot of the bed and went over to take her infant daughter from Sybil. She held her child close to her heart and gazed into her hazel eyes. "Did you have fun with Nana and Grandpa?"

"We did," Brittany answered for her baby sister.

Galen unclipped his ringing cell phone from his belt. "It's business. I'll just be a minute." He walked out of the bedroom to take the call.

"Mommy, we saw Grandma Virginia," Brittany said.

Mindy closed her eyes for a second and took a deep breath. "Where?"

"After dinner, Grandpa took us to Sundae Scoop for ice cream and she was there," Kyle said.

"I'm sorry, but I wasn't with them," Sybil said in her own defense. "I stayed at home with your mother and Gia. If I—"

"You have nothing to be sorry for, Sybil," Mindy assured her before turning to her children. "Did you talk to your Grandmother?"

They both nodded, then Kyle spoke. "She said she misses us, and she said that she was going to call you to see if we can spend some time with her during the summer."

"Can we, Mommy?" Britt asked. "We only have two more weeks in school."

"We'll see." Mindy wasn't going to lie to her children and give them an affirmative answer until she'd discussed it with Galen, their father. Virginia had never wanted them to have the Grainger name so now they proudly carried the hyphenated last name of the man who had adopted them—Carmichael-Andretti.

"It's a school night, and I think you both have homework, right?" she asked, to avert anymore talk of Virginia.

"Yes."

"I do."

"Then it's time to hit the books. Your father and I will come say good night before we leave."

"Do you want me to take Gia?" Sybil asked after Kyle and Bitt left. "I wouldn't want her to throw up over your gown."

"No. I'll keep her for a little while. If you don't mind, I'd like you to help the kids with their homework instead. Can you take Geoffrey, too?"

"Of course. Come on, Geoffrey," she said, picking up the toddler from the floor and calling for Bacon to follow.

Sybil was definitely worth her weight in gold, Mindy thought as the family nanny disappeared with her younger son. Sybil was knowledgeable in all of Kyle and Brittany's school subjects and had taken the pressure off both Mindy and Galen when it came to helping them. When she'd first met Sybil, to clear the air, Mindy had brought up the little incident Galen had told her about. Sybil had apologized and had promised that it would never happen again. There hadn't yet been an occasion for Mindy to doubt her sincerity and she hoped there never would be.

Virginia, however, was a different story, Mindy thought as she walked over to the sliders to gaze out over Crystal Lake. "Oh, Gia," she groaned as her daughter turned her head, nuzzled her face into Mindy's bosom, and began to whimper. Immediately, Mindy's breasts swelled and tightened as her milk glands began to fill up.

Knowing that she'd be uncomfortable until she relieved the pressure, she laid Gia on the sofa and, unzipping her Valentino dress, she carefully stepped out of it, and draped it on the back of the sofa. She then sat down and spread the blanket over her body before arranging her baby on her lap. Moments later, as Gia suckled away, Mindy allowed her mind to rewind.

Last year, even after Mindy's warning, Virginia had still tried to declare Mindy an unfit mother and had filed for full custody of her grandchildren. She'd thought that because she shared their blood, she had more rights than Galen who'd been in the middle of adopting them at the time. Mindy's lawyer, one of the best money could buy, had discovered that in his will, Dudley Grainger had left a sizable amount of money from his insurance policy for Mindy and his grandchildren. Money that would have made life so much easier for her kids and her.

Virginia, the executor of the will, had decided not to inform Mindy that she and her children were beneficiaries. And on top of that she had secretly been planning to kidnap her grandchildren and take them to live with her on the west coast. Subsequently, Virginia had found herself in a heap of legal trouble that she was still trying to dig herself out of. In addition to using the money she'd stolen from Mindy and her kids, she'd had to sell her house to cover her legal fees and was now living in an apartment in the not-so-nice side of town. Virginia was a living example of the Biblical proverb about pride going before a fall. Mindy felt no sympathy for the woman who'd brought on her own destruction out of spite and hate. But it pained her that Kyle and Brittany had to see their grandmother in such a state.

When her kids had asked why Virginia wasn't living in her big house anymore, Mindy had just told them that Grandma had to work through some personal issues before she could see them again. After all, Virginia was still their grandmother, and they loved her. However, the court had prohibited her from having any contact with her grandchildren until it was satisfied that she posed no danger to them.

Sometimes people had to hit rock bottom to really reflect and change their wicked ways. Mindy hoped that Virginia would change so that she could have a relationship with her grandchildren. The ball was in her court. Again.

Mindy trembled as she felt Galen's warm hands caressing her back and shoulders from behind. Then as if he knew she needed a hug at that very moment, he wrapped his arms about her and the child their love had created. They stayed like that for long silent moments, just drinking in the essence of each other's presence and basking in the deeper level of bonding their suckling offspring had brought to their lives.

Gia Safi Carmichael-Andretti—named after one of Galen's paternal ancestors and Mindy's best friend—was just the first of many children Mindy hoped would be created from her and Galen's love.

They had been using the rhythm and body temperature method for birth control. Today was definitely not a day for them to take chances, she thought, as a spark generated deep inside her womb. But earlier, when the time had come for Galen to withdraw, Mindy had locked her arms and legs about him, and he'd had no other choice but to shoot his seed inside her.

"Are you really ready for another one?" Galen had asked as they lay basking in the afterglow.

"I am," she'd responded, running her fingers through the mat of hair on his damp chest. "I want to give you a son, and then perhaps another daughter soon after so they and Geoffrey can be close in age like Kyle and Britt are."

Mindy pressed her lips against her baby's forehead, grateful that she would never have to fight anyone for her.

"She's really beautiful isn't she?" he asked, bending to kiss his youngest daughter's cheek and caress her head of soft dark curls. "She looks so much like you and Britt." His voice shook with emotion.

"Except for her eyes," Mindy said. "I really want another one soon," she spoke those thoughts out loud instead of discussing Virginia's request. She would tell Galen all about it on their way to the center. "I think siblings who are close in age and who experience the same growing pains together have closer relationships in life. I think if Billy and I were closer in age we would have a better relationship. We hardly spoke to each other when we lived together. He was in one world and I was in another. It's even worse now since he moved away."

Galen walked around the sofa, sat beside her, and draped his arms around them again. "I believe you. Sometimes people ask me if Kyle and Britt are fraternal twins. They're so attentive to each other. Even though they love Geoffrey and look out for him, the age difference does make a difference. Since you are the one who has to carry them and labor to bring them into this world, the timing is up to you, love."

"Well, the timing is probably out of my hands already after today," she said smiling into Galen's eyes. "It's possible that in nine months we'll be sitting here with Gia's little brother in our arms."

Galen took their daughter's tiny hand in his and rubbed his thumb along her arm. "I wouldn't mind many more of these little angels, actually, if it pleases you."

As if to agree with him, Gia released Mindy's nipple, looked at her father, and smiled, then blew bubbles before latching onto her food source again.

"There. Our daughter has spoken," she stated, turning her head to receive Galen's deep soul-bonding kiss that shook Mindy to the very marrow of her bones.

She, Galen, her children, and her mother had gone through hell and back to get to this very moment. And in spite of all the heartache, the pain, and the struggles, Mindy would do it again in a New York minute, just to have what she had, to enjoy what she'd accomplished in life so far. To say she was truly pleased was an understatement. "We're so blessed," she whispered against his mouth.

"Yes, love. We are."

And there in the quiet sanctuary of their bedroom where the din and noise and mundane concerns of the universe seemed a million miles away, the spark of life shone brilliantly in the silence of Galen and Mindy's love.

THE END

Dear Reader,

I hope you enjoyed following Robert and Yasmine on their journey *Happily Ever After* in **Loving Yasmine,** the first book in my ***Beyond Granite Falls*** series.

I wish you all the best in your search for that one special "Someone", and if you've already found him/her, then continue to revel in happiness.

Blessings,

Ana

Visit me: www.anaeross.com
Email me: ana@anaeross.com

ABOUT THE AUTHOR

New York Times **and** *USA Today* **Bestselling Author, Ana E Ross,** was born and raised in the Caribbean where she began indulging in romance novels at a very early age.

Ana holds a Bachelor's degree in English Literature from the University of New Hampshire, and a Master's of Education degree from Lesley University, Massachusetts. She is a former Writing and English Literature middle and high school teacher, and a College Freshman Writing Composition professor.

Inspired by the strong heroines and flawed alpha heroes in the stories she read as a young girl, Ana resigned from teaching, and now crafts sophisticated and drama-filled contemporary romances, featuring charming, powerful, larger-than-life heroes and beautiful, strong, independent women who fight and love with equal passion.

Ana lives in the Northeast, and loves traveling, tennis, yoga, meditation, everything Italian, and spending valuable time with her daughter.

www.anaeross.com

ॐ

Made in the USA
Middletown, DE
08 November 2021

51474903R00191